IN THE BEGINNING . . .

"Oh, Nurse, I think it's coming," Abigail said.

Joy and Carol stared at Abigail Hornsby's bottom. They could see it was too late. One more push and—Carol could only do as her maternity-nursing textbook had instructed and as she had seen the doctor do. Before Abigail could push again, she placed her hand on Abigail's perineum and exerted slight pressure there. She felt the baby's neck to see if the cord was wrapped around it. It *was*.

Carol tried to loosen the cord enough to pull it over the baby's head, but she couldn't. "Joy, go tell Dr. Peusy the cord's around the neck."

Joy flew out of the room. Seconds later, Dr. Peusy rushed in. He maneuvered the baby's head enough to lift the cord from around its neck, and one more uterine contraction delivered the infant's body. In spite of her horror and fear, Carol heard Abigail say "Whew!" Dr. Peusy's hands were a blur as he clamped the cord twice and cut it, suctioned the baby's mouth and nose, and handed him to Carol.

Baby boy Hornsby was bellowing furiously when Carol held him up for Abigail to see. Abigail said affectionately, "Aw, look at that. Ain't he just like a man? It was us that did all the work, and he's the one complaining."

EXCITING BESTSELLERS FROM ZEBRA

PASSION'S REIGN by Karen Harper   (1177, $3.95)

Golden-haired Mary Bullen was wealthy, lovely and refined—and lusty King Henry VIII's prize gem! But her passion for the handsome Lord William Stafford put her at odds with the Royal Court. Mary and Stafford lived by a lovers' vow: one day they would be ruled by only the crown of PASSION'S REIGN.

HEIRLOOM by Eleanora Brownleigh   (1200, $3.95)

The surge of desire Thea felt for Charles was powerful enough to convince her that, even though they were strangers and their marriage was a fake, fate was playing a most subtle trick on them both: Were they on a mission for President Teddy Roosevelt—or on a crusade to realize their own passionate desire?

LOVESTONE by Deanna James   (1202, $3.50)

After just one night of torrid passion and tender need, the dark-haired, rugged lord could not deny that Moira, with her precious beauty, was born to be a princess. But how could he grant her freedom when he himself was a prisoner of her love?

DEBORAH'S LEGACY by Stephen Marlowe   (1153, $3.75)

Deborah was young and innocent. Benton was worldly and experienced. And while the world rumbled with the thunder of battle, together they rose on a whirlwind of passion—daring fate, fear and fury to keep them apart!

Available wherever paperbacks are sold, or order direct from the Publisher. Send cover price plus 50¢ per copy for mailing and handling to Zebra Books, 475 Park Avenue South, New York, N.Y. 10016 DO NOT SEND CASH.

MATERNITY NURSE
BY PATRICIA RAE

ZEBRA BOOKS
KENSINGTON PUBLISHING CORP.

ZEBRA BOOKS

are published by

KENSINGTON PUBLISHING CORP.
475 Park Avenue South
New York, N.Y. 10016

Printed in the United States of America

To my editor, Leslie Gelbman

Where did you come from, baby dear?
Out of the everywhere into here.
                    —George Macdonald

ONE

"Scalpel."

Having already inserted the knife blade into the handle, Carol now placed the scalpel gently into Dr. Simon's hand.

"Now . . . I have on a pair of surgical gloves, Carol, and I can feel through these gloves just fine. But if you'd sort of slap the instrument into my hand—not hard, just firmly so that I know it's there . . ." Dr. Simon poised the scalpel above the patient's distended abdomen with its white spiderlike stretch marks branching out from the umbilicus. Then he brought the knife down and cut. The skin of Rebecca Johnson's abdomen separated in an incision that began two or three inches below her umbilicus to just above the pubic bone. The scalpel, having now come in contact with the skin which could not be sterilized, was considered contaminated, and Dr. Simon dropped it into the specimen basin.

"Sponge."

Carol took a gauze four-by-four from the Mayo

stand beside her and placed it firmly in his hand. This isn't my bag, she was thinking in a state of near panic. Surgery isn't my—

"Another please," Dr. Simon said as he sponged the blood that welled up into the surgical wound.

As Carol placed another gauze sponge in his hand he said, "I generally do not like to be handed the scalpel, Carol, but I find it helpful when teaching a nurse to assist, and normally my scrub nurse places what I'll be using on the Mayo stand even before I need it. Sometimes I'll get the instrument myself, sometimes I'll ask for something, depending on what's going on in the surgical wound." Dr. Simon cut through what Carol knew was subcutaneous tissue, yellow adipose tissue, *fat,* and exposed the pink-white anterior fascia which covered the muscle of the abdomen like a thin layer of tissue paper.

"Hemostat . . . yes . . . hemostat . . . clamp, please."

Carol handed the hemostats, clamps called Halsteads by some surgeons, passing the instruments with the handles toward the surgeon's hand, tip showing, so that he could clamp the bleeding vessels which he had just severed. *If I'd known I'd have to assist with C-sections occasionally—*

"Ligature."

Ligature . . . ligature, material to tie off the bleeders. She'd studied the procedure in her med-surg textbook. *You hand the ligatures holding both ends so that the surgeon can grasp it in the middle—*

"Cautery, Dr. Simon?" Mac asked. She was assisting also. Mac had worked in labor and delivery for eight years and usually scrubbed for the obstetricians, but today she was on the other side of the table from Dr. Simon because Carol was learning to assist.

"Probably, but not yet." Dr. Simon made an incision

8

into the fascia, and the blue-red muscle tissue appeared in the now gaping wound. "Hemostat . . . sponge. No, the Gelfoam sponge to seal off the capillaries. Hemostat."

God, I'm running out of clamps. Carol hesitated briefly before she handed the doctor another hemostat. Perspiration was slipping down between her breasts. *If I'd known I'd have to scrub and assist in surgical procedures, I'd never have chosen labor and delivery. We did not learn any of this in nursing school.*

"Suction that, Mac."

Mac took the sterile suction catheter and suctioned fluid and blood from the wound. *Sssssssst.* And Dr. Simon tied vessels with the surgical gut ligatures and released the hemostats. "Scissors." After he had cut the ties he took the scalpel and made a deft incision into muscle tissue. "Clamp . . . sponge . . . suture."

Suture? Does he mean ligature? Carol handed him the needle with its threaded suture.

"No. No. The ligature to tie the vessels. God, Carol, don't pass me what I say, pass me what I *want.*"

While Carol passed the doctor the ligature she silently cursed, expressing her favorite obscenities, the same ones she always used in the most trying of circumstances: *shit, damn it,* and *hell,* in that order. Before nursing school she never would have allowed herself to think curse words, having come from a strict religious family, much less actually *say* them. Age did that to people—she was twenty-six—and so did nursing.

A hemostat clattered into the basin. "Ligature."

The world caved in upon her when she dropped the ligature on the floor.

"Never mind," Mac said to her. "That's why we have so many of them. Just hand him another."

9

"Ligature," Dr. Simon said with a hint of impatience.

Her face burned as she handed him the ligature. Dr. Simon tied off a persistent bleeder. "Scissors. By now I shouldn't have to ask. . . ."

Her hand wavered over the Mayo stand for a second until she located the scissors and handed them to him.

Dr. Simon said under his breath, "If you tie something, Carol, you've got to cut it, and the only way to cut it is with scissors."

I'll quit, resign, just as soon as this surgery is over. I'll—

Suddenly, activity accelerated.

Clamp, suture, scissors. Clamp, suture, scissors, sponge. Cautery. "Sponge . . . scalpel."

Carol perspired and obeyed. Her eyes widened as Mac applied two retractors to the open wound, spreading it wide, stretching it open. Retractors looked like giant shoe horns. And suddenly the stirated blue-red uterus appeared in the wound.

"Saline sponges, now, Carol."

Carol froze.

"Saline sponges, please."

She dipped the sponges in the warm saline which Robbie, as circulating nurse, had just poured into the sterile basin.

As Dr. Simon took the sponges from her, he said, "Do I mumble, Carol?"

"No, sir."

"You can't be slow. A split second can sometimes mean the difference between a patient hemorrhaging and not hemorrhaging." He packed the warm, moist sponges around the uterus, then picked up the scalpel and held it over the uterine muscle.

Carol felt tears welling up in her eyes, willed them

not to spill; for where would they go? They would contaminate her mask, her surgical gown. She saw the small deft cut in the uterine muscle.

"Bandage scissors."

Dr. Simon cut the uterine muscle now with the bandage scissors, because their bottom blade was flat and less apt to injure the fetus. His gloved finger slid along the wound behind the scissors as they cut. Mac had the suction catheter ready. Dr. Simon nicked the amniotic sac. *Sssssssssssstttt.* Dr. Simon hooked the suction catheter back between Mac's third and fourth finger; she was still applying the retractors. Then the obstetrician dipped his hand into the uterus, tugged gently, and brought out the head of the wet, squinty-eyed fetus and pulled it from the uterine cavity.

Carol handed Dr. Simon the bulb syringe and he suctioned the infant's mouth and nose quickly, then swatted his bottom once to make him cry. Mac clamped the umbilical cord while the doctor held the infant upside down; then, placing baby boy Johnson upon his mother's chest, he applied a Kelly clamp three inches from the cord clamp. A minute later he brought out the placenta. Carol handed him the placenta basin, then the scissors for cutting the cord between the clamps. A glance at Dr. Pashi, the anesthesiologist, showed Carol that he was adding oxytocin to Rebecca's IV, a medication that was meant to cause uterine contractions so that the uterus would clamp down on the bleeding vessels where the placenta had been released from the uterine wall.

The infant mewled wetly, and suddenly Dr. Bordeaux was there taking him in his hands. Joy would aid the pediatrician in taking care of the baby's immediate needs, just as Carol had done twice before. The pediatrician would suction the infant's mouth and

11

trachea, apply oxygen if it was necessary, place the disinfectant drops into his eyes, place him in the isolette, and take him to the newborn nursery. Normally, a pediatrician did not have to be present during a C-section if it was a normal, elective Caesarean section, but baby boy Johnson was premature.

"What do you think?" Mac asked Dr. Simon who was applying Gelfoam sponges to the surgical wound.

"I think he weighs around five pounds," the doctor said as he inspected the uterine cavity for any placental fragments that might be left. The placenta seemed intact, but it never hurt to make sure.

"Normal?"

"From all appearances."

"Think she could have delivered vaginally if she'd gone full term?"

"The kid was transverse lie and I couldn't get him turned. Who knows whether or not he'd have turned himself by her due date?"

Dr. Simon held out his hand to Carol. Her own hand wavered again over the Mayo stand and came up with the strongest catgut suture, threaded, needle held by needle holder. It was a guess, but it must have been right, for Dr. Simon took it and began to suture the tough, thick, uterine muscle. While he sutured he said, "Carol, normally I use the low segment Caesarean incision because there's less blood loss, et cetera, et cetera, but today I did the classical because the kid was transverse lie." He held out his hand, and Carol passed him the scissors.

Luckily, the anticipated types of sutures and needles were prearranged on the table, in more or less the order in which the doctor would need them. Carol had only to use her own judgment as to whether the next suture in line was the one he would need or not. *Only* her own judgment? She'd never learn it all. *I'll quit OB, go to work on the floor, then eventually to CCU.* She wasn't meant to be an OR nurse. She had memorized the needles, though; straight, curved, half-curved, tapered, cutting . . . and the sutures: surgical gut, silk, wire, cotton, linen, nylon, polyester, even kangaroo tendon . . . and the suture sizes from 0000000, which was 0.038 millimeters in diameter, to number seven which was 0.965. Each needle and each suture had its own purpose. Besides all that, each surgeon had his own preferences. She'd never learn it all. Never.

As he closed the surgical wound layer by layer, Dr. Simon's scowl vanished along with his shining red layer of perspiration. Three layers of sutures in the uterine muscle; then the peritoneum, using round needle and continuous stitch like darning a sock; and the abdominal muscle—interrupted stitch, each tied— the fascia, same stitch but using a cutting needle; subcutaneous, and skin, and all the while Carol handing him the sutures he asked for.

Suturing was incredibly slow and painfully tedious. Sometimes the doctor forgot to say which suture he wanted, and it irritated him that she couldn't read his mind. But since this was the first time she had assisted him, he *had* to tell her. How else could a nurse learn? You had to begin somewhere.

For the next forty-five minutes, she alternated between hating Dr. Simon and admiring him. When he had finished, he said nothing to her, merely turned and strolled out the door of the delivery room, peeling off his dirty gloves and whistling, "If I Were a Rich Man" from *Fiddler on the Roof.*

"Well?" Mac said across the operating table as they were applying the last tape to the dressing over

Rebecca's abdomen.

"I was awful," Carol said as she pulled the damp mask down from her face. *"He* thought I was awful too."

"No, he didn't," Mac said. "Kid, *he* was the one who insisted that we L&D nurses learn to assist in C-sections, so the obstetricians wouldn't have to rely on the surgery department in cases of emergency sections like today."

"But he was cross with me."

"He always gets cross when he's down to the uterus," Robbie said as she paused beside Carol with the placenta basin in her hand. "It's a scary time. You did O.K. for your first scrub on a C-section."

"No, I didn't."

"Yes, you did," Mac said. "You expect too much of yourself. You did fine. You handed instruments well, and near the end, you were anticipating what he would need. That's the trick, anticipating the surgeon's needs."

Dr. Pashi, the anesthesiologist, spoke up. "Can you anticipate *my* needs, Carol?" He made his eyebrows go up and down.

The nurses laughed because it was a well-giggled-about fact that Pashi, who was only forty-one, was loyally married and had seven kids. Dr. Pashi had been Dr. Simon's silent partner during the surgery. Pashi seldom said much, and the obstetricians seldom conversed with him during a Caesarean, but he was their first choice as an anesthesiologist. Carol would never forget that Pashi had taught her how to start an IV when she was observing her first surgery as a student nurse.

Pashi was an Indian, dark with black eyes, a soft voice, and a disfiguring scar slashing from the left corner of his mouth to his left sideburn. At the moment, he was holding Rebecca's head tilted back after having removed the endotracheal tube through which he had administered the anesthesia; his big hands were spread over the side of her face, his fingertips touching the carotid arteries in her neck; not only was he watching her breath, keeping an eye on her coloring, but he was monitoring her carotid pulse as well. Carol knew that Pashi would watch Rebecca closely until she was well awake, then would accompany her from the delivery room to OB recovery.

The delivery room was a mess now. Feeling reassured by Mac and Robbie that her first performance as a scrub nurse was satisfactory, Carol's spirits shot up to an all-time high, and she quietly began to gather the dirty instruments and place them into basins for cleaning and autoclaving. Martin, an elderly widow who had risen through the ranks from housekeeping to labor and delivery aide, would wash and wrap and autoclave the instruments. Marty was indispensable to the OB crew, for it was she who did the dirty work—washing instruments, wrapping them, autoclaving them, cleaning up labor-room messes, remaking labor-room beds, unloading new equipment off the carts brought from central supply, and placing this equipment in the proper cabinets. She appeared now in the doorway of the room.

"Can I call housekeeping yet?" she asked.

Dr. Pashi said, "Give me five, Marty."

Martin scowled and hobbled back out of the room. She always scowled, pretending to be inconvenienced, but it was a defense mechanism to hide a too-soft heart and a vulnerable patience. Marty liked to be complimented on her work, though, like everybody else.

"Hey, Marty?" Dr. Pashi called on second thought.

15

When Martin stuck her head back into the doorway, he said, "Go ahead and bring the stretcher, will you, sweetheart?"

Martin's mouth twitched into a ghost of a smile and disappeared again.

Pashi started patting Rebecca's face gently. "Wake up, Rebecca. Hey, hey. It's all over."

"Mmmmm," Rebecca said hoarsely.

Carol touched her cool arm and bent down to her ear. "Hey, Becky. It's all over."

Rebecca's lips parted, and she croaked the inevitable, "What . . . is it?"

"You had a boy."

"A . . . live?"

"Of course, alive. 'Bout five pounds." Now *this* was nursing. Just this patient contact, just this little bit of reassurance, this seed of comfort. And she liked it much more than assisting doctors. Most nurses liked assisting doctors best, but not Carol. And not Joy either.

"Word from the nursery says he's five pounds and two ounces, actually, dear heart," Robbie told Rebecca; then she picked Dr. Simon's gown off the instrument table and danced away with it, one sleeve over her shoulder.

The nurses were experiencing the temporary high that always comes after periods of prolonged tension. Rebecca had been lying in the labor room for thirty-six hours. Because her labor had started a month early, Dr. Simon had ordered an alcohol drip to try to stop her contractions, but it hadn't worked. The nurses had been under tensions on all shifts because of it. Two hours ago, her labor contractions had increased in frequency and intensity, so Mac had called Dr. Simon. They knew that the baby was transverse lie, its body lying across the cervix, its shoulder presenting at the pelvic inlet. Sometimes in such cases the doctor could manipulate the baby to a head-down position, but in Rebecca's case, Dr. Simon had been unable to do it. The only choice left to him had been to do a Caesarean section.

Luckily nobody else was in labor at the time so all four nurses were able to go to delivery leaving Martin to answer the telephone at the nurses' station. Release from the rigors of assisting with a C-section caused them to feel almost euphoric.

While Carol and Robbie continued to clatter dirty instruments into the basins and to wrap these in surgical towels, Martin came in pulling the stretcher. When Mac brought the sheet blanket fresh from the warmer, Carol went to the stretcher and stepped on the brakes at the head while Mac did the same at the foot.

"O.K., Rebecca," Carol said. "We're gonna slide you onto the stretcher and take you to recovery. O.K.?"

Rebecca nodded.

Carol and Mac grasped the bottom drape on which Rebecca was lying and Pashi placed both hands under Rebecca's back.

"One, two, three," Mac said. They slid Rebecca off the delivery table and onto the stretcher in one motion.

"Scoot into the middle. My way, Becky," Mac told her.

Rebecca gritted her teeth, her hand going to the thick abdominal dressing on her abdomen, and edged herself into the middle of the stretcher, gasping, "Oh . . . oh . . ."

Dr. Pashi tapped her on the hand and held up one finger. "In recovery, you can have a pain shot, O.K.?"

The patient nodded.

As they wheeled her from the delivery room with

17

Dr. Pashi at the head of the stretcher, Mac at its foot, and Carol trailing along behind, they met Martin in the corridor before they reached the nurses' station. Martin said, "Dr. Simon got a call from the emergency room just now."

Pashi went on with the stretcher, but Mac paused to look at Martin blankly.

"Somebody named Melinda Curtis."

Carol and Mac looked at each other. "Lord, what for?" Mac asked.

"I dunno," Martin said shrugging. "All I know is Dr. Simon still had on his greens. He'd pulled his mask down, but he couldn't get it untied; and after he got the phone call, he yanked it off, breaking the ties, and left here running."

Carol blinked at Mac. Both of them knew Melinda Curtis from prenatal classes. She was a beautiful, petite girl in her early twenties, married to a young college professor.

"How far along is she, Carol?" Mac asked.

"I think six months."

Mac groaned. "You'd better go on to lunch, you and Joy. I won't be going to lunch today because I'm on a diet."

"Again?"

Mac patted her hips and continued on down the corridor with Dr. Pashi and the stretcher bearing Rebecca Johnson.

"Where *is* Joy?" Carol asked Martin.

"Went to ER to see what's happening, I reckon."

"Need anything before I go to lunch?"

"No, I'd rather you went on to lunch, 'cause by the way Dr. Simon was acting, all hell may break loose in here any minute. Joy said she'd join you in the cafeteria."

Carol picked up her lab coat from off the back of the

desk chair and pulled it on over her scrub pantsuit.
"Page me if you need me, Marty."

"Don't worry, I will," Martin said. "I've got this feeling that something's gonna happen. Something . . . something—"

"Out of the ordinary?"

Martin nodded. "And bad."

TWO

She was a nurse. A registered nurse. After two months as a graduate nurse and four as an R.N.—six months in all—the idea still blew her mind.

Over four years ago she'd registered for prenursing courses in preparation for nurse's training because of her moral ideals. She wanted to help people. But she was smart enough to realize that her desire to become a nurse, to help the sick, was not just a selfless sentiment; there were selfish motives involved. She wanted more out of life than being a secretary in an insurance firm as she'd been the four years since high school. The secretarial position was O.K., but—

When she had been in high school, her mother had had a hysterectomy, and Carol had entered a hospital for the first time, as a visitor. From the moment she had walked through the hospital doors she had felt something, something different—a vibrancy, a pulsating aliveness she had never felt before. There was life. There was illness and death, too, somewhere on some floor of the hospital, behind some door. But the nurses and doctors and other medical personnel were busy, hurrying, intent, doing something—she did not yet know what—to help the sick, the dying. There were the smells, too, many smells—medicinal. There were sounds: machines, equipment, people talking, working. What were they doing? What mysterious things?

The nurses who had come into her mother's room to take her blood pressure and pulse had been busy, hurried. Some had been friendly. Some had not. Most had worn crisp white uniforms; others' uniforms had not been so crisp and white. And the doctor had been so hurried, so authoritative, so brusque and brisk and loud and self-assured and friendly. Briefly friendly.

Then there had been a man, across the hall from her mother's room, who had had a heart attack while Carol was visiting. Medical personnel had converged upon the room, and a lot of noise and excitement had followed their arrival.

The old woman next door had cried out often, and Carol had wanted desperately to know why.

Drama.

White uniforms.

Strange equipment.

Busy people.

Mystery. Intrigue.

Fascinating.

It had taken four years working as a secretary for Carol to gather the courage—and the funds—to enter nursing school. She had paid the initial costs herself, and when her parents saw that she was serious about going to school, they had paid for the rest; though her mother had often said, "I just can't see you as a nurse, Carol. I don't think you have the stamina."

But she had set her Welles jaw, determined to do it and succeed.

Nursing school. A bittersweet experience for which

21

she wouldn't take anything in the world. Nursing-student friends, friends forever. And there was Duane, Duane in the exciting, exhausting, struggling years of medical school; now he was lost to her.

To love nursing was to love people, to appreciate oneself better for caring for people. To Carol, the pride in being a nurse went below the cutaneous surface of necessary employment; it came from the subcutaneous giving of a lot of oneself, of one's learned skills, personality, time, and patience—and maybe some-times even of one's soul.

She folded her arms across her chest as she paced down the corridor, looking around her at the beige-painted walls, impersonal corridor walls, and polished tile floors. Nothing here to really love, and yet she loved it because it was a part of a wonderful, miraculous whole—Bennet Memorial, one of the largest medical complexes in the entire city, in the entire state.

She was enjoying basking in the euphoria of knowing that she had just assisted in surgery as a nurse, too; she had reached for a star and found the sun. Even the puzzling foreshadows of something ominous concerning Melinda Curtis now in ER, shadows that hovered like a storm in the horizon of her euphoria, did not obliterate this sun. But they did threaten. *And bad,* Marty had said.

She bit her lip and pushed open the swinging doors to the cafeteria.

Bennet's cafeteria was huge. Most of the personnel there were lined up to choose their lunches from the long steam table which displayed steaming entrées and side dishes, or salads and soups and soft drinks. Many others stood in the little cattle chute–type areas where they waited to select cold dishes such as sandwiches, chef's salads, potato and corn chips, slices of pie, cake, or Jell-O from a giant stainless-steel revolving display unit.

Carol chose to wait in the line at the steam table for a hot lunch, and when she had selected her entrée and vegetables, and had placed her iced tea on the tray, she went into the eating area where there were many laminated tables and booths full of white-clad personnel.

Carol paused, holding her tray, sweeping the room with her gaze, looking for Joy. The din in the place was ear-shattering, people talking, laughing, cutlery clattering on dinnerware. The smell was always the same, something close to the smell of hot cheese and stale bread.

"Dr. Hamblin . . . Dr. Ruben Hamblin, please," came the page over the paging system.

Carol spotted Joy, who was motioning to her, and she wove around the tables until she came to the booth which Joy occupied, guarding it jealously with a profusion of her personal paraphernalia—lab coat, handbag, small make-up kit—to discourage other people from sitting there.

"Hey, sit down. Have I got something to tell you!" Joy said happily. Joy was well-named in Carol's opinion. She was never deeply troubled about anything, never deeply worried or afraid or concerned. Joy was just not deeply *anything*. "Scatterbrained," Dr. Simon had grumbled once. "Makes me nervous," Dr. Moss had said. "Oh, I got Joy in the mornin' and I got Joy at night. I got Joy when I need her and that makes Joy exactly right," Dr. Jackson would sing often.

"Darn it, Joy," Carol said plopping her tray on the table. "Why didn't you come back and tell us what's going on with Melinda Curtis in ER?"

"I figured something's gonna blast loose so I'd better

23

eat and get back to L&D."

Joy was Carol's age, twenty-six, with curly, shoulder-length auburn hair. She wasn't pretty, but "She has an interesting face," Dr. Blasingame had said. It was roundish, pink-cheeked, and made interesting because of her sensuous mouth and huge green eyes.

Three of the nurses on the seven-to-three shift in L&D had red hair, various shades; Mac's was dark red, Joy's was auburn, Carol's was reddish blond. Only Robbie, whose real name was Robin, had mousy brown hair. "Isn't that a bitch?" Robbie would say when somebody would laugh about all the redheads in L&D. "I'm the only one who has a legitimate reason to be a redhead, because of my name."

Dr. Jackson once pointed out that robins have red breasts, not red hair. He had a way of getting to the crux of that kind of thing.

Now Joy said, "The resident on duty in ER thinks Melinda has a perforated bowel."

Carol screwed up her face. "Oh . . . Lord . . . no!"

"How do you do an abdominal tap to see if there's fecal material in the abdominal cavity on somebody who's six months prego? I tried to see, but they wouldn't let me in the room. Anyway, the resident called Dr. Simon to ER. He didn't know if part of her pain was labor or what. When I left ER just a few minutes ago, Simon was antsy as hell. Seems Melinda has been complaining of stomach cramps the last two checkups. Says she's had diarrhea for two weeks. She's in real severe pain, but it's not birth pains. It's gut. Last I heard, they were taking her to x-ray."

Carol started shoveling her food into her mouth faster than she could chew or swallow, silently cursing her esophagus for being too small. The more Joy talked, the faster Carol shoveled.

"She's really sick. Vomiting, even screaming in pain.

We know from prenatal classes that Melinda's not the kind to scream for no reason, don't we? I mean not for just a stomach ache."

"That kind of abdominal pain can cause contractions to begin," Carol said.

"Well, Simon says—"

"Thumbs up."

Joy and Carol looked up and smiled at Corey Brewster, the male nurse on day shift in ER. He was standing with tray in hand. "May I?"

Carol scooted her tray and herself over to make room for Brew.

"What did they find out, Brew?" she asked. "About Melinda Curtis?"

Brewster sat down. He was the ugliest male in Bennet, maybe in the world. Oversized freckles, sharp, irregular features—everything on Brew's face was crooked: his large, pointed nose, his mouth, his jaw—and because he was tall and lanky with enormous feet, the obstetricians called him Ichabod. They did not have much to do with anyone in ER generally, but because Brew could judge just by a patient's behavior what phase of labor she was in when she came to ER on the verge of delivering, they knew him and had to respect him. And Brew was sharp, sharp as his nose. He knew ER procedures, first aid, and critical-care emergencies better than most M.D.'s.

"She's got diverticulitis," Brew said. "I thought so from the beginning."

"Diverticulitis?" Joy said, her eyes dancing with a mixture of excitement and trepidation.

Carol was remembering that diverticulitis was inflammation of a diverticulum, an abnormal sacklike dilation in the colon. It usually occurred in the middle-aged patient or the elderly; the cause was unknown. If it was severe enough, it could cause perforation of

25

the colon.

"We called Dr. Hamblin and Whitehall himself. I was hoping Whitehall would call Basil Novak," Brew said. "Maybe he has by now."

"Who's that?" Joy asked.

"Chief resident in surgery."

"Why a resident?"

"I know him," Carol put in, remembering . . . remembering . . .

"Novak has more surgical intuition in a minute than Whitehall does in a year," Brew said. "I worked with Novak a lot in ER. He's sharp. Anyway, they were debating whether to take her to surgery. If the bowel has perforated, then she's apt to get peritonitis."

Carol covered her face with her hand. Peritonitis was an inflammation of the peritoneum, the tissue lining the abdominal cavity. Peritonitis was usually due to a bacterial infection caused by a perforated gastric ulcer, a perforated colon, or a ruptured appendix, and was extremely painful and often, *very often,* fatal.

"Peritonitis and pregnancy is a doubly lethal combination," Brew said, voicing what Carol was already thinking.

She had lost her appetite. By now she was accustomed to talking about diseases and other gross things at lunch so that did not affect her appetite. It was that her stomach was knotted in apprehension for Melinda, and refused to accept any more food. She dropped her fork onto her plate. "Brew, pardon me. I'm going back to L&D."

"Hey. Why?" Brew said looking hurt. "This is the first time I've ever sat next to you, something I've dreamed about since you were a student in ER, and you want to leave me?"

Carol knew Brew's flirtatiousness was half friendly

26

bullshit and half-genuine. "I feel nervous just sitting here—"

"She feels nervous sitting beside me," Brew told Joy cheerfully. My sex appeal is causing her to become apprehensive that she'll lose her self-control."

"Actually, I feel perfectly safe beside you, Brew; it's just that—"

"Now she feels safe beside me. That speaks very well for my masculinity."

"She *has* a boyfriend," Joy said half-irritably, bored with the whole thing. "Another male *nurse*. Works at Veterans'."

"I know. I already asked around." Brew got up and watched as Carol scooted with her tray across the cushioned booth's seat and stood up. "I had her pegged as minnow bait, though."

Carol stood holding her tray, looking up at Brew. "What kind of bait?"

"Minnow bait. Med-student or resident bait."

Carol shook her head and told Joy, "I'll see you later."

As she made her way among the tables and shoved her tray through the kitchen window where the black conveyor belt slid by like a dirty tongue, Carol was thinking, Minnow bait. I *was* minnow bait once. She and Duane had become lovers while he was in med school and she was in nursing school. A classic situation for a soap opera, really. But because she had persisted in writing her term paper about the preventable death of Mr. Proctor, a patient who had entered Bennet to have a simple surgical procedure done on his prostate and had left Bennet feet first from the morgue, Duane and she had had their terminal fight. He had been afraid her persistence in checking into the case might cause the doctors involved to link her with him

27

and put his residency at Bennet in jeopardy. That was about . . . nine or ten months ago, and though she'd been employed in Bennet's L&D for six months now, she hadn't yet seen Dr. Duane Duren, sure to be interning somewhere within the hospital. And he had never called again, just as he had threatened. Both of them stubborn. Both selfish. But he had called her a pipsqueak, too, and a piss ant. Her face burned with fury even now at the thought of it.

Though she dreamed of him occasionally and he was seldom ever completely out of her thoughts, she wasn't sure how she would react if she ever did see him again, how she would be able to endure the impact of his looking at her again.

Her thoughts went to Bret and to his job at Veterans'. Bret—loyal, good-natured, easygoing. And he loved her. But he'd not been able to take Duane's place in her heart, not even to make one there of his own.

L&D was on first floor, the same floor as the cafeteria, but Carol had to pass from Dowell through Baskin to the Markson building. Bennet was a two thousand eight hundred-bed medical complex made up of twelve buildings, old and new, connected by corridors and underground tunnels. It was a maze, each building a different size and height from the one next to it so that one could not always connect with an adjoining building on the same floor.

L&D nurses seldom had to go elsewhere anyway, for the post-partum floor and newborn nursery were just down the corridor from labor and delivery.

Now going through Baskin's 1950s corridor to Markson's 1960s one, Carol thought of Melinda Curtis. Melinda had attended every prenatal class since the first session had begun in September. Her first and second trimesters had been normal with no complications. She was a cheerful, vivacious girl excited about her pregnancy, striding into class with her husband, John, in tow, her eyes sparkling, referring to herself as "we," having no qualms about discussing her pregnancy or any of its aspects. To Melinda, being pregnant was a marvelous miracle and she had commented that she had never felt more beautiful, healthy, and alive. She was the ideal OB patient, if there was an ideal, and the OB nurses, who participated in prenatal classes and who knew Melinda, had agreed that they were looking forward to her labor and delivery.

Carol went through the double doors with the sign that read:

LABOR AND DELIVERY
NO UNAUTHORIZED PERSONS PERMITTED

As she approached the nurses' station, she was shocked to see Mac sitting with her head in her hands. Mac looked up at her and Carol knew instantly that something out of the ordinary—and bad—had happened.

"Melinda?" Carol said.

Mac blinked at her. "She's in surgery. I talked to Dr. Simon just now on the phone. Dr. Whitehall, the chief of surgery himself is doing the surgery. They think it's a perforated bowel. If so, she's in a heap of trouble. Simon's going to assist him along with half a dozen other assorted doctors and residents."

Carol slowly sank down into a desk chair beside Mac. Robbie came out of the coffee room behind the nurses' station, still carrying her cup of coffee.

Mac was silent a moment, lost in her own thoughts. Then, "Damn it. Why did *I* have to be the one in charge of L&D at this particular time? Why *me?*"

"What's the matter, Mac?" Carol asked softly.

"Dr. Simon says if Melinda gets out of surgery without aborting the baby, she'll be brought back here. He's conferring with Dr. Jackson as chief of OB, also the nursing director, about turning one of the labor rooms into a room for Melinda." Mac shook her head. "Nobody's ever done that before."

"Maybe the situation has never come up before."

"It hasn't. So, why me? I've only been in charge back here for three months. Simon says we'll have to set the room up for isolation if she comes back here, to keep from carrying any disease to the other patients . . . while we're trying to fight diverticulitis, peritonitis, and"—Mac began to rub her face with both hands—"and premature labor." She groaned. She raised her head from her hands. "And me? I'm supposed to see that all these precautions and responsibilities are carried out on all shifts."

Carol said, "If Melinda does end up back here, Mac, you know we'll all help; we'll do our best."

Mac was still shaking her head. "God, that poor little girl. That sweet, bubbly little thing . . . Why did this have to happen to *her?*"

The telephone at the desk jangled suddenly, startling the nurses. Mac picked up the receiver. "Labor and Delivery. MacMillan speaking." She listened, then said, "O.K. Thanks." Her face was very pale as she replaced the receiver. She stared at the clock on the wall across the hall from the nurses' station, then looked at Carol. "That was Broughman, the supervisor of OR. It's a perforated bowel."

Carol put both hands on either side of her face and breathed, "Oh no."

With a Kleenex, Robbie began to wipe up the coffee

she had spilled on the top tier of the desk. She shook her head.

"She'll get peritonitis. Watch and see. And if she survives, she'll almost certainly lose the baby," Mac said softly.

Carol and Mac sat silently a few moments, and finally Mac's fist hit the desk. "Damn it!" she exclaimed. "I've got to get out of this negative attitude! Room eight! Room eight's the one we'll use. It's at the end of the hall, and it's larger than the others. It'll be a sort of intensive-care room." Her eyes shone as she thought, pondered. "Yes, labor-and-delivery intensive care."

"L&D ICU," Robbie mused uncertainly.

Martin had hobbled over to stand beside the desk. Joy had appeared, too, beside Robbie. Mac continued, "We'll read, we'll have conferences, we'll learn how to take care of a critical patient—whatever it takes." She looked at Martin. "You'll have a heap of sterilizing to do, Marty, every day. Blankets, sheets, instruments—" She looked at Carol. "We'll get the surgical ICU supervisor down here to show us how to manage equipment." She looked at Joy. "There'll be a specific nurse assigned to her each shift. We can do it."

"We're not critical-care nurses," Robbie reminded her.

"We can do it. We can be what we have to be," Mac said.

"We can do anything the intensive-care nurses do," Carol offered.

"Can we?" Joy asked brightly.

"We can if somebody will show us how to do some things," Carol replied.

"Well," said Martin scowling, "looks like I didn't retire soon enough."

Mac smiled, her face flushing. "Why not? We can fight for a life if we have to, can't we? *Haven't* we? That's what all this amounts to, isn't it? Only . . ."

The other nurses waited, and finally Mac suddenly paled again and stared blankly at the clock. ". . . only let's hope and pray she doesn't . . . doesn't go into *labor.*"

THREE

"Diverticulitis, as you know, is the inflammation of a diverticulum. Before one can have diverticul*itis,* the inflammation, one must first have diverticul*osis,* the abnormality." Dr. Whitehall was using the earpiece of his own personal stethoscope—or one stolen off a ward somewhere—as a pointer. He had hastily sketched the ascending, transverse, and descending colon upon the chalk-blurred chalkboard; hastily because his time as chief of the surgical department was very very valuable. If administration would rotate the nursing staff through other departments instead of letting them graze in only one area for years, such emergency briefings would not be necessary, he was thinking.

"A diverticulum is an abnormal pouch or sacklike protrusion, protruding out from the lumen of the bowel," he continued. "The etiology, or cause, of this abnormality is unknown. Perhaps it's a weakened place in the wall of the colon. These diverticula are apt to become obstructed with feces and become inflamed."

They had indeed discovered during yesterday's surgery that Caleb Simon's patient had a perforated colon due to diverticulitis, and he, Herman Whitehall, was expecting generalized peritonitis. He personally would have preferred that she be admitted to surgical ICU where she belonged; but Simon had thrown a fit, Jackson had backed him up, and Hamblin had gone along with them because he was antsy about managing a pregnant patient. And, of course, the pregnancy itself was threatened, no doubt about that. Simon had contended that ICU nurses were not specialized in dealing with pregnancy or threatened abortions. Whitehall himself had argued that neither were labor-and-delivery nurses specialized in caring for critically ill surgical patients. While Simon's patient lay for three hours in surgical recovery, the administration had met with him, Simon, Jackson, Hamblin, and the nursing director concerning where she should be admitted. Quite simply Simon, Jackson, the nursing director, and Hamblin had won. It was decided that all L&D nurses were to attend an emergency briefing in this empty room on the telemetry floor; that the nurses would set up a room in L&D for the patient under the direction of Simon and Jackson. In Whitehall's opinion, having a diverticulitis patient in a labor room was inviting the transmission of infection to the well OB patients. Of course, the patient would be in isolation, but could one depend on nurses to adhere strictly to the rules of isolation? Could one teach in one briefing the principles involved in the patient's case? Indeed, did anyone *know* the principles involved concerning her case in its entirety?

He looked at Elaine Bryant, the nursing director, a tall, thin, attractive woman about his own age, with prematurely white hair, sitting as if her body had been starched along with her wrinkleless uniform. It was amusing that Elaine had one foot in the old school of nursing and the other in the new school; she was torn between supporting the nurse-as-doctors'-handmaiden image and the new nurse-as-doctors'-colleague image, which, in his opinion, gave her a rather spraddle-legged mentality. Sometimes you could reason with Elaine and sometimes you couldn't.

And there sat Gwenn, the damned ICU supervisor, a sharp, admittedly beautiful girl with a gorgeous figure—top-heavy, as a matter of fact—and slightly crazy. He'd about as soon tangle with a mountain lion as Gwenn. He'd had a tussle or two with her in the past, and not particularly the kind he might have enjoyed either. She was forever thinking one of the patients in one of the ICU units was being neglected or something by their surgeons. It made him shudder when his receptionist would tell him that Gwenn Hutton wished to see him. Once she'd even burst into his office unannounced—

Then there were the other nurses now sitting in the metal folding chairs set up in the vacant room. OB nurses. All looking interested. God, had *he* ever made *them* sit up and take notice! When they were filtering into the room a short while ago, he had overheard some of the evening- and night-shift nurses complaining about the emergency meeting, about having to get out of bed early, et cetera. That was before he had really let 'em have it about the scope of their responsibilities in taking care of a critical surgery patient. *Woke 'em up, all right.* He continued his briefing:

"Melinda had diverticulitis, unknown to her or her physician; more than one diverticulum which may have been caused by or aggravated because of pressure from the gravid uterus, causing impaction, inflammation, and eventually, perforation of the bowel through the diverticulum. Intestinal contents spilled into the abdominal cavity, and as you know, the intestine is not a sterile organ. It harbors *Enterobacter aerogenes,*

35

Enterococci, and especially *Escherichia coli.* Although Dr. Novak and I lavaged the peritoneal cavity with antibiotic solution, this is no guarantee the patient will not contract peritonitis." He waited for the impact of that to soak in as he glanced at his wrist watch. "Now, because I've a surgery in ten minutes, ladies, with your permission, I'll let Dr. Novak brief you on peritonitis." Whitehall bowed slightly. "Dr. Novak is chief surgical resident, my right-hand man. He has much more time to brief you than I, and—it hurts my pride to admit it— he's also much better looking than I."

The nurses laughed and Whitehall smilingly exited the room half-expecting applause.

Dr. Whitehall's right-hand man stood up, stuck his hands in the pockets of his trousers, and glanced at the chalkboard. A slow smile spread across his mouth.

Carol perceived instantly that Novak *was* one of those men who inspired female fantasies. He was tall, handsome in a careless sort of way, smoky-blond. His eyes, which were moving slowly along the two rows of seated nurses, were baby blue and a little melancholy. But what struck her most was his affability, his lack of arrogance, rare in a handsome man, especially since he was also a surgeon.

He turned and slowly erased Whitehall's hastily sketched diverticulosed colon; then he picked up a piece of chalk and faced the nurses.

"The peritoneum," he said. He turned and suddenly his long, thin fingers sketched the outline of a human body, female; he even drew the triangular-shaped pubic area, minus the pubic hair. Joy giggled, but Novak didn't seem to hear. He sketched the abdominal cavity into the outline, and as he did so, he said, "The peritoneum is the largest serous membrane of the body; the outer layer lines the abdominal cavity and folds in to encase the viscera, forming the inner layer." As he

36

spoke he drew the membrane, and under his sleight of hand, the small and large intestines appeared. "The mesentary is an extension of the peritoneum and attaches the intestines to the posterior abdominal wall." He turned to face the nurses. "I won't go into the different omenta that connect the organs; suffice it to say that the peritoneum connects organs, encases them, and lines the abdominal cavity. The fundus of the uterus is encased in peritoneal tissue." As he paused, his eyes seemed to dance in the light coming from the overhead recessed fixtures, and the nurses glanced at each other. "In peritonitis," he went on, "the invading organisms infect the peritoneum and cause inflammation of the peritoneum. Sometimes the infection is localized; sometimes it is generalized." He used the side of the chalk to draw the infection spreading through the entire peritoneum.

"Melinda had one area of perforation, here in the descending colon. Fecal material and digestive enzymes and a few other nice things were discovered in the fluid of her abdomen." Novak raised his brows. "When Melinda arrived in ER at 11:32 yesterday morning, she was in severe pain, vomiting fecal material and a small amount of blood. Her abdomen was rigid with rebound tenderness. Her blood pressure was ninety over forty-two; her temp was one hundred two degrees. The resident in charge of ER suspected a hot appendix until he discovered blood in the emesis. Dr. Whitehall conferred with Dr. Simon, Dr. Hamblin, and me, and we decided emergency surgery was indicated. We located the perforation and sutured it. We had a difficult decision to make: to resect—or remove—about a foot of the descending colon which was diseased, and anastomose—or suture—the two ends together. Or we could *not* suture the two ends of the colon together where we removed part of it, and give

37

her a colostomy instead. Or we could repair the perforation and hope the diverticulitis would improve with medical treatment." Novak clicked his tongue. "A tricky decision in this case because she's six months pregnant. We finally decided to repair the perforation and give medical treatment a chance, which is mainly where Dr. Hamblin comes in on this case. We closed." Novak turned to his excellent sketch again and drew three coiled lines coming from the abdominal cavity. "We put a drain here, here, and here." He turned back to face the nurses, his eyes falling upon Carol. "These drains require meticulous management; you will need to keep them patent to drain purulent fluid and as a means of infusing antibiotic solution from time to time." He shifted his weight to his other foot. "Ladies, we've got a fight on our hands with Melinda. We're fighting diverticulitis to begin with, and we're trying to prevent peritonitis . . . and premature birth. I also don't have to remind you that the surgical incision could easily dehisce, or split open, if she goes into labor."

As he was speaking, Carol was remembering the one time she had been close to Novak. He had been an assistant chief resident then, and it was her first day to observe surgery as a student. She had tied his gown in the operating room, and he had said, "Well, Carol, next time I see you in surgery, I'll expect you to be scrubbed and know how to gown and glove me."

And had he been the cause of the death of her nursing student friend, Shelly? Had he led Shelly on to believing he loved her? Or had it all been Shelly's fantasy as the other students had suspected? This man was the cause of Shelly's death, of the despair which had caused her to drive her Toyota off the bridge on the Interstate because he had not attended her graduation ceremony—fantasy or not. Carol was torn between

38

admiring Novak as a surgeon and hating him as a horse's ass, *if* Shelly's story was true.

"Any questions?" he asked now.

Of course there were a few, half of them serious, half of them silly. When Novak had answered them all thoroughly, he left the front of the room and went to the back. Before he exited, he turned at the door, as if having second thoughts, and leaned against the door frame as Gwenn Hutton stood up with her clipboard under her arm. She motioned for Mac to roll the IV stand to the front of the room. Gwenn was beautiful, big-busted, violet-eyed, and commanded the other nurses' attention because they knew she knew what she was talking about. She also knew how to present information. Most ICU and CCU nurses at Bennet were certified. To be certified they had to attend regular inservice classes on various aspects of critical care, and pass the exams. Gwenn taught most of the courses, or at least directed them. Certified critical-care nurses made the best salaries in the hospital.

As the nurses watched in awe, Gwenn demonstrated the use of the CVP manometer. "CVP means central venous pressure," she began. A small catheter was threaded through a vein into the superior vena cava or the right atrium of the heart, and the other end of it was connected to a water manometer. The manometer looked like an oversized thermometer and was attached to the IV pole. The water for the manometer usually came from the patient's IV. One branch of the catheter went to the patient; the other branch went to the manometer. To take a reading of the central venous pressure, the nurse had only to turn a stopcock to shut off the IV solution going to the patient and allow it to flow to the manometer. Once the reading was taken, the stopcock was shut off to the manometer and turned on to the patient.

"Neat," the nurses said. They had learned all this once, but it was a well-known medical fact that if you didn't use certain equipment or perform certain procedures occasionally, you forgot them.

Gwenn told them that CVP readings were the best method of assessing circulating blood volume and the heart's pumping action. CVP would be installed in Melinda's case so that the doctors could better monitor her fluid intake and prevent either overhydration or underhydration.

While the L&D nurses stared at the simple-looking manometer that was scaring them to death, Gwenn briefed them on the drains, all Hemovacs, catheters threaded into the abdominal cavity, each sewn to the skin with a couple of sutures to keep them in place, the other end of each going to a little accordion-like device which expanded as the fluid in it increased. The accordion created a low suction which facilitated drainage. When Gwenn asked if there were any questions, the nurses were too awed to reply.

Then Mac stood up and explained the setup in labor room eight. The regime, unprecedented in Bennet's entire sixty-six-year history, was well-planned. In room eight lay Melinda Curtis, six months and two weeks pregnant, fifteen hours postop. The nurses would have to gown, glove, and mask before entering her room; then dispose of the gowns, gloves, and masks outside room eight in the red, plastic bag marked DISPOSABLE; and wash their hands. When the nurse caring for Melinda changed her bed linen, towels, washcloths, and hospital gowns, she would have to place them in a red plastic bag marked LINEN located in the room. This would later be placed in the red plastic bag, also marked LINEN, outside the room, to be carried to the hospital laundry. Any IV tubing, empty IV solution containers, syringes, and dressings would be disposed of in the same way, Mac said, only they wouldn't be carried to the laundry. Here the nurses laughed with Mac. Aside she said, "Imagine the laundry getting a bagful of syringes and dirty Hemovacs . . ."

After everybody had laughed again, Mac went on: Melinda's room would be cleaned once a week only by designated housekeeping personnel, and the mops and dust cloths used in Melinda's room would not be used in the other labor rooms. These isolation precautions were not to prevent Melinda from incurring disease, but to prevent the nurses from carrying the disease from her to other patients; to prevent them from contaminating charts, desk, and so on and then carrying the disease to well OB patients. Only one nurse would be allowed to care for Melinda per shift, and any nurse taking care of Melinda was not allowed to enter another labor room or the delivery room, or to touch any other patient during the shift on which she was assigned to Melinda's care. Any nurse who wished to visit with Melinda, while not caring for her, would have to gown, glove, and put on a mask, and while in the room should avoid touching anything. Any nurse, who visited Melinda and touched her or any of her equipment, would have to go directly to the nurses' lounge, change into different scrub clothes, and scrub as if she were going into the delivery room. Extreme measures, but that's what had to be done in order to assure the safety of well OB patients.

Mac went on to say that all nurses on all shifts would take turns being assigned to Melinda's care. Drs. Simon, Whitehall, and Hamblin were to manage her care. They were the best Bennet had. They were the best the city had. Gwenn, the ICU supervisor, would be on call to help manage drains, CVP, and any other equipment, in case there was a problem.

When Mac finished her speech and asked if there were any questions, the L&D nurses, both fascinated by their awesome responsibilities and chagrined, were speechless. *"Anyone have anything else to say?"*

Oh the drama! The wonder of it all! While the nurses and supervisors meditated in a momentary vacuum of silence, sober and reflective, Hank, a three-to-eleven nurse stood up. Hanky was her last name; Hank fitted her better. She was tall, lanky, breastless, the only LVN in labor and delivery, but she was the veteran of the crowd. She'd been in Bennet's L&D for eighteen years. New procedures befuddled her for a while, new innovations irritated her. She was always full of good-natured complaints and resigned sighs. She was also the unit's clown. Slouching now against the back of the chair in front of her, she raised her hand.

Mac said, "Yes, Hank?"

Hank drawled, "Well . . . *I'd* like to say a few words about Texas."

The room exploded. It was an old line every Texan knew. It came from an old joke everybody had forgotten. But it was all that the nurses needed to release them from the tension of the situation just presented to them. They fell apart laughing, and suddenly the task before them didn't seem as insurmountable.

The nurses began to file out of the room now and Carol was reflecting that this unprecedented rally of specialists and nurses to the care of a single little OB patient was not entirely motivated by a sense of duty and dedication. The doctors found it a challenge, something they could learn from and brag about later. The nurses were learning new techniques in case they ever left OB—and it broke the monotony. But whatever their motives, they were nevertheless determined to do their best to help Melinda.

Melinda Curtis had become more than a patient to them now. She was a battleground.

As Carol came near the door, Basil Novak noticed her; his eyes did their little dance in the light as he seemed to recognize her. He stroked his chin and, interrupting one of the other nurses who were chattering at him, pointed a finger at Carol.

"Do I know you?"

Carol paused, enjoying the other nurses' stares. "I tied your gown once in OR."

He blinked, not remembering.

"I was a student."

He frowned.

"Reba Flowers was the patient."

He pointed at her. "The patient who decided on a hysterectomy even though she was three months pregnant."

"Yes."

"I remember you now." He smiled, glanced at the nametag pinned to her scrub top. "I see that you made it, Carol Welles, and that you didn't choose surgery."

On the one hand Carol was hoping he wouldn't remember that she had almost fainted in surgery that day and had had to leave the OR; and on the other hand, she really didn't care.

"So you chose labor and delivery."

"I actually chose the cardiac-care unit, but I found out that Bennet doesn't allow new graduates to work in critical-care areas until they've worked in some other departments for a year or so."

He opened his mouth to say something, but was interrupted by the nursing director who came up to him saying stiffly, "Dr. Novak, we do so appreciate your coming to talk to us today." And Carol turned away.

43

She had always detested people who stride up and interrupt others in the middle of a conversation, but in this case, she was glad, and left Bryant chattering to Novak.

Duty called anyway. The nurses from the post-partum floor had been watching Melinda and the one patient in labor while the L&D nurses attended the forty-five-minute briefing. Mac had hurried back to L&D and so had Joy and Robbie. The L&D nurses from other shifts had either stopped in the corridor outside the room to chat or had disappeared.

Carol started back to L&D with mixed feelings. She felt that Melinda Curtis was going to have to fight too many battles. If she survived, surely the baby wouldn't, even under the care of Drs. Simon, Whitehall, Hamblin, and all the nurses who had been briefed and were committed to her care.

Carol lagged behind the others, apprehensive and yet sort of hoping Mac would assign her to Melinda. She glanced at her wrist watch. Seven A.M.; time to get to work.

Hoping to snatch about five more minutes alone in order to think before she fell into the hectic throes of L&D, she decided to take the elevator down to the first floor instead of the stairway as the others were doing. For Basil Novak had brought back memories of a few months ago, when the telephone had rung and it had been Duane asking to take her out to dinner. *. . . Calling it "dating" is old-fashioned. 'Fifties stuff. Now you call it "getting together" or something.* That first evening when they had gone out he had told her about his first day in surgery as a medical student. And she had so quickly fallen in love with him.

The pain of losing him was still there, still there although she hated him.

44

She pushed the button near the elevator, wondering what would happen when— She never stopped looking for him. It was never out of her mind, the possibility of seeing him in a corridor, in the cafeteria . . . or even in an elevator.

It happened like a dream in which she had willed his appearance. When the elevator door opened, there he stood; and she was not even surprised.

He was alone as was she. While the automatic elevator door remained open to admit passengers, she stood in the corridor unable to move.

He was standing like a statue, not moving, tall, handsome, thinner than she remembered. His expression, changing slowly as he looked at her, was a showcase for a thousand feelings: astonishment, horror, love, hurt, torment, and more, all there as he stood unmoving, looking at her.

And she, she felt the hurt all over again, and the love, and the hopelessness, and that first night together, and other nights, and hate, and desire.

But what eventually surfaced and engulfed her was *loathing*.

He must have seen it. For as the elevator door slid shut with him still inside and her still standing in the corridor, she saw the same agony of love-hate in his cocoa-colored eyes.

A searing pain shot through her abdomen and made her feel faint. She leaned against the wall for a moment thinking how unreal it was—how like a dream that when it finally happened it was exactly as she had dreamed it. She went to the stairway, descending slowly.

My little nurse. I love you for your femininity . . . . Carol, sometimes I think I almost hate you. . . . I love you, I love you and I want you. I want—I want—

Compared to a man like Tyree you're nothing. Nothing. As a nurse compared to Tyree, you're a pipsqueak! I love you and I want—

When she stepped into the corridor from the stairwell, she was half-afraid he would be waiting there. He was nowhere, nowhere in the corridor.

It surprised her to feel one hot tear sliding over her cheek.

Mac was on the telephone when she walked through the swinging double doors of L&D. Joy and Marty were wheeling the one patient in labor to the delivery room.

Mac slammed the receiver of the telephone down. "Carol, there's a patient coming from ER! Brewster says she's about to precip," she said hurrying from behind the desk. "I'll set up the delivery room if you'll check her." Mac ran toward the delivery rooms. She would scrub and put on mask and cap, go into the delivery room, and open the pack of instruments and arrange them on the table near the delivery table.

No sooner had Mac disappeared leaving Carol still standing with her mouth open near the nurses' station than the doors bumped open and a wide-eyed orderly wheeled the patient in. "She's . . . she's . . ." he stammered at Carol.

Carol recognized the glazed eyes, the panting of a woman in the latter phase of the first stage of labor. The second stage of labor was *delivery*. Carol said nothing, but grabbed the handles of the wheelchair and rushed the patient into labor room two.

"Your name?" she asked as she helped the woman to stand.

"Glenda Hopkins," the patient replied standing up shakily.

Carol recognized the name. The obstetricians always

46

sent copies of their patients' office charts to L&D a week or so before their due dates so that the nurses could make up their charts in advance.

"Dr. Jackson's patient?"

Glenda nodded gasping, "Oh, God—"

"Up on the bed quickly," Carol interrupted. "Can you take off your panties, Glenda?" she asked as she pulled on an examining glove. She snatched the bottle of pHisoHex off the shelf in preparation for squirting some on Glenda's vagina so she could do the vaginal exam.

"My water broke in the car so I took 'em off—"

Carol didn't have to examine. When she glanced between Glenda's legs, she could see that the baby's head was already visible with Glenda's contraction.

"You're crowning. I'll get the stretcher, and we'll go to delivery," Carol said pulling off the examining glove. "You've had three other children?"

"Yeah."

Super. That meant that one more push and Glenda could deliver the baby right in the bed. No time to be gentle and nurselike. No time for examinations, enema, prep. "Glenda, please don't push. Pant instead," Carol admonished as she hurried out the door. She heaved the stretcher from the corridor into the room. "Are you panting, Glenda?" she asked cranking up the bed.

"Trying to-oo-oo-oo—"

Glenda was in her mid-thirties, not a large woman; neither was she small, but she looked to Carol to be broad through the pelvic area. She wished she could remember if Glenda had a history of rapid dilation. Her guess was yes. Lord, would she make it to the delivery room? Carol stepped on the brakes of the stretcher.

"Slide onto the stretcher, Glenda," she commanded. No time to be polite.

Glenda scooted from the bed leaving a small amount of blood-stained amniotic fluid behind and Carol glanced once under her nightgown to see if the baby was delivered. Not yet.

Frantically she pushed the stretcher into the corridor and past the nurses' station into the corridor lined with delivery rooms.

"Mac! Mac!" she called. "Here she is and she's crowning. I'll shove her on in and get my mask on."

"Un-ngh . . ." grunted Glenda.

"Glenda, *please* don't push," Carol pleaded irritably as she wheeled the stretcher to just inside the delivery-room door.

Mac looked up from the table where she was laying out the instruments. "Lord, Carol, get your mask and hurry!"

In a blur of horror Carol did. Usually a patient had time to change into a hospital gown, have an enema, have her perineum prepped, her doctor notified, her contractions timed, the delivery room set up . . . .

"Carol!"

Carol ran into the delivery room with her hands still dripping from the rinse after the scrub. Mac was getting Glenda to scoot from the stretcher onto the delivery table. Carol ran over and grabbed Glenda's right leg, while Mac took her left, and together they lifted her legs into the towel-draped stirrups.

"It's coming! It's coming!" Glenda screamed.

Mac dropped the stainless-steep prep basin with a clatter. No time to even prep the perineum with Septisol scrub.

"Unhgh-ngh," grunted Glenda, and the baby's head was clearly visible at the labia minora.

Mac positioned herself immediately between Glenda's legs and pressed gently with one hand on Glenda's perineum between the vaginal opening and the anus in order to minimize any tearing, the other hand she placed just above Glenda's pubic bone, and before Glenda could push again, Mac gently delivered the baby's head. With practiced fingers she felt around the baby's neck to make sure the cord wasn't wrapped around its neck. It wasn't.

"Ungh." And baby girl Hopkins was delivered with the next terrific push.

Swearing under her breath, Mac took the slippery blue creature in both her hands. Carol handed her the bulb syringe and she suctioned the infant's mouth and nose saying with a forced cheerfulness that was a bit shaky, "It's a girl, Glenda!"

From somewhere above, in the vicinity of Glenda's head came a weak, expressionless, "Hurrah . . ."

Mac glanced at Carol. "Damn Dr. Jackson; he ought to have been here by now. Brewster said Glenda called him from home."

Mac had delivered babies before, but it never ceased to frighten her; for one never knew when something might go wrong. . . .

Glenda spoke up. "He's probably got to get rid of his girl friend first." She giggled.

Mac and Carol knew what Glenda meant. Dr. Jackson's wife had divorced him six months earlier, after having left him and their two teen-aged girls to run away with a dentist. Dr. Jackson did not object. Neither did he mourn. Indeed, he changed overnight, grew a mustache, bought snappy clothes—mostly suedes and leathers—a new motorcycle, and grew his hair longer. Dr. Jackson was forty-two, not handsome, but was an athletically built six feet four.

Carol had clamped baby girl Hopkins' umbilical cord in two places, near Glenda's body with the Kelly clamp and four inches from the baby's body with a blue plastic umbilical-cord clamp.

Mac cut the cord between the clamps. What worried them both was the placenta. They were hoping the placenta would not deliver for a few more minutes because most of the danger of hemorrhage was after the placenta was delivered, the third stage of labor.

While Mac worked she kept glancing at the door with *Damn Dr. Jackson* written all over her face, and while Carol took baby girl Hopkins so Glenda could see her, Mac released the Kelly clamp and filled the test tube with cord blood.

Baby girl Hopkins was crying when Carol held her up for Glenda to see. The delivery of infants in the movies always shows the doctor swatting the baby on the bottom to cause it to cry, but in reality this is seldom necessary. Most babies begin to breathe and cry at almost the same instant that their bodies are delivered. Doctors' opinions differ on why this is so; but Carol reasoned that the baby's chest and body were compressed as it pivoted its way through the birth canal and that once the infant was expelled, its chest cavity expanded causing it to take a deep breath, to stir, and begin to cry; the expulsion from the birth canal did the trick. But occasionally an infant did need to be stimulated to cry, and many were often stimulated to make them continue to cry. In these cases the nurses would have to thump their feet. Baby girl Hopkins was howling and pinking up as Carol showed her to her mother.

At that moment, Dr. Jackson appeared in the doorway, his eyes wide, his hair wind-blown. He was in his scrub clothes and tying on his mask saying, "What's going on?"

That was his usual greeting. Whether hell was breaking loose in L&D or whether nothing was going on at all, it was always, "What's going on?"

"What do you *think's* going on?" Mac demanded irritably, but she had to smile; you couldn't help smiling at Dr. Jackson.

As Carol laid the infant in the warming crib, Mac was busy delivering the placenta. Actually, one more contraction of the uterus expelled the placenta and all Mac had to do was hold the umbilical cord attached to it and let it fall into the placenta basin.

Looking surprised, Dr. Jackson came on into the room. "What the hell's all the hurry?" As if the nurses and the patient had conspired to have this delivery before his arrival.

Mac and Carol laughed. Dr. Jackson was likable, even lovable, always upbeat, always in a good humor. The buxom snow-headed matronly nurse on the night shift had said of him, "He'd go to hell and back for one of us if he had to." And the nurses all knew it was true. Dr. Jackson, as chief of the obstetrics department, was proud of his L&D nurses and often told them so.

He came into the delivery room now and pulled on the sterile gloves, still looking bewildered. While Carol put the silver nitrate drops in the infant's eyes, Dr. Jackson checked Glenda's uterus to make certain there were no remaining placental fragments which might later cause hemorrhage. He looked up at Mac. "Where *is* everybody?"

"Dr. Moss is delivering in room one," Mac said. "Joy's in there. Robbie's in Melinda Curtis' room, and Marty's probably cleaning up the labor rooms."

Dr. Jackson withdrew his hand from Glenda's vagina and inspected the slight tear in her perineum.

51

He selected a needle and suture off the sterile instruments table.

"And where were you all this time?" Mac asked.

His eyes smiled over the surgical mask and he sang, "What you don't know won't hurt you, and what you do know I don't care. Whatever I do, one thing is certain, this burden of guilt I won't sha-aa-re."

Probably Dr. Jackson was as close to a cowboy doctor as you could get. For some reason Carol had never seen a doctor who claimed kinship with anything country-western. Even here in the Southwest, until recently, anything country-western was *generally* considered lower middle class. Doctors were above the lower middle class socially, monetarily, and culturally. Dr. Jackson had come into L&D one day, laughing because a friend of his had flown into the city from Ohio and had asked him why nobody was wearing western clothes. Dr. Jackson had told him that the only people who wore western clothes in the city were people from the Northeast. Actually, this was only partly true. Occasionally a real rancher, cowhand, or rodeo buff did come into town dressed in western garb. And there were a few ordinary folks who just liked to dress that way because it was fun. The rest were from the Northeast.

Jackson helped Mac slide Glenda from the delivery table onto the stretcher. Jackson himself went to the blanket warmer and brought a heated blanket which he spread over Glenda and tucked around her.

Mac decided to take the baby to show Mr. Hopkins herself. While Dr. Jackson was whistling a western tune he wouldn't be caught dead whistling anywhere outside of labor and delivery, she pushed the stretcher bearing Glenda through the double doors and into the corridor. Her eyes glanced around as she paused and let Mr. Hopkins see his wife, and she could not help but glance around as she pushed Glenda on to the end of the corridor which ran into the corridor of the post-partum floor where the OB recovery room was. *She would never know when she might see him again. . . .*

After delivering Glenda into the competent hands of Iris, OB recovery nurse, she went back to L&D, experiencing a feeling of pleasure in the thing she'd just accomplished, a thing well-done even under difficult circumstances. Emergency delivery—precipitous delivery—it happened more often than the general public knew. It wasn't fun at the time, but it did break up the monotony of routine. Routine or no, Carol was still pleased that she was part of it all.

No tears this time as she pushed open the double doors of labor and delivery; instead she was surprised at her own unconscious smile.

Labor and delivery. It was one of the happiest places in the hospital, second only to the post-partum ward and the newborn nursery. It contained seven labor rooms exactly the same size, ten-by-ten, and another about ten-by-twelve, all lined up on one side of a hallway across from the long, laminated counterlike nurses' station. Another hallway began at the side of the nurses' station and extended behind it about forty feet. At the end of the hallway was the scrub area: two large stainless-steel sinks with phenol-saturated scrub brushes, a shelf containing disposable paper masks, caps, and conductive booties. Nobody used the conductive booties, however, because the nurses wore their own conductive shoes. The walls here were painted in two shades of green which the nurses called vomit and pseudomonas green. They hated the new paint applied just two months ago over the original nondescript beige.

On either side of the hallway halfway between the scrub area and the nurses' station were the four delivery rooms, two on either side, large, tiled in oatmeal beige, well-lighted, almost airy.

In an alcove to the left of the scrub area was the autoclave room where extra instrument trays were kept, also clean folded wraps, gowns, caps, masks, booties, and, of course, the autoclave unit for sterilizing instruments.

To the right of the scrub area was the "dirty" room where used instruments were carried to be soaked, scrubbed, and rinsed; where dirty linen was put, later to be carried to the hospital laundry.

Carol loved it. At one time she had thought she might want to work on the surgery floor; at another she had thought she wanted to work in CCU, and maybe she would someday. Meantime she loved L&D. And now that Melinda Curtis had been admitted to room eight in serious condition, Carol wanted very much to care for her. But today, Mac had assigned Robbie to her care. But that didn't mean she couldn't visit.

She decided to do it, to visit Melinda and see for herself how the room was set up for her care. She dreaded seeing the bubbly young girl, so proud of her pregnancy, in serious condition. She began to pull on the disposable paper gown, aware that the first awful shock of seeing Duane again had already passed and had left her with a dull headache. He had looked thin, weary. She knew he must work hard, try hard, but she also knew he loved it all, loved medicine far more than he had ever loved her. Well, she loved nursing just as well. Wasn't that really what the fight was all about?

Carol, if you go to Medical Records—if you write your paper—if you pursue this, I'm walking out that door and I'm never coming back.

Perhaps it was inevitable that they part from the

beginning. They had a lot in common; that was the rub. They were both stubborn. And they were both dedicated to their own professions—coexisting professions—but they were socially miles apart.

Now gowned, masked, and gloved, Carol fixed a cheerful smile on her face for Melinda's sake, and opened the door to labor room eight.

FOUR

Vaguely she realized that this thing that was wrong with her was serious. She *hurt*. She hurt badly—but not as badly as she had when she was drying dishes, when she was feeling so sick, when the sharp pains tore through her; not as badly as when she had dropped the dinner plate on the kitchen floor and screamed for John. It had hurt so awfully then that she had almost fainted and he had helped her to the bed.

Before that, she'd had diarrhea with nausea and vomiting for two days, stomach cramps for a month. But *that* day the pain was unbearable, and she hardly remembered John carrying her to the car and driving to the emergency room. She was almost unconscious when they put her on an examining table in the emergency room and nice Dr. Gizarde examined her, taking her blood pressure and listening to her abdomen. She could remember his saying that he wasn't sure whether the pain was labor or not, and then the buzzing had started and everything had gotten blurry—sounds, people's faces, lights and shadows and movement all mixed together in a painful smog.

The next thing that she had been aware of was this quiet room. When she had seen Dr. Simon, he had explained that she had had surgery for a perforated colon. That she had diverticulitis. She remembered that her mother had had diverticulitis years ago, but it had never caused a perforation in her colon.

Melinda was aware of the danger of internal infection because that distinguished surgeon—Dr. Whitehouse? Whitewall?—had told her about it when she had awakened in this room last evening. Dr. Simon had explained, too, that so far the baby was O.K. That was what was *really* important.

Now, thinking of John, she let tears trickle from her eyes. Poor John. How scared he had looked when they had let him, all gowned and gloved, into this room. He should know that she was all right. That everything would be O.K. Even now she could feel the baby moving—a foot, maybe, slid from her navel to her right hip bone. She smiled. Everything was going to be O.K. Mom would know. Mom would tell John how strong she was, how she had seldom been sick as a child, and when she had gotten colds, how easily she had thrown them off.

She lay with her eyes shut listening as the nurse, Robbie, did something with the blood that was going into a vein in her left arm. But even with her eyes closed she could picture her room. A nurse had told her she was in a special room in Labor and Delivery and that it had been all fixed up just for her. All that trouble just for her.

There were all kinds of equipment in the room which she didn't understand; some kind of special blood-pressure thing that was also her IV, and she had a tube in her bladder draining the urine. It didn't hurt, but it made her feel like she needed to urinate. There were three smaller tubes draining the fluid from her

57

abdomen, and there was a tube running blood into her vein; but the tube that was the worst was the one going through her nose and down her throat into her stomach.

Oo-oo. It was all scary! She was afraid to look even. That's why she kept her eyes shut most of the time, so she wouldn't have to see. And she was thirsty, so thirsty, but all the nurses could do was wet her lips with a swab or moisten her tongue. Her lips were rough even though they kept putting ointment on them.

But she was so lucky because she knew some of the nurses. She knew Ms. MacMillan and Robbie Parks on the day shift because of the prenatal classes. There were others who had assisted in the prenatal classes. Maybe she'd see them too. They were all so smart, so nice. With them taking care of her, she *knew* she'd be O.K. *So lucky to have taken the classes knowing Ms. MacMillan . . . and Robbie . . . Carol Welles . . .*

". . . Germlike spermatozoa wriggle up the vaginal canal and surround the ovum which has just been released by the ovary and traveled into the Fallopian tube. . . ." MacMillan says as she turns from her drawing of the spermatozoa and ovum on the chalkboard during their first class. She is a dark redheaded, middle-aged, pleasant lady, super as a lecturer. She makes things so plain and she knows so much. You really believe she knows more than anybody in the world about pregnancy.

And Carol Welles is a new nurse, cute as a cricket, reminds me a little of myself only she's prettier. I had to laugh when she explained about the spermatozoa lying in wait for the ovum to float down the Fallopian tube, how the sperm surrounds the ovum and one of them, with its X and Y chromosomes, penetrates and impregnates the ovum with its two X chromosomes. So it's the sperm that determines the sex of a child because

58

the ovum has only female chromosomes, but the sperm has male and female chromosomes. . . . Then the fertilized ovum travels on down the tube and attaches itself to the lining of the uterus. Carol makes it seem so simple, but she blushes sometimes, bless her heart. . . .

Robbie isn't as good at explaining things, but she is super at teaching the exercises . . . a smattering of the Lamaze techniques of breathing slow and deep when the contractions begin . . . the deep knee bends to help strengthen the perineal muscles. . . .

The surgeon's face swims above her in the surgery suite. "We're going to have to operate, Melinda. . . ." Dr. Simon is saying. "So far the baby is fine. . . ."

So far! Oh dear Lord! Dad is a preacher, Mom was once a practicing nurse; please, Lord, I have so much to be thankful for. But . . . please, dear Lord? Will you also let my baby live?

When Carol entered, the room painted in light green was bright with sunlight filtering in through the cream-colored Venetian blind at the window. Melinda lay still on her back, the head of her bed rolled up about sixty degrees. Her face was extremely pale, the sprinkling of freckles across her nose and cheeks paler than Carol remembered. Her eyes were shut, but Carol knew they were gray-green; her lashes were golden as was her hair. She was petite, maybe a size six or seven, about average height. She could have been Carol's sister, for they resembled each other; except Melinda was prettier and vivacious, bubbly, even effervescent, while Carol tended to be moody—laughing and talkative one minute, introspective and silent the next. And where Melinda's hair was pale gold with streaks of ash blond, Carol's was pale reddish blond. Carol's eyes were amber with flecks of green.

There was an IV of D5W infusing into Melinda's

right arm with the Y-shaped IV catheter also running to the CVP manometer on the IV pole beside her bed. In her left arm a unit of packed cells was infusing.

Robbie was bent over the small oblong tank of water on a cart where coils of IV tubing were submerged to warm the packed cells. Packed cells—blood with plasma removed—was supposed to be moving slowly through the tubing into the coils submerged in the warm water, and circulating in the coils and out into the extension tubing and into Melinda's vein. But it wasn't.

Robbie looked up at Carol scowling. "Have you ever given packed cells before?"

"No."

"You should try it sometime. It's loads of fun trying to get packed cells to go through all this damned tubing."

"Did you try infusing a little more of the saline with the cells?" Carol offered tentatively.

Robbie looked up at the cells hanging from the IV pole attached to Melinda's bed. "I never thought of that. Damn it, Carol. I'm not an ICU nurse, and I'm not a floor nurse. If I'd wanted to work in ICU, I'd have applied for ICU!"

Carol glanced at Melinda whose eyes blinked open and hoped she hadn't heard Robbie's remark. Melinda's eyes focused first on Robbie, then moved to Carol.

Carol said, "Hi, Melinda. How do you feel?"

Melinda's cracked lips spread slowly into a smile. "Yuk." She pointed at the nasogastric tube, one end of which was attached to the low, intermittent suction device on the wall above her bed; the other passed through her left nostril and down her esophagus and into her stomach.

"Feeling any pain?"

Melinda nodded but shrugged, smiling.

What a lousy deal, Bret would say. Melinda couldn't have much in the way of pain medication because of the baby. Major surgery plus diverticulitis and very little pain medication. *Jeez!*

Suddenly Robbie threw up her hands. "I give up! This damned blood won't infuse, and now there's a damned clot!"

"Clot" was a word that scared patients about as badly as the word "critical," and Melinda's eyes flew open again. She stared at Robbie.

Carol resisted the temptation to touch her. "Don't worry, Melinda. Robbie means it's a small clot, microscopic almost, nothing to worry about." Then Carol bent to inspect the catheter where it narrowed and went into Melinda's vein. As a student in ICU, she'd watched a nurse aspirate the injection site with a syringe to remove a clot of blood. The nurse had told her that sometimes the technique worked and sometimes it didn't, but Carol told Robbie how to do it. She told her to take a sterile syringe with an eighteen-gauge needle from its package, to open an alcohol pledget and swab the rubber valve near the site of infusion, to insert the needle into the valve and draw back on the syringe. Robbie followed instructions, but nothing happened. She raised up and gave Carol a glare.

"Try again," Carol suggested.

Robbie did and suddenly blood came into the syringe. "Christ look at that," Robbie said, grinning as the blood began to drip from the blood bag. She adjusted the flow rate of the blood, of the saline which was attached by a Y-shaped catheter to the blood tubing, then beamed at Carol. "Hey, you *have* infused blood before."

"No, I've just observed," Carol said feeling smug. She wanted to loosen the covers over Melinda's feet, to offer to swab her mouth with the glycerin swab, to *do* something, but she could not. Rules. She glanced at the vital-sign sheet on Melinda's overbed table. Her temp had risen one degree since her admission to L&D. Carol was like everybody else in L&D these days—tense, wondering if Melinda would spike a temp signaling the beginning of peritonitis.

Melinda meantime was watching, first Carol then Robbie. Carol knew why; she was scared. Melinda had never been in a hospital before and did not understand all that was happening to her. The doctors had informed her of the possible imminent danger of peritonitis; therefore, she seemed alert to any indication by the nurses that it was beginning.

Carol had been a nurse only six months, but during that time she'd learned to try to take time to explain procedures to patients to allay some of their anxiety and to listen to what they had to say both verbally and nonverbally. Melinda was not a complainer so most of the time the nurses had to interpret her shrugs, her nervous smiles, her frightened eyes, clenched fists, rigid position.

"You think the nasogastric tube's yukky?" Carol asked her.

Melinda said, "Blah-ah."

"The nasogastric tube is draining fluid from your stomach to keep you from vomiting. Your intestines aren't working yet—you know, making that wormlike movement to push food and fluid through. It's called peristalsis, and until peristalsis begins again, we'll have to keep the tube in to keep your stomach empty."

Melinda nodded. "The baby?"

"He's O.K. We're giving you IV fluids, and in a few days we'll start you on a liquid diet."

"When Perry Stalsis starts," Melinda said, her eyes sparkling with a hint of mischief.

Carol laughed. "Right. Maybe you should tell Perry

to hurry up."

"What if he doesn't?" Melinda's eyes grew suddenly sober. "What if it doesn't start?"

Carol glanced at Robbie still fussing over the coils and the blood, trying to regulate the drip rate of both blood and saline. "Then I think Dr. Whitehall will want to install a feeding tube directly into your veins, and we'll feed you a liquid diet that way."

Robbie gave Carol a foreboding look. "Christ's sake. That's all we need."

Melinda shut her eyes and swallowed. The naso-gastric tube was uncomfortable, and Carol knew that by now Melinda probably had a sore throat from it. "The drains?" Melinda asked.

"They're draining secretions caused by the surgery," Carol answered, but didn't add *and pus, blood, lymph* . . .

Suddenly the door opened, and Mac stuck her head inside. "Good news, Carol," she said, happily sarcastic, "Dr. Peusy is sending over two patients in labor. Dr. Moss has one coming in at any minute."

Melinda looked at Robbie to see what her reaction was, obviously sensing that she would rather be out there with *them,* with happy mothers having healthy babies, than in here with her and all her germs.

Robbie caught her expression, and in spite of her occasional lack of tact and insensitivity to patients' feelings, she had her better moments. She smiled at Melinda, nodded toward the door and said. "Ever hear of hell breaking loose, Melinda? Well, out there is where it all begins."

Carol laughed, and Melinda smiled hugely. "See you later," Carol told her.

Melinda gave Carol an O.K. sign with her thumb and finger, causing her bottle of IV solution to swing perilously on its pole. Then her hands formed fists again as the door closed behind Carol, who was going out there where all the good things were happening.

By now Carol had the routine of admitting patients down to a fine art—if you could call giving enemas, shaving pubic hair, and collecting urine specimens a fine art. Mac was admitting Dr. Peusy's first patient to room one while Joy was "setting up" two of the delivery rooms. An orderly from admitting rolled Dr. Peusy's second patient into L&D via wheelchair just as Carol was washing her hands after having taken off the gown and gloves she'd donned before entering Melinda's room. Quickly, she proceeded with the usual admitting procedures.

First she introduced herself to the patient, took her to room two, and instructed her to remove all her clothes and put on the hospital gown which was lying neatly folded on the overbed table. After the patient had done as she was instructed, Carol would take vital signs, do a vaginal exam, give the enema, do the perineal prep, time contractions, and watch.

In the meantime, Abigail Hornsby, enormous with her third child, would entertain her.

"Ain't that just like a doctor?" Hornsby told Carol as she pulled off her sweater. "The first thing they always tell you to do is take off all your clothes." Abigail Hornsby was built like a dirigible; tall, broad-shouldered, musclebound, bosomy, thick through the middle even when she wasn't pregnant, but there was no fat on her; she was all muscle. Her eyes were large and deep-set, sunken as if she were recovering from a long illness or a hangover. "And the best they can do to let you cover up is give you one of these gowns that show your fanny. Half the damned time it's a paper gown at that."

Mac looked in on Abigail as Carol was tying her

gown in back and when Carol went out to write Abigail's name on the chalkboard on the wall across the hall from the nurses' station, Mac said in a low voice, "Your patient, Hornsby . . . did you ever see such a woman? Boy, her husband had better walk the straight and narrow, or she might just whip his ass."

When Carol went back into Hornsby's room, she was still stewing. "Ever hear of a doctor telling a *man* to take off all his clothes?" she demanded as she crawled into bed. "No. It's always the women. Honey, now I left that specimen of weewee in the bathroom like you told me."

While Carol took Abigail's vital signs Abigail said, "These OB doctors have us by the ass. They see to it we have to go to their damned office for a checkup at least once a year. Write up a prescription for our birth-control pills so's we can get 'em filled for a year. Then after the year's up we have to go back into the office again else he won't prescribe more pills. That way ya gotta pay for another office call; otherwise, no pills. We got no choice. They got us by the ass."

Carol took Abigail's blood pressure and recorded it on the vital-sign sheet on the overbed table; then she took the fetoscope—a stethoscope fitted with a head brace—and stuck the earpieces in her ears, but Abigail clamped a mighty hand on her arm.

"Forty dollars."

Carol took one of the earpieces out of her ear. "I beg your pardon?"

"Forty dollars a whack every time I walk into Dr. Peusy's office. Peusy. Did ya ever hear such a name as that? What do you nurses call him behind his back, honey?"

Carol chuckled, but she didn't dare answer that. Instead she placed the diaphragm of the fetoscope on Abigail's bare, distended abdomen. The fetal heart was

65

loud; the head brace of the fetoscope, acting as a conductor of sound through the bone of her own skull, caused the fetal heart tones to be more audible than they would have been with an ordinary stethoscope. *Clop, clop, clop, gallop, gallop.* A good strong heartbeat, one hundred forty-two beats per minute—probably a boy because it was on the low side of normal. Girls' heartbeats were usually faster, around one hundred fifty-eight. This was no absolute way of telling the sex of a fetus, of course, but it held true more often than not. Carol removed the earpieces from her ears.

"Forty dollars for the privilege of sitting in one of his moth-eaten office chairs. Then he gets to look at my bottom. They stick me on that hard table, spread my legs, put my feet in stirrups and there my ass is, exposed to the world. He gets between my knees and prods and pokes down there sticking cold things in. Hell, you'd think he was watchin' TV and changing channels every few seconds. He does that and feels of my breasts, then has the gall to charge *me* forty dollars. I oughta charge *him.*"

While Carol was doing the vaginal exam, she asked, "Your membranes are intact, aren't they?" her voice sounding sweet, high, and clear after Abigail's raucous tirade.

"Speak English, honey."

"Has your water broken?"

"No, but it will. When I'm dilated six, you watch. Pow! I take a durned bath in my own water every time. So I'd advise you to hurry with the enema."

Carol pulled off her examining glove and began filling the plastic enema container with water.

"You know why I'm pregnant?" Abigail said when she was lying on her left side and Carol was holding the nozzle of the enema tubing in her rectum.

"When you feel full, breathe slowly and deeply, but if it gets too uncomfortable, tell me and I'll clamp off the water for a second."

"O.K., honey, but do you know why I'm pregnant?"

"Uh . . . well . . . not the details."

"I didn't go in for my yearly checkup, that's why. No forty-dollar trip, no pills. Bingo! I'm knocked up. Ought to have a hysterectomy except I don't believe in them. Then you know what?"

Carol was laughing softly. "No."

"They got us there, too. After the hysterectomy if you don't get your yearly checkup, you get no hormone pills. No hormone pills and you get nerve problems and hot flashes."

Carol would have explained to Abigail that yearly checkups were necessary for hysterectomy patients so that the doctor could keep tabs on the effects of the medication on the patient's health and well-being, but she didn't have a chance.

"Honey, now I've taken all the water that I can hold. So if you'll stand back, I'll make a dash for the bathroom, and when I come out, I'll be dilated six."

She was. And her membranes had ruptured while she was expelling the enema.

"How's Hornsby?" Mac asked Carol when she wrote *six* beside Hornsby's name on the chalkboard.

"As you see she's dilated six."

"So's Dr. Peusy's other patient."

Carol noticed then that Mac had written on the chalkboard too.

ROOM	NAME	ADMIT	GRAVIDA	DILATION
1	Ragsdale	11:45	III	6
2	Hornsby	11:50	III	6

"They're neck and neck," Mac said. "Dr. Peusy's

been inducing labor again."

Carol looked back at Mac. Dr. Peusy was an old-fashioned obstetrician and Carol knew that he did not believe in inducing labor. He was a soft-spoken, gentle man who generally did not like to rock the OB department's boat, so he didn't say much. But the nurses in L&D had picked up on the fact that he considered pitting patients—inducing labor by introducing Pitocin into their IVs—barbaric and unnatural. However, he seldom used forceps during delivery, which was to his credit; for some of the obstetricians used forceps to hurry the baby along when patience like Dr. Peusy's would have been better for both mother and baby.

"Did Peusy give Hornsby castor oil?"

Carol said, "I don't know."

"I'll bet you lunch they both went in for their checkup yesterday and he told them to go home and take castor oil last night."

Carol went back to Abigail's room and began to open the perineal prep kit. The kit was small and simple, containing a plastic tray, a disposable drape, a small package of Betadine solution, four gauze sponges, a razor, and gloves.

"It's men," Abigail said watching Carol open the prep kit. "Ever hear of men having to go in for a yearly checkup on their balls and penises?"

Carol had to laugh. "No."

"Ever hear of a man going in for a yearly checkup, stripping down to his birthday suit, putting on a gown, climbing up on a table, and spraddling his legs so a doctor can poke and prod his privates? No. But us? Once a year. What a racket."

Still smiling, Carol placed the drape under Abigail's muscly buttocks to protect the bed sheets, then opened the package of Betadine prep and poured it into the appropriate little compartment in the tray. Then she pulled on the gloves, took a gauze sponge, dipped it into the solution, and began to swab the pubic mound and perineum. She knew Peusy's routine orders—a *complete* prep. That included not only the perineal area, but also the entire pubic mound as well. Prepping the pubic mound was old-fashioned; most obstetricians required their patients to have a half-prep, perineal area only. The prep was done for the purpose of cleansing and shaving the immediate area about the vagina to prevent pathogenic bacteria from entering the birth canal.

"They've got us by the ass, and there ain't a damned thing we can do about it."

"Abigail, have you ever thought of having your tubes tied?" Carol asked as she made the last few gentle scrapes on Abigail's perineum.

"Why should I? Hal can go have *his* tied. Why should *I* go through that? Why is it always the woman? Not me, honey. He can go have a . . . a . . ."

"Vasectomy?"

"Yeah. One of them. Hell, the doctor can tie a knot in the whole damned thing for all I care."

"You can have a tubal ligation," Carol said, observing her handiwork. Doctors had been known to make a nurse scrape one lone hair off a patient's perineum right in the delivery room. If the doctor's mood was foul enough, it could happen anytime.

"Speak English, honey."

"The doctor can give you a caudal or spinal or a general anesthetic, then make a small incision in your abdomen and tie each of your fallopian tubes. Or he can insert an instrument which will cauterize the tubes, and there're new procedures like that which can be reversed if you decide—"

"I won't decide, honey. Nope. Now don't get me

wrong. I'll love this kid and he'll never want for nothin'. I'd work my fingers to the bone for him like I've always done for my others, but I don't want no more kids. Nope. Hal can have a vast-ectomy."

It occurred to Carol that not once had Abigail winced or complained of pain. And yet Carol had timed her contractions and they were five minutes apart. Vital signs were still good. Fetal heart tones were strong and fluctuating between one hundred thirty-eight and one hundred forty-two.

"Aren't you having pain?" she asked after she had taken her vital signs again.

"Sure. That's why I'm bitching. Every time I feel one coming on, I bitch. It helps."

Carol took Abigail's rough hand in hers briefly. "Can I get you something for pain? Dr. Peusy has ordered Demerol for pain."

"Old-fashioned ain't he? Most of my friends' OB doctors use them spinals now. I'd change, but you see he's from Oklahoma like me and we have a sort of association, know some of the same folks and he's delivered my other kids. Naw, I guess I don't need a shot yet, honey. Maybe later."

Carol laid her own hand on Abigail's abdomen, felt it harden and rise slowly beneath her hand as another uterine contraction began. "Would you like your husband to come in now?"

"No! He'd faint. I'm like them ERA women. Every man should have menstrual cramps once a month and have to clean toilets once a week."

"By any chance did Dr. Peusy have you take castor oil last night?" Carol ventured, glancing at the clock.

"Yeah. One of them castor-oil cocktails. Castor oil in orange juice. Bla-ah!" Abigail laid her hand on Carol's arm again. "Listen, honey, I've changed my mind. It's getting about time for me to push and I'd be obliged if

70

you'd fetch me my shot now."

Indeed, Abigail's pains were now three minutes apart. Carol took an examining glove from the package off the shelf and snapped it on.

"Let me check first," she said, "so I can keep the scoreboard up to date."

As Carol squirted the pHisoHex solution on Abigail's vagina and slowly inserted her middle and index fingers, Abigail said, "Wouldn't you think they'd figure out a better way to check for dilation than this?" And she patted Carol's arm. "It's not your fault, honey. You're just doing your job."

The cervical rim was completely effaced now. Having thinned out quickly, it was now almost nonexistent. The dilation was over eight centimeters. No wonder Abigail was feeling ready to push. Carol withdrew her hand. "Abigail, I'm sorry, but I think it's too close to delivery for you to have a shot. I'll check with Dr. Peusy, O.K.?"

Abigail turned her head to look at Carol. "You tell him I don't want no gas. By the time I get to the delivery room it's all over but the shoutin'."

Carol flew from the room intending to page Dr. Peusy, but he was already at the desk with Mac.

"Hornsby's dilated over eight," Carol told Mac.

Dr. Peusy was a handsome middle-aged doctor with black curly hair and thick eyeglasses. His eyes went to the chalkboard at the same time Carol's did. Hornsby and Ragsdale were still neck and neck, both dilated eight-plus.

Dr. Peusy stood up. "Get them both to the delivery rooms, please. I'll go in with Mrs. Ragsdale because she has a history of rapid delivery." He paused and frowned in thought. "But so does Hornsby." He stood for a moment undecided which patient should have his attention first, but Ragsdale helped him make up his mind.

71

A low moan issued from room one that rose to a screech, propelling Mac toward the room and Dr. Peusy toward the scrub area.

Joy appeared immediately and helped Carol get Hornsby onto the stretcher while Martin helped Mac get Ragsdale onto hers. The two stretchers met in the hallway in the final stretch. "I'll go with Dr. Peusy, you and Joy get Hornsby ready," Mac instructed.

As she limped beside Hornsby's stretcher, Martin told them, "Dr. Moss' patient is on her way from admitting."

"Superterrific!" Carol told Joy.

They donned their caps and masks and scrubbed hurriedly while Martin watched Hornsby just inside delivery room two. Minutes later Hornsby, with Carol's and Joy's help, heaved her own body from the stretcher onto the delivery table. The two nurses then lifted her legs into the stirrups.

"Oh, Nurse, I think it's coming," Abigail said.

"Oh, Mrs. Hornsby, you mustn't push," Joy said flitting around the table while Carol grabbed the prep basin.

The prep basin had been half-filled with Septisol solution for the final perineal prep. With gloved hands, Carol took the basin with its gauze sponges and began. One swipe from the top of Abigail's vagina down over the anus and the sponge was dropped into the bucket on the floor. Another sponge, from the top down across the anus and into the bucket. Moving outward one swipe at a time Carol prepped Abigail's left perineal area and part of her inner thigh. Then she proceeded doing the same on the right until she had used eight sponges, and Abigail's perineum was painted a rusty brown.

Meantime Martin was limping from the door of one delivery room to the other watching. "It's still neck and

72

neck, but Ragsdale is gaining," she told Carol just as she finished the prep.

"Unghh," grunted Hornsby, pushing, and the fetus's head was bulging the perineum.

Carol gaped, swallowed, said, "Marty, please tell Dr. Peusy that she's—"

"Unghhh!"

Joy was staring at Hornsby's bottom, her mouth open. Both nurses could see that it was too late. One more push and— Carol could only do as her maternity-nursing textbook had instructed and as she had seen Mac and the doctor do. Before Abigail could push again she placed her hand on Abigail's perineum and exerted slight pressure there, placed her other hand over Abigail's pubic mound and did the same which caused the head to be delivered. Had Abigail pushed one more time, the head would have been propelled out and would have torn the perineum. Most people did tear a little which is why the doctor always did an episiotomy, cutting the area because it would heal better than a tear. Abigail tore slightly, but that was the least of Carol's problems now. She felt around the baby's neck to see if the cord was wrapped around it. It *was*.

"Oh . . . . Joy, the cord's around the neck—"

Joy's face paled above her mask and she did a little dance of indecision at Carol's side.

Carol tried to loosen the cord enough to pull it over the baby's head, but she couldn't. "Joy, go tell Dr. Peusy the cord's around the neck."

Joy flew out of the room. Seconds later, Dr. Peusy rushed in pulling off his blood-covered gloves. Joy held another pair for him and he snapped them on almost simultaneously.

In his panic he asked Carol, "Did you do an episiotomy?"

Of course she hadn't. Nurses weren't allowed to do surgical procedures, she didn't know how, and there hadn't been time anyway. She stepped back.

Dr. Peusy maneuvered the baby's head enough to lift the cord from around its neck, and one more uterine contraction delivered the infant's body. In spite of her horror and fear, Carol heard Abigail say, "Whew!" And Dr. Peusy's hands were a blur as he clamped the cord twice and cut it, suctioned the baby's mouth and nose, and handed him to Carol.

Baby boy Hornsby was screaming his rage as Carol took him to the hooded warmer to finish suctioning his mouth and trachea and Martin appeared in the doorway shouting, "Mac's delivered the baby!"

Dr. Peusy shot up off the stool, finished delivering Hornsby's placenta, then, peeling off his gloves, ran out of the room again.

Baby boy Hornsby was bellowing furiously when Carol held him up for Abigail to see. Abigail said affectionately, "Aw, look at that. Ain't that just like a man? It was us that did all the work, and he's the one complainin'."

Five minutes later Dr. Peusy came in and changed gloves so that he could check Abigail's uterus for any remaining placental fragments; then he began suturing the small tear beneath Abigail's vagina.

Later, as Joy wheeled baby boy Hornsby from the delivery room and Carol helped Abigail slide from the delivery table onto the stretcher, Dr. Peusy informed her, smiling tremulously, "Both Mrs. Ragsdale and Hornsby delivered at 12:05. Hers was a girl."

As he left the room pulling down his mask, Abigail, misty-eyed with fatigue, looked up at Carol who was placing a warm blanket over her. "Yeah. We women did all the work, but guess who'll get the pay?" Abigail said. "The damned doctor."

Carol laughed as she pulled the stretcher from the delivery room into the hallway. As a matter of fact, the day-shift nurses had delivered three babies within two days, but she wouldn't tell Abigail that. In fact she wouldn't have admitted it to anybody—she was still too new as a nurse—but all the things Abigail Hornsby had been saying since she had come into L&D, did have a grain of truth in them.

FIVE

Basil Novak was leading the way to Labor and Delivery. It was early, 7:10 A.M. The charge nurse of the day shift of L&D had notified Whitehall that Melinda Curtis had spiked a temp of over one hundred three. They'd been afraid of that. Peritonitis, probably.

The most frustrating thing about that was, they were giving her two broad-spectrum antibiotics to which the normal intestinal organisms were sensitive. Why the hell then was she spiking a temp? Bladder infection? Like Duren said, you don't usually spike a temp that high that fast with a bladder infection. Then could she be going into septic shock? God forbid.

Pregnant, peritonitis, perforated colon. Poor girl. The diagnoses were almost like sounding a death knell for two people—the girl and the fetus.

Whitehall was going to be in conference all day and had instructed him to consult with Hamblin and Simon to decide what to do about the elevated temp; he also had four residents under his wing with whom he had to make rounds. Melinda Curtis' case was an auspicious learning situation, but that's not why he was bringing the residents along. Actually, he was only interested in bringing one of them along—Duane Duren. He had personal reasons for wanting to expose him to the most difficult cases, to find out what made him tick. Duren was no dummy. Second in his graduating class. He also possessed the ingredient Basil was looking for—ambition. Not pecuniary ambition, not necessarily glory; an ambition for—what? To make history? To be the best, to make a consequential contribution to medical science only for the sake of making the contribution? Maybe. Or maybe he had a gargantuan ego to feed. Did it matter? That depended.

Next fall, *only* next fall, Novak was going to have to establish his own private practice. Like most young doctors he'd probably become an associate of some established surgeon, which was why Whitehall was courting him. But Basil wanted to go it alone as soon as possible, after two years—or three—and take on a younger associate himself, somebody with the same ambitions and vision, like Duren.

For he had dreams, dreams of his own cardio-vascular team, a brilliant associate; trained, preferably specially trained, R.N.'s; his own anesthesiologist—an office staffed entirely by nurses trained in giving stress tests, performing lab tests for research . . . But that was in the future and this was today and as chief surgical resident, he had to lead the interns and junior residents around by the nose and expose them to as much experience as possible.

Outside the wide double doors of L&D Novak paused and the six junior residents came to a halt. He turned and looked at them one by one. *Junior resident Michael Hall thinks he wants to become an internist, but is taking extra surgical rotation to be sure. Eddie Denham, not too sharp, but thinks he wants to go into Oncology. Kent, nicknamed Clark, is ambitious to be*

Bennet's first black orthopedic surgeon. Bowie and Fuizat don't know where they're headed yet. That leaves Duane Duren, by far more brilliant than the others, more so than myself, ambitious to become a surgeon.

Basil had said to them earlier, when they had met for coffee before rounds, "You've all rotated through Labor and Delivery at one time or another in medical school, so I'm sure the goings-on in L&D won't be a surprise to you, but I have a case in there that *will* surprise you." And he had proceeded to run through the details of Melinda Curtis' case.

Now, as they stood outside the doors to Labor and Delivery he said, "Doctors, you are about to enter an area every bit as specialized as the intensive-care and cardiac-care units. The nurses who work in here are specialists, and they know more about labor and delivery than you'll ever know as a doctor—which brings a point to mind I think I should pass on to you. If you value your professional relationships, never talk *down* to a nurse. You may need her advice sometime." Then he backed through the doors and the others followed.

The red-headed charge nurse of L&D looked up from a chart on the desk before her. A fleeting look of distress came and went on her face when she saw the residents striding in. Basil couldn't blame her. He approached the desk and even *he* was surprised when his deep baritone voice came out sounding like that of a small boy asking for a cookie.

"Ms. MacMillan?" He indicated the six eager residents behind him with a sweep of his hand. "Drs. Hall, Denham, Kent, Bowie, Fuizat, and Duren would like to assist me in checking Melinda Curtis."

MacMillan said, "Well, you'll have to wait, Dr. Novak. The nurse is giving her a bed bath."

"Oh." Novak cast a look at Duren who was attempting to conceal a smirk, then he picked up Melinda's chart and flipped through the sheets pretending to read the nurses' notes, aware that he was not experienced enough, or arrogant enough, or doctor enough—yet—to be very assertive in matters of this sort, but that flipping through a chart always gave people the impression you were studying something or looking for something in particular.

The nurse looked at the crestfallen faces before her and took pity. Standing up, she said, "Look. Dr. Moss is doing an extra interesting delivery. A breech birth. The patient is a primip." When Mac saw their blank expressions, she explained, "A primipara, you know; this is her first delivery. Would you like to observe?"

The resident doctors looked at each other. Basil, surreptitiously peering up from the chart, read in their faces that they wouldn't.

"If you'll hurry, you'll have time to scrub and go in. Dr. Moss won't mind," MacMillan said.

Basil hated to act like a snob, but they weren't on L&D rotation. They were supposed to be on surgical rotation.

A woman moaned in one of the labor rooms and Eddie moved closer to Basil, looking over his shoulder. Hall forgot and scratched his privates.

Basil said, "Thanks, nurse, but we'd better just come back later." He noted the look of horror on the faces of the residents and read their expressions again. *Let a bed bath keep doctors from seeing an important patient? What kind of wimp* is *the chief?*

MacMillan read their thoughts too. "Just a second and I'll see if the nurse is finished with Melinda's bed bath." She hastened from around the nurses' station and down the short hallway to labor room eight, opened the door, peered in, said something to somebody inside, nodded, closed the door, and came back to the nurses' station.

"O.K. Melinda's nurse says you can go in, in about five minutes."

Novak thought he heard a collective sigh of relief from the residents. "Good," he said feeling his sense of authority returning. "We'll read her chart after we see her. How is she?"

"Temp is up, one hundred and three point two. But no other signs of infection. We've taken a culture of the drainage, but of course the results won't be back for several hours. She's in good spirits. Vitals stable. FHTs normal."

Basil saw Eddie nudge Duren. "What's FHTs?"

"Fetal heart tones," Duren mumbled.

Basil smiled and led the way to room eight where MacMillan oversaw their gowning and gloving—they had already abandoned the use of masks as being unnecessary—and when they were ready, she opened the door and the residents filed in stepping on each other's toes until the door closed behind them.

The overhead ceiling lights were on because it was just dawn outside when they entered the room. Novak took in the CVP manometer, the NG tube with fluid fluctuating in it—tan-colored and normal—the urinary catheter bag with the normal straw coloring of urine; then the patient herself, pale but smiling, large-eyed and watching. The nurse, who was bending over Melinda's sheet-covered abdomen listening to fetal heart tones with the fetoscope, raised her head and straightened slowly. She was the nurse he'd spoken with after the inservice meeting. The one whose name he'd seen last spring on the medical records check-out sheet. Carol Welles, the new one. Novak had to smile to himself as the residents gawked at her. She wasn't a movie star or model beauty, but she was cute and fresh and young.

Something else too. She was staring at Duren, and he was staring at her—both shocked-looking.

What was this? Duren knew her. A love affair? A mere acquaintance? A relationship?

She turned pale; her hand trembled, but she was looking at Basil. "Dr. Novak?" she said with a pert lift of her chin. "Will you doctors please step away from the bed? I would prefer that you not all crowd around so close, please."

Duren's eyes flashed, his jaw set. Uh-oh. *That* kind of relationship, Basil thought. The residents all stepped away from the bed except for Duren who stood his ground even while the nurse glared at him, and a slow blush began at her throat and went up.

The patient hadn't missed any of it.

Basil stepped closer to the bed. "How are you, Melinda?"

She croaked a hoarse, "I'm fine."

"Sore?" he asked lifting her gown a little as the nurse's gloved hand flew quickly to aid him to uncover her abdomen, but keep the sheet over her pubic area to preserve her privacy as much as possible. He began to peel one side of the dressing off the incision.

Melinda nodded. "I've had major surgery and you ask if I'm sore?"

The residents laughed, but Melinda put her hand on Basil's. "I *am* sorer today, though."

"Nauseated?" he asked as he checked the surgical incision.

"A little," Melinda answered as Carol covered the wound again.

Basil palpated her abdomen. Naturally it was tight, but tighter than a mere gravid uterus, perhaps. Perhaps. He checked the drainage from the three tubes draining her abdomen—fluid still dark brown and

81

scanty. Nothing you could call unusual there. *But the look on her face. God, that look on her face . . .*

While Novak stood beside the bed holding his stethoscope, he noticed Duren again, then Welles, then Duren again. Duren was studying the vital-sign sheet on Melinda's overbed table. He looked up at the nurse.

"Last temp was when?" he asked her.

"Seven-ten just as it says on the vital-sign sheet," she replied politely. But politely like a petunia with frost.

"But according to the vital-sign sheet her pulse is normal," Duren said.

"Yes."

"Elevated temperature but normal pulse is unusual."

"I know."

"Normally when a patient spikes a temp the pulse increases."

"I know."

Duren acted as though he wanted to say something else, but couldn't think of anything.

In a small voice Melinda asked, "Is there infection?"

Novak suddenly felt like hell for momentarily forgetting his patient and said, "We don't know yet, Melinda. Maybe. Maybe not. Most people spike a temperature for several days after surgery." He placed the earpieces of the stethoscope in his ears and bent down to listen for bowel sounds on the right side of her distended abdomen. All he could hear was the *swish, swish, swish* of placental circulation, the same pulse rate as the patient's, about eighty-five per minute. He moved the stethoscope up. Nothing. Over the umbilicus. Nothing. Down. Nothing. Down some more. *Thump, thump, thump,* came faintly but rapidly; the fetal heart, almost inaudible because a six-month fetus' heart was hard to hear with the usual stethoscope. He moved the diaphragm of the stethoscope on down. Nothing. No bowel sounds. He motioned for the nurse

82

to turn Melinda on her side.

She caught on instantly and placed both her hands on Melinda's side, saying, "Melinda, turn toward me. I'll help you."

The patient rolled over slowly, painfully, with Welles's hands on her back helping her turn—thin hands, long slender fingers. Novak noticed that Melinda's back was clear, no red areas. Evidently the nurses were turning her frequently as he had hoped. Couldn't expect L&D nurses to remember to turn a surgery patient every two hours, so he'd written the order. He had reasoned that they would probably remember; but there was usually a careless one in the bunch who would forget, so you always had to write the order to remind the careless ones. He listened from the side, the back. No bowel sounds. Then he moved the stethoscope over the posterior thorax. Lung sounds were clear. That was a break. He raised up, and the nurse came to his side of the bed telling Duren, "Pardon me," making him step back on Eddie's toes while she tucked a pillow behind Melinda's back so that she could rest her back against it as she lay on her side.

So what had he learned? Nothing. He turned to the others. "Any questions anyone wants to ask Melinda?"

They shook their heads, Melinda's obvious pregnancy having awed them into silence. All but Duren, who went to the bed again, laid a hand on her arm gently, said, "Got your Christmas shopping done yet, Melinda?"

The other residents looked at each other thinking, What the hell does that have to do with anything? Basil knew. Duren was checking her orientation. *The look on her face.*

Tremulously, hesitantly, Melinda replied, "No. But I've got lots of time."

"Have you?" Duren asked.

"Thanksgiving. It's not over yet. Is it?"

"Isn't it?" Duren persisted.

"I don't know. I don't think so," Melinda said softly.

Duren had been gently brutal, wrenching the evidence of her disorientation from her softly. "It's only two weeks till Christmas, Melinda," he said almost angrily and turned to face Welles. "The nurses will keep you oriented to time and place from now on, Melinda. It takes . . . so very little effort to do that."

Zap. There was no mistaking the malignant electric current popping between Duren and Welles as they stood face-to-face glaring at each other. Basil hastily jerked his head toward the door, and the residents followed him from the room.

Outside the door they pulled off their gloves and gowns and stuffed them carefully into the red plastic bag, while Basil was thinking, Duren's a better doctor than I am. He has the natural instincts. The look on her face was the look of confusion, and nobody but Duren had thought to test her to see if she was becoming disoriented, one of the first signs of shock, or impending coma, and a dozen other nice things.

Sometimes vital signs and lab tests were not enough to catch the beginning of a complication in its early stages; if you were alert enough, though, you could catch subjective symptoms before they became apparent. Duren had. Well, so now what would they do? Call another conference with Hamblin, Whitehall, Simon, and himself. And this time, Basil was going to see that Duren attended.

As he took Melinda's chart from the nurses' station and into the coffee room behind the nurses' station in order to review her case with the other residents, he couldn't help but remember the slow blushes and the pallor alternating on Duren's and Welles's faces as they stared at each other. Subjective symptoms—of what? An aborted love affair? Basil Novak moistened his lips with his tongue and eyed Duren who was pouring himself a cup of coffee from the carafe of the coffee maker.

"Duren, once again I ought to remind you that it's better not to talk down to the nurses," he said pointing his thumb over his shoulder toward the labor area. Novak was a little irritated at him and unable to conceal the irritation.

Duren lowered the cup from his lips, glanced slowly around the coffee room at the other residents who were looking at him speculatively. "I couldn't help it. She was shorter than me," he said smiling grimly.

"Come in. You're late. I couldn't wait for you any longer. I've already eaten. Enchiladas and nachos and Coke. Want some?"

Bret paused on the threshold between Carol's porch and the inside of her apartment. "Did you make 'em?"

"Yes, using Mom's recipes."

"Then I'll have some."

"That surprises me, since you haven't turned down any of my food yet."

He caught at her arm, but missed as she skillfully avoided him on her way to the kitchen. "What I want to know is, how you can work all day and come home and make a Mexican food dinner. That's a hell of a mess to make and takes a lot of time. Mmmm. Smells good though."

"Sit down at my brand-new dining set and I'll bring you some."

"No, you sit down at your brand-new dining set and I'll get my own food."

"Thanks. It's in the oven."

When Bret brought his heated plate to the table, he

sat down and looked across at her. "I'll bet Mac gave you Melinda today," he said. "I can see it in your face. Nothing but a new learning experience can light your face up like that."

"First time. Bret, I loved it. I loved taking care of Melinda. I didn't realize how much I have been missing. In L&D we see such a small area of nursing."

"I knew you'd like it," he said, shoveling in a mouthful of enchilada.

"Some medical residents came in this morning to see her briefly. One of them discovered she was slightly disoriented; her temp keeps going up. Dr. Hamblin is getting panicky, I think. He's the internist, you know. He keeps saying he wished he'd specialized more in abdominal diseases."

All of Melinda's vital signs had been normal since surgery three days ago except for the sudden spiking of her temp early that morning. And now after Duane had discovered she was becoming disoriented, Dr. Hamblin kept sitting at the nurses' station shaking his head, poring over her chart, acting almost rude to Melinda, almost accusing her of pretending disorientation. Only a nurse with a little experience would know why doctors acted rude like that at times, the same reason Duane had acted angry with Melinda—they were angry at the disease, not the patient.

"I'm surprised it wasn't you who discovered she was disoriented. You've still got the student-nurse syndrome; ultraperceptive, ultraanxious to absorb everything you can," Bret said.

"And I hope I never change. No, darn it, it wasn't me who discovered it. I had noticed she was extra quiet, lethargic, and I had tried not to talk to her too much, to tire her. No, it had to be Duane that—" She stopped, took a deep breath, blushed.

Bret stopped chewing and looked up from his plate

at her. Her face was flushed. She hadn't intended to tell him, to mention Duane at all.

"Duane," Bret said watching her. "He finally made his sashay back into your life."

She didn't answer, but perspiration broke out on her forehead. She concentrated very hard to keep her face from showing the emotional upheaval going on inside her. "Yes. Briefly."

"Was it the first time?"

"No. I saw him day before yesterday. He was in an elevator I was about to go into. I took the stairs instead." Carol silently cursed her shaky voice which betrayed her when her expression didn't.

Bret laid down his fork and leaned back in his chair. He looked to the side and beyond her, out the window at the gathering dusk, the gray-blue dusk of the southern sky, his arms hanging limply at his sides, his eyes misting. He sighed. "You still carry the torch for him."

Carol picked at the frilled place mat on the table before her. "No. No I don't."

"Yes, you do. You do. I've known it all this time." Bret shook his head slowly, still looking out of the window.

What could she say? A year ago Duane had come into her life, met her when she was a student nurse taking pediatrics at Children's and he was on pedi rotation, a third-year med student.

. . . *I can't fall in love, Carol. I can't get involved,* he had said. But they had gotten involved, eventually— very—only to break up because he was afraid that damned term paper of hers would expose a certain surgeon's mistake and that someone would associate him with her, which would jeopardize his residency at Bennet. They'd had a terrible fight, and he had walked out of her life, had not seen her again.

Bret had been a student in the same graduating class as Carol and had come to her on graduation night because he was lonely and knew that she was lonely; he had offered her comfort—and himself.

Their relationship these seven months had been good, comfortable, uneventful.

"Every time you let me take you in my arms and make love to you, I kept telling myself that you were beginning to love me. But I should have known—I did know that you were probably—" Bret stopped, looked at her, his blue eyes full of hurt, full of anger.

"Probably what, Bret?"

"That you were probably pretending that I was *him.*"

She stood up and went to him saying, "No, no," and pressing his head to her breasts. "No, Bret. I didn't. I was enjoying you. Please believe that. Don't belittle our relationship."

"Relationship," he said, letting her hold his head. "Not love, just . . . relationship."

She let him go, but remained beside him. "Please eat. Mexican food's not very good when it's cold."

"Neither is sex, Carol. Besides, I've lost my appetite." Bret slowly pushed the plate away from him. "For both."

Carol watched as he stood up slowly, tiredly. He was not quite six feet tall, but was built solid, broad through the shoulders. As a student, Carol had come to realize the value of male nurses to the profession. They could handle belligerent male patients whom the female nurses couldn't; they could lift, pull, shove, and roll patients all by themselves where it took two female nurses to do so. She had thought of male nurses only as brawn then; but since, she had observed others and realized they had brains as well, and intuition, and were capable of sympathy and tenderness.

"You're jealous, Bret," she told him as he leaned on

the table with his fists.

"Yeah, I am. Damned stinking jealous, Carol. Because of the look in your eyes, on your face . . ." He turned, went to the living room, and picked up the coat he'd draped over her chair. "I've got to go for a walk."

Carol ran and took hold of his solid arms. "Bret, Bret, I do care for you," she said and meant it in a mixed-up sort of way.

He stood, looking down at her, his face expressionless but his eyes alive with a million unspoken emotions. "Like a puppy or a kitten, or maybe a brother?"

And now all the strength of her protests left her even as she said, "No. More."

He took a deep breath. "Let me go on home, Carol. I've—I've got work to do."

She clasped her hands and shut her eyes tightly. "I've lost you. I've lost *you* too."

"No. I'll still be around. I just can't—" He went to the door, put his hand on the doorknob. "I'll call you tomorrow, O.K.?"

She nodded and he left. She stood beside the door listening as he went down the stairs outside her apartment, his steps slow at first, then faster, faster as if fleeing something. Then she heard him start his car and pull slowly out of the parking lot.

She turned and looked about her.

New. The apartment was new; the entire apartment complex was new and Carol was one of its first tenants. Once she had gotten her first paycheck as a nurse, she had rented it; it had an L-shaped living-dining area, a bar separating the living area from the compact, modern kitchen, papered in a green-trellis and gold-flower design on a white background, and equipped with a butcher-block counter top, white appliances, even a dishwasher. Pale beige carpet, off white walls, large bedroom. Her aunts had come through with a good used sofa, some chairs, a color TV, end tables. She had bought the little round dining table and matching chairs herself, and Bret had helped her move from the old apartment to this.

She folded her arms and walked toward the window in the dining area. Bret had helped her hang the curtains, too, and had helped her unpack. *Wow! What's this pink thing, Carol? Camisole? What's a camisole? Model it for me?*

He would have moved in if she'd invited him, but she hadn't. Against her principles. Principles? *What* principles?

She'd used Bret to get over Duane and now that she'd seen Duane again Bret's friendship just sort of paled beside the vivid memory of Duane, in spite of her hating him and his arrogance. And Bret was loving, decent, and kind.

But she had wanted him to go tonight, to leave her alone. She hadn't wanted him to stay, hadn't protested much when he had decided to leave. She'd felt sorry for him, wanted to hold him, to love him. But she couldn't. Not tonight.

Why, why, why was it Duane who had discovered that Melinda was becoming disoriented? Why hadn't *she?* Why hadn't Dr. Hamblin? Why hadn't Basil Novak?

Somehow the incident overwhelmed her. She was overreacting to it; she knew that. An hour later she, or one of the other doctors, might have discovered it. Why did *Duane* have to be the one? She hated his self-assuredness, his brilliance, *him.* Now she sensed that Novak would bring Duane back on rounds. She'd have to see him again. And again.

How could she? How could she keep seeing him and not fall apart or fly into a rage at him?

I'll tell you why, Carol Welles, she told herself. Because you've got to remember that you're a professional. You've got to chuck your personal life into a corner, especially when you're on the job. You've got to concentrate on your patients, on your work, to absorb and learn and then give, give all the help and comfort you can. It's why you chose nursing as a profession. Sure, she was aware she was dramatizing everything, still idealistic, still what Dr. Blasingame had accused her of being when she was only a graduate nurse in L&D—nunlike, he had called her. "You remind me of a nun."

I have to be the best or die, Duane had said once.

Well, she was determined to match his ambition with her own, her dedication with his. She'd be damned if she'd let him become a better surgeon than she was a nurse.

Nunlike, nunlike, nunlike . . .

Carol suddenly turned from her window angrily, away from the image of Duane Duren in her mind, an image that followed her, stayed with her, and in her growing fury she gave that image an obscene gesture, waved it in the air. "To you, Duane Duren!" she cried. "To you. And here's anything else insulting that your kind can think of, to you!"

Then she took Bret's plate to the sink and scraped it off vigorously into the disposal side, her mouth tight with determination, her eyes shining with the brilliance of hate mixed with tears.

SIX

Carol had learned that maternity patients often thought they were in love with their obstetricians. She had tried to analyze this, wondering if it happened because an obstetrician spoke tenderly with his patient about her most intimate problems, probed her most secret places? No, because most obstetricians weren't particularly tender, and when they probed the secret places, they were likely to be talking with the nurse about last night's football game or something. Nevertheless, most maternity patients were intensely loyal, if not fond, of their obstetricians. And Dr. Blasingame's patients were the fondest of all.

They adored him.

In fact, their devotion was a standing joke at Bennet. Many of his patients would come to Labor and Delivery, ready to give birth, dressed in filmy negligees, bodies perfumed, hair elegantly coiffured, faces meticulously made up, some even wearing false eyelashes. Why, Carol would never know; because of the ten obstetricians on staff at Bennet, Dr. Blasingame deserved their adoration the least.

He wasn't even handsome. Well, he *was* sort of. He was mid-thirtyish with black curly hair and brown dog eyes, not very tall, a bit cocky. He was Dr. Jackson's associate, and although the nurses in L&D and on the maternity floor liked Dr. Jackson, they detested Blasingame. But Carol had been prejudiced against Blasingame from the beginning.

When she was in nurses' training, her friend, Mae, had observed Blasingame doing cryosurgery on a patient for vaginal infection. Mae had said that the patient had adoringly told him "night-night" and had gone sweetly to sleep with only a whiff of the anesthetic administered by the anesthesiologist. However, she had not gone deep enough and had gagged on the endotracheal tube when the anesthesiologist had tried to insert it into her trachea for continuing anesthesia. With the hair curler–type instrument in hand ready to apply it to the patient's vaginal mucosa, Blasingame had said to her, knowing she would not hear or remember, "Don't like that, sweetheart? Too bad. Take her down, Roger." When the anesthesiologist had reminded him that there was a student nurse present, Blasingame had said, ". . . She might as well find out how it really is." Because of that incident, Carol disliked him, but she would not have liked him anyway because of his lack of consideration for his patients. She'd never understand why Dr. Jackson tolerated him as an associate. Maybe Jackson wasn't that aware of Blasingame's hostility toward women; and maybe Blasingame only showed his true colors to the nurses. Who knows?

At the moment Blasingame was suturing Harriet Guthry's episiotomy. His caudal anesthetic hadn't worked on poor Harriet—probably because he hadn't gotten the catheter in the right place—and she had to be given gas in the delivery room. Robbie had administered the gas, which was unlawful for nurses to do, but she was supervised as well as possible by Blasingame. It was just a "whiff" to help Harriet through the last stages of delivery.

"Nothing could be fina than to be in your vagina in the mo-orning," Dr. Blasingame sang under his breath.

Robbie and Carol looked at each other. Robbie was injecting Deladumone-OB—an estrogen-androgen combination—into Harriet's hip to suppress the release of prolactin and, therefore, prevent breast engorgement; for Harriet was not going to breast-feed her infant. Carol was placing baby boy Guthry into the isolette preparatory to taking him to the newborn nursery. Robbie rolled her eyes in disgust with Blasingame, and Carol wanted to tell him that they'd heard other obstetricians sing that little ditty before and they didn't think it was cute. But she didn't. It was better to ignore Blasingame because he could be vindictive when the black mood was upon him.

"Toodle-oo," Carol told Robbie as she rolled the isolette past her. Robbie would be stuck for another ten minutes in the delivery room with Blasingame while he finished suturing the episiotomy. "Have fun."

Robbie gave Carol an obscene gesture, at her side where the doctor couldn't see.

Carol was still laughing when she rolled the isolette out of the delivery room and into the corridor where, pulling off her mask, she met Mac. "What did Guthry have?" Mac asked as she bent down to peer into the isolette. "Ah, a boy. I want to see the daddy's expression when you show him."

While Mac walked with Carol from the corridor to the hallway in front of the nurses' station, Carol asked, "What did Hamilton have?"

"Boy. It's boy day. All four deliveries have been boys."

94

"And Blasingame's day," Carol said pausing as Mac opened one of the double doors for her. "Why did he pit three in one day *this* time?"

"Christmas vacation. He's going to Vermont on a skiing trip tomorrow night and won't be available in case one of his patients goes into labor. I guess he's doing Jackson a favor since Jackson will be on call for him while he's gone." Mac shrugged. "I don't know. Who knows?"

"Is Bonham still in labor?"

"Naturally. She was green. Not ready for delivery and should never have been induced." They were pacing down the corridor toward the waiting room next to the post-partum floor. "She'll be in labor for hours. When the cervix is green, it won't dilate easily, Pitocin or no Pitocin."

They paused outside the waiting-room door as Mac called, "Mr. Guthry?"

Mr. Guthry, a burly young man dressed in a neat flannel shirt and blue jeans, followed anxiously by his mother-in-law, rushed from the waiting room into the corridor. He approached the isolette grinning foolishly and bent down to peer inside. "This . . . is this . . . ?"

"Your son," Carol said smiling.

"My son." Guthry was exceedingly pale. The Guthrys had a girl two years old; this was their first boy. "Aw-w," he said, "look at it. Aw."

Harriet's mother nudged him giggling. "He's not an it, Ernest."

"He's a dead ringer for Dad."

"Look at his feet!" Harriet's mother looked at Carol. "How much does he weigh?"

"Probably around four thousand eighty-two grams, or nine pounds. They'll weigh him in the nursery. Harriet's doing fine," Carol said. This was one of those happy times in L&D, the happiest of all, probably.

"Did they give her something for the pain?" Harriet's mother asked.

"Gas. She's groggy, but she'll be just fine."

Guthry's face had gone pale again and he was pointing to the squawling infant in the isolette. "His . . . er . . ." Then his face flushed and his eyes moved from Carol's innocent young face to Mac's experienced middle-aged one. "His . . . uh . . . scrotum . . ."

Mac glanced at infant Guthry. "Large. Yes. That's normal. Baby boys' scrotums are swollen for the first few hours after delivery. Nothing to worry about. Perfectly normal." When Mac saw that Guthry was still uncertain about his infant son's endowment, she added conversationally, "In Italian infants and Latin Americans, Negroes, any nationality with darker skin coloring, and in some Jewish infants, their scrotums and nipples are dark, very dusky at birth. That certainly scares the fathers sometimes."

Harriet's mother giggled nervously.

Mr. Guthry sighed with relief and his eyes then moved to Carol who had attended his wife throughout her labor and delivery. "Harriet. When may I see Harriet?"

"We'll be taking her to recovery in about ten minutes," Carol told him. "After they get her situated there, the nurse will let you visit for about five minutes. But if you'll wait right there, we'll roll her by here on the stretcher, and you can say hi."

Carol and Mac let the father and grandmother look at the infant a moment longer; then Carol told them congratulations and began to wheel the isolette to the nursery. Mac went along and, before Carol had gone very far, stopped her in the corridor.

"Carol, I want to tell you something," she said.

Carol, as a new nurse, was still uneasy about her job

status. She *thought* she was doing good work, had caught on fast in L&D, but there was always that nagging doubt: *but am I good enough?*

As Dr. Blasingame had told her when Mac had introduced her to him on her first day in L&D, "I hope you can catch on fast, dear. Back here we either make 'em or we break 'em."

Comforting.

Well, screw him. But what did *Mac* think? Carol was overdue for her sixth-month evaluation and she was wondering if this was the anticipated conference. Mac was so solemn. . . .

"Carol, I had thought we should take turns being assigned to Melinda Curtis, but as you know, Robbie hates it. Joy is . . . too flighty. I'm afraid she'll miss something or forget something. You seem to have good rapport with Melinda and don't seem to mind caring for her. Do you?"

Carol stared at Mac, relaxed, said, "Certainly not. I enjoy it."

"That's what I thought. I'm nervous as a whore in church about all this, and I'd feel a lot better if you'd do most of the caring for Melinda on day shift. I realize that it's grueling and confining, but if you'll work say . . . three or four of your five days with Melinda, I'll let you have a break now and then to have other patients. O.K.?"

"Fine with me, Mac."

"Whew. Boy! Thanks, Carol. I wasn't sure. I've been after Bryant to hire us more help in L&D for months; we're grossly understaffed as you know, and now with Melinda to take care of, maybe we'll get more help. We *have* to have more help."

Carol sighed and nodded.

"And about your six-month evaluation . . ."

Carol swallowed and tensed.

97

"There's a copy of it in your locker. It's good, incidentally, and you'll be getting a raise." Mac smiled at Carol's suddenly beaming face. "Now I gotta go check Bonham," she said, starting back to L&D.

The conductive-treated canvas shoes had developed springs as Carol resumed pushing the isolette toward the nursery. She pictured herself now as she savored this glorious moment: a slender girl with hair put up in a loose bun at the back of her neck, dressed in baggy surgical scrub dress that didn't quite conceal the swell of her young breasts and the curve of her well-developed behind, and green canvas sneakers with bottoms that had been treated with conductive material to prevent causing sparks in the delivery room when someone was being given gas or oxygen. She sported a big secret smile, maybe a little smug, and she had bright funny-colored eyes. Carol had gone straight from nursing school to L&D. Lately she had begun to realize that because she hadn't had any floor experience, there was a world of things she didn't know, hadn't experienced as a nurse. L&D was just one small, confined area of nursing. The routine of patient care was the same for each patient, except that some were Pitocin-induced and you had to monitor them closely, and others were not. Most had caudal or epidural anesthesia; a few didn't. But the labor and delivery processes were mostly all the same. She loved L&D and it was extremely interesting. If only she'd decided to work on a regular ward first, though, perhaps she could be more content.

In nursing school you were exposed only briefly to *some* of the disease processes, to *some* of the surgical procedures. She knew a lot about labor and delivery, but what about gall-bladder disease, for instance, and cancer, multiple sclerosis, emphesema, heart attacks, abdominal-surgery patients, thoracic-surgery patients, neurological and vascular disorders? She wasn't learning about those. Only one small part of her nursing career was growing; the rest was withering on the clinical vine.

She pushed baby boy Guthry into the newborn nursery, and big, buxom Bess met her at the door. "Hello. Guthry, right?"

"All of him."

L&D nurses always called the nursery when a patient was admitted to L&D for delivery, so the nursery nurses could put together a chart on the prospective new arrival in advance.

Bess opened the top of the isolette, reached in, took him out. "Hello, buster," she said running practiced eyes over the infant's squirming, cheesy body. "Cuppa coffee says he weighs nine pounds, six ounces."

Carol knew better than to match wits with Bess when it came to guessing birth weights, but it was standard procedure and she said, "You gotta bet. I say he's closer to nine even." She watched as Bess took Guthry to the scale, laid him on it, adjusted the weights. Meantime, she was aware of the din in the place. Babies were screaming frantically, newborn hoarse cries full of furious panic and explicit demands. She glanced at her wrist watch. No wonder; it was one o'clock, *feeding time*. She remembered, when she was a student in the newborn nursery, how the babies had yelled while being carried to their mothers, how they had come back asleep and silent, tummies full, contented.

"Nine pounds seven and three-quarter ounces," Bess called.

"O.K. I'll treat you whenever," Carol conceded happily.

"I'll hold you to that, Welles."

Going back to L&D pushing the empty isolette, Carol reflected over her months in maternity nursing.

99

Full, fun, and frantic. Now there was Melinda to break the routine. And because of Melinda's elevated temp, which Joy couldn't get down even with tepid baths, it looked as though L&D was also going to become tense and tedious.

If she clenched her teeth hard, the burning wasn't so bad. Joy was trying to cool her off with damp cloths, but she felt the heat all around her—everywhere. Drs. Hamblin and Novak had flushed some antibiotics through the drainage tubes in her abdomen yesterday, and Dr. Novak had said it was supposed to go into her abdomen where the infection was beginning.

Her back hurt. Her stomach burned.

"Melinda, please don't throw your arms around. Remember your IVs?" Joy said.

Poor Joy. What an awful time she was having with her today. Melinda shifted to her left side, but it hurt so badly that she rolled back onto her back.

I'll be careful, Joy.

There was an antibiotic in the IV going into her right arm, an aspirin suppository in her bottom. And John had come in this morning to see her, all gowned and gloved like the doctors. Poor handsome John.

Oh, how her back hurt, and every nerve in her arms and legs was jangled, twanging like the strings of a guitar; yet the baby was still, in his sacks of warm water. If she dared to open her eyes, the room would grow and get larger and Joy would grow smaller and smaller and farther away and everything would look tiny. So she kept her eyes shut and drifted in and out of sleep as the ocean waves flow to and ebb from the shore, but these were hot waves; she hoped the baby wasn't too warm in his little sacks . . . the little sacks which rocked him . . . rocked him. . . .

. . . Carol to tell you about . . .

. . . The fertilized ovum begins to multiply into many cells and travels from the Fallopian tube to the uterine cavity where it floats around for about four days until it attaches itself to the uterine lining. . . .

. . . When the cells become embedded in the uterine wall they continue to multiply and gradually form three layers of cells; the outer layer is called the ectoderm, the middle layer the mesoderm, the inner layer the entoderm. From the ectoderm is formed skin, hair, nails, mouth, nose . . . from the mesoderm muscles, bone, kidneys, ovaries, testes, heart, blood . . . from the entoderm come the digestive tract, respiratory tract, bladder . . .

. . . A fluid-filled sack develops around the layers— which are now called an embryo—and the bag of water in which the embryo floats is called the amnion. The outer membrane of the sack is called the chorion. The two membranes are the membranes which rupture during labor. . . .

. . . The placenta, or afterbirth, is formed and clings to the uterine wall. The placenta is a flat disklike organ which supplies the embryo—now called a fetus—with nourishment. . . . Placenta sends villa into the uterine wall, tapping maternal sources of nourishment. . . . Placenta and fetus are connected by the umbilical cord . . . about twenty inches long and containing two arteries and one vein twisted together. . . . From the mother the fetus derives nourishment . . . floats in amniotic fluid. . . .

. . . Which rocks him, rocks him . . . sleep in heavenly peace. Sleep in heavenly, heavenly . . . p—

"Melinda? Mel, honey? It's Mom."

From somewhere, she didn't know where, she emerged, opened her eyes, and blinked at the asbestos-tile ceiling wondering if she had fainted in prenatal class. Where had Carol gone?

"Mel?"

Mom's voice. She saw Mom bending over her and pulled her dry lips apart to whisper, "Mom?"

"Mel. Here, let me moisten your lips."

Coolness on her lips. Oh, the wonderful coolness.

Mom looked tired; she wondered when the wrinkles had appeared in Mom's face. "Do I still have the baby?"

"Of course. The baby's fine. How do you feel?"

Melinda summoned her strength, knowing at the time that what she said didn't make sense, no matter how hard she tried, that it had something to do with the heat around her and the infection inside her. "I don't feel so hot," she croaked drowsily, barely able to keep her eyes open. But she summoned a spark from somewhere that caused her to hold up one finger and say, "Correction. I feel hot as hell."

Dad would croak if he heard her say that. Swear words, contribution to her vocabulary by John.

But Mom smiled. "The doctor says I can stay awhile. Only John and I can come in, one at a time once a day."

"Swell," Melinda said, and the *l*'s stuck in the back of her throat on the stomach tube.

But the baby kicked and made her smile.

"What's left? We've done it all and done it promptly and correctly, haven't we?" Basil Novak said. He looked at Hamblin. Physicans' consultations with each other always gave him a pain in the ass, especially if a consultation included an internist. But if the internist was Ruben Hamblin, it was slightly more tolerable than it would have been with most of the others. Whitehall and Hamblin respected each other's expertise as specialists, but hated each other's guts as personalities, so Whitehall had demurred attending the conference and sent Basil instead. Novak in turn had brought along Duane Duren because . . . well, because. But as an intern, Duren would have to keep his mouth shut and listen and learn. Although Duren was sitting off sort of in a corner to himself, he was nevertheless attentive and neither Simon nor Hamblin questioned his presence.

This was Basil's third conference with the internist and the obstetrician and already he had them pretty well pegged. Hamblin was sharp, plain and simple, but he bucked every suggestion he or Simon made, thinking he was running the show. Only trouble was, he didn't know a whole lot about surgical procedures and complications.

Simon, on the other hand, was simply scared. Basil felt sorry for him. He was a middle-aged man in his fifties, medium height, partially bald, mostly aloof, smoked a pipe constantly that stunk as if he were smoking cabbage leaves. Simon's pipe smoke always smelled like somebody had let a fart. But he liked Simon.

"Oh," moaned Simon now as he took his pipe out of his mouth. "Oh, how I wish I were still a used-car salesman."

Simon was prematurely wrinkled anyway, and the longer he sat in the chair of the conference room discussing Melinda Curtis' case, the deeper his wrinkles became and the shorter he shrank until he was beginning to look like some medieval gnome. All he lacked was the beard.

Hamblin said smiling, "I'm not sure I agree with you, Basil, when you say that everything has been done promptly."

Basil knew what Hamblin was getting at, that Simon should have responded more energetically to Melinda's first complaint of abdominal pain on her last OB checkup. But Basil could see that a single complaint of abdominal pain and nausea from a pregnant woman was not one to panic about unless it became severe or prolonged. And in Melinda's case, she wasn't a complainer and had endured abdominal distress until the diverticulitis became severe and perforated the colon.

Simon knew what Hamblin was referring to also and had his weapon ready. He pulled his pipe out of his mouth, studied it, said, "Some things have been *over*done, too, as I understand." He looked up at Hamblin. "And it took a nurse to bring it to our attention. It's occurred to me that maybe we ought to bring one of the Labor and Delivery nurses in on our conferences."

Everything got quiet. The three of them had decided yesterday to introduce kanamycin solution intra-peritoneally, which Novak had done with Hamblin standing by, but then Hamblin had ordered Valium IM because Melinda was getting more and more restless. When the nurse, who was assigned to Melinda, had read the order for Valium on Melinda's chart, she'd telephoned Hamblin and said she couldn't give Valium if kanamycin had been given intraperitoneally because of the danger that it could possibly cause respiratory arrest. Evidently, the nurse was still new enough to look up drugs in the *Physicians' Desk Reference* to check the warnings and side effects, and had discovered that you couldn't give a muscle relaxant concomittally with intraperitoneal kanamycin. Hamblin had sheep-ishly discontinued the order for Valium.

Basil had to smile. Earlier that morning he had told the tale to his pack of new residents, and Duren had said, "Same nurse we saw there yesterday, on the day shift?"

Basil had smiled at him. "Yeah, Wills," he said

104

baiting him.

"Welles," Duren had corrected.

Basil glanced at Duren now. Duren hadn't batted an eye, nor had his expression changed.

"I really don't believe Valium is a potent enough muscle relaxant to cause respiratory arrest in this case. I think the *PDR* was referring to major muscle relaxants such as carisoprodol or metaxalone and such; but the nurse refused to give the Valium, and her charge nurse backed her up," Hamblin said.

"And you didn't press the issue," Simon said.

"No."

Simon struck a match on the bottom of his chair. "Because you weren't absolutely positive that Valium *wouldn't* cause respiratory arrest."

Hamblin shrugged and watched Simon relight his pipe.

"I objected to the kanamycin in the first place," Simon said, "because it's a risk in a pregnant patient."

"All the antibiotics are a risk. That's why we've started out with smaller doses than normal, and kanamycin's the best, isn't it? For intraperitoneal instillation?" Hamblin challenged.

Basil wanted to get to the point and get the conference over with. He tapped the shoe on his right foot which was resting on his left knee. "We've given kanamycin IV, IM, and intraperitoneal. According to the cultures, *E. coli* has been controlled, but not any of the other bacteria. What now?"

Yeah what now? There were hundreds of antibiotics on the market, but you couldn't just indiscriminately order a couple of them to be given to your patient. Different disease microbes were sensitive—or susceptible to being destroyed—by only *certain* antibiotics. Basil had explained it once to a patient. The process was sort of like killing insects; an insecticide that would kill a roach would not necessarily kill a scorpion. You could pretty well predict what antibiotics to give for certain diseases—like streptococcus infection, for example—but for others, especially the intestinal microbes, you couldn't always be certain a particular antibiotic would destroy them. That's why you sent cultures to the lab, to determine the microbes causing the infection and the antibiotics to which they were sensitive.

Basil was made aware for the millionth time how important the work of a laboratory technician was.

Using a swab, a nurse on the eleven-to-seven shift in L&D had taken a sample of the drainage coming from Melinda's abdominal drains and had placed it in a culture tube, which she had then sent to the lab along with a requisition slip for a C&S. In the lab, the lab techs had smeared the drainage sample from the culture tube onto a culture medium, usually an agar plate, to allow the microbes to proliferate and grow into colonies. Sometimes that took only hours, sometimes a week or so depending on the microbe. Once growth appeared—and you could see the growth of the colonies by the naked eye—the growths were smeared on slides, stained to permit better visualization, and studied under a microscope. The organism was thus identified; then came the sensitivity tests.

Although in vitro, or test-tube, tests weren't always absolutely reliable, much of the time a microbe's sensitivity could be determined by introducing a small amount of certain antibiotics to the agar plates containing the colonies. After twelve hours, the lab tech could see which of the antibiotics he had added to the plates of microbes had killed the colonies. He would then check off, or write, the name of each antibiotic that had killed each microbe colony on a lab slip; and that was the guide that the doctors went by. In

Melinda's case, the three major pathogenic microbes involved were sensitive to twelve antibiotics.

"Omnipotent" doctors, himself included, had had to rely on a nurse's skill at taking the culture in the first place, and the lab tech's expertise in determining the microorganisms responsible for the infection and the antibiotics to which they were sensitive.

Now, the doctors had to decide which antibiotics to give, dodging the ones that could cause certain undesirable side effects in Melinda's case, which was complicated because of her pregnancy. No wonder it took three doctors and repeated conferences. Who the hell would want *all* the responsibility involved for a pregnant young woman with surgical complications?

Hamblin finally spoke up. "Can't give streptomycin or Garamycin because we're giving kanamycin and you can't give aminoglycosides together; they'd cause toxicity. What about Neobiotic?"

Duane Duren, whom Novak had recognized weeks ago as one of those walking encyclopedias that came along once in a while, spoke up. "That's another aminoglycoside."

Hamblin stared a moment at Duren, with not too friendly a demeanor, but Duren never changed his expression.

"I still say penicillin is safer in pregnancy," Simon said.

"Not as effective against fecal bacteria as kanamycin, though," Novak offered.

"We can combine them. Give kanamycin IV and penicillin IM," Hamblin said.

"But can you give them together?" Simon asked. The doctors all looked quickly at Duren.

Duren said, "Yes." And Novak suppressed a grin.

It wasn't that the doctors weren't up on the latest drugs; it was simply that out of the thousands of drugs on the market, it was damned difficult to remember which ones you could give concomittally, together; or sequentially, one after the other. Only a supersharp doctor, or pharmacist with a photographic memory, who was new and up on all the latest findings on the interactions of drugs, could know for certain what drugs could be given with what, without looking them up in the *PDR*. You even had to consider what vitamins a patient was taking when you ordered the administration of antibiotics—or any other drug. For instance, Melinda was receiving injections of vitamin B_{12}; therefore, one of the best antibiotics for intestinal microbes, neomycin, had to be ruled out immediately. If you gave a patient neomycin while she was taking B_{12}, the neomycin would prevent the absorption of the vitamin. Of course, that rule applied to B_{12} which was taken by mouth, and Melinda was receiving the injections instead; but they weren't sure about the interaction of B_{12} and neomycin when both were given IM, so they ruled it out to be safe.

Also, you couldn't give penicillamine or the tetra-cyclines because the two chemicals combined would be poorly absorbed or inactivated. If Melinda was taking food by mouth, they'd have to consider what oral meds were compatible with what foods. It was all compli-cated because all drugs, even vitamins, are chemicals, and most chemicals are incompatible with other chemicals, which can cause drugs to become inacti-vated or to produce side effects.

What a mess—like fighting your way through a jungle of thick underbrush. Because of these inter-actions people ought to take as few medicines as possible. Even aspirin had its incompatibilities with a host of foods and other drugs.

"That's it then? Kanamycin IV and penicillin G IM?" Novak asked. It was a solution, he knew, but he couldn't act too knowledgeable. After all, he was still only a resident himself.

"Let's try them," Hamblin said.

"I still don't like the kanamycin," Simon muttered darkly.

Simon was right too. There were damned few drugs that weren't risky to the unborn fetus. In fact, there was no conclusive evidence on any of the antibiotics concerning the risks involved if administered to a pregnant patient.

So, for the next forty-five minutes they sat in the conference room on the second floor of Markson and tiptoed lightly among the antibiotics, analgesics, and tranquilizers, while Melinda lay disoriented and restless, with a steadily increasing temperature.

After the conference, Basil and Duane were striding back to the surgical floor in Jenson, and although his mind was aching with medical dilemmas and disquiet, one curious question hung in the miasmic jumble in Basil's head like a single star in the sky on a dark, blustery night. He grabbed at it. "Duren, curiosity overwhelms me. How did you know the name of the nurse who is assigned to Melinda on day shift, the one who refused to give the Valium—Wills?"

"Welles," Duane corrected. "I—it—her name was on her nametag—you know, pinned to her."

"Oh." Basil nodded, glancing at Duren as they both stopped before the elevator on Jenson's second floor. Duren never batted an eye, the liar. Basil rubbed the itch on the side of his nose as they stepped onto the elevator. So Duren *did* know the little nurse in OB. He couldn't have read her name on her nametag in Melinda's room that day, because one of the isolation rules for nurses assigned to Melinda's care was: don't wear nametag because of the possibility of transmitting disease from Melinda to other OB patients via the nametag.

Hmmm. Well, so that was established and he could get back to thinking about the case. With Melinda's three doctors as grumpy and nervous as they were because she had spiked a temp and the cultures from the drains had shown a suspicious elevation of intestinal bacteria, Basil wondered what it would be like if she *did* develop peritonitis, become critical, or did go into labor.

Panic probably.

SEVEN

Bret called to her from the sofa, "Listen to this, Carol," as he rattled the newspaper. "'Joany has just been tested and it was discovered that she has an IQ of 152. Within twenty-four hours after her birth in 1970, *the doctors* pricked her heel and collected a few drops of blood. From these few drops of blood *the doctors* were able to determine that Joany had a condition known as phenylketonuria and were able to prevent mental retardation by placing the infant on a protein-restricted diet.'"

Carol brought the sandwiches in on a tray and set it on the coffee table—gift of Aunt Emma—in front of the sofa—gift of Aunt Sally. "Sounds like the article is referring to the PKU test and whoever wrote it is as naïve as Alice in Wonderland."

Bret dropped the newspaper on the floor. "Wouldn't you think that a newspaper staff medical writer would know better? Doctors don't prick the babies' heels; the nursery nurses do. It's as routine as changing their diapers. Sheeeeeee—"

"And the doctors don't determine if the kid has

phenylketonuria either; the lab technicians do." Carol sat down beside him and he automatically put his arm around her. "It's the public, Bret. In the movies you never hear much about hospital personnel, just doctors. Nobody hears about the respiratory therapist, the lab tech, x-ray tech, the other therapists and technicians it takes to diagnose and cure people. When medical miracles happen, it's always just *the doctors*. Now eat your sandwich." While she sipped her tea, she thought back over the day.

Medical miracles. Medical miracles are wrought by playing a sort of Russian roulette with treatments and medicines, like the two antibiotics the doctors decided on for Melinda. And they were winners; kanamycin and penicillin G. Forty-eight hours after the intra-peritoneal instillation of kanamycin and the first infusion of penicillin, Melinda's temp had declined and cultures taken from the abdominal drainage had shown a decrease in intestinal microbes. Then Burnett on the eleven-to-seven shift had detected the squeaking and gurgling of peristalsis in Melinda's intestines. She had reported it to Whitehall, who had some choice words for the nurse who had wakened him at 3:00 A.M.; nevertheless, he ordered the NG tube pulled at 7:30. Carol had been assigned to Melinda that day and the honors were hers. She had never pulled an NG tube before. It was scary.

When she heard from the night nurse that the NG tube was to be discontinued at 7:30, Carol had run the procedure through her mind in a kind of dazed panic; everybody had taken it for granted that she'd done it before and knew how. Well, it wasn't difficult or anything, but you did have to do it correctly; otherwise Melinda could have aspirated some of the fluid in the NG tube as it came up out of her stomach. No big deal, but scary if you hadn't done it before.

112

It had been simple. Melinda had held her breath while Carol had pulled the tube from her stomach, esophagus, and nose—with one steady, swift-but-not-too-swift pull, caught it as it came out with a towel.

"Yuk," Melinda had said. Gastric contents had clung tenaciously all up and down the tube, but Carol had caught it with the towel and had whisked it away to the bathroom wastebasket before Melinda could become nauseated just by looking at it.

Dr. Hamblin had then ordered Melinda on a liquid diet to begin with, so she had feasted luxuriously on broth, Jell-O, and hot tea.

"Your mind is still on the incident with Blasingame, isn't it?" Bret asked now as he lifted her chin to look into her eyes.

"Not at this precise moment, but thanks for reminding me. I'm trying to forget," Carol said. "It really isn't something you forget easily."

"I know. I've been through it too. Only I was in a position to tell the doctor to go to hell. And *you* should have walked out. You should have turned around, gone to the nurses' lounge, changed into your uniform, and walked out of Bennet forever. Or at least gone to the nursery director and asked for an immediate transfer."

Carol shook her head, smiling, and leaned over to pick up a sandwich and napkin off the tray. "That would have solved nothing."

"No, you should have thrown something at the son of a bitch," Bret said and then bit into his sandwich furiously.

Carol had to laugh now, because Bret really was angrier than she was. He was like that; warm sympathetic, concerned for her. He loved her, that's why. At times like this, she wished she could return his love.

Seven days. Melinda had been free of her nasogastric tube for seven days, and now that her condition was less serious and the isolation procedures would soon be discontinued, Robbie didn't mind being assigned to her so much, and Carol was able to spend more time with other patients.

Today had begun innocently enough. Clara Smith had been sent to L&D by Dr. Blasingame, who, from his office, had phoned in orders for the nurses to hang an alcohol drip. Clara was seven months pregnant; the alcohol drip, alcohol injected into an IV solution, was a conservative measure to stop her premature labor. Some time during the Victorian days, doctors had discovered that if a woman drank a large enough amount of alcohol to intoxicate her, there was a good chance that her premature labor would cease and she would go on to carry her infant to term. Now in the days of IVs and doses, alcohol is instilled via IV and often results in anesthetizing the uterine muscles enough to cause labor to cease.

Carol had never prepared an alcohol drip before, but that, too, was simple. Mac oversaw her injection of the alcohol into the IV bag, and the IV solution was ready by the time Clara arrived in L&D.

Clara was a short, pudgy, red-headed, very freckled young woman with pea green eyes and a soft voice. She was a gravida two, para zero—which meant she had been pregnant twice, but had not yet delivered a viable fetus. In other words, she had miscarried during her first pregnancy—and was trying to miscarry this, her second.

Nervously, Carol read Dr. Blasingame's orders as she made up Clara's chart at the nurses' station.

IV alcohol drip as per routine.
Complete bedrest.

Liquid diet.
No vaginal exams.
No enema.
No perineal prep.
Vital signs q. 30 min.
Fetal heart tones q. 15 min.
Record frequency of contractions.
Report bloody show, rupture of membranes,
  or increase in frequency of contractions.

The nurses in L&D knew all this, but Blasingame thought he had to remind new people or forgetful ones or nurses filling in from the nursing pools. Bedrest was the main thing for Clara.

Carol started the IV and regulated the drip rate. Starting IVs on young mothers with fat, juicy veins was usually easy. Starting IVs on the elderly or on a patient with low blood pressure was hard, but Carol had succeeded in starting one on an elderly lady in ER as a student, and on her friend Charlotte when she was in a diabetic crisis. Still, in starting IVs, no matter how good you were, you couldn't always be certain you'd get a vein every time. Most of the time it was easy, but occasionally Carol went for several days without being able to start one. There was no explanation for it. It was a cycle that happened with every nurse, Mac had told her, like menstruation; you had days when there was absolutely no excuse why you couldn't start an IV; you just couldn't. Then the failure part of the cycle would pass, and you started getting a vein every time. Weird.

Sweet Clara Smith was gentle and subdued, afraid of losing this, her second, child. The IV had infused five minutes when Carol asked, "How do you feel now, Clara."

"Dizzy." Clara giggled. "My alcohol intake is limited

to an occasional dinner wine. Don't tell my husband I can't hold my liquor." And she giggled again.

Clara was trying to be brave, trying not to panic or cry, trying to be positive, to believe that now that she was in the hospital everything was going to be all right. She was also getting tipsy.

At that moment Joy stuck her head in the door. "Hey, Carol?"

Carol excused herself and left the room. Better that Clara rest anyway. Out in the corridor Joy whispered loud enough for the entire hospital to hear, "Dr. Blasingame is pitting two patients, Dr. Moss one, Dr. Simon one."

"Rats! Why don't they get together and plan these on different days? Blasingame knows we've got Clara and that's a handful for one nurse."

"I don't know. All I know is Mac and I have to have your help, what with Robbie tied up in Melinda's room. Got your alcohol drip stable?"

"Yes. Who's going to be the doctor in house?" The rule at Bennet was that whenever a labor was being induced by oxytocin, one of the obstetricians had to be in the hospital in case of an emergency, namely the rupturing of somebody's uterus. Pitocin, the oxytocin of choice, was relatively safe, but like most other drugs it had potentially dangerous side effects.

"Blasingame," Joy whispered loudly, "and he's in an awful mood. He lost two babies last week on the three-to-eleven shift, both premature, and almost lost a mother. Remember the Caesarean he did on the night shift? She hemorrhaged post-partum. None of it was his fault, but he's really schizy and in a black mood. When your patient came in, he canceled all his office appointments today to stay in the hospital. Approach him with caution."

"I have no intention of approaching him at all."

116

"You don't like him, do you?" Joy said, smiling. "Neither does Robbie, but I think he's cute. Sometimes he's gross, but most of the time he's nice."

"Blah."

"Look, you take rooms two and three, and I'll take four and five."

Carol nodded. Mac had admitted both patients in rooms two and three, Carol found out, which meant they had been put to bed, examined, and each had already given a urine specimen. Mac was now probably setting up the delivery rooms, but had written each patient's info on the chalkboard across the hallway from the nurses' station.

ROOM	NAME	ADMIT	GRAVIDA	DILATION
2	Grant	8:05A	I	0
3	Blalock	8:10A	II	0

Gravida referred to the number of pregnancies a woman had had, including the present one; so Edith Grant was pregnant with her first child, Loretta Blalock was pregnant with her second.

At the nurses' station, Carol glanced over both patients' charts, noted Dr. Blasingame's routine admit orders; same as always, he'd not penned in any different instructions.

Carol went to Edith Grant first in room two. As a gravida one, Edith was scared, and her huge brown eyes watched Carol anxiously as she entered the room. Six months as an OB nurse had given Carol a certain confident air, although she was still confident only part of the time, well-aware that she still had a lot to learn. As a nurse she'd learned to assume a professional demeanor for the patient's sake; knowing there was surely nothing more disconcerting to an anxious patient than an inexperienced nurse.

"Hi!" she said hurrying into Edith's room. "Given your urine specimen yet?"

"Yes, ma'am," Edith said. She was lying in bed clutching her top sheet as if she were afraid someone would suddenly whisk it away and leave her lying bare and vulnerable.

Carol approached her bed. "Did Mac, the nurse who admitted you, explain the procedures?"

"Procedures?" Edith breathed. "What procedures?"

"Oh, just the enema and the shave."

Edith stared. "I've never had an enema before."

Bennet Memorial's L&D kept all their routine supplies within the department and one of each kit and instrument needed in each of the rooms on a shelf above the room's sink. Carol had only to take the prepackaged enema kit off the shelf.

"I'll give you the enema and when you're through expelling that, I'll start your IV," Carol said as she unwrapped the kit. O.K., she was thinking, Edith's terrified. Some were, some weren't. Whether or not a patient was scared when she was admitted for delivery depended on a lot of things; what tales she'd heard about hospitals or labor and delivery, and how well-informed she was about her hospital admittance and the processes of labor. Edith wasn't one of the patients in the prenatal classes, so no telling how much she knew, or more importantly, how much she didn't. Carol had another patient to prepare, and she had Clara to watch, but these first few seconds of Edith's admission were important and could decide to what degree she could relax. Carol sat down on the side of her bed.

"This is the enema kit," she said, showing it to Edith, and she explained how she'd fill the plastic bucket and how Edith would lie on her side while Carol ran water through the tubing and into her bowels.

118

Edith swallowed. "Will it hurt?"

"The enema?"

"The IV."

"Well, there'll be a brief stick, naturally, but hopefully only one. After that, the IV shouldn't be painful."

Edith was really uptight, but cooperative, so Carol gave the enema chatting about babies, the weather, husbands, until she had instilled the half liter of warm, sudsy water into Edith. *Click.* She snapped off the tubing. The enema was finished now, all but the grand finale.

"Please try to hold the water as long as you can, Edith. Then go to the bathroom when you can't hold it any longer, O.K.?"

"It's over?" Edith asked, glancing over her shoulder at Carol.

"Sure. The rest is up to you."

"My scene, huh?" Edith laughed nervously, her eyes flashing with anxiety and whatever awful sensations a lower intestine full of sudsy water gave to a patient. For Carol had never had an enema either.

"While you're doing that, I've got another enema to give, then I'll start your IV," Carol said as she washed her hands.

"I can't wait," Edith said scrambling from the bed. Carol didn't know whether she meant the IV or the enema, but she smiled as she left the room and Edith slammed the door to her bathroom.

Loretta Blalock was a gravida two. She had produced a viable fetus and this was her second pregnancy. Her first glance at Loretta told Carol that she was one of Blasingame's *girls.* She was a beauty too; slender with a flawless complexion, but heavily made up with foundation, rouge, lip rouge, mascara, and eyebrow pencil. Her very dark hair was pro-

119

fessionally done, her nails manicured.

"Hi, Loretta," Carol said going into her room. "I'm Carol, and I'll be your nurse through your labor and delivery. Ready for your enema so we can get this show on the road?"

Loretta smiled patiently at Carol's nursiness. "Well, I'm not actually *ready,* but whatever it takes."

Carol took the enema kit off the shelf over Loretta's sink and mouthed Loretta's next words, even as she said them.

"Does Dr. Blasingame know I've been admitted yet?"

Carol turned toward her. "Well, actually he's at home, you know, and we probably won't be calling him until we're ready to start the Pitocin." She glanced at the clock on the wall opposite the foot of Loretta's bed. "I'll call his secretary in his office as soon as I can. There're three of his patients here today, including you."

"Really? When will he be in?"

Carol began running water into the enema bucket. "When one of you is ready to have the caudal done." When she glanced at Loretta, the woman was staring at the ceiling.

"I thought he'd be here through my labor."

Fat chance, Carol thought, but said, "Well, he'll be in the labor-and-delivery area, but probably won't visit until you're dilated maybe five or six centimeters. Then we'll call him and he'll probably rupture your membranes and do the caudal."

"That may be hours," Loretta protested, scowling.

Loretta pouted all through the enema, and Carol was glad to leave the room. Time to check Clara again. Boy! It was going to be a harassing day. Oh, how they needed another L&D nurse! Or even two.

She bustled hurriedly into Clara's room. "How's it

120

going, Clara?" she asked still feeling uneasy from her sojourn in Loretta's room. One glance at the IV showed her that the drip rate of the alcohol solution was steady.

Carol counted the drip rate for fifteen seconds as Clara replied, "Hun-ky dory. Hu-unky dory!" Then drawled, "Say, when's ziss pain s'pose t' stop?"

Carol laid her hand on Clara's abdomen and watched the clock. "I hope very soon."

"Wull-ll-ll, it's all very sad. Very sad. T' lose my firss an' t' lose my second's about more'n I kin take, lady."

"I know," Carol said, suppressing a smile. Clara had one contraction, but it was weak. Carol waited for another while Clara began to sniffle.

"'Ve ya got a Kleenex?" Clara asked.

"Sure. Just a second and let me finish timing this contraction." Five minutes. The contractions were five minutes apart, the same as they were on admission, but they were weaker. She got Clara a tissue off the shelf and handed it to her.

Clara blew her nose. Red-eyed and sniffling she said, "T' lose my first and t' lose my second's the shids. Y'know that?"

"I know," Carol said wrapping her hand around Clara's arm. "But your contractions *are* weaker."

"They are?" Clara looked up at Carol.

"Yes. But that doesn't mean they'll stop." She took the fetoscope off the hook at the head of the bed and placed the earpieces in her ears as Clara smiled, wept tears of happiness, and intoned something about Carol being the kindest most wunnerful human being in the who-ole world. The pains'd stop. Juss you wait'n see.

The fetal heart tones were a bit low, one hundred twenty-eight, but nothing to worry about yet. Carol recorded the FHTs and left the room hurriedly, wishing she could spend more time with poor Clara, but . . . she had the preps to do and the damned IVs to start on Edith and Loretta.

When she briskly entered Edith's room, Edith was back in bed with the top sheet pulled up under her chin. "That was an experience," she told Carol. "What next?"

Carol smiled and, turning to her, held up the prep kit. "The shave."

"This is terribly embarrassing," Edith said moments later as Carol swabbed her perineum with the soapy solution.

Carol raised her head to look at her. Actually, when you really thought about it, it was gross. Her head was between Edith's bent knees, her face not three feet from her most secret places. Jeez, she thought, what you've gotta do is concentrate on the work at hand; even after doing hundreds of these preps it could really gross you out if you thought about it much. So you didn't think about it; you just did your job; which was cleaning and shaving all the perineal hair in order to minimize the possibility of introducing infection into the birth canal. "Ahh, we do this a hundred times a day," she said shrugging, and went back to her work. No wonder the obstetricians say that they never get a charge out of seeing women's bottoms because they all look alike— with variations only in complexion and padding. It was the women's *personalities* that the obstetricians said they might find attractive. "Bullshit."

"I beg your pardon, what did you say?" Edith asked.

Carol raised her head again to look at Edith's face. "I said 'full shift.' It's a good thing we have the full shift on today."

Edith nodded thoughtfully, and Carol went back to her work.

Later, Edith said, "I've never had an IV before. Are you sure it doesn't hurt?"

Carol had tied the tourniquet on Edith's upper arm

122

and was bent over her arm, palpating a nice vein in her wrist. "There'll be a brief stick as the needle punctures the skin. After that, you shouldn't feel a thing."

Ten minutes and three sticks later, Carol got a vein in the other arm.

"I'm sorry, Edith; usually—"

Edith nodded. "I know. My veins roll. That's what the lab technicians always tell me when they draw my blood."

Carol's confidence was shattered by then, but she concentrated on adjusting the drip rate on the Pitocin just so. When all else fails and your patient's confidence in you is teetering on the brink of disaster, you always count the drip rate of the IV and pretend to regulate it. To patients there is something mysterious and fascinating about IVs; they assume anybody who knows anything about them must know *something*.

She wasn't yet completely comfortable about inducing labor, however. According to the routine L&D procedure, Carol had drawn up a minute amount of Pitocin from a vial and injected it into a bag of 1000 cc of D5W. She had turned the bag upside down a few times to mix the Pitocin in well, then started the IV. Ideally a nurse should stay at the bedside during the administration of Pitocin, but that would take one nurse per patient which was usually impossible. Carol started the Pitocin at five drops a minute and watched the drip rate, timing it carefully to make sure it was steady and did not fluctuate.

Oxytocin, a hormone normally secreted by the posterior pituitary gland, is released slowly into the bloodstream and begins to stimulate the uterine smooth muscle. A peristalsislike movement of the uterine muscle, a wavelike contraction, begins at the upper segment of the uterus and moves down. Pitocin, a synthetic oxytocin, stimulates the beginning of this

123

movement and produces powerful rhythmic waves which cause labor pains, and which should increase in frequency and intensity until the explusion of the fetus.

Every patient had her own tolerance to the uterine stimulant and you never knew what that tolerance would be. First, you had to get the uterine contractions going; then you could regulate the number of drops it took to keep the contractions increasing in frequency and intensity. But as in all medical or surgical procedures, inducing labor with Pitocin had its danger. The danger was in giving too much. If a contraction was allowed to be sustained for more than ninety seconds, there was a danger of the uterus rupturing—a fatal occurrence. Also, during the height of each strong contraction, the blood supply to the fetus is cut off, and if the contractions are too frequent and too strong, the baby's ability to restore its supply of oxygen between contractions is insufficient and the baby will become distressed.

There is a third bad side effect to the administration of Pitocin, a tendency for the mother's blood pressure to drop, but this is a transient side effect and doesn't last long.

Carol finished checking the drip rate and looked at Edith. Both Edith's hands were on her abdomen. "Here it comes," she announced.

"A contraction?"

Edith nodded. "Does it start this soon?"

"Many times."

The next step was to check Edith's BP to make sure it was normal. Carol did that first thing. It was normal. Then she placed the fetoscope head brace on her head, put the earpieces in her ears, and listened to the FHTs. They were normal. Carol timed the interval between the first contraction and the second—eleven minutes.

She listened to fetal heart tones during the second contraction. Usually during a contraction, because of the compression of uterine muscle on fetal circulation, the FHTs slowed. This was normal. But a slowing of FHTs below one hundred twenty during a contraction signaled possible fetal distress. Happily, the FHTs during Edith's second contraction were lowered only about five beats per minute.

Ideally, Carol should stay at Edith's bedside continually for the duration of her labor, for although the first fifteen minutes of the induction had gone well, complications could arise anytime. Here's where the patient's husband could help.

Carol hurriedly went to the father's waiting room just off the corridor outside the double doors of L&D and summoned Roger Grant.

Roger Grant sprang to his feet and joined Carol in the corridor, saying, "How is she?" He was a funny-looking fellow with a comic-strip grin, like that of the character on all the *Mad* magazines, and he wore an old-fashioned flattop.

"She's fine. Now I have to leave her for a few seconds and need your help," Carol said going into Edith's room with him. Some fathers paled when a nurse in L&D said those words, but some, like Roger Grant, brightened. She asked him to time Edith's contractions and the duration of each. This was actually Carol's job, but—L&D was short of help as usual, too many patients, an old story. Besides, timing contractions gave the father and the mother something to do, something to do together to help bring the progress of labor along.

Roger grinned and, pulling a chair up to the bedside, took his smug-looking wife's hand in his as Carol checked the drip rate of the Pitocin again. It was steady at five drops per minute.

Now for Loretta.

"I did the prep myself," Loretta told her, as she glanced at herself in a compact mirror she had produced from somewhere, probably from her overnight case.

Carol stood with her mouth open for a second. "You . . . *did?*"

"Last night. You didn't notice when you gave the enema, did you? Since I had my back to you."

"No, I didn't notice."

"Well, I did it. How does my hair look? Is it mashed in back?" Loretta raised her head up off the pillow and patted her coiffure.

"It's perfect. Now may I check to—uh—make sure everything—I mean even if there's one small hair left . . ."

Loretta sighed and rolled her eyes. "Go ahead. But will you raise the head of my bed up a little first, please?"

Bennet had relegated their old crank-type beds to the L&D department and to the intensive- and cardiac-care units. This had been done because in L&D the doctors didn't want a patient to be able to raise and lower her own bed because caudal and spinal anesthesia required that she lie in a certain position or at a specific angle, and if she were able to raise her own bed, she might raise the head of it to a disadvantageous position. In the ICU and CCU units, electric beds could interfere with the electronic functions of the cardiac and arterial monitors.

She went to the foot of Loretta's bed and started cranking.

"That's enough," Loretta said. "Just a little lower. O.K."

Then she went to Loretta, tentatively pulled down the top sheet, and lifted her gown. *Oh God! She'd done*

126

a full prep, and Dr. Blasingame always ordered a half-prep. Shit, damnit, and hell.

Well, she'd just have to tell him that Loretta had done it herself at home. However, Carol did check to make sure she'd done a good job of it where it counted. She had. She let Loretta pull down her gown and yank up the sheet while she turned to the IV setup.

It took only one stick to get Loretta's IV started—*there simply was no justice*—and she adjusted the drip rate carefully. In two minutes Loretta's contractions began.

"I really thought Dr. Blasingame would be here. I really feel very uncomfortable that he isn't," Loretta complained.

Carol was timing the duration of her contraction. A good "working" contraction, one that was strong enough to cause the effacement and dilation of the cervix, caused the abdomen to become very tight. At the height of a good contraction, the nurse should not be able to make an indentation in the abdomen with her finger. Loretta's first two contractions were ten minutes apart. Vital signs were good, FHTs normal. Now to check Clara.

"Nurse."

Carol turned back to Loretta.

"I think if I'm paying this enormous amount for a labor room, I ought to at least have a visit from my doctor."

Carol said, "I'll telephone his secretary and tell her that you're admitted."

This seemed to pacify Loretta, but it meant nothing, actually. Blasingame probably was already in the doctors' lounge, or eating breakfast in the cafeteria. That Loretta Blalock had been admitted to L&D wasn't going to make him tremble with anticipation. But Carol telephoned his office and reported to his

127

secretary that Edith, Loretta, and Clara had all been admitted and that labor had been induced on Edith and Loretta. Blasingame was more likely to check with his secretary about things than he was to check with Labor and Delivery. If he called Labor and Delivery, somebody might pester him with some goofy problem or other. If the nurses needed him for anything important, all they had to do was page him.

The morning wore on. Loretta predictably dilated more quickly than Edith, and Carol paged Dr. Blasingame at 12:05 to report Loretta's progress—not because Loretta was ready for a caudal, but because she demanded it. It angered Carol to be ordered to do something, but—O.K., if a patient demands something, you have to do *something*. Blasingame took his time getting there and by the time he got there, Loretta was dilated six centimeters, was ready for the caudal, and was furious.

Blasingame trudged into the room in a foul mood. When he was in a foul mood, he didn't speak to anybody except to give orders. By the time he entered Loretta's room her lipstick had been eaten off, her mascara had given her two black eyes, and her hair was flat on the sides and back.

"Damn you," she told him. "I hurt. You promised that I wouldn't." But Loretta managed a feeble smile.

Carol bit her lip and began to place several extra disposable pads under Loretta's hips while Blasingame smiled his most charming smile and said, "Aw, you won't hurt once I give you the caudal." And he told Carol, "She's one of my *girls.*"

Still biting her lip, Carol handed him the amniotome, which he took, still smiling fixedly while he sat down on the side of the bed.

"Bend your knees and spread your legs," he said.

Carol carefully pulled down the sheet and slowly

raised Loretta's gown.

Blasingame became very still. His smile waned slowly until his face was absolutely expressionless. His voice was very steady as he asked, "Who . . . did . . . the prep?"

Carol said sweetly, "Loretta. At home."

A tremor went through Blasingame as he attempted to control his rage. You couldn't rage at patients, only at nurses and lab techs and such. But his hand was steady as he inserted the amniotome and pricked the bag of waters, rupturing the membranes so that amniotic fluid flowed onto the disposable pads to thoroughly soak them. Then he did a quick vaginal exam.

While he grimly washed his hands, Carol took the FHTs. After the membranes were ruptured there was always a danger of the umbilical cord prolapsing into the vagina and becoming compressed between the baby's head and the mother's pelvic inlet, cutting off fetal circulation. FHTs were neither too high nor too low.

Carol hung the fetoscope on the bedrail, whisked away the soaked pads under Loretta's hips, and produced Blasingame's very own hospital-packed caudal tray. All the other obstetricians used the ones that were prepackaged by a manufacturer, but not Dr. Blasingame. He didn't like the needles in the prepackaged ones, or the gloves, or the syringes, or the catheter. So Martin had to pack and wrap and autoclave Blasingame his very own caudal tray. And this wasn't unreasonable. Each of the obstetricians had his own preferences; Dr. Simon didn't like the paper disposable gowns, so the nurses always made sure there was a sterilized cloth one on the delivery-room instrument table. Dr. Moss hated plastic placenta basins, so the nurses always saw that a metal one was

129

on the table. Some others had idiosyncrasies, too, but nothing that couldn't be complied with easily enough. Only Dr. Jackson could work with any gown, basin, caudal tray, or instrument; he didn't care.

Carol unwrapped the tray, careful not to contaminate it or any of its contents, then went around to the other side of Loretta's bed and told her to turn toward her, on her left side, and to bend her right knee up, leaving the left one straight.

Dr. Blasingame pulled on his gloves and sat down in the bedside chair. His brown eyes examined the caudal tray to see if all the equipment was there. As he picked up the swab and dipped it in the Betadine solution, which Carol had just poured into the small basin, she opened a new vial of lidocaine. He then swabbed an area about the size of a dinner plate at the base of Loretta's spine.

"Oh-oo," Loretta moaned with pain from a contraction.

Frowning with concentration, Blasingame picked up the 5-cc syringe, and Carol held the vial of lidocaine as he stuck the needle of the syringe into the rubber top of the vial and drew up 5 cc of the anesthetic. After he dropped the syringe back onto the sterile tray, he selected the Tuohy needle and began to palpate for the caudal hiatus, a small area at the very base of the spine just where the spinal nerves flare out fanlike from the spinal cord. There was a trick to finding it; the doctor had to enter the exact space at just the correct angle. Blasingame inserted the needle.

Loretta jumped, but Carol was there again to hold her still, saying softly, "A stick. Stay very still. Now he's going to inject a little air, and you'll feel a little pressure. . . ."

Blasingame injected 5 cc of air from a syringe into the needle. Carol knew that if there was no resistance to

130

the passing of air from the syringe, it was properly placed. But Blasingame frowned, drew the needle out part of the way, injected more air, tightened his mouth, and finally threaded the twenty-inch-long small-lumened catheter into the needle. Then he withdrew the needle leaving only the catheter—hopefully—in the caudal canal.

Carol tore wide adhesive tape off the roll, while Blasingame secured the catheter to Loretta's sacrum, or lower back, with the tape until it was firmly in place. Then Carol told her to roll onto her back while Blasingame attached the syringe of lidocaine to the catheter and slowly injected the anesthetic into the catheter.

Carol was already having Loretta raise her hips so that she could tuck a pillow under them when Loretta whined, "My legs. I can't move my—"

The effect of the anesthetic was almost instantaneous. Loretta should be anesthetized completely, pain-free, from the level of the umbilicus down, and also paralyzed in the same area. Carol straightened her legs as Blasingame wordlessly placed one piece of tape on the syringe and catheter, securing it to Loretta's abdomen. As labor progressed and Loretta began to feel pain again, Carol would have to inject a few more ccs of lidocaine into the catheter to maintain the anesthesia.

Blasingame waited for Loretta's next contraction with his hand on her abdomen, while Carol quickly took her blood pressure, respirations, and FHTs. Mixing caudals with Pitocin could cause respiratory difficulties occasionally. The vital signs were normal. Carol then checked Loretta's feet, which were glowing pink, indicating that the caudal was working.

"Feel that?" Blasingame asked Loretta when her next contraction began.

Loretta frowned. "On the right side a little."

"Ah. It'll go away," he said, going back to her sink to wash his hands.

"What if it doesn't?"

"It will."

"But I've heard that sometimes people can feel pain on one side."

Blasingame smiled wryly and looked at Carol. "Not with *my* caudals. Unless a nurse accidentally pulls the catheter out a little and it gets in the wrong place."

Loretta's huge brown eyes fastened on Carol, and Carol's greenish brown ones fixed on Blasingame. *Turd.* What he had just said wasn't true. He *did* miss once in a while, and so did the other doctors. He had probably missed the caudal space and was going to let Loretta blame it on her.

"C'mon, Welles. Let's go do Grant's caudal. She's probably there by now."

Fuming silently, but with a fixed smile on her mouth, Carol followed the doctor from Loretta's room into Edith's.

That day, with four patients being induced and all having caudal anesthetics, only one caudal did not work. Loretta's, which "took" only on her left side. Knowing it was hopeless, Carol nevertheless reported it to Dr. Blasingame who was having lunch in the cafeteria. He instructed Carol to turn Loretta onto her right side. It did not help so she called him again, this time in the doctors' lounge. He sighed and said he'd be in shortly, but he did not show.

When Carol met Mac in the hallway at 1:05, Mac said, "Jenkins is ready to deliver and Dr. Moss is in delivery now with Vicente. But Joy says he's doing the episiotomy, so—how's yours?"

"I've called Dr. Blasingame twice because Loretta Blalock's caudal took only on her left side."

132

"He got the catheter in the wrong place, then, and just won't admit it."

"What can we do?"

"Give moral support, I guess. Small comfort. By the way, I just checked Clara. She's still having low back pain."

Carol rolled her eyes. "I know. And I'm worried."

"So am I. See you around, kid." Mac hurried on down the hallway to get a stretcher for Jenkins.

By two o'clock, Mac's patients had delivered two boys. Loretta had delivered a girl, Edith a boy . . . and Carol had determined that Clara was now in true labor.

It had been a typical day in L&D, moderately busy, mostly routine. Four patients delivered.

Clara's case was not routine, but neither was it rare. Mac entered Clara's room quietly, her brows raised. Carol raised her head to look at her. "Four minutes apart," was all she said as she held the emesis basin under Clara's chin.

"I've called Dr. Blasingame again."

Clara retched suddenly into the basin, coughed, took a deep breath. Her concern over losing the baby was but a fog that surrounded her now; the focus of her concern was upon herself, her pain, her nausea, her fear.

Mac took the damp washcloth from her throat, rinsed it in cool water at the sink, and replaced it on her throat. A cool room and cool cloths on the throat were two of the best ways to assuage nausea.

"Did he say . . . anything about . . . caudal?" Carol asked trying not to say too much about it for fear of causing Clara any more fear.

Mac shook her head. "But he ordered Phenergan for nausea." Mac put her hand on Clara's arm. "Clara, Dr. Blasingame ordered something to keep you from vomiting, O.K.?"

Clara nodded and retched again into the basin, and there was a sudden sound like someone had thumped a watermelon. Carol and Mac stared at each other a moment. Then, apprehensively, Carol lifted the top sheet. It was there on the disposable pads and still trickling from Clara's vagina. She looked at Mac and told her what they already knew. "Her membranes have ruptured."

Mac's eyes went instantly to the fetoscope; for the first thing now was to check fetal heart tones. But Carol, who had already reached for the fetoscope, now placed it on the X she'd marked on Clara's abdomen to indicate where the FHTs could be heard the best. Fetal heart was low, one hundred, and Clara wasn't having a contraction. Carol listened, frowning, while Clara's abdomen began to tighten, to harden. She couldn't believe what she was hearing. She raised her head and looked at Mac. "FHTs are eighty-six with a contraction. One hundred without."

Mac took a weary, deep breath, turned toward the door, and said, "I'll notify Dr. Blasingame."

Carol was aware of her own tense body as she listened again. She'd attended probably a hundred or more patients as a nurse, and never had the rupturing of a patient's membranes been accompanied by a prolapsed cord, but she knew that it did happen occasionally. As she listened while the next contraction came, the FHTs slowed, slowed to eighty at the height of the contraction. She wet her lips, kept listening. With the subsiding of the contraction the fetal heartbeats rose again to one hundred twenty. The next contraction came within four minutes and the FHTs slowed to ninety.

When Mac entered the room again; she was pushing the electronic monitor, a device about the size of a bedside table or nightstand, called an electrohysterograph and fetal cardiograph—or EHFC.

Mac smiled at Clara. "Sweetie," she said effecting a casual cheerfulness she didn't feel, "we're going to monitor your contractions and compare them with your baby's heartbeat. Just a sophisticated way of keeping tabs on what's going on."

By then Clara was too sick and in pain to care.

The nurses in L&D seldom had to use the electronic monitor. It was a terribly expensive machine, and its use would cost the patient—or her insurance company—a great deal of money.

Carol and Mac strapped the monitor's electrode, a device about the size of a pack of cigarettes—to Clara's abdomen. Then Carol flipped on the switch. The readout graph paper, much like an electrocardiograph or EKG, began to move along and the stylus recorded Clara's next contraction; the duration of the contraction in seconds and the number of fetal heartbeats per minute. At the height of each contraction the fetal heart dipped below eighty-five.

Mac left the room at a run and paged Dr. Blasingame *stat*.

The next few minutes were a blur of controlled panic.

Looking horrified, Dr. Blasingame came hurrying into the room, yanked the fetoscope off the hook on the wall, and took the monitor readout from Mac; he read it, then bent to listen to Clara's abdomen. Then he raised his head and said to her, "Clara, I'm going to have to do a Caesarean. We think the umbilical cord is prolapsed and we've got to save the baby." Without waiting for Clara's reaction he turned to Mac. "Call Dr. Pashi. Get the delivery room set up for a C-section. Dr. Jackson's out of town, so you'll have to assist me. Who else is here besides Carol? Carol can't scrub yet."

"Joy."

135

Blasingame tossed the EHFC readout on the floor. "Shit! Get Robbie. She's experienced. Carol can circulate."

"I'm sorry, Robbie is in Melinda's room and can't assist. The rule is . . ." Mac glanced at Clara and motioned for the doctor to go out into the hallway with her. Blasingame followed Mac out of the room. Carol knew that Mac was telling him that Robbie couldn't assist with another patient that day because she was taking care of Melinda.

". . . don't give a damn. We need one nurse to circulate, one to scrub. Carol's new, and Joy's scatter-brained. . . ." came Blasingame's voice from the hall.

Carol was caught up in trying to comfort Clara, only half-aware of her own words. ". . . General anesthetic . . . you're seven months along . . . . The baby will have a pretty good chance. . . . When you wake up it'll be all over. . . ." But Clara's anxious eyes, dimming periodically with pain, turned away from Carol's compassion, became introspective, withdrew. Amazed at her own capacity for pain, she was emotionally becoming a fetus herself. Dr. Blasingame's voice was saying, "I'll go to the nursing director about this, Mac. Just see if I don't."

"The nursing director was the one who made the rule, Dr. Blasingame. . . ."

"I could have you all fired. . . ."

"Fine. You do that."

Furious as a thundercloud, Blasingame came storming into the room and snatched up an examining glove. He was in a rage at Mac for not obeying his commands, furious with Joy for her lack of skill and at Carol for not being more experienced at scrubbing for C-sections, and irritated at Clara for complicating his day.

"Spread your legs, Clara. You ought to know what to do by now," he told her as he pulled on the examining glove.

Carol glared at him and Clara moaned with her next contraction.

The doctor did a vaginal exam. "She's seven, can't feel the cord, so it's up high." He pulled off the glove and stalked out of the room without meeting either Clara's gaze or Carol's.

Mac readied a delivery room for a C-section; Dr. Pashi came into L&D just as Carol was pushing the stretcher from Clara's room, and Pashi helped her push it into the delivery room. Dr. Bordeaux appeared and went to the scrub area.

In the delivery room, Mac was to assist, Joy to scrub, Carol to circulate, and Dr. Bordeaux to take care of the baby.

Carol had acted as circulating nurse only twice, and both times with Robbie's help. But she felt confident about what to do. She had only to bring what was needed to the instrument table, to keep the table supplied, to run any errands that needed to be run. Dr. Blasingame, with thunderous expression and hands shaking from weariness and frustration, began his work. Pashi was silent; so was Bordeaux. From Carol's vantage point, she couldn't see the incision, but knew from the instruments Joy passed to Dr. Blasingame—or from those he called for her to hand him—about where he was in the operation. Pashi was monitoring the anesthetic, Clara's vitals, and the fetal heart tones.

"FHTs?" was all Blasingame kept demanding.

Pashi would say, "Eighty during a contraction."

"Shit."

Dr. Bordeaux was checking the oxygen tank on the isolette. One of the L&D nurses' jobs was to see that the

137

two oxygen tanks attached to the isolettes were always at least half-full. The pediatricians always checked to make sure. On the warming hood he now laid out the infant's resuscitation equipment; tiny laryngoscope, small endotracheal tube, suctioning equipment, oxygen mask, breathing bag.

"Suction," Dr. Blasingame commanded of Mac.

Ssssssssst.

"FHTs."

"Wait a minute," Dr. Pashi said.

"Well, goddamnit, give me the *last* FHTs."

"Eighty-two."

By the acceleration of activity among Joy, the doctor, and Mac, Carol knew when he was down to the uterus.

At last he dipped his hand and brought up the fetus. She could hear the bulb syringe suctioning; the infant whimpered. The cord was clamped and cut, Dr. Bordeaux placed himself behind Mac; she handed the baby to him without contaminating her gloves.

Then suddenly, Martin, masked, was standing in the doorway motioning to Carol. Carol told Mac, "Marty's motioning for me; I'll see what she wants."

Mac was suctioning the surgical incision and nodded; Joy handed Dr. Blasingame the placenta basin. Carol could hear baby boy Smith whimpering as she walked out of the delivery room.

"It's Mr. McCabe," Martin said to her. "He wants to speak with Dr. Blasingame on the telephone."

McCabe? Carol didn't know a McCabe.

"He says it's an emergency," Martin said.

Shaking her head in harried amazement, Carol hurried down the hallway to the nurses' station, pulling down her mask as she went. She picked up the receiver of the telephone and answered, "Hello, this is Carol

138

Welles in Labor and Delivery. Dr. Blasingame is in the delivery room at the moment; may I take a message?"

A man's voice stammered over the line. "My wife . . . she's eight months . . . Dr. Blasingame's patient? She's . . . she's bleeding. A lot."

Carol's hand went to her head. "What do you mean 'a lot,' sir?"

"Soaking her gown . . . with blood. Now she's having a lot of pain."

Carol shut her eyes, opened them. "Mr. McCabe. Get your wife to the emergency room as fast as you can. Don't wait to change her clothes or anything. Do you understand?"

"Yes, ma'am."

Carol hung up the receiver, dialed the emergency room. The admitting clerk answered, and Carol said, "Please have Corey Brewster come to the telephone; this is important."

Brewster came on the line, and Carol said, "Brew, I've just got a call from a Mr. McCabe. His wife is eight months pregnant and she's hemorrhaging. I've instructed him to bring her through emergency, and I'm counting on you to bring her into L&D without all the red tape."

"You didn't identify yourself, Carol dear, but I recognize your voice. I'll get your patient on a stretcher and get her to you pronto. Whose patient?"

"Blasingame."

"God almighty! Hasn't he had some hell of a week?"

"Yeah. Tell me about it. Gotta go. We're in the delivery room. Dr. Blasingame's doing an emergency C-section right now."

"God . . ."

Carol pulled up her mask and hurried back into the delivery room. She paused about six feet from the

139

delivery table. Joy was handing Dr. Blasingame a suture. Carol said, "Dr. Blasingame?"

He said, "What do you want? What do you want?"

"A Mr. McCabe just telephoned and says his wife is bleeding. I questioned him, and it sounds like hemorrhage. I instructed him to bring her to the hospital immediately, through the emergency room."

An instrument clattered to the floor. Blasingame seemed to freeze for a moment. Then his frame shuddered as he shouted, "Goddamn it! Goddamn it! Goddamn! Hemorrhage? Goddamn you, Carol! You come in here and tell me this . . . Get out of here! Get out of here and don't come back in here!" He turned toward her, raised a towel clamp in his hand as if to throw it, then paused and lowered his hand.

Meantime Pashi was staring at the doctor, Mac was petrified, and Dr. Bordeaux, horrified, was looking at Carol.

Carol was suddenly on fire, but cold at the same time. This was a nightmare. This couldn't be happening.

Back here we either make 'em or break 'em.

"Get out," Blasingame said without feeling.

Carol did not move, but the room swayed. Her heart was thudding in her chest, her pulse beating in her head. Her voice was hoarse when she finally found it, and while the OR crew stood frozen in a diorama of horror, Carol said, "I must have orders for your patient, Doctor."

Blasingame's rage was but a simmer now. "You . . . I . . . start an IV," he said softly, his voice shaking. "Start an IV . . . 1000 cc D5W . . . six million units penicillin . . ." His voice drained away as he shook his head over and over.

"Is that all, Doctor?"

140

"That is all."

She turned and ran out of the delivery room. No, it was not all. The delivery room must be set up. Carol set up the room and then injected the penicillin into the IV solution, and by the time Brew pushed the stretcher into L&D bearing Myra McCabe, Carol had the room and the IV ready. Brew helped her get Myra from the stretcher to the bed and started the IV while Carol checked under Myra's blood-soaked robe. A little watery blood was still trickling from the vagina. Carol grabbed the fetoscope, and, saying comforting little meaningless things to Myra as she worked, she began to listen for FHTs. There were none. She glanced at Brew and he read her expression.

Brew had the IV started in seconds, and as he left the room, passing her, he said, "I got it started for you because you're shaking, and I didn't figure you'd get a vein like that."

"Thanks, Brew," she said, only half-aware that Brew had left the room as she took Myra's vital signs. Her pulse rate was rapid, but not dangerously so; BP was high, respirations a little high; FHTs—none.

When she looked under the sheet again, the prolapsed cord was protruding six inches from the vagina. It was not pulsating. Carol jerked the oxygen mask off the wall and strapped it on Myra's face saying, "Myra, I'm going to give you a little oxygen. Now, you're just fine, but the baby's not, as you know, and maybe this will help."

While Carol regulated the O_2 at the meter on the wall above the head of the bed, Myra was saying, "O.K., do what you have to. Oh, dear Lord. What's going to happen?"

Mac paced into the room then, questioning Carol with her eyes. Myra was intent on wincing from a

141

contraction, so Carol was able to shake her head as she handed Mac the fetoscope. Mac placed the head brace of the fetoscope over her head, bent down, and placed the diaphragm of the instrument on Myra's abdomen. She listened, moved the diaphragm down to the right, to the left, upward, near the umbilicus, and at last raised up and met Carol's gaze.

At that moment Dr. Blasingame came in, face tight with tension, not looking at Mac, not looking at Carol. Mac handed him the fetoscope, and he pushed her hand away. He already knew without listening.

"What happened, Myra?" he asked.

"I woke up bleeding, Dr. Blasingame, a little at first. Then when I got up, it really started and my water broke and the pains started and while we were getting into the car, the pains got really awful."

He lifted the top sheet. Carol could see blood on the disposable pad under Myra's hips; not much there, so most of the bleeding had evidently already occurred. The doctor palpated her abdomen and told the nurses, "Get a delivery room ready."

"It's ready," Carol told him.

"Let's get her on in then."

Mac went to tell Myra's husband that she was going to the delivery room, and then joined Carol in time to get Myra's legs up in the stirrups in the delivery room.

The delivery of the dead infant was awful. Dr. Blasingame did not carefully apply forceps or wait patiently for Myra to deliver. He simply pulled the infant from her, feet first, for it was breech, as Dr. Pashi gave her a little gas. Silently, Blasingame clamped the cord, cut it, handed the infant to Carol.

It was warm and she laid it under the warming hood. Her hands went instinctively to the bulb syringe in the warmer, hesitated. She wanted to do something, to

142

bring it back. But Mac, who was holding Myra's hand, looked at her and shook her head. The infant had been dead probably two hours by now.

Carol laid the sterile blanket over the body of the infant. She had assisted with the delivery of perhaps a hundred or more infants in her six months as a labor-and-delivery nurse; Mac had delivered two, Carol had partially delivered one; there had been emergency C-sections and two elective ones, and several premature births; but this—this silent, cyanotic infant was the first real tragedy.

Later, after Carol had taken Myra to OB recovery, she came back to the nurses' station. The three-to-eleven crew was there already in their scrub clothes, silently standing around, respecting the fact that the day-shift nurses had had a hell of a day. Carol greeted them, then went into the lounge to change into her clothes. Mac was there stepping into her corduroy slacks and for a moment she didn't say anything, respecting Carol's humiliation, her depression. Finally she said, "I've got to go shopping today for something to wear to the Christmas party. But I'll be damned if I'll buy a party dress just to wear one time."

Carol smiled and said nothing.

Mac said, "Dr. Blasingame's a horse's ass, you know, at the very least. But also this was the fifth tragedy or near-tragedy he's had in two weeks. It's like everything else: when it rains, it pours."

Carol tossed her head as she pulled the scrub dress free of her hair. "But he had no cause to curse me, Mac. There is no excuse for that."

"No, there really isn't. And our profession is one of the only ones—if not the only one—in existence where that kind of verbal abuse is tolerated."

"I had no idea—"

"Some people tolerate toxic substances potentially damaging to their lungs, or radioactive materials, or some sort of physical danger, but we have to tolerate the verbal abuse sometimes. Reminds me of the sweat factories in Europe."

Carol, with tears still in her eyes, slipped her sweater over her head and pulled it down over her shirt. She unpinned her hair, which was gathered in a chignon at the back of her neck, and let it fall to her shoulders in a shower of soft threads that caught the lights from the fixtures overhead. "The verbal abuse is hard to take, Mac, but I think I can learn to live with it. But the baby—"

"Yeah. That infant. This is nursing, though, Carol. You knew when you went into nursing that you'd be dealing with death. Even in OB we're not immune to tragedy."

Robbie came in just then with a sigh. "Heard you guys had a busy day," she said as she pulled her scrub top up over her head. "Well, so did I. This makes me so nervous, Mac. Please assign Melinda to somebody else for a while." She stood in bra and half-slip, looking at Mac. "You'd just got through asking me all about how Melinda was doing, and her vital signs were O.K. *then.*"

Preparing to leave, Mac had hung her handbag over her shoulder. She paused and looked at Robbie.

Robbie said, "They were O.K. then. But I just now took them again. She's spiked a temp, from one hundred one point two to one hundred four in less than an hour."

Carol turned from the mirror, saw Mac's frown. "Did you report it to the three-to-eleven crew so that they can report it to Dr. Whitehall?"

"Yeah. Hank's assigned to Melinda today. She's

144

already calling him."

Mac stood silently a moment, then sank down into a chair and said thoughtfully, "Damn. Damn. *Damn.*" And Carol knew that Mac would stay for a while longer to check on Melinda.

But she had to leave. You couldn't hang around to see how a patient was doing after the three-to-eleven shift arrived; they would think you didn't believe they could handle the situation.

And now with her head on Bret's solid shoulder, thinking back over the most horrible day of her life, just past, she was wondering who had shown the dead McCabe baby to the mother and father; for Myra had asked to see it. Thank God, she was spared that task!

"You should have told Blasingame what an ass he was and walked out. Except I agree with you that you had to stay and do something with the hemorrhaging patient," Bret said.

She smiled. "You won't believe this, Bret, but I feel sorry for Dr. Blasingame."

Bret didn't answer. Maybe because he could see her point, maybe because he also had seen doctors break under pressure because he, too, was a nurse.

And I am a nurse; I have witnessed birth and death, happiness and tragedy. I cried when Dr. Blasingame yelled at me, but I did stand my ground for the sake of the patient. I know OB routine now, but I have so much more to learn. She wondered if her mother had been correct in the beginning. *I just can't see you as a nurse, Carol. I just don't think you have the stamina.*

Did she?

Now Melinda Curtis had spiked a temp again. *Peritonitis?* Carol took Bret's hand in hers, held it, brought it up to touch her cheek. He was a comfort to her, a ready listener, someone who empathized with

145

her and with whom she could share her nurse stories. "Mac said that even in OB we're not immune to tragedy," she said softly.

"Nor is anyone else anywhere else in life," Bret said. "But at least people like you and me, Carol . . . well, we're in the best position in the world for fighting it."

EIGHT

It didn't seem fair that her own life should be so exciting and so fulfilling, while Melinda lay burning with a fever that had climbed steadily since Friday, when she went off duty, until today, Monday. One hundred five degrees was dangerously high, and although the nurses had given her aspirin and acetaminophen every three to four hours all weekend in an attempt to bring her temp down, neither of the analgesics with their antipyretic side effects had succeeded. These tepid alcohol-and-water soaks had not succeeded either. Carol wished the doctors would hurry and do something else to bring the temp down. Melinda was almost delirious. The FHTs remained on the rapid side of normal.

Carol continued the baths using a basin of tepid water—not too cool lest Melinda become chilled—with rubbing alcohol added for its cooling effect. With the top sheet she had covered Melinda's body, except for her arms and legs, which she had placed on disposable pads and towels so that the cool washcloths placed on her arms and legs would not get her sheets wet. The tepid bath was a continuous thing; you kept it up stopping only to take vital signs, change the IV, take CVP readings, and record everything on the chart which lay on the extra overbed table placed at the foot of Melinda's bed.

The girl lay flat on her back now. Her face was extremely pale, her hair damp and tousled, her head moving back and forth on her pillow. She was stiff, afraid to move because of the intolerable pain in her abdomen. Melinda suffered from every symptom of peritonitis. It made Carol depressed just to look at her. It wasn't fair.

Carol lifted Melinda's left arm, rinsed the washcloth in the tepid water, bathed under her arm, her upper arm and forearm, taking special pains to let the cooling water trickle over the antecubital space and radial area of her arm, the places where the blood vessels came closest to the surface of the skin, trying to cool the blood which raced at one hundred two beats per minute through her delicate veins.

They *must* get her temp down.

The antibiotics weren't working anymore; and Carol tried to fathom why—because at first the combination of antibiotics had worked. Melinda's temp had taken a plunge downward and had stayed that way for seven days. Now . . .

Superinfection. It was the only answer; pathogens, which had been reduced and controlled for seven days, had become resistant to the antibiotics. Now the doctors would have to try to find a new antibiotic, one which they could give safely to a pregnant woman, one which would control the particular organism that was causing the infection.

On Sunday, Hank had taken sample fluid cultures again from the drainage tubes in Melinda's abdomen, the cultures were being grown and studied in the lab.

Once the lab discovered which disease-carrying microbes had become resistant to the antibiotics, the doctors would have to rummage about in their minds again, or in their journals or *PDR*'s, for an antibiotic that would destroy those particular organisms.

It wasn't fair.

Carol, bathing Melinda's face, saw a faint smile on her lips, though she would not open her eyes. Melinda bore her pain and illness with the patience of Job. Better than Job; Job had complained a lot, Melinda never did. Always upbeat—pain, fever, danger, the unknown quantity of whether the antibiotics and pain medication had damaged the fetus already—all of it she endured with hope and as much cheerfulness as she could manage.

Carol talked to her as she worked almost constantly, nonsensical things, just to let her know she was there. Melinda knew about the party Saturday night, and it was the only thing of which she had spoken since Carol had come into the room an hour ago to take over her care.

"Did you go to the party?" Melinda had whispered.

Carol's heart fell to see her glazed eyes, cracked lips, and dry mouth, to smell the musty sweet odor of her breath.

"Yes," Carol had replied, and Melinda had given her a small smile before she had drifted off to sleep again—or wherever it was she drifted off to.

Carol applied a glycerin swab to her lips again, then resumed giving the bath.

"The party was lovely," she began as she squeezed water from the washcloth into the basin, her own mind going back as she gently bathed the distended throbbing carotid vessels in Melinda's neck. "First, when I left work Friday, my friend Bret Harris met me, and we went shopping for a dress."

149

Bret was a super shopper, Carol told Melinda. He hadn't been at all embarrassed to stand and wait in the ladies' ready-to-wear department while Carol had looked at dresses among the racks of beautiful things. He had even offered to help.

As she had pushed aside one dress after another, examining styles, sizes, colors, Bret would say, "Here's a pretty one."

She'd politely look at what he had selected; it might be four sizes too large or have an atrocious style, but he would like the color or something. Only thing was, Bret was color-blind. Looking at dresses on a rack, Bret hadn't the faintest idea how they would look on the person.

It was discouraging looking for something young yet sophisticated, an attractive style, the right color, the right size. Thousands of dresses, yet there were so many particular things you had to look for. The dresses on the models who floated about the store were too flamboyant for Carol; floating layers of crimson red crepe de Chine, taffeta bell-shaped skirts with exotic red cummerbunds and plunging blousy tops. No, Carol knew what looked best on her: something with a nipped-in waist. Not a square neck either because her jaw was sort of square.

"Put on a dress with a square neck and I'd look like a boxer ready to whip somebody's ass," Aunt Sadie had said of herself once—and the family all agreed that Carol had Aunt Sadie's jaw, minus a few inches of fat.

V-necked. Black wasn't for her or orangy reds or brown or gold. Something plum or blue-red, or green or blue-green.

"I ended up with a gorgeous crepe de Chine aqua with a V neck, very slim all over until it comes just below the hips where it flares out. And I have this pair of real lizard slippers, very high heels."

Melinda's gray-green eyes opened for a second revealing the red sclera, the feverish glaze of a girl in pain, almost delirious, afraid but listening, listening to Carol's droning monologue as she softly painted a picture of party clothes.

"Bret dressed in a tan sports jacket and brown slacks. He's not very tall, not much taller than I am, but very handsome with straight brown hair and blue-gray eyes." She had felt beautiful at the hospital Christmas party held in the Inn of Tropicana's tropical room where a small but excellent band played a mixture of pop tunes, watered-down rock, and dressed-up country-western; a mixture guaranteed not to displease anybody.

There was food galore on the tables, compliments of Bennet's super volunteer auxiliary, and there was a wonderful punch and champagne and eggnog.

Carol and Bret were hungry when they arrived, so before they danced they took a plate of hors d'oeuvre to the fountain. It was colorfully lit with red and green lights, and surrounded by real palm trees and giant ferns which were decorated with red velvet ribbons and red and gold ornaments.

"Sounds ludicrous, but you should have seen it," Carol told Melinda as she bathed her face. "Tropical palms decorated as if they were firs or pine trees. They were gorgeous."

Shortly, they had been joined by other hospital personnel, one of the med vets, who had graduated with Carol and Bret; Nancy, who had been Carol's partner on the very first patient they had been assigned as student nurses—Nancy now worked at Bennet on the urological floor—and others drifted over.

The party was for all Bennet personnel, from housekeeping and maintenance people to nursing

151

supervisors and hospital board members. Doctors on staff at Bennet were there, too; probably a higher percentage of doctors attended than anybody else.

Carol had expected to see Duane, and she did. Her face reddened as he entered with a tall willowy blonde on his arm. It wasn't that she was jealous of the painted-up blonde; she was jealous of Duane's cheerful flippancy, that same uncomplicated, self-centered enjoyment of himself that he had once shown in *her* presence. The turkey pâté went suddenly flat in her mouth.

Suddenly, as Nancy and Bret talked, and Gary, the med vet, tried to impress Carol with his wit, all her moral, puritanical indoctrination flushed through her mind. When she was six years old, the little boy across the street had asked to see Carol's privates and offered to let her see his; but shyness had overpowered her natural curiosity, and she had fled the chicken house in fright and told her mother. That's when she got her first talk about sex. "Never, never let a boy see inside your panties. It's very, very bad. It's a very bad *sin.*"

Carol had asked if it was O.K. if she just took her panties off. Her mother had dropped into a chair and fanned herself, for she was pregnant with Carol's little brother at the time. "Oh, dear Lord," she had gasped, "she'll never make it. Never!"

And later, when she first began to have her period, she had overheard her mother telling her Aunt Agnes, "Carol's had her first period last week."

"Well, beware, Jewel. She can have a baby now," Aunt Agnes had philosophized.

"If it gets around that you let a boy do anything with you, Carol, you'll be ruined for life," her mother had confided once.

"Nobody will want to marry you then," Aunt Jane had offered.

By the time Carol had reached high-school age, she was so sexually inhibited that she was sure she was the only girl graduating who had never even petted, and she wouldn't have touched her own genitals for a hundred million dollars, much less anybody else's!

By the time she had met Duane six years later, she had gained a little experience at that sort of thing, short unimportant infatuations. Lovers for a few months and then eventually by mutual agreement the affair was over. She did not tell Melinda any of this, only recalled it silently. It was all so pale in her memory beside the more recent memory of Duane.

Let me in, Carol; it's cold out here. . . . Duane, go home. Please . . . No way. Carol, I've made up my mind. I'm going to spend the night with you. . . . I love you; I love you and I want you. . . .

"I feel like dancing," Carol told Bret suddenly as they stood beside the fountain listening to Nancy match wits with Gary.

Bret as a dancer was O.K. Carol wasn't so swift herself in that department, but they did get out on the floor where the majority of other people were dancing. The older people—people in their thirties and forties and fifties—were in the majority, so a lot of the music the band played was for slow dancing; kind of O.K., if you were in a melancholy mood as she was at the time. But watching the dancers soon lifted her spirits until she was actually giggly.

Doctors were dancing with nurses, but it wasn't the sort of thing you saw in the movies—handsome young doctors dancing with beautiful young nurses. Actually, it was hilarious.

Old doctors who had been at Bennet for a hundred years danced with young nurses while their wives looked on. Young residents danced obligatorily with seasoned nurses they were hoping to win to their side so that they'd be more helpful when they were on the wards. Doctors danced with their wives. Dr. Simon tried to persuade Martin to dance, but she shook her head violently and blushed. Dr. Pashi danced with Mac, after asking Mac's husband's permission. Whitehall danced with Gwenn Hutton from ICU, who looked bored.

It was much more entertaining to Carol to see who was dancing with whom than it was to be dancing herself.

A jolt brought her attention back to Bret, and to the couple who had bumped into them. Carol laughed inexplicably when she saw that Basil Novak and the girl whom Duane had brought to the party had bumped into them.

"Welles," Novak said. "Just the lady I wanted to see."

They were in everybody's way as the four of them stood in the center of the floor surrounded by hilarious dancers; but flushing, Carol made the introductions, "Bret, Dr. Basil Novak. Dr. Novak, my friend, Bret Harris."

"My pleasure," Novak told Bret.

"And mine," said Bret, who had to look up a bit into Novak's eyes; and while Bret studied him, he introduced his partner to them.

"This is Carla Collins. Carla, Carol Welles."

Carol sized up Carla Collins; tall, willowy, flat-chested—a real airhead. "Glad to meet you."

"Pleased to meet you too. Seems like I've heard your name—" began Carla.

Novak interrupted asking Bret, "Mind if we switch partners, Harris? I've got some business to discuss with Carol."

Bret's eyes moved to Carol, and seeing that she was

154

willing, he nodded and looked back at Carla.

The last glimpse she had of Bret, as Novak whirled her away, was of Carla and Bret dancing, Carla a head taller than Bret; and she laughed as Novak led her through the throng of dancers while the band played a jaunty tune about "raindrops falling on my head," perfect for amateurs to two-step by.

Carol was delighted—sort of—that Novak had asked her to dance. Somehow, she hadn't pictured him dancing or partying. That he had a personal life—a social life—outside the hospital had never occurred to her. It did occur to her that this man might have led Shelly Wilkinson to despair and death. Up close, Novak was nicer looking than she had expected. He was dressed in a vested suit the color of his hair, a sort of tannish gray, and his blue necktie was the same color as his eyes. Yes, she could see why Shelly had fallen so much in love.

"My motives for asking you to dance are not purely because you are an attractive girl," Novak told her, smiling.

She liked his hands; long fingers, pale, the hands of an ideal surgeon. His hand was light on her waist.

"It's curiosity," he went on.

"That's really astonishing," she said smiling sarcastically.

"Nosiness, actually."

Carol laughed in spite of herself. "Now you've got *me* curious."

"There're two things I want to know," he said whirling her around gracefully as she gracefully followed. "What motivated you to refuse to give Valium to Melinda Curtis after we treated her intraperitoneally with kanamycin?"

"All I did was look in the PDR. It cautioned about

155

administering a muscle relaxant during or soon after intraperitoneal instillation of kanamycin. So I refused to give it."

"Do you look up every drug before you give it?"

"Yes. Especially if I haven't given it before. I guess I'm still inexperienced enough not to be acquainted with every drug, so I look them up. Besides, I think you doctors ought to become more acquainted with drug interactions and pay more attention to side effects."

"Oooof. Right in the solar plexus." Novak laughed. "But you're right. Difficult to do with all the drugs on the market—"

"Dr. Jackson advises his patients to take iron tablets wtih milk, for instance. You can't give iron with milk because the components of dairy products and iron mix and cause the iron to be poorly absorbed."

"I suppose you pointed this out to him."

"No, but Mac did."

"His reaction?"

Carol bit her lip, her eyes dancing. "I can't repeat it, but the crux of it was that it was a bunch of malarky."

Novak smiled. "He's right, you know. The problem is only with powdered iron or liquid iron . . . mostly . . . but not entirely, I guess."

"There, you see? Now *I* have a question," she said.

"Be my guest."

"When I went off duty yesterday Melinda Curtis had just spiked a temp from one hundred one point two to one hundred four. I called this morning to check on her, since it was my day off, and her temp is still high. Is it superinfection, Dr. Novak?"

Basil said, "I would guess it is, but—"

"But it could be septicemia too?"

"Good thinking. Infection of the bloodstream. But we've taken a blood culture so we'll see."

156

"How do you feel about Melinda, Dr. Novak?"

"How do I— Carol,"—his eyes caught the lights from the overhead fixtures as they so often did—"I— would you mind just calling me Basil?"

"O.K. But how do you *feel* about her?"

"Sorry. A little angry."

"But what about her prognosis?"

"It's grave, of course. She's got a lot against her."

"I know. But what's your *gut* feeling about her?"

Basil regarded Carol with a half-smile. "I'll be darned if you aren't the most persistent nurse I ever knew. I'm supposed to diagnose and prognosticate by employing scientific principles and astute medical judgment. Intuition figures into it too. But gut feeling?" He laughed softly. "Yes, I believe in gut feelings, too, and my gut feeling is . . . that she'll make it. Although the odds are more and more against her every day."

Carol smiled up at him. "I'm glad your gut feeling is positive. So's mine. How is she today? Or were you off duty?"

"I was on duty. I'm always on duty. God help me, Carol, I don't even know when my last day off was." Novak pulled the tail of his coat back and she could see the beeper attached to his belt. "I'm on call even now."

"And you're only a resident."

"Doesn't matter. Residents are on call more than the staff physicians are. Medical residency is a survival of the fittest."

"I know. And speaking of survival, I have another question."

"O.K."

"A name, actually."

"Speak."

"Shelly Wilkinson."

Novak winced, and his hand tightened on her waist.

157

"Shelly was in my graduating class," Carol said.

Novak did not smile, looked beyond her at something else, did not acknowledge her statement. Then, when she remained silent, he said slowly, "Ah, yes. Shelly."

"Interesting case, right?"

He looked at her again. "One of my first."

"So interesting that you had to follow up on it later. Right?" Carol was shocked at herself for pursuing this, but she couldn't seem to control herself; she hadn't realized that Shelly's crush on the brilliant resident surgeon who had assisted with the removal of parts of her colon, which had resulted in an ileostomy; Shelly's subsequent pursual of him; his possibly leading her on for whatever reason; his rejection of her, if he had led her on; and Shelly's ultimate suicide had been eating away at her for months. For it was *she* who had identified Shelly when she had been brought in, crushed, blood-soaked, and dead on arrival in Bennet's emergency room on graduation night.

Novak's eyes had gone sad. Did he feel something for Shelly then? Love, remorse, *guilt?*

"It wasn't an accident, you know," Carol persisted.

Novak stopped dancing. Blue, blue eyes searched hers, deeply, making her cringe inside and making her wish she had not set herself on this course of conversation. He stood while the other dancers bobbed ridiculously around them. A doctor, dancing with his wife, said over his shoulder, "Run down already, Basil?"

Basil ignored him. "Why?" he began softly. "Why are you telling me this?"

Carol couldn't speak for a moment. Then, "Shelly was in love with you. That's why she killed herself."

Basil stood holding her hand, touching her waist.

158

His expression was sad, a little angry; it was as if he were trying to comprehend what she was saying. Didn't he know? Or was it all in Shelly's fantasies? The lights from the overhead lights danced in his eyes. Then his gaze left her, and he turned suddenly and grabbed an arm. "Duren! I need to talk with Haggins."

It was unbelievable to her, but it was Duane whom Basil caught, Duane dancing with a nurse, who worked on the three-to-eleven shift in ER. Duane and the nurse stopped dancing; his eyes went to Carol.

"Wait a minute," Carol protested.

Basil told her, "It was my pleasure, Miss Welles. Excuse me while we change partners. I'll see you later on."

"Basil . . . look . . ." Duane protested, his eyes darting from Novak to Carol.

Basil said to Carol, "This is question number two. What reaction will Duren have if he has to come in contact with you on a social occasion?"

Novak took nurse Haggins in his arms, leaving Carol and Duane standing face-to-face on the dance floor. Then Duane turned to say, "Why the hell should you care?" But Basil only smiled and whisked Myrtle Haggins away from them as the band swung into a slow waltz.

Embarrassed and furious at being abandoned on a dance floor, and hating Duane and Novak and all men, Carol turned to leave, but he caught her arm.

"Oh, no, you don't, Carol," he said. His firm hold on her arm brought her round to face him, and he caught her to him, closer probably than anybody else was dancing, possessive even in his rejection of her. "You're not going to embarrass *me* by walking off the floor and leaving me."

"Still worried about your image, aren't you?" she

159

said falling into the rhythm and sway of the dance. "Are you sure that Dr. Tyree or Dr. Benson or Dr.—"

"Shut . . . up," he said through his teeth. "Somebody can overhear you."

". . . Mr. Proctor and his farce of an autopsy," she went on.

He was red-faced with fury. That was what their terminal fight had been all about, her term paper on Proctor. Carol had witnessed a CPR on Proctor, who had been admitted to Bennet for a simple transurethral resection of the prostate. Because Dr. Tyree, his urologist, had inadvertently nicked the bladder, irrigation fluid had leaked into Proctor's abdominal cavity causing him to go into shock. Nurses in charge of the floor and the private-duty nurses had not recognized or paid attention to the signs of shock, and Proctor had died as a result.

Carol had then witnessed the cover-up of the surgeon's error at Proctor's autopsy when the urologist, Tyree, purposefully tore the bladder so that evidence of his error was forever obliterated. Carol had decided to do her term paper on the case.

Duane, having just been accepted for residency at Bennet, had panicked, afraid that her research into Proctor's case might be noticed by the doctors involved—Tyree, the urologist; Benson, the young pathologist; and Coleson, the resident who had attended the CPR—and would link her to him, jeopardizing his residency or, at the very least, his reputation at Bennet. They had argued violently. And he had slammed out of her apartment forever.

Now she noticed with disgust that his touch still had the power to paralyze her, and it was as if they'd never been apart for nine months.

He said, "Still determined to ruin me, aren't you?"

"I was *never* determined to ruin you."

"You chose to do a paper that would have."

"I chose the paper, but there was no danger of it hurting you."

"There was a risk and you knew it. You chose a term paper over *me,* Carol."

"And you called me a pipsqueak and a piss-ant. You belittled my nursing."

"You made your choice."

"So did you."

"Then we have nothing else to say to each other."

"You're absolutely right."

The song was nearing its end, so Duane led her through the dancers, off the floor to the French doors near the table of snacks and punch. In summer the doors would have been open. Tonight, because of the blustery-cold winter air, they remained shut, but the lights of the city—more brilliantly colored this time of year with Christmas lights—twinkled in the frosty air.

"It's been my . . . misery to have had the opportunity to dance with you," he said bowing slightly.

"And mine."

He left her then, standing alone by the door.

She danced with Bret shortly after that. Bret must have watched her dancing with Duane, but said nothing; he knew their story. He also knew Shelly's and Novak's story, at least as much of it as Carol herself knew. She also danced with Dr. Pashi, after having met his beautiful, tiny, dark-eyed wife; and with Dr. Jackson, who was an awful dancer but a hilarious conversationalist; and with Brew from ER, Mr. Perkins from maintenance, a general practitioner, named Campinelli, who was recently divorced and on the make; and finally with Novak again.

"Is your curiosity about Du—about Dr. Duren and

me satisfied now?" Carol asked smiling.

"Well—not really," Novak replied. "You see, I couldn't help noticing the white-hot sparks leaping between you and Duren in Melinda Curtis' room that day, and I was nosy. Duren never mentioned any relationship between you. I have to confess, I'm not usually interested in people's love affairs, but Duren is a curious person to me. He's brilliant and ambitious. I say this to you because you obviously already know it. He had never shown any . . . affinity for the opposite sex . . . for *any* sex. This . . . hostility between you made me wonder what the relationship was, or had been. I'm his chief. He'll be under my wing only part of this year. This year he'll rotate through all the departments to gain a sort of haphazard general knowledge of practicing medicine. Next year he'll mostly specialize in surgery."

"I perceive also that your curiosity about Duren is motivated by selfish interests," Carol said trying to understand why this disappointed her so.

"You have perceived correctly. I have designs on Duane's future career. But I want him to fall into it naturally, not be influenced too much by my own ambitions, until later."

"I'm curious. What are your designs on his career?"

Novak smiled. "Since you two are obviously on the outs, can I trust you not to tell him?"

"You can trust me never to speak to him on a personal basis again."

"Open heart surgery. Later, developing a method of repairing damage to cardiac muscle and vessels, a method more effective and permanent than coronary bypasses. Or developing a method of replacing the heart entirely." Novak smiled. "Sounds like a pipe dream, doesn't it?"

Carol thought about that. "Yes, it's a pipe dream, and it sounds perfect for him."

"I'm pleased you agree."

She looked up at him, studying him. "Are you really?"

"He's in love with you, of course, and if I'm not mistaken, the feeling's mutual. You probably know him better than anybody else. If you say it's perfect, then I'm greatly pleased."

She laughed softly, incredulously. "Tell me, why is it that you, the almighty physician, deign to confide in me, a lowly nurse?"

Novak threw back his head and laughed; then he took her by the arm and led her off the dance floor. Near the fountain with its pool where goldfish swam drowsily in their placid pond, Novak said, "First, I haven't been a doctor long enough to reach the almighty status yet. Second I perceive you're as ambitious in your own profession as I am in mine. And you're smart." He smiled, and his eyes laughed at her as he said, "Besides, you're pretty and within four or five years of my own age."

She tossed her head. "Bah. What has that got to do with anything? Stick with the truth, Dr. Novak."

He shrugged, still laughing at her. "You are the only person I could have mentioned Duane Duren to . . . and obtain a little insight into his character from. I would look for more information concerning Duane from you because he doesn't—*won't*—talk about his personal life, but I can see you won't be too informative."

"Your perception is correct."

Novak nodded, pondered, looked at her. "I did not know about Shelly's death."

Carol didn't answer. She waited for him to say more,

but he seemed to consider, then to change his mind. Looking beyond her, he said, "Here comes your escort, so I'll say thanks for the dance, Carol. If you were not spoken for this evening, I would have liked—"

Bret was there, so Novak politely excused himself and went away.

I would have liked—to ask more questions? To take her out somewhere for dinner? To try to gain more insight into Duane's character?

The party ended shortly with Maximilian from respiratory therapy getting up on the table to do a striptease, down to his undershirt, as the band played a sexy go-go tune.

And she did indeed enjoy the party, the dancing, and watching the other hospital personnel; how their characters changed in a social setting, and then changed back in the clinical situation; Dr. Simon giving Martin businesslike orders to set up an epidural tray for one of his patients; Dr. Jackson rushing into L&D, looking wild, and saying, "What's going on?" Joey Maximilian plodding sleepily down the post-partum corridor and pushing an IPPB machine before him. Novak himself checking Melinda and referring to Carol as "Nurse" or "Miss Welles." All businesslike now and you could catch only a glimpse of the personalities the hospital personnel had displayed at the Saturday-night Christmas party.

Melinda smiled softly as Carol opened her fist and placed the cool washcloth in her hand.

"Then Bret and I rode around and looked at the Christmas lights. People have decorated their houses beautifully this year, now that they aren't so energy-conscious," Carol concluded.

Melinda's fingers squeezed Carol's hand, a feeble gesture to let her know she had heard it all and had liked to hear it—that she was glad to hear it.

So glad . . .

But the Christmas lights are so hot to think about, and my heart is beating so hard I'm afraid it will break the beautiful lights. And the baby is so still I wonder if maybe it's because it is snowing in my face—my face which is dying.

NINE

Basil Novak is smart, but he hasn't been as assertive as he should be in this particular case, Herman Whitehall was thinking. He should realize that treating the mother is first and foremost, because if she dies, both die. Fetal consideration must come only after maternal consideration . . . and he shouldn't let Caleb Simon push his weight around so.

Whitehall lit his pipe, puffed, and, one by one, furtively studied each of the doctors sitting in the conference room on the second floor of Markson.

Simon, his bottom lip stuck out, was associated with Benjamin Moss, both in their fifties with lucrative practices. Just to walk into their offices cost a patient forty bucks before even seeing the doctor. Caleb lived in a colonial mansion, almost, in Humphrey Park, and Moss drove a Rolls to work every day. God only knew what his wife drove. *I'm one up on them, though, because neither of them has a full-time maid. But they're attentive to their patients, both of them, even possessive. For OB-Gyn men, they are both excellent physicians.*

Whitehall chuckled to himself. He'd never forget the time Moss had diagnosed a patient of his as having a tumor of the uterus and prepared to do an abdominal hyst on her, but when he got in, he had found out she was pregnant.

Then there was Ruben Hamblin, internist, who was associated with Nicholas Michaelson, both in their early forties. Ruben was tall, lanky, humorless. Whitehall just couldn't relate to anybody who didn't have a sense of humor. Both had flourishing practices, treating mostly cardiac patients which meant they sent most of their potential open hearts to Greenburg; Greenburg, who was trying to lure Basil Novak into cardiovascular surgery. *Very* lucrative specialty. Hamblin was intelligent, as internists go, but had the personality of a turnip. His after-shave smelled like one too.

Whitehall took the pipe out of his mouth. And there was Novak, ambitious but not assertive enough; and his new sidekick, Duane Duren, a pretty-boy intern with a brilliant mind, though he'd never ever let him know he thought he was brilliant. He had an ego and ambition—he'd go far in surgery if he didn't burn out in the next two years.

Novak had just read Melissa Carter's chart, or whatever her name was, read it to them aloud; the latest lab reports and last night's vital signs and intake and output. Whitehall had him repeat the last few hours of vitals and I-and-O's.

Whitehall crossed his legs and sighed. "Doctors, the antibiotic of choice, since the predominant strain cultured in the lab from Matilda's drainage tube is *Enterobacter aerogenes,* is gentamycin."

Simon said, "Who's Matilda?"

Whitehall knew it irritated Simon that he kept referring to his patient as "the patient" so in order to pacify him and get along, he was trying to refer to the patient by name. Evidently, he had missed.

"Melissa, I mean," he said laughing genially.

Not looking at him, Simon raised his brows, tapped some tobacco into his antiquated pipe, and said, "Who's Melissa?"

Novak interceded. "Dr. Whitehall, we discussed gentamycin before you arrived, but there's a question about neonatal toxicity with gentamycin."

He smiled. *Dr. Whitehall.* Physicians called each other by their first names, but a resident didn't dare. Not until he had finished his residency and set himself up in private practice, but coming from Novak, the Dr. Whitehall business sounded ridiculous somehow. He already considered Novak a colleague.

Of course, they all wanted to keep from harming the fetus, but they also wanted to save the girl, so they launched into a discussion of antibiotics, new and old; at one point Hamblin left the room and came back with a *PDR*. The *Physicians' Desk Reference* listed every medication on the market and gave a rundown on all of it, each drug's dosages, side effects, contraindications, and interactions with other drugs and even foods. There were a lot of antibiotics you couldn't mix, like the aminoglycosides, which were the "mycins." Many of the penicillins you could give concomitantly with each other, but there were others you couldn't mix; and you could seldom mix the "cillins" with the "mycins." Therefore, the drugs of choice for Belinda's diverticulitis could not be mixed with the drugs they needed to combat peritonitis. Because some drugs canceled out others, they were chemically incompatible, or they were antagonistic. Just about the time they thought they'd found a couple of antibiotics they could give together, they discovered they would be potentiated excessively by Demerol, which Belinda had to have because of the pain. Or else Simon said thumbs down because of the fetus. There were two phases in a woman's pregnancy in which drugs could cause damage to the fetus, in the first trimester when the fetal organs are differentiating, and in the third trimester because the fetus could be born with drug toxicity since its own organs wouldn't be mature enough to detoxify drugs. Theoretically, a pregnant patient shouldn't take *any* drug, even aspirin. Since the thalidomide tragedy in the 'fifties, OB-Gyn men were antsy about giving anything, especially new drugs. Nobody wanted to be responsible for creating malformed infants!

But the new antibiotics *were* new possibilities. The *PDR* was full of them, and they had to refer to it often to look for side effects. The intern, Duren, seemed more acquainted with the new drugs than Simon, Hamblin, or himself. Novak, too, was more up-to-date. A throwback from medical school for Duren, and keeping-up by Novak. Nine times out of ten, one or the other of them knew the new drugs and their inter-actions and side effects.

Yes, the new drugs had the same old problem of interaction. It was high time to forget the fetus, or at least to consider it secondarily; otherwise they were going to lose the patient.

Whitehall rested his ankle on his knee, his wrist on the arm of the chair. "Doctors, Doctors, Doctors," he said softly, his eyes shut. "Possible damage to fetus must now be put behind us. Certain death of the patient must be considered first. Peritonitis has a ten-percent mortality rate. Yes, these drugs are dangerous to the unborn. Maybe they can even cause miscarriage, which would almost certainly kill the patient, in my opinion, because her abdominal pain is already unbearable. Now, I'm for giving massive dosages of antibiotics and a normal dosage of Demerol for the patient's sake." He looked at each of them sadly. "It may be good-by to the fetus. Let's face it." He looked at Simon. "Caleb?"

"Only as a last resort," Simon said not looking at him.

"Don't you agree then that we have come to that . . . last resort?"

Simon answered affirmatively by not answering at all.

Whitehall looked at Hamblin. "Ruben?"

Hamblin nodded. "I know the two drugs I want. One is new, the other is old; they are compatible. I want one given IV, the other IM. Massive doses—" He glanced at Simon. "And possibly damaging to the fetus."

Whitehall looked at Novak. He appeared to be slightly disconcerted. Then he looked at the intern, Duren, who must be learning a hell of a lot during this session. He was lucky, the young upstart. He wished *he* had been able to sit in on conferences like this when *he* was an intern. But that was in the days when— Well, he liked Duren. In fact if Novak went over to cardio-vascular—if— *Oh shit!*

Whitehall stood up abruptly, causing the others to look up, startled. He said, "I have a conference in ten minutes and surgery in thirty, plus rounds. Now that we've agreed that—that we have to proceed no matter the consequences to the unborn, I'll leave it in your hands, Caleb, Ruben. Whatever you have in mind in the way of antibiotics and palliative therapy." He strode quickly for the door of the conference room, turned, and said, "If you need my help, though, please feel free to call me, no matter what."

Hamblin regarded him silently. Simon did too. Novak looked puzzled, and Duren—damn him—was that a smirk on his smart-assed mouth?

Whitehall went out, shut the conference-room door behind him, and began to stride down the corridor

170

toward Jenson, thinking, Well, Basil's puzzled because I conceded so quickly after being previously assertive on having my say about antibiotic therapy. I have a few pet antimicrobials myself that I wanted to try and was going to fight to have them. But Basil knows which ones, and he can have a give-and-take with Hamblin and they'll come up with something compatible for Belinda . . . or Melissa . . . or whatever the hell her name is. But as I told them, I've got a damned conference and surgery and rounds yet. Besides, he had seen Duren look at him with a funny expression on his face, and he had looked down to see if his fly was unzipped. Goddamn Elvira again! He'd had his right foot resting on his left knee when he'd looked down to see if he was unzipped, and he'd seen that one of his socks was navy, then that the other damned sock was black!

She isn't me, but she's my other self. When the others . . . now I forget their names because the heat makes me forget . . . when they leave me, she comes because she is my other self. She takes care of me.

But her name is Carol. She's another person, a nurse, the one who taught us about conception and the growth of the embryo in utero.

. . . At seven months the fetus measures about fifteen inches in length and weighs about two and a half pounds. If born at this time its chances for survival are about one in ten. . . .

. . . Oxygen passes into fetal circulation and fetal carbon dioxide diffuses into maternal circulation through the placenta. The placenta acts as the fetus' lungs, since the lungs do not function as such until after birth. Glucose, minerals, proteins, and fats diffuse into the fetal circulation through the placenta also.

. . . Most drugs are able to pass through the

placental membrane to the fetus, at least to a certain degree. . . .

. . . A fetus whose mother has become addicted to narcotics may demonstrate withdrawal symptoms soon after birth, and if the symptoms are undetected, the infant may die . . . die . . . die. . . .

Melinda's eyes flew open, but the lights were too bright so she shut them again, only to become aware of a sudden cramp in her left leg. *Robbie had said . . . Robbie had said . . .*

. . . Leg cramps in the calf muscle, so remember to turn your toes up, pointing them toward your chin as far as they'll go, and push the back of your knee against the mattress. . . .

. . . Gas after the baby comes, or any other time when you aren't pregnant, try lying on your abdomen and turning your toes inward . . .

. . . One of the questions we'll ask you when you come to Labor and Delivery is, have your membranes ruptured? We mean has the bag of waters, the amnion and chorion, burst? . . . How will you know? Believe me, Melinda, you'll know. . . .

. . . At birth the placenta weighs approximately one pound. . . .

. . . The umbilical cord which connects the fetus with the placenta is approximately twenty inches in length and contains two arteries and one vein twisted together. . . .

. . . And connected to Grandmother who is surely with God in heaven. But somebody keeps twanging on the cord and making it vibrate. It isn't me. Not me. I can't move else the pain overwhelms me and the other self fades in and out sometimes and I can't see. Mother, help me. Oh dear God, everything will be O.K., John says . . . all right . . . baby fetal heart roaring in my head with Daddy thanking Carol and lights too bright

172

the head I surge I surge through this pain and my gums
are tightening on my teeth until the teeth fall out on my
bed the fetal heart so sick surge . . . surge . . . surge. . . .

"It's a new antibiotic," Dr. Hamblin told her morosely. "It is an extremely painful injection, but to our knowledge it has no antagonists or problems with interactions. We'll try two other newer antibiotics in conjunction with it. I'll write all this on her chart. When exactly did she assume this fetal position?"

Carol glanced at Melinda and replied, "Yesterday. Monday, about noon." The girl's pain was unbelievable. She was now lying on her side, her abdomen supported by a small, flat pillow, the same pillow which the nurses put under patients' heads who have just had caudals. Her legs were drawn up toward her abdomen. One small white fist clutched the bottom sheet even in her sleep, the other had a viselike grip on her gown.

"I'm increasing the Demerol to fifty milligrams q. four to six hours."

"The baby—"

"We aren't worried about that now."

Carol glanced at Melinda again. She felt so guilty, so awful. Guilty because—she didn't know why. Maybe because she was well and Melinda was so ill in such awful pain. Yet she knew she shouldn't feel guilty. Nobody had tried harder to help Melinda than she.

Robbie had all but refused to take care of her. When Mac had tried to assign her to Melinda this morning, Robbie had said, "All right. I'll take her today." But then she had started crying. "For Melinda I'll do it, but I hate it, Mac. I hate it. If I'd wanted to take care of ICU patients, I'd have applied for ICU. If I'd wanted to give bed baths I'd have been an LVN."

By now Mac was under so much pressure she was losing her patience with everything and everybody.

173

"Robbie, for God's sake *why* did you get into nursing then?"

"I'm like everybody else, Mac. There're some things about nursing that I don't like. I picked L&D so I wouldn't have to deal with terminal patients."

Mac had turned moist eyes to Joy. "What about you?"

"Mac, I'm afraid to do the CVP and I'm scared of that new cold-blanket thing."

"Carol?"

She had been thinking, Every area of nursing has its drawbacks and its pluses. It's like every other profession; it depends on what you like, what area you want to work in. Carol liked to learn. Everything. She had said, "Please, Mac. I want to work with Melinda."

"Are you sure you don't feel closed in? It's not getting to you is it? You seem kind of tired."

"Sure, I feel closed in. It's also tiring. I worked hard; no need to lie to you about that. I had to bathe her constantly, all shift long. I never sat down. But I've learned so much, and I'm so fascinated by all of it. And I feel so personally responsible for her. I *want* to take care of her, Mac."

"O.K. But tomorrow it's Robbie's turn . . . or Joy's . . ."

Now Dr. Hamblin was saying, "We're also going to instill a different antibiotic directly into the peritoneal cavity."

It was eight o'clock Tuesday morning and Dr. Hamblin was on rounds. The doctors had met sometime yesterday evening on the three-to-eleven shift, and Hamblin had come in to give orders for Melinda to be placed on the hypothermia blanket.

The hypothermia blanket was actually a mattress of sorts. Hank had told them that all four of the three-to-eleven nurses had been involved in getting the mattress

174

under Melinda and the bottom sheet over the mattress, while Gwenn Hutton, the ICU supervisor, had come from her home to instruct them on the blanket's use. Then, everybody except Amy, who took care of Melinda on the three-to-eleven shift, had to change scrub dresses and scrub with phenol.

Two large tubes were connected to the head of the hypothermia blanket, and coiled to a small boxlike machine on wheels. The machine cooled the water and quietly circulated it to and within the coils inside the mattress. It was automatic. A rectal probe attached to the machine had been inserted into Melinda's rectum. The probe was a thermometer, and since the nurses had set the machine's temperature gauge on ninety-eight point six degrees, the machine would keep circulating cool water until Melinda's temp came down to ninety-eight point six. Then it was supposed to shut off.

There were drawbacks to the machine's use, of course. One of them was that the machine wasn't infallible. You had to watch Melinda's skin to keep her from getting cold burns where her skin touched the blanket; you had to make sure the machine was full of water. Melinda's temp had not yet come down to ninety-eight point six, so the nurses had to set the dial on a higher temp, otherwise, the constantly circulating cold water might cause cold burns no matter how often they turned her. Melinda's temp had declined from one hundred five degrees to one hundred one point six.

Dr. Hamblin was studying this morning's vital-sign sheet which was lying on Melinda's overbed table. Carol knew he was seeing that Melinda's temp was one hundred one point six; her pulse ninety-eight and thready, and her blood pressure high, one hundred seventy over eighty-eight.

Dr. Hamblin looked very depressed. But then, he always looked depressed. Carol realized he was a nice person, though, and a good internist and she trusted his judgment. He went to Melinda now and touched her arm. Even that small gesture caused her to wince. He felt her pulse, watched her expression, took his stethoscope from his pocket, and bent down to listen to her chest, first in front as best he could, then in back. He moved the diaphragm across her back, straightened, clicked his tongue, looked at Carol, and said, "I'll write the medication orders now if I may borrow her chart."

"I'm sorry, Dr. Hamblin, but her chart has to stay in the room because of the danger of contaminating—"

"Oh, yes. I forgot."

"But after you've disposed of your gown and gloves outside the door, you can take a new doctors' order sheet from the nurses' station and write the orders. Mac will mix the medications, and I'll give them."

Usually a nurse mixed any meds she gave, but in this case—

"Yes. Yes. I appreciate your nurse's caution in this, Ms. Welles," he said and left the room.

Jeez, Carol thought, somebody actually appreciates all this?

Dr. Hamblin was met in the doorway by Dr. Novak and his entourage of residents, all gowned and gloved. Carol felt her face flushing as they entered, not briskly this time, but quietly, almost tiptoing.

Novak smiled broadly at her and went to look over the vital-sign sheet on the overbed table. Carol ignored the other residents, but was aware of Duane's disdain at finding her in the room. Without looking up, Novak asked, "When did she become semicomatose?"

"Last night about 11:45."

He looked up, at Duane, at the others. "Typical symptomology," he remarked in a soft voice. "The position . . . shallow respirations because of the abdominal pain. White-cell count is grossly elevated."

176

"Shouldn't the head of the bed be elevated more?" Duane suggested glancing at Carol.

Novak studied that. "Probably." He looked at Carol. "Is she passing flatus? Any bowel sounds?"

"Bowel sounds, yes."

"Then we haven't paralytic ileus at least." He went over to Melinda and touched her arm. To Carol's surprise her eyes flew open. He bent down to her. "Melinda?"

"Please don't touch me," she panted.

"I need to check your incision—"

"Please don't touch me," she said speaking rapidly. "If you'll wait I'll turn on my back all by myself."

"I can check your stitches where you are, if—"

"No. I want to help. I want to help. Please. But I have to move slowly," she gasped and screwed up her face. "Oh, dear Lord. Oh, dear Lord."

Novak stared, moistening his lips with his tongue as Melinda pressed the small pillow to her abdomen and began to turn slowly onto her back.

Carol noticed that both Duane's hands had become fists, but his face remained expressionless.

"Oh. Oh. Oh," Melinda cried as tears rolled down her face.

"Dr. Novak—" Carol protested.

"There. There," Melinda said. "I'm on my back. But can I keep my knees bent?" In spite of her hundred one point two temperature, perspiration beaded her forehead.

Novak looked at Carol. His eyes asked her clearly, *Forgive me. I didn't intend to cause her pain.* He looked back at Melinda, did his obligatory oscultation of her breath and abdominal sounds, had Carol peel back the abdominal dressing so that he could glimpse the healing surgical wound, felt her pulse—the same things Dr. Hamblin had done except for checking the

177

abdominal wound.

She knew Novak was doing this because Whitehall was busy and Novak was acting in his stead. He would have to chart something in the doctors' progress reports for Whitehall to see. She felt sorry for Novak, but still this was a learning experience for him, wasn't it? And for Duane? And for the other residents?

He touched her abdomen which Carol realized was distended more than it would have been from her seven-month pregnancy, distended with infection, gas, collecting fluids, and pain. Hard to the touch.

"Nurse?"

Carol looked at Duane. *Nurse!*

"I believe when she turned over she pulled out her IV," Duane said calmly.

She had. The IV tubing had become disconnected from the hub of the catheter going into Melinda's vein. Exasperated because she would have to start the IV all over again, she rushed over to the other side of the bed to the IV pole and shut off the stopcock. Then she grabbed an alcohol pledget, tore open the package, and, removing the catheter from Melinda's arm, pressed the pledget over the vein where the catheter had penetrated.

While she pressed the pledget to the vein, Novak looked at Duane, then at Carol. "Since you need the practice, Duren, I'll let you start this IV while the rest of us continue on rounds."

Duane eyed Novak soberly and said, "I don't really need the practice, Dr. Novak."

Basil smiled at him. "Sure you do. It takes constant practice, starting IVs, doesn't it Car—Miss Welles?"

Carol saw what Novak was doing, trying to get them together. Why? She tightened her mouth but didn't answer because the reply that came to her mind was inappropriate.

Basil told her, "You've kept good records, Miss Welles." He looked back at Melinda who was already dozing, then, looking somber, he jerked his head toward the door and the other residents followed him out, leaving Duane alone with Carol.

Men. They were worse busybodies than women. Novak thinking he was doing them a big favor. Ha! Carol got the IV tray, which contained all the necessary paraphernalia for starting an IV, from the shelf above the sink. Her eyes made a quick survey of the tray, checking to see if everything was there that would be needed. Two packages of new tubing. She opened one while she checked the rest of the contents. Four sizes of intracaths, two different types of intracaths, alcohol pledgets, four-by-four gauze sponges, Betadine ointment, two kinds of tape—cloth adhesive and paper tape—and two sizes of each. She bustled briskly around the bed and placed the tray on the overbed table while Duane's eyes followed her insolently; then she stepped back from the overbed table, folded her arms, and looked at him.

They both knew that getting a new vein on Melinda would be difficult. Though her blood pressure was up, which usually caused veins to engorge and therefore made them easier to find and penetrate, the best veins had already been punctured, and once you'd punctured, you had to move up the arm, not down, to a new place. Poor little Melinda had been stuck dozens of times for blood samples for lab work, mainly in the bend of her arm, the antecubital space. The veins in her forearm were small, and they, too, had been punctured for IV infusions and blood transfusions, the cutdown for the CVP.

Duane came to the bedside table slowly, like a prisoner to the gallows. He glanced briefly at Carol, then bent down and examined Melinda's arm, looking

179

for a vein.

"I really should ask Mac if you can do this," Carol said.

He rose to his full height and looked at her. "Since when does a doctor need permission from a nurse to start an IV?"

"Doctor!"

"That's right. Doctor." He bent again to Melinda's arm, and poked gently at three different veins, then reached for the tourniquet and tied it on her upper arms.

Suddenly, the tourniquet reminded Carol of an elongated condom. She was instantly furious. "Are you even aware . . . Doctor . . . of what the IV solution contains? You're starting an IV without knowing what the solution is; that's like giving a medication without knowing what it is."

Not looking at her, Duane sighed patiently. "The solution is approximately six hundred cc D5W with no medication added. According to your own *well-kept* records, the IV is merely a keep-open for the administration of antibiotics and other medications when they are due to be given."

He was correct.

"But you haven't any authority to start this IV."

He rose again, slowly, and looked at her. "I have authority, Nurse, because I happen to be on rounds which unhappily includes Labor and Delivery. Much to my dismay. Although Melinda's case is important and I—"

Carol glanced at Melinda who was moving her shoulder as if the tourniquet hurt. Duane's eyes moved from Carol's face to Melinda's. Then he began to open the package which contained the IV intracath, a plastic catheter threaded through the lumen of a needle. The needle would puncture skin and vein, then the flexible catheter would be threaded into the vein, the needle discarded, *if* he knew what he was doing.

Carol watched him as he attached the hub of the intracath to the connection to the new tubing, slowly removed the contaminated tubing from the bag of IV fluid on the pole, attached the new tubing, then bent again to Melinda's arm. Sort of backward, but— She folded her arms again *daring* him to contaminate the IV site, or to miss the vein.

He proceeded smoothly at first, opening the little package containing an alcohol pledget, palpating a vein, swabbing the area. His hand was shaking as he removed the needle with its tiny catheter from the sterile package. Pausing with the needle over the fat vein, he hesitated.

She read his thoughts. *Damn her. I'm a doctor. How dare she stand there being judgmental like that. I'll show her.*

He said, "Cut four strips of tape, Nurse, about six inches long."

Nurse! She unfolded her arms slowly. *Nurse! You turd, you slept with me a dozen times or so. You told me you loved me, you horse's ass. You—*

"And tape them to the bedrail where I can reach them," he added.

He waited and, when she didn't respond, looked up at her, raised his brows, and said, "Tape?"

Furiously she did as she was told. Not for his damned sake, for Melinda's. She tore the paper tape from the roll—and stuck it on the bedrail very near his thigh, again and again, four times. She did not miss the perspiration that suddenly beaded his forehead either.

He was slow, not half as fast as she would have done it, but he did it. Blood backed up into the catheter indicating he was in the vein; he released the tourniquet; IV fluid dripped rapidly. Yes, he was in.

181

She adjusted the flow rate as he taped the hub of the IV catheter to Melinda's arm, and in a moment of insanity, she was careful to let her thigh brush his. *Nurse,* you bastard, she kept thinking.

Finally, IV secure and dripping, he turned and went to the door, but there he turned again to glare at her, his face damp and red, his eyes very bright with hate. She could see the vertical vein in the center of his forehead standing out, and she knew that the only time that happened was when he was sexually aroused. "Damn you, Carol," he whispered; then he turned and left the room.

Damn me? You've damned me before, Duane Duren, and I've survived. Look at me sometime, Duane, and see that I have survived.

She would have cried with rage then, if Melinda hadn't begun to retch for the first time in days.

TEN

"Sometimes when we're like this you're with me. Sometimes, you're somewhere else. If I were more of a man, I'd resent that enough to leave, or at least protest. But because I love you, I pretend I don't notice. And I do love you, Carol."

They were warm, damp, spent, boneless, weightless, mindless—floating in the ethereal aftermath of love-making.

Mother would say she was ruined forever. Dad would say she had fallen by the wayside. Her multitudinous aunts would be shocked.

Carol was not a virgin, hadn't been since her second year as a secretary for Times Mutual and Trust.

She appreciated Bret, and at times like this, she loved him. Bret was a girl's dream lover: lusty, masculine, handsome. She loved him, but she was aware that she wasn't *in love*. There was a difference. Perhaps the sin of premarital sex was in having sex with someone you weren't in love with . . . that was when she felt guilty.

She had never felt guilty with Duane.

She held Bret's tousled head to her breasts, cradled

him in her arms. With him she felt secure, secure in a love she had done nothing to earn, one for which she had never made any promises.

Actually he was a purge. Each painful confrontation with Duane, however brief, sent her home to her apartment burning inside from a mixture of fury and sickness in the pit of her stomach. And when Bret came over as he did every evening, she would need his love.

"Do you know I've never spent the entire night with you?" he murmured.

"I know."

He said nothing more, afraid, perhaps, to say anything more. She sensed that Bret could not endure much more pain in his life. She'd learned he had lost friends to unspeakable deaths in Vietnam, and he'd witnessed medical atrocities and miracles by the thousands in the hastily set up hospitals there, and even in the hospitals in the States. But it was not the miracles that had propelled him into the nursing profession. It was the atrocities.

"There are some lousy things going on in some veterans' hospitals that I'd like to see changed," he had said once. And another time, "My grandfather was a grand old man, a veteran of World War I. He had cancer of the colon. In a veterans' hospital they removed his colon and gave him a colostomy, but the cancer had metastasized to his liver. I can remember a fat male nurse with dirty shoes coming in to start intravenous chemotherapy on Grandpa and piggy-backing the chemical into his regular IV, not bothering to swab the valve with alcohol to kill the germs. I could read that nurse's mind: *He's just an old man and he's going to die anyway. What difference does it make if he gets an IV-introduced infection?*"

Bret had seen yards of intestines removed unnecessarily from veterans so that young doctors could

184

practice. A neglected shrapnel wound had almost caused Bret to lose his own right leg.

"But I'm sure there's medical and nursing mismanagement in every kind of hospital, Bret," she had told him.

"Yes. I'm sure there is. But the veterans' hospitals are the ones I'm after, the ones I want to help change. You take care of the others." He had smiled then and said, "Let's talk about something else."

Medical mismanagement? Well, she'd seen some of that at Bennet. Dr. Moss doing a hysterectomy, at the patient's demand, on a woman who was four months pregnant. Dr. Tyree perforating the bladder of Proctor and covering up the evidence at autopsy. Dr. Blasingame making fun of patients to the nurses, applying forceps unnecessarily and too soon, literally pulling the baby out instead of being patient and waiting. Nurses in the nursery despised him because his babies came in with forceps marks, deep blue ones, more often than any other doctors'. And there was nursing neglect, too.

But considering the number of doctors and nurses who worked in the hospitals and the volume of patients who came and went, mismanagement was probably very minimal. It was never the good medical and nursing care which patients received routinely that one heard about. It was always the bad that was advertised. She wondered, if Melinda survived, if the extraordinary care she was being given would be known by anybody besides her family.

"I really don't mind, Mac. In fact, I really prefer to work with Melinda."

Robbie gave a sigh of relief and Joy brightened.

It was 6:45 Wednesday morning. There were no other patients in L&D but Mclinda. The three-to-eleven and the eleven-to-seven shifts had had a busy

185

night. Twelve kids had been born. Marty was upset at the moment because the eleven-to-seven shift had left all the instruments for her to wash and autoclave. Since the day shift was usually the busiest—that was when the doctors usually induced labor—Marty had been assigned to help with cleaning, wrapping, and autoclaving instruments. The other shifts did their own cleaning up because they were not as busy.

On some nights, however, they often did not have time to take care of the instruments, and they would leave them for Marty to do.

"If we have anybody come in ready for delivery, we won't have any instruments," she told Mac as she cast a dour glance at Hank. Then, shaking her head, she hobbled hurriedly back to the "dirty" room where the instruments were soaking in a basin.

"Sorry, Marty," Hank called to her. "I'd help, but I was assigned to Melinda."

Mac said, "Never mind, Hank. We can help her until a patient shows up." Then to Carol, "You really don't mind taking care of Melinda, do you? But this will be your third day in a row."

"That's O.K."

"And she's been vomiting, but the doctors haven't ordered an NG tube, because we can still hear bowel sounds," Hank said. "Her temp is up a little in spite of the blanket. By the way, the blanket's on the blink. It won't shut off. You'd better watch, else she'll get cold-burned for sure. On the three-to-eleven shift, Melinda's husband asked to visit. They let him for a couple of hours. Whitehall didn't like that when he found out. He came in here real cheerfullike, as high as a cowboy's ass at the Fourth of Jew-ly rodeo, said everybody must really have the Christmas spirit because the hospital staff kept laughing and calling 'Merry Christmas' to him in the corridors. None of us had the guts to tell him he had Christmas-tree icicles stuck all over the back of his pants. Anyway, he didn't like her husband visiting so long in Melinda's room, and he wrote orders that only her husband and her mother can visit and only once a day each for just ten minutes."

Mac said, "That's not very much."

"He says all these people going in and out of her room cause a greater risk of spreading infection."

"Then he should not allow these miscellaneous interns to go parading in there," Carol said.

Mac smiled. She wasn't blind. She'd noticed Carol's behavior around the one intern: her blushing, her hostility, her dancing with two of them at the Christmas party. "Maybe we should mention that to Dr. Whitehall."

"Or Hamblin," Carol said. "He's more reasonable."

Moments later Carol entered room eight. Melinda looked much thinner and more pale. She lay on her left side, her knees drawn up to her abdomen. She was sleeping heavily, seemed comatose. Carol's spirits plummeted. In the white, fluorescent lights of the room, Melinda looked already dead. She lay rigid, unmoving, blue-white. When Carol touched her she did not move and her skin was hot to the touch, and dry. The nurses, who cared for her on all shifts, gave her skin care, smoothing lotion over her skin, though now even that small movement caused her unspeakable pain. Taking her vital signs caused her intolerable pain. Bumping her bed produced a moan of agony, or she simply wept.

Carol proceeded with taking her vitals. First, the rectal temp. That was simple; she had only to check the gauge on the hyperthermia machine. She took her pulse. That wasn't so bad either, but when she tried to lift her arm to wrap the blood-pressure cuff around it Melinda awakened, gritted her teeth, and endured the pain with her usual patience.

"How do you feel, Melinda?" Carol asked.

Before, the answer had always been, "Better." Today Melinda smiled weakly up at her and said nothing.

"Cripes," Hank had said earlier. "If the girl wasn't so sweet and upbeat and positive, I think she'd have gone bad before now."

Today Melinda didn't seem so upbeat.

Carol took her blood pressure as quickly as possible. Then she noticed on the chart that Dr. Hamblin's new antibiotic was to be given at 7:00 A.M. Hank had ordered the med, and it was ready in the room. Carol examined it. It was in powder form, so it had to be reconstituted with normal saline. Hank had everything she needed on the shelf, because she had already given one dose of the medication. Carol prepared the solution, injecting saline into the vial of powder. The med was to be given intramuscularly. She had already looked it up in the *PDR* before she had come into the room—after Hank had mentioned that the antibiotic had arrived from the hospital pharmacy and was in the room. Carol injected the med into Melinda's right gluteal muscle. Melinda didn't flinch. Carol then helped her turn—the hardest job of all because of Melinda's pain—and positioned her on her right side. Then she began to prepare Melinda's bath. She brought the basin from the sink to the overbed table, took a washcloth, rinsed it in the warm water, and bent over her intending to begin by washing her face.

Something was wrong.

Melinda's face was red, and she was perspiring. Perspiring! Carol glanced at the gauge on the hypothermia machine. Her temp was still one hundred one.

An alarm went off in Carol's head, and words kept bouncing back and forth in her brain as she took the blood-pressure cuff off the bracket on the wall: *shock*

. . . labor . . . dilation? Premature . . . bacteria . . .

She wrapped the blood-pressure cuff around Melinda's arm and pumped it up, expecting the BP to be where it had been the last two days, hovering around one hundred twenty. The mercury on the wall manometer slid down slowly, slowly until it reached ninety-eight. Carol couldn't believe it. She pumped the cuff again, the mercury slid down. Ninety-eight. She let the mercury move on down to register the diastolic pressure. Forty-two. She raised up and, taking the earpieces of the stethoscope out of her ears, went to the foot of the bed to check Melinda's last blood-pressure reading. At 6:30, her BP was one hundred eighteen over fifty, normal. Before that, it was one hundred twenty-two over forty-eight. Why was her BP suddenly dropping? Her pulse was one hundred. Shock? Septic shock?

Hurriedly she listened for bowel sounds and couldn't hear them. *Oh, dear Lord, please no.* Carol hastily wrote down the last vital signs, trying to think what to do next.

Suddenly the door of the room opened and Novak and Duane entered. For the first time, Carol was glad to see them. She handed Novak the vital-sign sheet. He grew sober at the look on her face, took the sheet, and studied it. His mouth became a grimace, and he said softly, "Crap!" as he handed the vital-sign sheet to Duane.

Novak went to Melinda, took her pulse, looked at Duane, and jerked his head toward the door. Hurriedly, they left the room. Carol wanted to follow to find out what was going on. She hesitated. Melinda, becoming restless, was constantly moving her feet. Carol turned and left the room, and by the time she had pulled off her gown and gloves, Novak and Duane had disappeared.

Mac looked up from the patient's chart on the desk in front of her.

"Where'd they go?" Carol demanded, hurrying to the nurses' station.

Mac frowned. "Dr. Novak and Duren are back in the coffee room. They didn't say anything. What's going on?"

"That's what I wanna know," Carol said as she passed the desk.

Novak was hastily pouring himself a cup of coffee from the nurses' coffee carafe on the warmer. Duane had propped one foot on a chair, his elbow on his knee, and was resting his chin on his fist. Both looked up when she entered the coffee room.

The room was a cubicle about seven-by-seven feet with a small cabinet which contained paper cups and plastic spoons, packages of sugar and sugar substitutes, and small packages of powdered coffee creamer. On the wall behind where Novak stood was a neat, homemade sign that read:

NURSES' GUIDE TO HELP SPOILED DOCTORS

Dr. Simon	black
Dr. Moss	half-pkg. sweetener
Dr. Jackson	cream and 1 pkg. sugar
Dr. Blasingame	2 pkgs. sugar
Dr. Wallack	hot tea, 1 pkg. sugar
Dr. Horwitz	black
Dr. Peusy	black
Dr. Barbera	1 pkg. sugar
Dr. Pashi	small amt. cream
Dr. Marsh	decaffeinated, 1 pkg. sugar

Most of them were obstetricians, but one was a GP who used L&D the most, and there was Dr. Pashi; but

Carol didn't see the chart now, only Novak's face.

"Is it shock?" she asked a little breathless.

Novak looked at Duane, then back at Carol. "Yes."

Her body tensed even more. "Which shock?" she demanded. "Gram-negative septic?"

"Not with a falling blood pressure," Novak said. "The blood pressure elevates in septic shock."

"Wait." Duane straightened. "If it's septic shock, the BP elevates at first all right, but drops later." He looked at Carol. "What has her blood pressure been for the past few hours?"

"Normal."

"What's normal?"

"Around one hundred twenty over forty-four or forty-eight."

"Are you absolutely certain?"

"Yes."

"And suddenly it started falling?" Novak asked.

"Yes. At 7:10."

"Can't be *E. coli,*" said Novak thoughtfully. "We controlled that, but all the intestinal microbes involved are gram negative—"

Shock. Labor. No flashed in Carol's mind like a blinking light. *Low blood pressure. Not high. Red face. Restless. Shock.*

"Dr. Hamblin," Carol said her eyes widening.

The two residents looked at her.

"His new antibiotic. I gave an injection at 7:05."

Duane jabbed a finger at her and demanded excitedly, "First injection?"

"Second."

The residents looked at each other; both said, "Anaphylaxis."

Novak pointed at Carol. "IV have any medication in it?"

"No!"

191

"Turn it up all the way," Novak told her speaking rapidly. "Give epinephrine one in one thousand, five-tenths milligram. Repeat once after five minutes. I'll order more if necessary. Get some O_2 on her."

Carol turned and ran. As she passed the nurses' station she said, "Mac. Epinephrine stat!"

"What?" Mac exclaimed.

Carol yanked on a clean gown and gloves and hurried into the room.

Anaphylactic shock. My God! she thought as she hurried to Melinda's bed. She turned the drip rate of the IV up, looked at Melinda. She was breathing rapidly.

"Melinda, a little oxygen, dear, to help you breathe better, O.K.?" Carol said as she took the O_2 mask off the wall and placed it over her mouth and nose. Then she turned the oxygen meter to—*what do you turn oxygen to in this case?* She'd never given oxygen before. But Mr. Bascum in ICU, her patient when she was a student, had always had his O_2 on at five liters. She turned the O_2 on at five liters.

Mac came rushing in, gowned and gloved, and carrying an ampule of epinephrine and a handful of syringes. Her face was still questioning. Carol said, "Anaphylaxis."

Mac's mouth dropped open.

Shaking violently, Carol took the syringe, which Mac handed her, and squinted at the lettering on the ampule of epinephrine, wondering how much epinephrine she would need to draw up to give five-tenths of a milligram. The label read: one milligram=one milliliter of one in one thousand. A milliliter was the same as a cc. She drew up five-tenths cc. Mac handed her an alcohol swab. Carol gave the injection in Melinda's left gluteal muscle.

She was just withdrawing the needle and Mac was

192

flipping off the hypothermia machine when Novak entered.

"Epinephrine five-tenths milligram given IM," Carol said.

Novak's eyes took in the dripping IV, the oxygen meter on the wall. "Up the O_2 to ten for a while," Novak told her. "Duren is notifying Hamblin."

Joy stuck her head in the door. "Mac, Boswell's crowning. What's going on in here, anyhow?"

"Shit." Mac bustled out of the room without another word.

Duane entered, and he and Novak talked softly among themselves as Carol drew up another five-tenths milligram epinephrine. By the time she gave the second dose of epinephrine, which is the generic name for Adrenalin, Duane was holding Melinda's wrist, taking her pulse, and Novak was lifting the stethoscope off the hook above Melinda's bed. The blood-pressure cuff was still on her arm from when Carol had last taken her BP.

Novak said, "Melinda, I need to take your BP, sweetheart. I'm sorry. We can't hear bowel sounds, and I need you to turn on your back. . . ."

Carol knew Novak was trying to get Melinda to turn onto her back to help ease her respiration more than anything.

"Oh," Melinda groaned hoarsely. "Oh, please no. I can't move. No bed bath please today. Please, please."

"We want to listen for bowel sounds," Novak said again. "We'll help you turn."

"No. No. No!" Melinda began to cry.

Novak swallowed and glanced at Carol. Even *he* was perplexed that a girl as cooperative and patient as Melinda had been, as psychologically stable, could be so horribly afraid of any kind of movement.

Carol bent down to speak in her ear. "Melinda. Dear

193

heart, we need to turn you again anyway because of the blanket. Remember? It could burn you. You've been on that side fifteen or twenty minutes, and Dr. Novak needs to listen to your tummy, for bowel sounds."

"Oh . . . Carol please don't make me. I'm sorry. I'm sorry. I'm a coward, but . . . oh please . . ."

"Melinda," Carol said gently, "Dr. Novak wants to listen to the baby."

Melinda's eyes fluttered; she thought a moment, and then reached a thin hand up to Carol. "Help me?"

Suddenly three pairs of hands dipped down and turned Melinda smoothly from her right side to her back. Two masculine arms supported her head and shoulders as she turned; muscular arms with smoky blond hairs supported her legs, her back. Gloved feminine hands touched the fingertips of those under her head and those under her waist.

The three of them straightened and began to breathe again when Melinda did.

Novak was still a very young man, perhaps thirty-one, and had been out of med school five years. This was his fifth year of residency at Bennet; he had not yet seen enough of pain and suffering to make him callous and completely objective. Perhaps he never would. He bent down and, placing the earpieces of the stethoscope on her arms, pumped the blood-pressure cuff.

Duane's hands, thicker than Novak's, adjusted the pillow under Melinda's head. His cocoa-colored eyes were very black.

Novak said, "One hundred over thirty," and moved the stethoscope down to listen to her abdomen. He listened for a long moment, then raised his head, looked at Duane, looked at Carol, and passed the stethoscope to Duane. Duane listened to Melinda's abdomen, moving the diaphragm around on it.

"Baby?" came Melinda's tiny voice.

194

"Your baby's heartbeat is one hundred fifty-eight beats a minute, Melinda. I think it's a girl," Novak said.

"Naw. It's a boy, it's too strong a heartbeat for a girl," Duane argued, smiling.

Melinda smiled too. Faintly.

Novak said. "Respirations are slowing."

"Pulse is too. God I'm amazed at how fast IM epinephrine is. Pulse is down to ninety." He kept his hand on her wrist.

Carol was worried that the talk over her might be disturbing her, but she seemed too lethargic to comprehend what was happening.

Dr. Hamblin stuck his head into the room; his face was red and morose. By then the epinephrine had almost completely reversed the shock, and Melinda was breathing deeper and slower. Her flushed look had disappeared, her BP remained a little below normal, but her pulse was normal, though somewhat weak. Hamblin motioned Novak to go outside the room.

Carol opened the door just enough to overhear their discussion.

"Why would she be allergic to this new antibiotic and not to any of the others we gave?" Novak was asking.

"I don't know. I just don't know," Hamblin said.

"How many kinds of shock can a person have at one time?" Duane asked.

"You mean to tell me you're thinking gram-negative sepsis?"

"She's moribund, Dr. Hamblin."

"I can only order another antibiotic and hope for the best."

Carol was still trembling. Melinda was going to die. She had known it from the beginning. There were too many things against her.

She sat down beside her bed, took her hand, and

waited. The bed bath was forgotten. And so were her own mixed up feelings. She sat holding Melinda's hand for a long time.

Finally Mac stuck her head inside the door. "How's it going?"

The doctors filed in at that moment, all of them: Whitehall himself, Hamblin, Simon.

"How're her vitals?" snapped Whitehall. He had only to look at the vital-sign sheet where Carol had recorded Melinda's vitals every five minutes.

"Pulse is decreasing; last was eighty-five. Blood pressure is now one hundred thirty-two over sixty. FHTs are one hundred forty-eight," Carol answered.

"Go ahead and remove the O_2," he told her and bent down to listen to Melinda's chest. He took her BP himself while Dr. Simon took the fetoscope off the hook above her bed.

Melinda, who seemed to be attempting to stay awake, to stay aware of what was going on said, "Baby?"

Dr. Simon listened to her abdomen, moving the fetoscope from one area to another. He raised his head and straightened. "Baby's fine, Melinda."

Whitehall prodded her abdomen gently, watching her face. Every time he touched her abdomen, she winced and her knees jerked up, and she winced when he touched her lower left side.

"Rebound tenderness in the lower left," he said softly to Dr. Hamblin.

Hamblin nodded. "Possibly localizing?"

"Hope so. It'll be easier to treat."

"What's the position of the fetus, Caleb?"

Dr. Simon hesitated. "I'm not sure without palpating, and it'll hurt like hell if I have to do that."

"Don't, then. I was just trying to determine if the infection is localizing."

196

Carol was thinking, Isn't any of them concerned with Melinda's state of mind? She held her hand, held it until Dr. Hamblin told her, "Melinda, we're going to have to put the NG tube . . . the tube that goes through your nose and down your esophagus into your stomach . . . we're going to have to put it in again, O.K.? You rest now, and we'll see you later." The doctors hesitantly left. Simon glanced over his shoulder at Melinda as he went out the door.

Melinda had stiffened, her nails were digging into Carol's palm. That was when Carol really wanted to cry.

ELEVEN

She was pulling Joy's trick, spreading out her lab coat, handbag, the pocket kit with its bandage scissors, pen and pencil set, over the booth's table to discourage anybody from joining her. Only she wasn't saving the booth for anyone. She wanted to be alone.

She wanted to think. The cafeteria was noisy as usual, and busy. She decided that hospital personnel were the noisiest people in the world in the cafeteria and in social situations. Pent-up emotions and tensions being released? Probably. But then every job and profession had its tensions, although maybe life-and-death tensions were worse. Who knows. She shrugged and sipped her iced tea.

Yesterday, when Melinda had become stable after suffering the beginning symptoms of anaphylactic shock—an allergic reaction to the new antibiotic—the doctors who were nervous, abrupt, loud, and demanding had written a list of orders, twenty-one in all, new antibiotics, IV, IM, and intraperitoneal. They DC'd the order for Demerol and ordered morphine, a sedative; a new antipyretic to bring her temp down if it went back up to one hundred four and above, plus a continuation of tepid baths, a blood transfusion of one unit of packed cells, a battery of new lab tests, and portable abdominal and chest x-rays. The rest of the day had been a nightmare to Carol.

Melinda had become rigid with pain when they had to tuck the x-ray plate behind her back. In her pain and near-delirium, the portable x-ray unit must have resembled a monster as the technician adjusted the machine over her in order to "take the pictures." X-ray techs were always gentle with the patients, though. Perhaps that made up for the portable x-ray unit's dinosaur look and the growling and whining sounds it made as the technician rolled it into and out of the room.

Dr. Hamblin had ordered hyperalimentation for Melinda, and that was when Robbie and Joy had really panicked. Carol had panicked, too, but she hadn't let anybody notice. Indeed, hyperalimentation probably scared the nurses more than it did Melinda. The doctors had conceded that they should have instituted hyperalimentation in the beginning, right after Melinda's surgery. But they had tried to get by without it, hoping Melinda could take fluids by mouth. Now hyperalimentation was the only answer. She couldn't live on IV fluids forever.

Hyperalimentation consists of infusing a hypertonic solution of glucose in nitrogen directly into the vena cava, the main vein of the body which drains the head, neck, upper limbs, and thorax and empties into the right atrium of the heart. Melinda was thin and weak because she was unable to eat and replace the protein and fats her body had used up in its attempt to heal itself and because of its high temperature. What she needed was calories, about one thousand four hundred calories a day. The body uses the calories in sugar

199

before it resorts to using protein and fats. Therefore sufficient sugar in the body saves the protein needed for the healing processes. Dextrose, the main sugar in the human body, and the major component of most IV fluids, is high in caloric content. However, it was not possible to infuse enough dextrose into Melinda's veins to provide the needed one thousand four hundred calories because that would have taken as many as four liters of IV fluid a day. Giving that much fluid on a day-to-day basis would have caused circulatory overload, a blood volume which would have been too high and she would have become overhydrated, which could lead to pulmonary edema or congestive heart failure. That's what monitoring by CVP was supposed to prevent.

In order to begin hyperalimentation, a cutdown is made into the subclavian vein near the clavical, or collar bone, on the right side, and a catheter is inserted into it, and through this catheter, hyperalimentation fluids, made by different pharmaceutical companies and mixed in the hospital's own pharmacy, are instilled into it. The fluids consist of calories and proteins. They would provide Melinda not only with nourishment, but would allow her injured bowels to heal as well, because they would not have to digest and absorb the nourishment.

Dr. Hamblin did the cutdown for hyperalimentation. Carol had never assisted with a cutdown before, but both she and Mac helped and seemed to do O.K. Hamblin was sympathetic, knowing the L&D nurses were not accustomed to helping with such procedures, and he told them exactly what he would need in the way of equipment as he proceeded, and when he would need it. He had been gentle with Melinda.

Melinda endured it all with complaisant exhaustion until Carol explained to her about the tube. That's when she put her foot down.

"Melinda, I'm sorry," Carol had said as Mac stood beside her and looked on. "We have to put the NG tube, the stomach tube, back in to decompress your bowels. They're filling with fluid and gas—"

Melinda was shaking her head violently.

"—And you've been vomiting. You can't go on like this."

"No-oo-oo," Melinda howled.

Carol looked at Mac.

Mac said, "Melinda, dear heart, listen to me." She sat down in a chair beside the bed and tried to take Melinda's hand. Now she would have to change her scrub clothes and scrub with phenol, but no matter. Elaine, the nursing director, had finally heeded Mac's pleas for more help on the seven-to-three shift; she had talked an old veteran charge nurse from the post-partum floor into transferring to L&D until the personnel crisis there was over. The nurse's name was Goodnature. She was a huge, bulldog of a woman with gray hair dyed red and had worked in L&D years ago when "there wasn't any of this nonsense about inducing labor, and when women yelled and hollered with birth pains." Now most patients did not yell and holler; they smiled their way right through delivery because of the caudal, epidural, and spinal anesthetics. Sixty years old, grumbling, good-natured Goodnature was a godsend. The doctors knew her and liked her and, "They'd better not tell her she's slow or yell at her, else she'll whip their ass," Hank said. L&D was the only ward in the hospital where the nurses were addressed by the doctors by their first names. That was because the same nurses assisted the same doctors day in and day out; whereas in other areas, there were more doctors, different ones admitting patients to different areas, and the nursing staff had a greater turnover. In L&D the nurses there were the personal possessions of the obstetricians, or so they thought. But they did not call Goodnature by her first name; they did not even know her first name. She was always referred to as "Goodnature."

So Mac had a little time today to spend with Melinda, for this was Goodnature's first day in L&D. "Look, Melinda, if you keep—"

Melinda shook her head violently, tears welling up in her eyes.

"—If you keep vomiting like this—"

"No." Melinda's hands clasped over her mouth.

"There's no other way to decompress the bowels, to get the fluid out, sweetheart. Your bowels have stopped working," Mac persisted.

Melinda kept shaking her head.

Carol had tried again. "Melinda, please try to understand. Peristalsis in your bowels has stopped, the way it did after your surgery. Remember we explained that peristalsis moves the food and fluid through your bowels? We can't just let the fluid and gas collect. And this tube is the only way we can help you there."

Melinda shook her head.

After thirty minutes of trying to convince Melinda to allow them to pass the nasogastric tube through her nose, Mac notified Dr. Whitehall, who was the doctor who had written the order for the tube. Irritably, he came to L&D with Novak and Duane Duren in tow.

Whitehall was tired of Melinda's nonsense, and he was disgusted with the nurses on all three shifts for not being able to insert an NG tube into a weak and helpless patient. Wordlessly he entered the room and selected a plastic NG tube from the collection of three—two plastic, one rubber—which Mac had brought in and placed on the shelf above the sink. He opened the package and ran warm water over the end of the tube to soften it, then he accepted the package of water-based lubricant from Carol, and lubricated the end of the tube with the gel. He moved his shoulders around to get the sleeves of his gown loose from the sleeves of his new tweed blazer and approached the bed. He would try the bully approach.

"Now, Melinda, the nurses say you have refused this nasogastric tube and in the meantime you've been vomiting," Whitehall announced. "We're through with all that nonsense. I'm going to insert this into your nose and throat, and I want you to swallow and keep swallowing."

Whitehall motioned for Mac to raise the head of the bed. He nodded to Carol to hold Melinda's head tilted slightly forward and to keep it still. Melinda was shaking her head no.

Carol put her hands on either side of Melinda's face, but Melinda tightened her lips over her teeth and kept shaking her head. Her small frail hands grasped the bedrail on either side of the bed.

In a split second of time, Carol observed the scene. Melinda had lost a great deal of weight until now she was very thin, and with her protruding abdomen and thin arms, she reminded Carol of pictures she'd seen of the starving children of Biafra, all skin and bones and swollen belly. There was a CVP line going into her right arm, an IV for her meds in her left; the hyperalimentation tubing in her subclavian, a catheter draining her bladder, and three drains coming from her abdomen. She was pale, blue-white; her eyes were moist. The room was bright with overhead fluorescent lights, for it was cloudy outside. There were three doctors in the room and two nurses.

"Here we go now, Melinda," Whitehall said as he brought the tube near her face.

Melinda shook her head violently. Whitehall drew away and said to Carol, "I said keep her head still, nurse!"

"I'm sorry," Carol said.

Whitehall told Duane, "Duren get over there and see if *you* can hold her head still."

Duane hesitated, threw Carol a look that was half-irritated, half-sympathetic, and did as he was told. He put both hands on either side of Melinda's face, held her head still. But Melinda's eyes grew wide as the tube approached her face again, and her hands flew to cover her face.

Whitehall sighed and stepped back. "Nurse, hold her hands."

Carol with tears in her eyes attempted to pry Melinda's hands from her face, but could not. Melinda was stronger than anybody thought.

"Dr. Novak, see if you can hold her hands." Whitehall sighed.

Red-faced he watched with tube in hand as Basil Novak, looking sorrowful, took Melinda's hands from her face and held them at her sides.

"Now." Whitehall knew that the easiest way to install an NG tube was for the patient to swallow, but NG tubes were put down comatose patients every day. The trick was to keep Melinda's head bent slightly forward so that the tube would go into the esophagus and not into the trachea. He proceeded.

He placed the tip of the tubing in Melinda's left nostril and began to thread it in. Melinda's eyes were wide, and she held her breath, watching Whitehall's hand approach. Then suddenly she wrenched her head free—and bit him.

The surgeon jumped back and dropped the tube onto the bed. He stared shocked at his hand. Melinda had drawn blood, even through his gloves.

"I'm sorry, Dr. Whitehall," Duane said shaking his head. "I—she—she only moved an inch."

Basil Novak ducked his head, bit his lip, released Melinda's hands. Her hands flew to her mouth, and she began to cry aloud, hysterically, afraid and ashamed.

Whitehall's face was scarlet; his mouth worked furiously but he couldn't speak. And everybody else was afraid to do so.

Finally he said, "Doctors, this is obviously not the way to proceed," and he strode from the room followed by the two sheepish residents.

"We'll sedate her down," Whitehall told the residents and Hamblin and Simon in the L&D corridor that afternoon.

"I object, Herman," Simon said. "That's an unnecessary risk to the fetus."

Whitehall, who had refused to let Mac apply an antibiotic ointment to the bite on his hand, not wanting to focus any more attention on it than possible, said, "The fetus. Lord God, Simon. It's either the girl now or the fetus. And Valium won't hurt the fetus anyway."

"The amount you're talking might possibly . . ."

The next order which came from the conference was for a rectal tube to be inserted. This would decompress Melinda's lower bowel, at least. It was a tube which would be inserted through the rectum and into the lower bowel. When Carol inserted the tube, feces, fluid and gas filled the bag attached to the other end of the tubing. She kept thinking, Another tube, another tube.

Whitehall meanwhile had lost his enthusiasm for inserting the NG tube himself. He told Mac, "Nurse, she must have the tube. You nurses try to persuade her, wear down her resistance. And . . . if you need any assistance just call me."

By then the three-to-eleven shift was coming on and the labor rooms were full.

That day the first few hours of the three-to-eleven shift were too busy to permit anyone to help Hank insert the tube. The rest of the shift was given over to persuading Melinda to let them insert it. Their efforts were to no avail.

This morning, when Carol had come on duty, she had been dismayed that nobody had yet gotten the tube down Melinda, who had been retching all evening.

Mac, looking hollow-eyed and tired said, "No, Carol. I can't let you take care of Melinda again today. You need a break. Robbie?"

"O.K., Mac. If you want her to catch this lousy cold . . ."

"Abigail?"

Goodnature shrugged. "I wouldn't mind except I don't know anything about hypothermia blankets or CVPs, or hyper—whatever that is."

Carol had said, "Mac. Please. I'll take care of her today."

So she had.

Today Melinda lay on her side, pale, her knees drawn up, her skin hot, her lips cracked, her eyes shut tightly, the emesis basin on the bed near her head. Her breathing was shallow and rapid, her BP low, the fetal heart rapid, pulse weak and rapid. *Why wasn't anything helping her?* X-rays showed no complications in the abdomen and no signs of pneumonia. Blood tests revealed no pathogenic organisms in the bloodstream. Electrolytes were somewhat abnormal and a few of the other lab tests were slightly abnormal, but nothing critical. *Why wasn't she responding to medication?* New antibiotics had been prescribed and she had been watched carefully for allergic reactions. She had none. Three antibiotics. *Why was she still moribund?*

Carol couldn't eat. Couldn't. Dr. Whitehall had

telephoned at 9:00, Mac had said, and told them he'd have to sedate her in order to get the nasogastric tube down. That he'd be in, in a couple of hours.

"I beg your pardon, Ms. Welles—"

Carol looked up. John Curtis, Melinda's husband, was standing beside her table holding his tray.

"May I join you?"

"Sure," Carol said and hastily removed her lab coat and collected her belongings as John sat down across the table from her.

He was a nice-looking young man—a bit older than Carol—with solemn gray eyes and a closely trimmed brown beard. Today he was dressed in a white shirt, open at the neck, with a tan leather jacket and blue jeans. He was looking at Carol; the sclera of his eyes were red. He kept looking at her, with his hands on either side of his tray.

"She's dying," he said. "Isn't she?"

Carol avoided John's eyes. "I don't know."

"Yes. She is. And . . . and we don't even know why."

Carol looked at him then. Eye to eye they looked at each other. "What do you mean?" she asked.

"The doctors. They don't give anyone but themselves credit for having a lick of sense," John said simply, evenly.

Carol remained silent.

John had visited Melinda once a day on the three-to-eleven shift. He was allowed ten minutes with her a day. He had never missed a day. Melinda's mother, who visited her in the morning, also was allowed ten minutes. Both John and Mrs. Bass were sick with weariness, worry, despair. That had been evident to the nurses in L&D for days.

"We're in the waiting room twenty-four hours a day," John said. "Mrs. Bass stays every morning. I stay every evening. Reverend Bass stays all night. About

207

once a day Dr. Hamblin gives one of us a report on Melinda, but after he leaves, we don't know any more about what's going on than we did before he talked to us. He seems unable to speak in laymen's terms, doesn't seem to want to take the trouble to explain. He says things like 'Melinda suffers from acute diverticulitis which resulted in perforation of the descending colon, which in turn resulted in extravasation of pathogenic microbes into the peritoneal cavity causing peritonitis. She is moribund.'"

Carol frowned trying to understand what John was saying.

"I'm an educated man, Miss Welles, but I don't know exactly what's going on. I try to remember the terms Dr. Hamblin uses and I go home to look all this up in my library, which happens to be extensive and contains a medical reference book. I don't remember half what he tells me."

Carol was thinking that college professors very often were knowledgeable on many subjects, but there were a few subjects on which they were completely ignorant. Medicine was often one of those subjects.

"Lately, I've started writing all the medical terms down in a notebook, and I look them up when I get home."

Carol remained silent.

"What I'm trying to say is, Hamblin talks like a medical textbook. It never occurs to him that I don't understand. Most of the time he talks to Mrs. Bass, who was a practicing nurse some fifteen years ago, and even she doesn't understand some of it. Whitehall sees Mrs. Bass and talks to her like she's a half-wit. 'Aw, Matilda—' He doesn't even know her name. 'Aw, Matilda's very sore because there's infection in her belly. She's very sick, you understand, and we're doing

208

all we can.'" John folded his hands in front of his tray of untouched food. "Much of the time the doctors sneak out without telling us what's going on. We've gone as many as three days without seeing one of them. I wonder how they would like going three days without having a report on the progress of someone *they* love."

Carol shook her head.

"Why doesn't Hamblin sit down and look me in the eye and explain what's going on? Why doesn't Whitehall give Mrs. Bass credit for having good sense? Whitehall talks down to me, too, like there's no use in telling me much; I wouldn't understand the highly technical terms which only an intellectual giant can understand. Miss Welles, most people *will* understand procedures and disease processes if the doctors would just take the time to explain it. We are an educated public for the most part. We are capable of grasping such things. I have three degrees, yet when I ask about Melinda, Whitehall says to me, 'Well, it's very complicated, Mr. Curtis. She had an infection in her belly. We had to wash her out with antibiotics because of all the dirty stuff that got in there from a hole in her colon and so on and so on. She's a very sick girl. We're doing all we can.'

"I want to know what 'all we can' means. *What* are they doing? What is all the equipment in the room? Mrs. Bass can explain most of it to me. But this latest tube, going into her near the clavicle— And what are Melinda's chances of recovery? Is she close to death, or is she eventually going to recover? What are the baby's chances? Why doesn't someone tell us what's going on? What happened in there yesterday? Why were all the doctors in there at once? I've tried asking the nurses, and they tell me to ask the doctors. Are they afraid to tell us because the doctors don't want us to know? Why all this mystery? Melinda's *my wife.*" John's voice cracked as he looked down at his hands. Then he looked up with tears in his eyes. "Why doesn't somebody give us credit for having good sense and for being able to cope with whatever crises Melinda's going through?"

Carol was surprised. She hadn't been aware of the family's distress herself. How easy it was to dismiss the family's part in Melinda's illness. She was ashamed. She reached out and laid her hand on John's. "Mr. Curtis, ask. And I'll tell you everything I know."

Later she told Mac. "The family has a right to know what's going on with Melinda. Why can't they stay in the room? If she . . . if she dies, the family ought to be with her. They should have been with her all this time."

Mac listened as Carol told her about what John had said in the cafeteria. Mac said nothing, but picked up the telephone and dialed. "Operator, please page Dr. Whitehall for four-six-two, please. Yes, Labor & Delivery. Thanks."

When Whitehall called back, Mac told him about the family's desire to stay with Melinda and asked for new visitation orders. They were denied.

Mrs. Bass happened to be sitting in the room during her ten-minute visiting time when Whitehall appeared with Mac, who was carrying a nasogastric tube in one hand and a syringe of Valium in the other. Melinda, lying on her back, began to cry when she saw Whitehall and clamped her hands over her mouth.

Carol, who had been cleaning the overbed table with alcohol when they entered, now rushed over to Melinda's bed. "Melinda, please," she said. "If you don't let him put the tube in, we'll have to give you this

210

shot. And it's a sedative."

Whitehall said, as he stood over her bed, "Melinda. Honey, it will go down fast, I promise. And as soon as—"

Melinda, delirious with one hundred point four temp, began to wail, the wailing muffled by her hands, and tears spilled down over her hands and face.

Everybody knew she'd had enough. How much pain and worry and illness and tubes and needles can one person endure?

For ten minutes Whitehall alternately pleaded, explained, and bullied. Then he motioned for Mac to inject the Valium into her IV.

While he waited for it to take effect, he listened to bowel sounds, chest sounds, took her pulse, and checked the abdominal wound, now free of its dressings, while Melinda continued to keep both her hands clamped over her mouth.

Valium ten milligrams IV would have sent a three-hundred-pound wrestler into a daze, but not Melinda. She'd had the tougher stuff for days now: Demerol and morphine.

"Here we go, Melissa," Dr. Whitehall said and tried to take her hand from her face.

She shook her head and kept her hands clamped to her mouth.

Mrs. Bass, meanwhile, had remained out of the fray lest Whitehall notice her and send her out of the room. But while she was sitting, she was remembering her daughter's pulse as she had held her hand earlier—that weak rapid, thready pulse—and Carol's expression, the urgency of the doctor, who had seemed rather nonchalant to her before. And she had made herself face a reality she had refused to face before. That Melinda was dying. She was suddenly furious with her

211

sick, frightened, and rebellious daughter for refusing a treatment. She stood up suddenly saying, "O.K., Mel. Enough's enough." She took Melinda's hands and pinned them easily on either side of her head. "Enough of this. You're being a brat. You're not going to die, and you're not going to let my grandbaby die either," she said firmly, glancing at Mac who was holding the tube.

Mac threaded the tube through Melinda's nose commanding, "Swallow! Swallow, Melinda!"

Melinda swallowed, swallowed again, gagged, gagged again. When Mac saw that the mark on the tubing had reached her nostril, indicating that the end of it was in her stomach, she commanded Melinda to hum. If the tube was in the trachea rather than in the esophagus, she would not be able to hum. Melinda moaned, Mac nodded, Carol turned on the intermittent suction on the wall, and dark brown fluid rushed up the tubing and poured into the collection canister on the wall. Mrs. Bass slowly released Melinda's hands.

Melinda let her arms fall to her sides. She let her knees unbend, she lay flat on her back—and gave up. Her eyes glazed over.

I'm dead. I'm dead and my baby too. I'll let them kill me now. I'm so tired. So tired. The baby's tired. He doesn't move much anymore. They can feed me, push medicines in me, and I'll die. I'll drift up and away, up through this hot sun. I'll let it burn me up. I'm already crisp. It's so hot. This life has burned me up. For days I've burned and my baby too. The heat and the pain is the hell Dad preaches about. I'm there. I've gnashed my teeth. I've begged for water like the rich man who begged Lazarus to dip his finger into water and touch it

212

to his tongue. I've been cast into outer darkness, returned to the white-hot heat of hell again.

Darkness and nothingness.

Sounds.

A light up ahead. Eternity? I'm coming, but you'll have to help me, because I'm too tired and the baby keeps holding me back, making me stay.

Hell roars around me. Hell roars with fire and the croaking of a million frogs. The devils jerk me. They turn me, causing me pain that also roars. I am hell with hell, I am pain with pain, fire with fire.

I lost God somewhere because He's out there, and I'm inside myself where the darkness is.

Darkness. Hell again. Darkness and nothingness.

Hell and pain again. I prefer the darkness. I want the darkness. Please. Please, the darkness, the nothingness.

Mom is not here. John is not here. But once in a while I can hear them. And somebody else whom I've forgotten.

Sounds.

Darkness. Nothingness.

Someone turns my body, someone with cool hands. Someone puts something cool on me.

I bathe in Mother's womb, but it's cool.

I drift up slowly and away, up through this hot sun, up to where the sky is blue and cool. There're meadows here and green grass. Nobody knows there're green meadows in the sky but me.

I carry baby Johnathan with me. In my arms. There's my kitten, Fluff. Johnathan will love Fluff.

Whispers. Melinda?

Whispering.

Somebody walks beside me. Someone talking. Melinda?

They want to share my cool place?

"Melinda."

Somebody else is here, somebody I love. Johnathan knows his voice, kicks in my belly, reaches for him.

I open my eyes.

It is John.

TWELVE

Tasha Packard's cervical dilation was slow so Carol had plenty of time to set up the delivery room. Delivery room three had been cleaned, polished, and disinfected after the last delivery. The oatmeal beige-tiled walls reaching to the asbestos-tiled ceiling were shiny. They were always shiny. The tile floor was polished. The stainless-steel delivery table—almost identical to the examining tables in doctors' offices, except for the handle grips and straps—was polished. The one six-foot-wide cabinet in the room was never touched by housekeeping personnel. It contained sterilized delivery packs, the prep solutions, IV solutions, forceps, retractors, sutures, needles, test tubes, extra bulb syringes, a few vials and ampules of select medications, syringes, infant-resuscitation kits, eye drops, and hopefully, a ballpoint pen.

Carol selected the usual instrument pack from the cabinet. It was a metal placenta basin packed with most of the necessary equipment and instruments needed for a vaginal delivery. The instruments had been washed and placed in the basin, wrapped in a thirty- by forty-inch green surgical drape, taped and autoclaved, either by Martin or by one of the three-to-eleven or eleven-to-seven nurses.

She placed the pack in the center of the three-by-five instrument table, tore off the tape, and unwrapped it; left corner, right corner, far corner, bottom corner. Now the table was covered with a sterile drape and the stainless-steel placenta basin sat in the center packed full of instruments and wraps. She tore open a package of sterile gloves and pulled them on.

Setting up the delivery room was one of her favorite tasks. Gowned, masked, and gloved, she could handle the sterile instruments using sterile technique.

The first item in the basin was the baby blanket which she placed on the upper left-hand side of the table. On this she placed two sanitary napkins, or "peripads." Next came the folded sterile drapes for the patient, which she placed on the upper right side of the table. On these she placed the doctor's gown and, opening a package of sterile gloves, placed them on top of the gown.

In front of the placenta basin in the center she arranged a urinary catheter, a blue plastic umbilical-cord clamp, a bulb syringe for suctioning a newborn infant's mouth and nose, and a test tube for a sample of the umbilical-cord blood. In front of these she arranged the medicine cup, a stack of four-by-four gauze sponges, two thumb forceps, the prethreaded sutures and needles for repairing the patient's episiotomy, and a small basin for the Septisol solution.

At the front of the table she arranged the instruments; from left to right, four towel clips, two scissors—one curved, one straight—a needle holder, two peons, two allis clamps, two curved hemostats, two placenta forceps, and two forceps rings.

Setting up the delivery room was a one-person job,

and anyone wanting to enter it while the instruments were uncovered must wear a mask. Out of the corner of her eye she saw Robbie or Mac enter the room slowly; she wondered if Mac was checking her sterile technique. Probably, because she was responsible for the performance of each of the nurses on the day shift, and their sterile technique was an essential part of their performance. That's why Mac was approaching quietly.

O.K., fine. Because Carol always used sterile technique in setting up the delivery room.

She stepped to the delivery table where she had opened the pack containing the Piper forceps. Generally, she would have opened Dr. Jackson's favorite forceps, Tucker-McLane, but Tasha's delivery was going to be breech and required different forceps. Each doctor had his favorite kind of forceps, and Carol had memorized them. She took the Pipers and laid them on the instrument table. She guessed that doctors, like everybody else, had their favorite instruments as well as their unfavorites. Dr. Moss liked a chromium double-0 suture for suturing episiotomies, and he liked the Luikart-Simpson forceps. He always ordered twenty units of Pitocin to be added to the patient's IV after delivering the placenta. Dr. Blasingame would request extra Russian thumb forceps and a Gelpi retractor, and he didn't like the curved needle holder, but preferred a straight one.

They all had their preferences, and if you couldn't remember them, you'd have to take off your gloves and refer to the index cards in the little index box in the cabinet, take out the required gloves, sutures, or instruments and open them. Then you'd have to open a new package of sterile gloves for yourself, put them on, and pick up the extra sterile objects and place them on the table.

Since it was Dr. Jackson's patient for whom she was setting up, Carol had remembered to open and lay on the counter top a pair of size eight and a half gloves (extra large), which she now picked up out of their sterile pack and laid on top of the sterile gown.

Now she pulled off her gloves, took the plastic bottle of Septisol from the cabinet, and poured it into the sterile basin. Taking care not to touch the inside of the sterile top drape, she spread it over the entire table.

Smiling she turned to Mac.

Only it wasn't Mac.

Mac was not six feet tall, nor did Mac have curly brown hair and cocoa-colored eyes. Carol pulled her mask down from her face, her heart thudding almost audibly in her chest.

He pulled his mask down, too, and they stood quietly looking at each other.

"Sooner or later it had to happen," Duane said, his lips curling up at the outer corners.

"What did?" she asked haughtily.

"That I had to do labor-and-delivery rotation."

"I'm sure it did."

"So far, I've been able to maneuver my obstetrics duties to the evening and night shifts. But today I . . . seem to be stuck here, because Dr. Jackson's patient is going to have a breech delivery."

"So why did you have to manipulate your schedule for night-shift duty?"

"I traded off with another intern and you know damned well *why* I didn't want the day shift in here."

She smiled, hurt and flustered, but nevertheless she managed a bright smile. "Because it's busier on days?" she asked.

"Because it's much more pleasant on the other shifts," he said. "That was a damned dirty trick you pulled on me last week in Melinda's room."

"Trick?" Carol said raising her brows as she tossed her gloves into the wastebasket. "What trick?"

"You know what trick. Twitching your ass around, as if I were interested enough to look."

"That's a trick?" She laughed.

He took hold of her arm, but she pulled loose from him, smiling, amused. "Is that what you came in here to tell me? How my twitching *didn't* affect you in the least?" she asked brushing past him toward the door.

"I came in here to tell you that I couldn't avoid day shift today."

"So why must you tell me?"

"I didn't want you to get the mistaken idea that I had arranged to be here today on purpose," he sneered.

"Why should I?"

He had no answer, so she smiled again and left the delivery room.

"Push, Tasha."

"Unghh!'

"Push!"

Carol was feeling super because she had detected the breech presentation earlier, all by herself. When Tasha had come into L&D from admitting via wheelchair, she had taken her to labor room four, had requested that she change from her clothes to the hospital gown, and had asked her to urinate in the specimen cup in the room's private bath. Then she had done the vaginal exam. The cervix, the neck of the pear-shaped uterus, was still thick; the internal os, or opening, of the cervix was dilated three centimeters, but the external os of the cervix was dilated only about one centimeter. For Tasha's labor pains to have been as intense and frequent as they were, the cervix had not dilated or thinned out as it should have. The cervix should have gotten shorter and shorter, but it hadn't. And she could not feel the fetal head. She had palpated Tasha's abdomen, however, and thought she could feel the head about the level of Tasha's umbilicus. She had checked the cervix again. The fetus was high, not yet engaged at the pelvic inlet. Membranes were still intact.

While she smiled and talked about the weather and other incidentals, Carol had taken Tasha's vitals and FHTs. They were all normal. Then she had gone to the desk and told Mac what she suspected. Mac had checked Tasha then and had confirmed Carol's suspicion. Breech. Mac telephoned Dr. Jackson.

Because of the inherent difficulties of breech delivery, Dr. Jackson had left his office sitting full of pregnant patients leafing through magazines and had breezed into L&D within fifteen minutes of Mac's call. Carol would never become accustomed to Dr. Jackson's lackadaisical manner. She expected him to enter, solemn and concerned over Tasha. Instead, he came in, hair windblown from riding over on his motorcycle—laughing.

He sat down at the nurses' station still laughing. Mac stared at him and had to laugh too. When Martin appeared, her face a portrait of agony from her effort not to smile, Joy, too, showed up at the desk, giggling; and Goodnature was standing in a labor-room doorway chuckling all over. Carol was no better. She caught herself laughing, too, as she approached the desk. It was hilarious; but nobody knew why.

Finally Dr. Jackson rubbed his hand under his nose, causing his mustache to bristle. "You'll never believe this," he said sweeping them all with an amused glance.

"Try and see." Mac chuckled.

"This morning,"—the doctor laughed—"I had this patient named Mrs. Dorsey come into my office for her usual checkup. As usual, my nurse, Ingrid, had her go into the bathroom and leave a urine specimen in a paper cup. Only thing, as we found out later, someone had used up all the toilet paper. So Mrs. Dorsey got into her handbag and found a Kleenex with which to wipe herself. Then Ingrid had her go into one of the examining rooms, disrobe, get into the disposable gown, and get up on the examining table. Ingrid put Mrs. Dorsey's feet up in stirrups, draped her, and got ready to clean the vagina; then she burst out laughing.

"Now Mrs. Dorsey is a very nervous lady, and she was perturbed at Ingrid, but Ingrid called me in. She was hysterical. I'm thinking, Ingrid's finally gone bananas. But I go in, sit down on my stool, fix my light, and undrape Mrs. Dorsey's bottom. What do I see?" Dr. Jackson laughed and framed an imaginary picture for them with both his big hands. "The usual female perineum. Only this time there're eight green stamps stuck to her vagina!"

Joy screamed with laughter, and Mac collapsed. Jackson roared, and Carol threw back her head in a throaty laugh.

"The Kleenex had green stamps stuck on it," Martin surmised with a grimace that passed for a smile. Her words made them all roar with laughter again.

After a few moments of this somebody remembered Tasha, and Dr. Jackson plodded into her room saying, "What's going on?" He confirmed that indeed Tasha's baby was going to be born breech.

Breech delivery, caused by an abnormal fetal position, presents a greater danger to fetus and mother alike. One breech infant in fifteen dies as a result of the delivery. Most of this is due to head trauma; and in footling breech, prolapsing of the umbilical cord is always a danger. Cervical lacerations are the most frequent complication to the mother delivering breech; not serious, but annoying.

Dr. Jackson had ruptured Tasha's membranes, and

the meconium stool from the infant had stained the amniotic fluid, further confirming breech delivery. Carol had been checking the fetal heart almost continually. And she and Mac had attached the EHFC monitor to Tasha's abdomen in order to better monitor the relationship between her contractions and the FHTs. The fetal heart tones were normal, and Tasha's vital signs remained stable.

Now the hour of delivery was at hand.

In a normal delivery the infant's head usually forms an excellent wedge that causes dilation of the cervix, but in breech other parts of the fetus are presented at the pelvic inlet. Tasha's was a frank breech, according to Dr. Jackson's calculations; the fetus' buttocks were presenting while its legs lay against its abdomen and chest. This was a better dilating wedge than the footling breech—feet first—or the complete breech. Still, it was an abnormal presentation, and Tasha had to help as much as possible.

"Push!" Carol commanded.

This was Tasha's second child. She knew what to expect and was not afraid. She did as she was told, knowing that the pushing meant that labor was in its last phase. She was clasping her legs, holding them up and bent.

"Unngghhh!" she grunted pushing.

An outsider might have viewed the scene as bizarre. Carol was sitting on the edge of the bed watching the vaginal opening while Tasha held her knees and pushed. "Unnnnghhh!"

Carol's gloved hand spread the labia trying to gauge the progress of the breech delivery. It was then that Duane appeared again. She ignored him as he moved to the foot of the bed, a vantage point from which he could see everything. He was already wearing a surgical cap and a scrub suit. "Frank breech?" he asked in a low voice.

"Yes. The baby's just rotating slowly through, so I think we're about ready. Tasha, this is Dr. Duren. He's going to assist Dr. Jackson in delivering your baby."

"Hi," Tasha said. "I've had a caudal so I don't hurt. All I can feel is pressure. Uh-oh. Here it comes . . ."

"Push, Tasha."

Tasha pushed, hard, very hard. Carol got a glimpse of the presenting part. It was time.

"Please tell Mac we're ready, will you, Doctor?" Carol asked as she covered Tasha's legs with the top sheet.

It took at least two nurses to get patients, paralyzed from the waist down from caudal anesthetic, from the bed onto the stretcher, but some innovative soul had invented rollers. Rollers were four six-foot-long metal cylinders covered with black rubber and attached to a frame at each end. All the nurses had to do was roll Tasha onto her side, tuck the rollers against her back, roll her onto her back again which put her on the rollers, and then pull the rollers, patient and all, from the bed onto the stretcher.

Mac had notified Tasha's husband that she was going to delivery, and he met the stretcher in the L&D hallway.

"Don't call me, I'll call you," Tasha told him smiling drowsily. Pushing was hard work and she was tired.

Mr. Packard took her hand. "Well, hurry, Tasha. I've got a golf date at three," he joked.

Goodnature watched the scene with awe. The new methods of anesthesia allowed this kind of relaxed banter, whereas in her day in L&D, a patient like Tasha would have been screaming, writhing with birth pains, or lethargic from having been given "twilight sleep," a Demerol and Scopolamine combination. She certainly wouldn't have felt like joking. And even in Good-

223

nature's day, she thought, medical science had come a long way, since husbands no longer paced before the open hearth fire shrinking at every scream their wives made, while maids carried kettles of boiling water up the stairs. Now, some hospitals even allowed the husband in the delivery room!

They rolled Tasha down the corridor and into labor room three which Carol had prepared.

Mac and Carol used the rollers to pull Tasha from stretcher to delivery table. Mac showed her the handles on the table for her to grip. Needing something to hold on to during delivery was something that had never changed through the ages for women. Simultaneously, Carol and Mac lifted both Tasha's legs into the towel-draped stirrups. Carol pushed the bottom part of the table under, until Tasha's bottom was at the edge of the table.

Mac prepped the perineum, while Carol recorded the time of Tasha's arrival in the delivery room in the Delivery Room Record Sheet.

Dr. Jackson strode in with Duane following, both capped and masked. "What's going on?"

Nobody answered him because he didn't expect to be answered. "Boy or girl, Tasha?" he asked happily as he took the sterile gloves off the table which Carol had set up.

"I don't care," Tasha replied as she watched him snap on the gloves.

"It's a girl," Dr. Jackson said. "It has a rapid heartbeat." He hooked the rolling stool with his foot and brought it expertly beneath his own bottom just as he sat down.

Duane was pulling on his own gloves, not looking at Carol or even Mac. Mac was adjusting the huge overhead spotlight to shine directly on Tasha's perineum as Carol recorded the time it had taken Mac to prep Tasha. She was acutely aware of Duane in the room, had been aware that he was in the vicinity since he had approached her here earlier when she was setting up. But her work had taken precedence in her mind, steadying her, causing her to view him as Dr. Duren, not *Duane whom I once loved, who once loved me, with whom I shared my bed, who caused me unspeakable pleasures . . . and pain.*

Now she drew up ten units of Pitocin into a syringe and then another of Deladumone, a medication which would suppress lactation and prevent engorgement of Tasha's breasts, since she was not planning to breast-feed her baby.

"Yes, yes," Dr. Jackson said examining Tasha's vagina. "A frank breech, classic frank breech." He watched as Tasha's next contraction bulged the perineum. Carol went to stand behind the doctor so that she could watch the proceedings.

It was another bizarre picture. With Tasha's contractions, a tiny buttocks appeared for a moment at her vagina, then retracted after the contraction.

"Dr. Duren," Jackson said standing, indicating the stool. "Be my guest."

Carol looked up at her former paramour. His forehead was pale.

"I've never—"

"You've delivered," Jackson said.

"Yes. Twice. But not . . . breech."

"I'll assist and advise. This is a rare opportunity. Please be my guest."

"Unngggh," Tasha said as Duane replaced Dr. Jackson on the stool.

Carol had dreamed of this once; Duane as the doctor delivering the infant, Carol assisting as his nurse. It could have been sort of . . . romantic, like a soap opera, or like *Not As a Stranger,* but it wasn't. Mainly

225

because every time Tasha pushed, the buttocks of the infant advanced a little more, presenting a shiny bottom, an anus, and a proportionately oversized scrotum.

"Sunny-side up," Dr. Jackson observed jauntily.

Carol didn't need that; she was already blushing stupidly and unprofessionally.

Duane didn't need it either. By the color of his face, she knew he was embarrassed too.

"'Moo-oon over Miami,'" sang Dr. Jackson, and even Tasha had to smile. Lackadaisical or not, he still had his professional eye on the proceedings, and Carol knew that if the baby wasn't delivered very shortly, he would have Duane use the Piper forceps.

But the buttocks was delivered with Tasha's next push. Excited and flustered, Duane grabbed the bulb syringe off the instrument table.

"I wouldn't advise your suctioning that," Dr. Jackson said. "Just support the body; that's right. Bend him up. He'll rotate to face-down position as you deliver the shoulders. But right now the legs . . . Exert a little pressure now, pull . . ."

"Push, Mrs. . . . Mrs. . . . ." Duane stammered in near panic.

"Unnngghh," Tasha grunted as she pulled on the hand grips of the table.

Duane looked up at Carol. "Please exert a little pressure on the fundus."

Carol obeyed, helping Tasha push by pressing down gently on the fundus of the uterus.

"Let him straddle your arm now," Dr. Jackson instructed Duane. "Up more, support that chin with your fingers as you deliver his head."

Carol, now almost face-to-face with Duane, saw the perspiration on his forehead, his strain, his intent brown eyes.

"Ah," Dr. Jackson. "How about that? It's a boy!"

Everyone laughed because that fact had been evident for at least ten minutes. And baby boy Packard added to their laughter by demonstrating his opinion of the entire proceedings; he let go with a stream of urine that arched up and sprinkled down the front of Duane's gown. Dr. Jackson had stepped back and now spread his arms and sang, "'Blue moo-oon, you saw me standing a-lo-one . . . .'"

Laughing to herself, Carol turned away to fill in more of the delivery-room record as Duane began to suction the mewling infant's mouth and nose. Dr. Jackson began to clamp the umbilical cord in two places; *click,* using the Kelly to clamp the cord about eight inches from the infant's abdomen, and *snap,* using the blue umbilical-cord clamp about five inches closer to the infant.

On the Labor and Delivery Record, Carol filled in as many blanks as she could, catching up the record while she had the chance.

To Delivery No. __3__ At 1:32 P.M. Prepared
  for Delivery at 1:45 P.M.
Anesthetic __Caudal__ by Dr. __Jackson__
Delivered at 2:21 P.M. by Dr. __Duren__
Normal __✓__ Low forceps _____
  Mid forceps _____ Presentation Breech, frank
Caesarean Section _____ Primary _____
  Repeat _____
Complications __None__

When she turned back to watch, Duane was holding the infant in his big hands, and Carol found herself smiling at him. He glanced up at her. "This isn't my bag," he reminded her above the lusty bawl of the baby.

He had cut the cord between the two clamps, and Dr.

227

Jackson was releasing the Kelly clamp filling a test tube with the cord blood. Duane handed baby boy Packard to Mac who received him in the sterile baby blanket. He then consulted Dr. Jackson. "Apgar eight?"

"I'd say so," Dr. Jackson said tapping the lid onto the test tube full of blood.

Carol would say so too. She recorded the Apgar score on the Delivery Room Records Sheet. The Apgar score is the index by which the doctors evaluate the condition of the infant at birth. The scoring consists of the number of points given for each "sign" one minute after birth and five minutes later. The signs evaluated are: heart rate, respiration, muscle tone, reflexes, and color. A perfect score for each sign is two. A baby scoring ten points would have perfect signs one minute after birth, but this was not usual. Most normal, healthy infants scored seven, eight, or nine.

Carol filled in the blanks on two tiny strips of stiff paper which were printed with the same number for the arm bands.

	Packard, Tasha	2:21 P.M.
08640	Boy 1/4/80	Dr. Jackson

Mac would clamp the arm bands on the baby's wrist and ankle. Carol recorded the arm band number on the Delivery Room Record Sheet.

While Mac finished suctioning the infant's mouth and nose and trachea, Duane delivered the placenta. Carol injected the Deladumone into Tasha's right hip and then injected the ten units of Pitocin into her IV. The oxytocin would cause the uterus to clamp down on the bleeding vessels left in the uterine wall when the placenta had become detached.

Next, Duane had to suture the episiotomy. This was

more to his liking; taking stitches in the incision. The tail sponges were inserted to occlude the bleeding, and with continuous sutures, which in sewing fabric would be called a whipstitch, he repaired the vaginal mucosa. Jackson suggested an interrupted stitch for the muscle and then the "whipstitch" again for subcuticular fascia. When most patients left the delivery room, they asked how many stitches they had had. Most of the time the doctors wouldn't know, so they'd just offer a number. In an unusually severe laceration, they might actually count the stitches, but most of the time they only guessed. It didn't matter. They took as many stitches as were necessary to close the wound.

At this, Duane was in his element, suturing, unaware of anything else going on around him. Dr. Jackson watched for a few moments, saw that he was not needed now, nodded, and pulled off his gloves.

Mac had taken baby boy Packard to the newborn nursery. Carol was straightening up the cabinet, putting up supplies. She'd gathered the instruments into the basin to help Marty all she could. Dr. Moss was delivering in room two, and there were two more patients, in the early phases of labor, in the labor rooms, so Marty would have a lot of instruments to wash, pack, and autoclave.

"Have you seen my new watch?" Dr. Jackson asked Carol as he pulled off his gloves.

She turned toward him. "No. You have a new watch?"

"Gift from a friend," he said and pulled up the sleeve of his gown, presenting his new watch for Carol to see.

She should have suspected something silly, knowing Dr. Jackson, but she didn't and bent to examine the watch—bent closer.

The watch was built like a Mickey Mouse watch, but instead of Mickey Mouse, a naked man and woman

229

were imprinted on its face, standing facing each other. The hands of the watch were the right hands of the smiling couple. His was at 3:00 o'clock and was covering the woman's breasts, hers was at twenty before and was covering the most intimate part of the man.

Carol gasped in surprise and stepped back, bumping her head on the overhead light. "Dr. Jackson!" she exclaimed more out of shock than embarrassment.

Dr. Jackson laughed uproariously. "I can always tell a virgin by her reaction to my watch," he said to Duane.

Duane looked up slowly to meet her gaze, and held it.

Jackson showed Duane the watch. Duane looked, nodded, turned away, did a second take. Then his face mask puffed out, and he exploded, threw back his head, and roared.

And Carol turned away to gather the instruments into the placenta basin.

The three-to-eleven shift came in on time to carry Tasha to recovery, so Carol, Mac, Robbie, Joy, and Goodnature were able to go home on time—which suited Carol just fine. She wanted to wash her hair and take a shower before the party. She didn't see Duane again after she left the delivery room.

Going home, she tried to evaluate her feelings for him. She couldn't. It was as if her psyche had thrown up some sort of roadblock to keep her feelings from running away with her. Duane had been near her for several hours, yet she had felt no delight in that, or any dismay. She was puzzled with herself.

At home she washed her hair, showered, dried her hair, and got into her jeans and a neat shirt. The beef brisket had been marinating in barbecue sauce as it thawed in the fridge for two days. That morning she had placed it in the oven at two hundred degrees, and now its aroma filled her entire apartment.

Joy would bring her boyfriend, Ricky, to Carol's casual party; the girl next door would bring hers. The philosophy prof from UTE would bring his girl, and there were others coming, ten in all, and each would bring a dish. "A dish or pot?" the professor had joked. She hoped nobody would bring pot. She wasn't into that. So far she had not digressed into anything stronger than dinner wine and an occasional Virginia Slims.

The apartment was spotless. She checked the fridge for drinks. Her mom and dad would die to see it. Wine and beer sat among the bottles of Coca-Cola and other soft drinks. She went to the cabinet and measured coffee into the filter of the coffee maker and soon the apartment smelled of coffee brewing. She lit a cigarette just as the doorbell rang. That would be Bret. She went to the door and unlatched the dead bolt. "Who?"

"Me."

She opened the door. It was Duane. Her smile faded and she started to shut the door, but he caught it, held it open. She let it go.

"You have a knack for bursting into people's doors, don't you?" she said, remembering the time when he had kicked open the door of her apartment and come in, that night when they had first made love.

"Only yours," he said coming in and shutting the door. He smiled at her grimly and looked around him. "You've come up in the world."

"What do you want, Duane?" she said with a lift of her chin.

He looked at her a long, quiet moment. "Since when did you begin to smoke?"

"Since when should you care?"

"It makes you look ridiculous."

231

She turned around and walked over to the couch. Yes, he was right. She was new at it and *felt* ridiculous. She squashed the cigarette out in the ashtray on the table beside her couch.

He still stood just inside the door looking around. He spotted the small bar with its stemmed glasses. "That looks ridiculous too. When I first knew you, you hadn't touched anything any stronger than Nyquil, and even *that* made you drunk."

She folded her arms with a jerk. "How did you find my apartment?"

"Telephone directory," he replied now moving about the room.

"And why have you come?"

"Cooking, too," he said wandering into her kitchen. "When I first knew you, you couldn't fry a hamburger."

She followed him into the kitchen. "Look here, Duane, I didn't ask you here. I don't *want* you here. I'm about to have a party, and I have things to do."

He smiled at her. "I'll bet you even have a boyfriend."

She tossed her head, causing her long hair to fall over her shoulders in a red-blond shower. "Of course."

He raised his brows. "Live-in?"

Suddenly furious, she pointed to her door. "Out! Get out or I'll scream."

Smiling grimly he studied her some more, shook his head. "I don't think so."

"I *will.*"

"I don't think I can make you scream."

"You just try me, buster."

"I have," he said, moving from her kitchen to the dining area. "And you were so inexperienced that if you now have a live-in boyfriend, it would be more than ridiculous. It would be ludicrous."

She pointed at the door again. "Out!"

He studied her, not moving; opened his mouth to say something, closed it, opened it again. "I haven't come calling socially, so you can relax about that."

"I won't relax until you leave through that door."

They were adults, but both inexperienced at handling the complex emotions they didn't understand, so they became children, and were aware of fighting like children.

"You really do hate me about as much as I hate you, don't you?" he said.

"More."

"It's a tossup."

"I didn't call you hateful names."

"No, you chose a term paper over our relationship."

"You hurt me when you called me a pipsqueak and a nothing."

"And you hurt me when you preferred a term paper over me."

Carol hadn't ever looked at it that way before, but she had chosen to do the term paper on Proctor, knowing that if she did, it would be the end of hers and Duane's relationship. Yes, it must have hurt him—or at least his pride. "I . . . hurt you?"

"I let you get under my skin too much. I deserved it." And for a moment, she could *see* the hurt. Then, "But that's over."

"Then why are you here?"

"I was passing by on the way to a friend's apartment. I—you—Carol?"

She waited.

But what he was about to say never got said. The doorbell rang, and she went to it and let Bret in. He stood quietly, not looking surprised, looking only at Duane, Duane looking at him.

Duane said, "I'll be going."

"You never answered my question about why you're

here," she said.

At the door, he and Bret looked at each other, not with any hostility, not even with any curiosity, just coldly, soberly. Duane said, "I didn't come calling socially, fella, so relax."

Bret folded his arms. "I'm relaxed. Always am. But I'm sort of like Carol, wondering why you're here."

Duane smiled, looked at Carol. "I had to work an hour longer than you, Carol, before I went off duty for the first time in twelve hours. The Gladstone lady had a girl. Beatrix Whatever-her-name-was had a girl too."

Carol snapped, "That's just fine."

"But what I came by to say is . . ." He looked at Bret. "I hate to ruin her evening like this."

She walked over to him. "O.K., Duane. What?"

He opened the door and turned toward her. "No matter what they tell you at the hospital, Carol—when I left, Melinda Curtis had just begun to have labor pains. Remember, it's labor pains," he said and went out the door shutting it behind him.

THIRTEEN

Being sick makes you act awful. With a great deal of shame Melinda was remembering how she had fought the doctors and nurses when they had tried to put the stomach tube in; but she had been almost delirious with fever and pain and didn't really know what she was doing. It was as if somebody else had taken over her body and was making her act the way she had. Now she knew what the Bible meant when it told about persons being possessed by demons. She was using her sickness as a cop-out. She *had known* what she was doing, in a foggy, vague, terrified way. But she hadn't been able to keep herself from acting the way she had. And after that, she had experienced her long, horrible nightmare, an unconsciousness that had lasted four days, through Christmas. Finally she had awakened to find John standing beside her bed. The roaring had stopped, the fever was gone, and most of the pain was gone too.

Now they said she had only a small amount of fever, and they said peris—peristalsis had begun and they had taken out that awful old stomach tube just this morning. But she was still tired; and she wouldn't admit it, but she felt a little nauseated, too, and sleepy, and there was a little bit of pain. She was very, very weak.

She had looked at her arm this morning. It was so skinny. But the baby was kicking, stronger than ever.

Last night Hank had told her not to be alarmed because of the false labor contractions that had gone on all yesterday. Someone had called Dr. Simon when they had started, and he had ordered shots. Morphine, she thought, because of the way it made her feel kind of high at first and blah later. She had had false labor before. She had first felt the labor contractions when she was five months along, little tightening sensations in her abdomen, but that was normal. The shots had stopped the contractions yesterday for a while. Now they were going again; but they didn't hurt, and they weren't regular.

She could remember the film in prenatal class about false labor:

> *False labor, called Braxton Hicks contractions after a famous physician who first described them, occurs after the first few weeks of pregnancy and continues until the onset of true labor. During the last few months of pregnancy these contractions can become quite strong and cause the patient some real discomfort. She may wonder if she is going into true labor. . . .*
>
> *. . . Ways to differentiate between true labor and false: true labor occurs at regular intervals; false labor is irregular. True labor intensifies with activity; activity has no effect on false labor. During true labor, the pain is felt primarily in the lower back; in false labor it is located in the abdomen. In true labor the pains or contractions increase in frequency and intensity; in false labor*

*their intensity remains the same. There is no
bloody show with false labor.*

So far her contractions had been irregular and had
not become more intense. She had felt them only in her
abdomen, which was still sort of tender from her
surgery and the peritonitis. She only hoped that the
discomfort in her back now was because she'd been
lying on it so long. Dr. Whitehall had written an order
for the nurses to sit her up on the side of the bed, and
she'd sat up twice since yesterday. He had told her she'd
be getting up to sit in a chair by tomorrow.

True labor intensifies with activity. . . .

Gosh, how could any woman tell if she was in labor
for sure if her contractions were as strong as *this*.
Melinda placed both hands on her abdomen and felt it
harden and rise beneath them.

Carol was taking care of her today, and she was glad.
They were friends. Carol probably understood her
better than the others. And Carol didn't know it, but
she understood Carol, too. She understood that there
was something going on between her and the intern
named Dr. Duren. Maybe an aborted love affair?
Wow! Just like on TV!

Also, she thought she saw something Carol didn't: a
certain look on Dr. Novak's face when he talked to her.
He respected Carol's opinions. He listened to her
explanations and suggestions as if she were another
doctor.

"What are you smiling about?" Carol asked now,
taking Melinda's wrist in her hand to take her pulse.

Melinda's throat was still sore from the tube, but she
croaked, "You'll never guess."

"Tell me."

"I will. Someday."

Carol placed a hand on her abdomen, felt the slight

tightening, glanced at her wrist watch. "Gonna be cagey, huh?"

Melinda smiled mischievously.

It hurt Carol to see the thin girl, the gaunt face, the sunken eyes. Melinda's once-glossy hair was now dull. And today her temp was up a bit from yesterday, according to the vital-sign sheet Robbie had kept so judiciously.

What Duane had said yesterday about Melinda Curtis wasn't exactly true. When Carol called the hospital an hour after he had left her apartment, Hank had told her, "No, she ain't exactly in labor. She's having Braxton Hicks contractions is all. Dr. Simon ordered small doses of morphine hoping to stop the false labor, and I think the first dose has worked. Go back to your party, Carol, and don't worry. Whoop it up for me, will ya?"

Carol had hung up the telephone in high spirits. So Duane was wrong. Why was he so sure? Or was he just trying to ruin her evening? And if so, why? Why had he *really* come by?

Well, he hadn't ruined her party. Everybody she had invited came, dressed in jeans, and ate barbecue and played country-western music on her stereo. People brought more tapes than they did dishes of food, but that was O.K. Now and then somebody danced, but mostly they just talked and sat around and littered her apartment with soft-drink bottles and glasses, or filled her trash can with paper plates, and her ashtrays with cigarette butts and ashes. Most left late to go to the Brass Chandelier, a high-class country-western club. She and Bret had elected to stay and clean up her apartment.

Bret never mentioned Duane's visit, but she could tell it was bothering him. Poor Bret, so good-looking, so good to her; yet standing side by side with Duane, he

238

did not compare favorably in good looks or dashiness. Duane dominated the scene without really trying.

"No matter what they tell you at the hospital, Carol, when I left, Melinda Curtis had just begun to have labor pains. Remember, it's labor pains."

Duane's words made her uneasy even now. Why *was* he so certain?

She looked at Melinda. Noted the time. The contractions were twenty-two minutes apart—and regular. Braxton Hicks maybe. Everybody said so, but the small dosages of morphine were no longer stopping them. She really wished she could get Dr. Simon's permission to do a vag exam or something. Because—it was a feeling she had. Duane had been so positive. Maybe it was a feeling *he* had too.

"Wow!"

Carol looked at Melinda again, who smiled timorously. By now she knew Melinda well enough to know she would not complain, but also well enough to note the little worry line in the center of her forehead; she saw Melinda's hand go to her abdomen. The hair on the back of her own neck prickled. She had been getting Melinda's bath ready, and now set the bath basin down on the overbed table and placed her hand on Melinda's abdomen.

The contraction was firm, firmer than the others had been, and Carol glanced at the clock. Twenty-five minutes this time. Braxton Hicks? Hell with that. She didn't believe it anymore.

Melinda was only seven months along. A baby born now would have a one-in-ten chance to live. Nature's way of "getting rid" of a defective fetus? That was a worry the doctors and nurses had had from the beginning, though they had seldom mentioned it. The infant could have a physical defect, or a brain defect, or both, from all the medications they had given Melinda.

Most of the time a mother's body would somehow detect and abort a defective infant. Most spontaneous abortions were because of defects in the fetus.

Melinda frowned.

"Kinda strong, huh?"

Melinda smiled. "According to film number five," she said taking a breath, "Braxton Hicks contractions are the uterus practicing up for the real thing. But if this is a false labor contraction, it must be a *dress* rehearsal."

Carol began to bathe her methodically. "Oh, we'll time the next one and see if it's as firm. You gotta remember false labor helps firm the muscles of the uterus for D-day."

"D-day?"

"Delivery day."

Melinda giggled softly.

The next contraction came when Carol was helping Melinda into a fresh gown. The contraction was firm and lasted twenty seconds and was twenty-five minutes from the last one.

Carol left the room, stuffed mask and gown into the red bag outside the door, and went to the desk. Mac was busy in a patient's room; Carol could hear her saying loudly, "Push, Octavia. Push!"

Joy skittered by carrying a catheter tray and disappeared into room one.

Carol scrubbed her hands with Septisol and went back to the nurses' station to telephone Dr. Simon's office.

"Mary?" she said when the secretary came on the line. "This is Bennet Memorial L&D. May I speak with Dr. Simon?"

"He's gone to the dentist and should be back by noon."

"Dentist!"

"Sure. Doctors go to the dentist like everybody else. He canceled all his appointments today because he bit down on a bone and broke off a tooth. He's in awful pain. What's wrong over there?"

"Melinda Curtis . . ."

"Uh-oh."

"She may be going into labor. All I want right now is permission to do a vag exam. We have an order directing us not to do a vag exam on her."

"Listen. I'll try to get him at the dentist's office, and I'll call you back. O.K.?"

"O.K. I'll wait. This is Carol Welles."

Ten minutes later Mary called back. "Carol? I can't find Dr. Simon. The dentist says he left there five minutes ago. I tried his beeper but it's not working. I've left word with his wife that he should call you if he comes home."

"I don't think this can wait," Carol said remembering that if a patient dilated more than three or four centimeters . . . well, that was the point of no return. "Is Dr. Moss in?"

"He's out of town."

Carol put her head in her hand. "Thanks, Mary."

"Look, Carol, I'll keep trying to reach him. O.K.?"

"Thanks."

Mac approached the desk now as Carol hung up the telephone; she raised her brows in a question. Carol told her her plight.

Mac said, "We're panicking, Carol. But if Melinda continues to have contractions like that, I'm going to take the responsibility and do a vag exam whether Simon gives orders for it or not."

"Simon won't like that. He was so specific about that order."

"I know, but he won't like it if she goes into premature labor and we just sit here with our hands

241

folded either."

It was a dilemma nurses faced in every department. You often had to weigh a patient's welfare, sometimes against a doctor's order. Sometimes the doctor's orders were just asinine. Sometimes they had solid medical reasoning behind them, and Simon's order against their doing a vag exam was one of these. Vaginal exams often stimulated labor. Still there was no way of checking to see if dilation of the cervix was taking place except through a vag exam.

Carol said, "I checked Melinda's vagina when I cleaned her. No bloody show or anything."

"Most of the time that's first, the bloody show . . ." Mac said thoughtfully.

"But we know that a lot of the time they can be three or four centimeters dilated before the show too."

"Shit," Mac concluded. She stood up and strode down the hallway to Melinda's door with Carol following. Both put on gowns and gloves and went in.

Melinda was wide-awake, eyes brighter than usual, perspiration beading her forehead and upper lip.

"Any more contractions?" Carol asked.

Melinda held up three fingers. "They're real, aren't they?"

Carol took her hand. "We don't know."

Mac felt the next contraction, shrugged, and said, "I've felt Braxton Hicks contractions this strong before."

But Carol wanted to tell her, Mac, I know this is real, though I've never experienced false contractions. But Melinda has. And we've had patients in with false labor before. But—I know. I just know. Besides, *Duane* knows.

At that moment, the door opened suddenly, and Basil Novak came to the rescue.

He nodded to the nurses and said to Melinda,

242

"What's this I hear about false labor?"

Melinda smiled. "I'm beginning to wonder."

Novak took out his stethoscope. "I'm not the expert on that, Melinda. These nurses are." He raised his brows and looked at Mac.

"They're firm. Getting closer together. No bloody show. I've seen false labor like this before," Mac said.

He looked at Carol.

"But . . . they are firm . . . and . . ."

"And you think she ought to have a vag exam."

"Yes."

Novak listened to Melinda's lung sounds, prodded her abdomen gently. "Of course false contractions will hurt more, Melinda, since your abdomen is still tender from the peritonitis, not to mention the surgery. Though I think we've just about whipped the infection. Still, the contractions are more painful, I'm sure."

"I hope that's it," Melinda said softly.

Novak nodded for Carol and Mac to precede him out the door. While they were pulling off gowns and gloves again, Mac's patient rang her bell, so she went down the hallway to answer it.

"Let's go to the coffee room," Novak suggested and he and Carol crossed the hall to the little kitchenette behind the nurses' station.

Carol leaned against the wall and said, "O.K., Dr. Novak. I understand that the peritoneum is still painful from the infection. But pain can *cause* real labor, and we've seen false labor itself develop into the real thing."

"Sure. And you're a better judge of that than I am."

"What do you think?"

"I agree with Duren. He told me yesterday that Melinda's labor was real." He poured himself a cup of coffee and turned back toward her.

"Dr. Duren? Who is he? A first-year intern with three days' experience in L&D," Carol said irritably.

Novak held the cup out to her, and she shook her head. He sipped the coffee himself and said, "Duren is a strange breed of cat, Carol." He looked at her intently. "He's sharp, ambitious, learns fast, studies hard, works hard. Did you know that he was number two in his graduating class in medical school?"

Carol looked down at her shoes and studied the spot of Betadine prep on her shoestring. "No. But I'm not surprised."

"No?"

"I believe we were talking about Melinda Curtis."

"But I'm talking now of Duren."

"I don't care about Duren. Time is important in Melinda's case and I—"

"I know," he interrupted. "I'm saying that Duren's not only smart, he's uncannily intuitive. And I'm one of those weird characters who believe in intuition with regard to medicine. He and I were in her room yesterday afternoon, and he believes she was in true labor even then."

"Yes, I know."

"Duren told you then."

"Yes."

"And he didn't bother telling anyone else. Know why?"

"No. I really don't care why."

"Because he knows you're intuitive also. If he had told the nurses on the three-to-eleven or the eleven-to-seven shift that he just *knew* Melinda Curtis was in real labor, can you imagine what they'd have thought?"

Carol smiled. "And said."

"Things like 'arrogant'? 'Who does he think he is?' and 'He's crazy'?"

Carol folded her arms. This was absurd. Doctors don't usually go around to particular nurses and reveal their intuitions privately about patients.

Or do they?

If so, *that's* why Duane came by her apartment. Because only *she* would believe him.

"Naturally, I notified Dr. Simon about our intuition. Simon's a super obstetrician, but he can't see the forest for the trees. We, Duane and I, are still new enough in medicine to have suspicions, speculations, and to examine possibilities—against all other evidence. Simon told us it was Braxton Hicks, and he was right then. Only we knew—or felt—that because of the pain of peritonitis, she was likely to go into real labor. We've seen it happen before; surgical pain, pain from broken arms or legs, or from lacerations causing pregnant patients to go into labor. Simon is seeing Melinda from an obstetric viewpoint; we're seeing her from a surgical point of view with OB rotation still fresh in our arrogant young minds." Novak pressed his lips together and shook his head. "No, I'm not making sense. Any physician hearing me would laugh." He looked at her. "I just think . . . that Melinda's in true labor. You're new enough to be flexible too. What do *you* think?"

"That she's in the first phase of true labor."

"Then we've wasted five minutes here deliberating."

"I appreciate your confidence in my judgment."

"Duren didn't say so, but if he had confidence that you would be persistent enough to pursue this, then I have confidence in you too."

Carol unfolded her arms and stood up straight. "Duren. It all goes back to him. Everything."

"Doesn't it?"

"All I want now is for Dr. Simon—or any doctor—to order a gentle, fast vaginal exam on Melinda Curtis."

Novak dropped his empty cup into the garbage can. "Simon may kill me, but I doubt it." He looked at

Carol again. "Ms. Welles, I'm ordering a one-time vaginal exam on Melinda Curtis. Stat. I'll write the order on her chart."

"Dr. Novak, thank you for your confidence in me, even if it *is* only because of Dr. Duren."

"That's only one reason, Ms. Welles," he said, and when he said no more, she went out the door and down the hallway, turned at the nurses' desk, and went to Melinda's door.

Yes, Novak was thinking, I trust your judgment, little nurse, for several reasons. One reason was that she was still new enough to be alert, not set in her ways and not fallen into the well-worn path of what is *usual*. She could still conceive of the unusual. Second, she was smart. Third, not every new nurse will refuse to give a medication ordered by a doctor. Fourth, as a student she had probed into the death of one of Larry Tyree's patients, a man named . . . Proffer? No, Proctor. She hadn't exactly been an average student nurse in that respect.

He had first seen her name signed *Carol Welles, S.N.* beside Proctor's name on the medical-records checkout sheet when he had gone in to read the medical history on one of his own patients. He remembered her name because it had struck him as peculiar that a student nurse would be checking out a patient's chart.

Later that same evening at Abernathy's party, Coleson had gotten stinking drunk and had cornered him and told him about a CPR he had managed on a wealthy oil man named Proctor, a patient of Tyree's; of how Tyree had covered up his surgical blunder at autopsy, even in front of a group of student nurses. Novak knew that one of those nurses must have been Carol Welles.

At the hospital Christmas party, when he'd maneuvered Welles and Duren into dancing together, he

246

had overheard two words of their conversation only, *term paper,* spoken with emphasis and a scowl by Duren.

He had put two and two together, thought about it, and come up with a solution. Carol had probably done a term paper on Proctor's case, and her research into the case had angered Duren because it had involved a surgical error and cover-up and because he feared somebody might associate her with him. And maybe Duren had thought the association might jeopardize his residency. If so, he was an arrogant son of a bitch.

Lately, Novak had begun to question why he was so nosy about Duren and Welles. He kept telling himself it was because he was interested in knowing what made Duane Duren tick. Interest in a future associate. Hopefully.

But now he was beginning to wonder if that was the only reason.

Melinda Lynn Curtis
Hosp. No. 086420
Ward: Labor and Delivery
Age: 26

NURSES' NOTES

January 7, 1980
7:00—Contractions continuing @ rate of one q. 25 to 30 min. C/O mild abd. pain @ height of contractions. No back pain. No bloody show. V/S remain stable except for slight elevation of temp., 101. B/P 128/40, pulse 85, resp. 18, FHT 148. Abd. soft.
7:25—Bed bath given. Contractions appear to be increasing in intensity. Attempt to notify Dr. Simon unsuccessful.

7:45—Dr. Novak here. Orders.
7:55—Vag exam revealed cervix dilated two centimeters with blood-tinged discharge.
8:00—IV alcohol drip begun as per order by Dr. Novak.

C. Welles, R.N.

I know now for sure that these contractions are for real. Dr. Novak explained it to me. Dear Lord, help me.

John was in to see me while they started the alcohol, and I'm glad he's gone because I don't want him to see me cry. I'll try not to cry, but—

I'm so tired. Why am I tired? Dr. Simon told me the baby might be malformed because of all the medicine I've had. He promised that when I feel better they'll do a sonogram on me to try to see if the baby's O.K. that way. But who knows how he'll be mentally?

Here comes another one and the alcohol has been going for three minutes. And I'm beginning to feel so warm, like the blood in my veins is all heated up.

It's funny that me, a preacher's kid who's not ever had a drink of alcohol in my life—well, only once or twice on the sly maybe—ends up having to have some like this. Ho-oo-hum. I'm sleepy, but kind of floaty too.

It's not the only time I had alcohol. When I was twelve . . . no thirteen . . . my friend Priscilla gave me some wine. Yuk. And I snuck a sip of beer once at a party.

Ooops. Carol heard me giggle. She told me 'while ago to be still and rest. She's looking at me out of the corner of her eye while I wave.

"Hi."

"Try to rest, Melinda. Don't mind me. I've got to tidy up your room a bit," Carol said.

Tidy. It never occurred to me before how funny that word is. Tidy. "Tidy." *Carol heard me giggle again; and she's trying not to smile, but I can tell she's about to.* "Hidy tidy." *Oh, it hurts to laugh. I forgot.*

Woo-oo-oops. My silly hand feels so heavy and aimless and knocked the call bell off the bed. Call bell. I never hear it ring, but they call it a bell. Ringy-ding-ding. Ringy-ding-ding . . .

What was it Humphrey Bogart sang in that movie when he got drunk? "Rrrrrinky-dinky-dee-ee. Rrrrinky-dinky-die."

"Shh, Melinda."

"Ya know what? I think I'm drunk." *I'll take the call bell in my hand and swing it back and forth.* "Carol Welles? Ding-dong." *There it comes again, the swelling up. The alcohol's still going though. It's gotta stop this. Wow, is the baby ever kicking! Ooops. Now he's got the hiccups. I don't believe it. He's got the hiccups!*

Here comes Dr. Novak in the door. I'll wave.

"Hi."

"Hello, Melinda."

That glance at Carol. I know what he's thinking. He's thinking I'm drunk and I'm still having contractions. He's also thinking Carol knows me better'n anybody. If anybody knows what's going on with me it's Carol. She's taken care of me more'n anybody else.

"If I'd known how good I'd feel with alcohol I'da tried it years ago."

He's holding my hand. "Still having pains?"

"Not much, but lots of this bunching up. You know, blowing me up. My abdomen. See?"

"Twenty minutes apart, the last six," Carol tells him.

And steady. No, they call it regular. Regular. That's what we told our gym teacher in high school when we were having our period and didn't want to dress out for gym. Regular. When she called the roll we'd say

249

regular. Now regular means real labor. And I want it to stop. I don't want to lose my baby. My sweet baby. My—

Dr. Novak pats my hand and says, "I've contacted Dr. Simon, Melinda and he'll be in shortly. Don't cry."

"I can't help it. My baby. My sweet baby."

"I know this has got to be difficult, but try to relax and rest. It might help."

"I want my mom in here. Can I see my mother?"

"Any time you say."

"I want Mom now." Now I'm bawling out loud like a baby, but I don't care. Don't care at all. What a troublemaker I am! What a bother! What a *mess!* "Ha-aa—oh hum!"

"Sleepy?" Carol says as she stands beside me.

I nod. Their faces are swimming above me and I know the alcohol's making me drowsy—And a little nauseated. The baby's still hiccuping. And I'm getting more nauseated. *No. Please dear Lord don't let me vomit. They'll put the tube back in. Oh no.* "Vomit!"

Carol can read minds; she has the basin by my chin. . . .

Green. I ate broth and green Jell-O for breakfast. . . .

Room's swimming. Keep my eyes shut. Somebody's putting cold cloths on my head and neck.

"Fifty of Phenergan for nausea," Dr. Novak says, and he stays with me while Carol starts fiddling with a little wee bottle of medicine and a needle. *No, it's called a sy-ringe. But I've gotta keep my eyes shut. Sleepy . . .*

Melinda ceased to focus clearly on what was going on, but some of what those around her said penetrated the fog which enveloped her.

Mom: Anything for premature labor besides alcohol?

Novak: . . . Try a progesterone solution if this doesn't work.

Carol: Second vag exam, she's dilated three centimeters.

Mac: Dr. Simon just came in and saw where I had written her name on the scoreboard and "three centimeters" under "Dilation," and he was furious. Wrote "Bah" in big letters all across the scoreboard.

Dr. Simon: All right, you were right, Carol. She's three . . .

Novak: Progesterone . . .

Simon: . . . To come this far to lose . . . age of astronauts and we haven't come up with a medication to delay premature labor . . . Progesterone . . . it's our last hope. . . .

John: I love you, Melinda.

Mom: Hang in there, honey.

"Progesterone IV and Demerol for pain. Phenergan twenty-five for nausea," Dr. Simon was saying when she opened her eyes again. She watched him as he went out the door of the room.

Wow, what a headache.

Yuk! What an awful taste.

But the pains . . . they aren't as intense. They never were real pains, just a tightening of my abdomen and a slight ache in my back.

Melinda turned her head to see who was holding her hand. It was Mom, and she was smiling in spite of the worry line in the center of her forehead.

"Boy, did you ever go on a binge!" Mrs. Bass told Melinda.

Melinda shut her eyes and groaned. "This is the first time I've ever felt sorry for anybody with a hangover," she said slowly. "Why do people drink? It isn't worth it."

Her mom laughed.

Melinda opened her eyes again and saw Carol hanging a bag of IV solution. "What's in it now?"

251

Carol smiled. "Progesten, a progesterone solution. Remember what that is? We've been giving it to you for about eight hours now. They started it on the eleven-to-seven shift. You slept for almost twenty-four hours."

"What happened to the alcohol?"

"Well, it made you go to sleep; your contractions slowed down, but didn't stop. Dr. Simon came in and checked you, and you didn't even know it. That was yesterday. On the three-to-eleven shift, he ordered this progesterone solution, and it was started just eight hours ago."

"Has it worked?"

"Well . . ."

Melinda looked at her mother. "I can't remember what progesterone is, Mom."

Mrs. Bass scooted her chair closer to Melinda's bed. "I couldn't remember exactly all it does myself. Since I haven't worked for several years and haven't read about it, I've forgotten what-all it does do. I read up on it last night. Progesterone is a hormone, as you know, and it does a lot of things, but one thing it does is relax the uterine muscle. In fact, the placenta secretes it in large amounts to prevent premature contractions."

"My placenta's letting down on its job then," Melinda said feeling the slight tightening of her abdomen.

"It's not your placenta," Carol said. "Remember how it's formed? It's the baby's placenta. Anyhow, the progesterone IV has helped."

Melinda took a deep breath, let it out. She felt so tired. And depressed.

A one-in-ten chance of survival. The baby would never make it, she decided suddenly.

And neither would she.

"No fair, parking on the employees' parking lot!"

Carol shouted across the top of four cars.

"I lost my little plastic card that lets me into the doctors' parking lot. Please don't tell on me, Carol."

She laughed and unlocked her own car's door, her hair blowing across her face. When she pulled it away from her face, Basil Novak was striding toward her.

"Fine day for January," he said flinging his hand heavenward as he approached her.

"The wind's a bit cold, though."

"Ah, but the sun's warm." He came to stand beside her grinning. Both were feeling giddy because it had been a tense thirty hours. Melinda's labor had continued for at least that long, and now that the contractions were all but gone, the nurses in L&D and the doctors were relieved. Maybe that's why Basil Novak said in the next breath, "If your friend Bret won't pursue me and shoot me, would you care to join me for dinner?"

Carol looked around her and said, "Dinner! But it's only 3:30."

"Is there a rule that says people can't have dinner at 3:30? I haven't had lunch and only a cup of coffee and a doughnut for breakfast." He pointed at her, poking her shoulder with his finger. "And you didn't eat lunch either. I know. I sat at the nurses' station with Simon and Hamblin for an hour and a half during the lunch hour, and you never came out of Melinda's room."

He was right. Carol had been regulating and watching the progesterone drip, and watching and counting contractions. Anybody else who could relieve her for lunch would have had to scrub and change gowns afterward. Usually she could leave for thirty minutes, especially if Mrs. Bass or John was with Melinda. Today . . . well, she just couldn't. What if Melinda's membranes had ruptured or something? John was in the room, but . . . well, men . . .

"Come on. Take your pick: steak, pizza, fried chicken, lamb—"

She was remembering Shelly. "No, really. I have on my uniform and—"

Basil Novak, Dr. Whitehall's right-hand man, the resident who turned female heads and caused young student nurses to drive Toyotas off highway bridges, was not accustomed to being turned down.

"I'm rude. I'm sorry. Naturally you wouldn't feel comfortable in a restaurant with your uniform on. Forgive me. Hamburger?"

She shook her head and opened her car door. "Really. I've got things to do at home, Dr. Novak."

"In private, call me Basil."

She slid in behind her wheel. "We'll never be in private, Dr. Novak."

He held her door open, the wind blowing his blond hair straight up like tufts of winter grass. His eyes were the color of the blue, blue winter sky. He squinted up at that sky, grimaced, showed two rows of perfect white teeth. Yes, handsome, but . . . "You'd better take me up on the dinner invitation. The weather forecasters are predicting a cold front due in today with rain."

"What has that got to do with having dinner with you?"

He looked back at her and shrugged. "I don't know, but *some*thing must."

"Thanks for the invite," she told him. "See you . . . whenever."

He smiled at her and said simply, "Proctor."

Carol blinked.

"It shouldn't have happened," he said.

As she stared at him, feeling the blood drain from her face, he said, "It's one of the things I like about you, Carol. You've got guts, going to the autopsy. Investigating the . . . was it really a cover-up?"

254

She stared. "Duane told you."

"No, he did not."

"He did. He *had* to."

"Nope. Scout's honor," Basil said holding up his hand.

"So?"

"So."

Carol leaned her forehead on the steering wheel. So, did the doctors know she had investigated Proctor's death after all? Was Duane right after all? *Would* they link her with him and suspect her of spying on Dr. Tyree and the others for Duane? Horror engulfed her.

"Steak, mashed potatoes and gravy, tossed salad, a glass of wine," Novak said.

She raised her head up off the steering wheel. "How did you find out about Proctor if Duane didn't tell you?"

"Strawberry shortcake . . ."

She stared at him with a mixture of despair and curiosity.

He said, "Stimulating conversation . . ."

She pondered, sighed, and said, "Get in, I'll drive."

Novak skipped lightly around the back of the car and slid in on the passenger's side beside her. He was smiling hugely at her as she started the motor.

"This is blackmail, you know," she said sarcastically as she backed out of the parking slot.

"Of the crassest sort." He smiled as she stuck her little plastic card in the machine at the gate and the barrier raised. "Turn left," he said.

She pulled out of the parking lot. "Where is this place?"

"Irving's on Sixth and Ross. I'm also taking advantage of your good humor. With Melinda's present crisis alleviated, we hope, your spirits and mine are at an all-time high. Right?"

255

"They *were.*"

He smiled again at the road ahead. "Only a few years ago all we had for premature labor was alcohol. Now we have synthetic hormones and also a few uterine relaxants that nobody wants to use because of their serious cardiovascular effects. We've come a long way. The uterine relaxants we have now relax the uterus and kill the patient."

She nodded as she pulled up to a stoplight. "If the progesterone quits working, then what?"

"Simon says that's it. And he should know."

"I wish I were a secretary again."

"Naw. Not now that you've had a taste of nursing."

He was right, of course. Damn him. She was thinking that she liked him in spite of herself. He was easygoing; some people said he was brilliant, unaffected, treated the nurses . . . well, as if they were human. Like colleagues, almost. And if Duane hadn't told him about her investigation of Proctor's death, who had? Curiosity overwhelmed her.

"Who told you?"

"About what?"

"Proctor."

"Over dinner. Not now." He smiled again, broadly, at the road ahead and had the audacity to take her hand in his. She took it away and placed it back on the wheel.

"You hate me because of Shelly," he said.

"I don't hate you. I'm just not accustomed to holding hands with strangers."

He looked at her. "We've been together a total of two hours a day for six weeks."

"In a professional capacity."

"But not as strangers."

"Aren't we?"

"From your serious and adept professional manner, your nursing intuition, and your spontaneous sense of

256

humor, I know you better than you know yourself, Miss Carol Welles."

She glanced at him. "Bullcorn."

He raised his brows a little and tilted his head. "Bullcorn," he said thoughtfully. "I like it. It's much more melodious than bullshit."

She pulled into the parking lot of Irving's, cut the ignition, and looked at him. "What do you really want of me, Dr. Novak?" she asked.

He thought about that. "I don't really know. For the present, conversation. I want to know what makes you tick. I want to know what makes Duane Duren tick. I want to know about your relationship with Duren. I want—"

"My relationship with Duane is not any of your business." She started up the car again and said, "I think I'll drive you back to the hospital before—"

"Proctor." He sighed.

She hesitated a moment and cut the motor again.

FOURTEEN

"Dr. Novak, please tell me that Dr. Coleson doesn't know that I know—or that Duane knows."

He flicked on his lighter and, from across the table, lit her trembling cigarette, then his pipe. After about six quick puffs on the pipe, he snapped the lighter shut and said, "You let the cat out of the bag on the parking lot awhile ago. Now I know Duane knows. I didn't know for sure that he knew until then."

"Dr. Benson, the resident pathologist, knows then."

"I don't know about that." Novak laughed. "This could get confusing, all this knowing. Let me put you at ease right away. Coleson got stoned at a party and told me about Proctor's CPR and autopsy. Earlier that day I had noticed the name, *'Carol Welles, S.N.'* where you'd signed out Proctor's chart in medical records."

Carol groaned and spread her hand over her face.

"Don't fret," Basil said reaching across the table to take her hand from her face. "As far as I know the only one who knows you went to medical records to read Proctor's chart is me. And I guess Duren?"

She nodded and withdrew her hand from his. "I did

258

my term paper on the case, but nobody knew except my instructor. And Duane."

Basil leaned back in his chair and looked around him. Irving's Steak House was located two blocks from the hospital and was a neat, well-run restaurant that advertised in the newspapers and on a garish marquee out front as having "the best chicken-fried steak in town."

A good chicken-fried steak was hard to find in the city because most restaurants fried the steaks the old western way, the way they'd been fried for a hundred years or more. They fried it until it was as dry and juiceless as a cow chip in July; they fried it until they decided it was burned up, then they fried it another five minutes on both sides. After that they smothered it with wallpaper paste which they referred to as cream gravy. Irving's didn't fry their steaks as long and you could actually cut them with a dinner knife instead of having to use a saw.

This small quiet restaurant was where all the interns and residents came to eat, if and when they got the chance. He nodded to a couple of them across the room sitting at the same kind of table he and Carol were. The little round tables with colorful cloths, which some perceptive soul had recognized as "batik," were scattered around like wet disks of watercolors in a painter's box. The cloths had Indianish patterns on them, not woven into the cloth, or painted on, but dyed into it. He didn't understand the process involved, but it was striking and gave the place a bright, south-western flavor. The artwork on the tops of the tables was protected with glass cut the same size as the table tops. The room was semidark at the moment, now that clouds were billowing in from the north. Ten minutes ago there hadn't been a cloud in the sky, which goes to show you that whoever had said, "If you don't like

Texas weather, just hang around for a while, it'll change," had hung around here for a while. Somebody had turned on the dim lights in the room. The longhorn steer horns over the small, dark bar, located on one side of the room, were still crooked, he noticed.

Basil puffed on his pipe, a nasty habit that would probably send him to an early grave, but it helped him think. "Duren interested in your paper?"

She was fumbling with her cigarette like an amateur smoker. By God, she *was* an amateur smoker. He watched as she took a drag without inhaling and almost choked, her beautiful eyes watering a little. "Oh, he was interested all right."

"Helpful?"

She didn't answer, so he decided that what he had guessed earlier was true; that they'd quarreled over her term paper because Duren was afraid somebody would find out about her delving into Proctor's case, would link her with him and—

Well, he wasn't interested in whether Duren was an ambitious, self-centered bastard or not. That just made him normal for a surgeon. He was only interested in his brains and what skills he might learn.

"Let me get this straight," Carol said, already squashing out the cigarette. She stuck out her tongue enough to pick a piece of tobacco off it, and he found himself staring at her mouth and wondering if it was as soft as it looked. "As far as you know, Dr. Coleson doesn't know anybody knows about Dr. Tyree's cover-up except Dr. Benson, the pathologist."

"Correct. And me, though I don't think he will remember telling me about it. He did mention there were students present, but he discounted the fact that one of them might catch on to what was happening."

Leaning back in her chair, Carol shut her eyes, opening them only because the waitress set their steaming plates down in front of them. "Good," she said. "Now that I've found out all that, I can leave." With a lift of her chin, she pushed her chair away from the table.

"Shelly."

She paused, pondered, then scooted her chair up to the table again and spread the napkin in her lap. "Yes, Shelly," she said picking up her fork.

"Now, let's see. Who's more curious to know Shelly's story? Me or you?" He watched her take a sip of her wine and said, "The nurse on three-to-eleven in the emergency room told me at the Christmas party that Shelly came in D.O.A. on graduation night. I asked her about it when you told me."

Carol nodded grimly.

"Tell me, Carol, what has that got to do with me?"

She cut her steak studiously, not looking at him lest he see the distrust in her expression. "You don't know?"

"No."

She looked up slowly and searched his face. It was a smooth face with a hint of a beard just beginning to grow, because it was getting late in the day and he must have shaved early. It wouldn't be a dark beard, but light like his hair, like the dark blond hair on the back of his surgeonlike hands, like his thick brows and too-long-for-a-man lashes. His eyes looked straight into her own unabashedly—lying? Or telling the truth?

"Shelly didn't keep it a secret that she was in love with you. Everybody in nursing school knew about her ileostomy, and several of us knew that you assisted Dr. Whitehall with her surgery. She also told us about your visiting her hospital room often after the surgery." Carol paused, watched his expression. "Did you?"

"Yes."

"Why?"

He opened his mouth to say something, closed it, said, "I was proud because it was my first ileostomy. I didn't assist, I *did* the surgery. Whitehall assisted."

Carol nodded. "O.K. We knew Shelly telephoned you often, sent you gifts."

Novak put his fork down. "Yes."

"And you accepted them."

"Yes."

"You gave her a bracelet?"

His eyebrows shot up. "Yes."

"That's getting kind of personal with a mere former patient, isn't it?"

Novak looked angry for a second, then smiled. "I've been admiring your audacity for investigating a surgical error and cover-up, and now *I'm* the defendant and don't like it."

Carol blinked, not having realized she was third-degreeing Basil, when his love affair—if that was what it had been—with Shelly wasn't even any of her business. Why was she so dead-set on finding out if Shelly's love affair with Basil Novak had been real or imagined? She looked away, out a nearby window at the clouds scudding by in a slowly lowering sky, a sky now the color of the wash water in which you've washed a brand-new pair of blue jeans. Because she *wanted* Shelly's affair to be in Shelly's fantasy only. Because she *wanted* to like Basil Novak.

"My turn," Basil said steadily.

She looked back at him, glad to see that he wasn't angry.

"Did Shelly think we had an affair going?"

"Yes. *Did* you have an affair going with Shelly?"

"Not from my vantage point I didn't."

"She thought so."

"About graduation night—"

"She felt—no, she was *certain* that if you attended

262

her commencement exercises, you loved her. You didn't attend. Shelly didn't show up at the party afterward. I happened to go with a graduate nurse friend of mine to ER that night. That's why I was there when they brought Shelly in D.O.A."

Basil winced, searched her face. "God, Carol. And you think—"

"She drove her Toyota off a highway bridge. I think it was suicide."

Basil looked pained, and he had lost his appetite for the dinner. "No wonder you distrust me." He pushed his plate away and leaned back in his chair. He suddenly looked very young, and very vulnerable. He studied the chandelier above their table, a five-armed, copper ring with five electric candelabra covered with amber globes.

"Did you have sex once with Shelly?"

He took his eyes from the chandelier slowly to look at her. "I did nothing . . . to give Shelly the impression that I was in love with her."

Carol was horrified again at her own—what did he call it, audacity?—in persisting with the questioning of this man. *But she had to know.* "Didn't you?"

"My turn," he said and his face looked haggard and no longer very friendly. "Did you have sex with Duren?" he asked more out of self-defense than of curiosity.

She did not flinch. "Yes."

His eyes moved from her eyes to her lips, up to her hair and to her eyes again. "And love?"

She stood up slowly. "Tune in tomorrow, same time, same channel for another episode of 'As the Worm Turns,'" she said dropping her napkin onto her plate, and then amazed him when she strode across the room and out the door leaving him alone, to walk to the hospital parking lot in a gently falling rain.

"Do you . . . uh . . . do this every time you sit down to eat?"

Duren had bitten into a soda cracker, and his eyes looked up from the pages of the *Southwest Medical Journal* without his having to lift his head. He finished munching the bite of cracker and answered, "Not every time."

Novak nodded. "That's nice."

"Am I annoying you? If I am, I'll stop."

"Oh no. No, I just wondered. We've had lunch together twice and both times you've read through it. This is the third time in two days we've eaten together, and if I'm not mistaken, this is the third journal."

Duane turned the journal upside down, pages open, and continued to eat his Irving's homemade chili with beans. "It's just that I'm always reading something somewhere . . . And besides, eating's a waste of time."

"Yes. I remember when I was in my first year of residency. Sleeping was a waste of time too. And I'm like you in that I'm always reading something somewhere, because I'm always reading—and seldom remember where I read a particular something. Right?"

Duane said, "Exactly." He smiled one of his rare smiles and Novak liked him a little better for it.

Their relationship was one of those rare ones in which they each were attracted to the other on a friendly and professional basis, but attracted as impersonally, as coldly, as two magnets. Normally the chief resident of a certain division remains aloof from his junior residents for many reasons, the first being that he doesn't wish to show favoritism or be accused of showing favoritism. Another has to do with a bit of intellectual snobbery. But Basil Novak showed favoritism to Duane Duren because he couldn't help it. He did not, could not, exactly figure out why Duane was as receptive as he was to his friendship, since he was so aloof with everybody else. Ambition? Maybe. But also Duren and he were the only two he knew of who could fall into a conversation as naturally as brothers. During Duren's rotation through surgery, they had gotten acquainted, and although Duren was rotating through the dreaded and hated outpatient clinic now, they kept running into each other, having coffee, and snatching a little time together for lunch.

At the moment, Duren was hiding from the chief resident in charge of the clinic because he'd been on duty ten hours without a break, doing vaginal exams on poor females: blacks, Chicanos, poor whites; checking for all the finer things in life like gonorrhea, syphilis, pelvic inflammatory disease, herpes, and unwanted or unexpected pregnancies; taking pap smears and cultures for all kinds of pleasant lab tests. Sooner or later every resident had to rotate through the clinic, and Duren had unhappily gotten stuck mostly with the GYN patients. The first two days of it, eight to ten hours at a stretch, he couldn't eat. But after several hundred pap smears, he'd gotten accustomed to it. You had to, to survive.

Basil was hiding, too, from everybody. He'd been on call for sixteen hours and felt bonged. Duren looked bonged too. Basil wasn't sure, but he thought the ladies in the booth across from them were casting wry glances their way thinking that they were both drunk. They looked it. They were drunk on work and pressure and hassle and what Duren had aptly called "birdshit." In laymen's language birdshit meant busy work—Doing nothing of much importance, not even anything important enough to qualify as being bullshit, or as Carol had said yesterday, bullcorn. *Which reminds me . . .*

"Proctor."

From his bowl of chili Duren raised his washed-out brown eyes that were sunken with fatigue; he would have blinked if his lids weren't so heavy. "Beg your pardon?"

"I know about Proctor," Basil said.

Duren blinked. "Proctor who?"

Either he'd guessed wrong or Duren had forgotten the name of the patient whose case Carol had studied for her term paper. Basil stirred his coffee slowly and decided on another approach. The day he had given the briefing on peritonitis to the nurses in L&D, he had noticed the little nurse sitting there listening intently to everybody who spoke. Something about her had looked familiar. When she was about to leave, through the door where he'd stationed himself out of curiosity, he had mentioned to her that she looked familiar. She had reminded him that she had tied his gown in surgery when she was a student nurse, and he couldn't remember that for a moment. Then he remembered those eyes, those green eyes with amber flecks—or sometimes, they were amber eyes with green flecks— and when she had told him her name, he still couldn't remember. Later, going back to surgery, he remembered. Carol Welles, of course! The one who had signed out the records on Coleson's CPR, Tyree's skeleton in the closet! He knew he had seen her face before; actually it had been only her eyes. And who could forget a face like hers? It was an all-American-girl face. While he was having these revelations about who she was, he got to wondering why a student nurse would sign out a dead patient's chart. Was Proctor her patient? Probably she was going to do a study on his case. If so, she was bound to see the progression of errors in medical and nursing management that had led to his death.

Now he said, "Proctor was the patient who had a

TUR over a year ago; Tyree was the urologist; Proctor went into cardiac arrest. There was an autopsy—"

Duren choked on his chili—choked and coughed and covered his mouth with his napkin. When he recovered, his face had gone yellow.

"Relax, Duren, nobody knows Carol Welles did a study on the case but me."

Duren's face went white, and his eyes went black. "Carol," he said gritting his teeth.

"No. I just happened to see her name in medical records, and Coleson, the one who attended the CPR, told me the story. Nobody knows about Carol's case study but the three of us."

Duane laid his spoon down on the table and leaned slowly toward Novak. "Why are you bringing this up?"

"Trying to find out why you two hate each other. Supposedly. I think I know now."

Duren studied him. "She chose a term paper over me."

"She shouldn't have had to make a choice."

"She was prying into a case that was—that was—"

"Questionable. And interesting."

"She had no business—"

"I'm not taking sides, Duren. Merely—"

"Why should you care at all?"

"You know that I've decided to get into cardio-vascular surgery."

Duren nodded.

"This morning Greenburg invited me to become his associate when my residency is finished here."

Duren's eyes widened. "My God," he breathed. "That's—that's—"

"An honor. And a dream come true. But anyway, after a year or two as his associate, I'll want to go it on my own."

"Greenburg will like that," Duren said sarcastically.

"Greenburg will be old enough to retire. When that happens I want to pick an associate of my own. And I want to train a really sharp nurse as an assistant, for office, rounds, and surgery. Also, I want my own crackerjack anesthesiologist—"

Duren was smiling. "Like the big-shot cardio-vascular men. You really *are* ambitious."

"The big cardiovascular men have whole teams working with them. Hand-picked, and specially trained."

"You seem to be thinking ahead," Duren said, half-mockingly.

"This is my last year. Since I've been working mostly with Greenburg lately in cardiovascular surgery, I'm certain this is what I want to do. But not coronary bypasses. Those will be obsolete soon as you know if you've been reading up on such things."

"I have."

"We'll be working with proton beams soon and balloons, artificial hearts. Read where some doctor in Idaho's experimenting with plastic hearts? Any day now he or someone else will transplant one into a live patient. And not only that—"

Duren smiled again, for the third time all evening, a real record for him. "You sound like a kid just before Christmas." But his smile ceased. "Let's get back to Carol and why my relationship with her should interest you."

"Carol's the nurse I want to assist me."

Duane laughed then. "You really *are* thinking ahead. But why Carol?"

"She's new enough not to be set in her ways, young enough to train, not hampered by marriage or the threat of being pregnant. She's sharp, has the curiosity and persistence it takes to venture into new fields of medical research." Novak leaned back in his chair and

268

said, "Besides, she's pretty."

Duren's eyes flashed from the overhead chandelier's light. "And stubborn. And mule-headed."

"And sexy."

Duren looked at him. "What the hell does that have to do with qualifying as an assistant on your surgical team?"

Novak shrugged and the carrot stick snapped as he bit into it. "Nothing. But it's another plus." And munching amusedly, he watched Duren's face go from subtle shades of fucshia to a gentle carnation pink.

So. He is in love with her after all. Right now he would just as soon smash my face with his fist as look at me. Which tells me all I want to know. She loves him too. I saw that yesterday. He loves her, she loves him. Which means Carol should be eliminated from my search for assistants. Can't have them working together. Duren thinks I'm just having pipe dreams about the surgical team. He'll find out in time that I'm dead serious and that I have a habit of thinking ahead. Way ahead. Like Pop always did with the stock market. And Pop made a small fortune on the stock market alone. I don't want to make a fortune, necessarily. I want to make history. And the time to lay the groundwork for that is now.

Which puts me in a quandary. I doubt that I can have Carol as an assistant. Personalities in teams like this have to be at least compatible. And I can't think about her on a personal basis either. They wouldn't be able to work together, and I'd sure as Hades alienate Duren if I tried to date her. Forget Carol altogether then?

It was too late for that. She kept intruding on his thoughts—pleasantly. He kept catching himself smiling when he remembered her trying to learn to smoke a cigarette; her wide, little girl's eyes; her hair blowing in the wind or swept up into a chignon at the

269

back of her head; her female form hidden, almost but not quite, in the baggy scrub dress, bending over Melinda Curtis. *Fetal heart tones good, Dr. Novak. Bowel sounds good. She's (blush) passing flatus now.*

She hadn't been assigned to Melinda Curtis this morning, but when he had gone into L&D on rounds, she had hurried from another room and approached him in the hallway. "Dr. Novak?"

He couldn't be angry with her even if only yesterday she had left him at the restaurant with his dinner half-eaten and hers barely touched and by the time he'd summoned the waitress for the bill and had paid it, she had driven off.

"I think we danced to something called 'Raindrops Keep Falling on My Head' once, Carol. I missed you when rain was falling on it again yesterday."

"I'm sorry about that," she told him impatiently, as if it were something of less importance than stepping on his toe. "But I need to ask you something about Melinda." She glanced around, took him by the arm, and sort of led him into the coffee room.

"Is this to make up for yesterday?" he asked, pretending to be hopeful for something unprofessionally related.

"She's in labor," Carol blurted wide-eyed. And then she broke down and, covering her face, began to cry.

Amazed, Basil watched her silently a moment and couldn't think of anything to say. He who had won seven trophies in debate at U.T. He just stared at her.

Sniffing, she took a Kleenex from her pocket and wiped her eyes and nose. "I'm sorry. It's just that—that she's been through so much." She smiled then. "But you know that. Why I cornered you—Dr. Simon is a good obstetrician, but younger doctors are more up on the latest meds. Isn't there—*God,* isn't there anything else we can try to stop her labor before it's too late?"

270

He was still staring. "Carol, Simon is up on the latest."

"But alcohol and progesterone—" She threw up her hands. "I'm sorry. Of course he's done everything. And I'm behaving very unprofessionally. She's dilated three centimeters according to Robbie. Her contractions are fifteen minutes apart. We're trying isoxsuprine now, but to give enough of it to relax the uterus, you risk causing cardiac arrhythmias, which have just started happening. She's having sudden very fast pulse rates, which slow to normal; then speed up again and become too rapid to count, Robbie says. She's frantic. Robbie, I mean, and we've got six—*six* patients in labor."

"P.A.T."

She frowned. "I beg your pardon?"

"Her sudden rapid pulse is called paroxysmal atrial tachycardia, or P.A.T. for short. It's not lethal, but it isn't good either."

"Dr. Hamblin and Simon just gave Robbie an order to discontinue the alcohol and ordered progesterone again." Carol wrung her hands. "But it won't do any good. Everybody knows it won't do any good." She smiled quickly glancing up at him. "I don't know *why* I thought you could think of something. Maybe because I haven't a great deal of faith in older doctors."

"Simon can't be over fifty."

"But you new men are more up-to-date."

"Not on every specialty. Are you up-to-date on the latest cardiac meds, for instance?"

She thought about that. "No, of course not. I'm just—"

"Grabbing for straws. And I never saw you behave in such a human way before."

Then, for some moments—no longer than a minute—they stood looking at each other. Something clicked or zapped, engulfing them both until neither of them was

271

certain where they were. They could have been in the Garden of Eden or on a hill on a starlit night. He wanted to take her in his arms. He could hear the organ music in the background even now. But the spell shattered like glass when a woman's high-pitched shriek brought them to their senses.

Her eyes widened. "Mrs. Shriemsher! Peusy's patient," she whispered, and disappeared from the coffee room in flash.

Basil had stood there confused—by her confidence in him, her emotional outburst, his feelings for her, and the mood they had just shared. Finally he came to himself completely and puzzled aloud, "Peusy?" and left the coffee room thinking, Poor man.

Carol's excitement had stimulated his own and had caused him to start trying to remember something he'd heard recently—strictly gossip, he thought—something that hadn't interested him much at the time he had heard it, but he couldn't quite bring it to mind. Deep in thought and a little confused, he went in to see Melinda.

Physically, she was improving. Last cultures of the drains showed no pathogenic organisms, and so, using his own discretion, he removed them. She was taking fluids, though dozing most of the time because of the morphine. But she was in labor, and by the time he left her room that morning, he was as sick about it as the rest of them.

That afternoon, the girl was still in labor, although it wasn't progressing. A few minutes after his afternoon rounds, he met Duren in the corridor of Jenson, and Duren asked about Melinda Curtis. Basil was still agitated at the time because of Carol's distress and said, "Well, remember I told you she was in labor. They've tried alcohol and progesterone and isoxsuprine, and none of it's working."

The pupils of Duren's eyes dilated, and his mind seemed suddenly far away as if he, too, were trying to remember something, something he'd read or heard that really hadn't interested him at the time he'd heard it.

"Duren, have you read or heard of anything—something about any new drug or—"

Duren had read his mind. That's why they were compatible; they *thought* alike.

"I don't know. It seems—"

"Look. Will you be able to get away for dinner?"

"No. But I *will,*" Duren had said with a wry smile.

They had agreed to meet at Markson's outside door as close to six o'clock as possible, and when Duren came striding down the corridor to meet him at 6:10, he was carrying a medical journal.

"Basil?"

Novak looked up at him now. Duane was finishing his coffee, his hand spread out on the pages of the medical journal which he had commenced to read while Basil had been daydreaming and thinking back over the day.

Duren set his coffee cup down with a clatter and grabbed the journal in both hands. "Listen to this," he demanded excitedly. "'. . . The doctors at Pacifant are excited about a new drug which they refer to as RH, which may help to curb one of today's highest death rates, that of infants born before term. RH is being tested in carefully controlled and selected cases in hospitals located in three cities in the United States. It is a sympathomimetic drug which acts by stimulating beta-adrenergic receptors in uterine smooth muscle cells and relaxing uterine muscles more effectively than the IV alcohol infusions, hormones, and other sympathomimetic drugs being used today.'"

Basil jumped up and went around behind Duren to read over his shoulder.

Although the drug is still in the experimental stages, RH has already doubled the number of infants born at weights of more than five and a half pounds, who might otherwise have been born one, two, or three months prematurely.

"Waiter!" Basil called to the smiling young man who had made it clear, when he had brought them their chili, that he was attracted to Basil.

Pursing his mouth, the waiter came over. "Don't tell me. Your *beeper* went off," he said.

"Give me the check, please. And quick," Basil ordered.

Dressed in Irving's uniform, a long-sleeved white shirt with pearl buttons, a string tie, and black jeans a size too small, the waiter looked very slim.

"Well, you're not in the hospital now, Doctor, but I will obey your order."

Basil bent back to the article where Duren's finger was.

IV RH increases the heart rates of both mother and infant, but can be regulated to infuse at a rate high enough to provide the necessary amount of uterine relaxation, while controlling the tachycardia and cardiac arrhythmias that may occur.

"Thank you and do come back," said the waiter placing the bill on the table by Duren's hand.

Basil wasn't even aware that Duren was paying the entire bill; Duren wasn't either. They hurried out the door and into the lightly falling mist.

"But the drug's not on the market yet, Duren. It's still in its experimental stages."

"I know. If you could get the drug, every obstetrician in the country would have got his hands on it by now."

"There's no way. There's a pile of red tape you have to go through to qualify for experimenting with a new drug."

"I *knew* I had read or heard something about this, and after you mentioned it in the hall this afternoon, it got to bugging me. But it's impossible. Why are we getting so excited, Basil? We can't do anything about this. Besides, what can *we* do? What can anybody do? Steal the formula and try it on Melinda? We'd have the Food and Drug Administration on our—"

"I wonder how you qualify to use it for experimental purposes. You can't just ask for it out of the clear blue— Did the article say anything about when the drug might be available?"

"It says hopefully it will be approved in 1981."

"Is that a very recent article?"

"This month's and it was tucked away three pages from the back of the journal in the section called, 'Drugs' in a two-column layout as unobtrusive as a witch's tit. You could easily overlook it."

The sidewalk was slick, and they had trouble keeping their footing. A rare snow was falling, mixing with the cold mists as they ran across the street. Bennet loomed geometrically against an inky sky a block away, its square windows light yellow and warmly glowing.

"And anyway," Duren said, "you couldn't indiscriminately try a new drug—"

". . . On just any patient," Novak said.

"Pacifant is the only hospital the article mentioned where the experiments are being conducted, and that's on the West Coast."

"Simon should see this article."

"Even if he did we'd not be able to—"

"Of course not."

They hurried through the double doors of Markson, and both stopped abruptly in the corridor.

"What can we do, Basil?"

"I'm going to call Simon and read the article to him." He held out his hand.

Duren handed him the water-soaked journal. "I don't see what he can do."

"I don't either, but we've got to let him know about this."

Duane followed Novak into Markson's doctors' lounge. Novak prevailed upon the switchboard operator to dial Dr. Caleb Simon's home phone number. Simon himself answered. The telephone number he had given the hospital switchboard was the one for the telephone in his study. It was an unlisted number, so when it rang, it was either the hospital or a wrong number. "Dr. Simon," he answered.

Novak identified himself and told Simon that he and Dr. Duren had just read an article in the *Southwest Medical Journal* that he might be interested in. Simon was silent, so Basil read the article from beginning to end. When he was through, Simon was still silent. Then he said, "Hmmm." Was silent some more. "Interesting." And Basil could almost hear the wheels beginning to turn in Simon's head, his enthusiasm gaining momentum like a rusty old locomotive.

"Doctor, is there a chance in the world—" Basil began.

"It isn't that I'm not up on the latest research, Basil, you understand."

Basil just listened with his mouth open, ready to argue or agree or whatever it took.

"But I didn't catch that article. You understand I've heard that somebody has been experimenting with this drug for over a year. But I had more or less discounted it, thinking it was another drug like isoxsuprine when I heard that it could cause cardiac— But this sounds different. I—you'll never believe this, Basil, but . . .

did you know that I know the chief of the obstetrics department at Pacifant?"

Basil stammered as he looked at Duane, who was trying to read his expression. "You . . . actually *know* the chief of obstetrics at Pacifant?"

"Gib and I graduated from Southwestern the same year. We kept in touch for years, but I haven't heard from him in . . . And I don't know what I'd have to do to get the drug . . . I'll call and talk to Gibson. My God, I can't believe this. You, Basil, contact Whitehall and Hamblin. See if you can't get their asses up there by nine o'clock. Call Pascal, we'll need the administrator there . . . and the chairman of the board. Call Jackson, we'll need the chief of obstetrics there."

The locomotive was getting up a full head of steam now, and Simon was actually panting. "Tell them to drop everything. The little patient's in labor, and God only knows when she'll get down to business with it. All we're doing at the moment for her is keeping her labor from progressing. We haven't got any time to lose. By God, that article had better not be a farce! Gib'll know. With my luck, he'll be out of town, but even then I'll . . . Basil?"

"Yes."

"This is a gamble. But I'm counting on you to get these people together. Get Pascal to think about what kind of releases he'll need from the family in order for us to do this experiment. Now I've got to hang up. I'm calling California."

FIFTEEN

It was like herding five bulls into the same pen.

Jackson was out and wouldn't answer his beeper, but the three-to-eleven charge nurse in L&D had a number that Basil could call, which no one else had, and some breathless female answered and reluctantly put Jackson on the phone. Basil presented the case. Jackson didn't believe it. He never had heard of any such drug except some gossip off and on about several uterine relaxants being experimented with somewhere. Basil read him the article in the *Southwest Medical Journal*. Jackson thought about it and said that the board would never agree to the experiment and that a hospital had to have the approval of the FDA before they could legally use an experimental drug and anyway Melinda's labor would probably be too far along by then and ... But he showed up in the conference room at 9:15 wearing a thousand-dollar smooth leather suit he had received as a gift at Christmas time. The line creasing his forehead was from the pressure of a too-small motorcycle helmet.

Dr. Hamblin was out to dinner and his baby-sitter

was reluctant to give Duane the telephone number of the restaurant. Duane had agreed to help Basil make the calls, and he had no patience with anybody who wasn't gung ho to hear about the article. "It's Dr. Hamblin's night off," the baby-sitter said. She must have been an elderly lady from the sound of her voice. "I mean Dr. Michaelson, his associate, is taking his calls tonight."

"Listen here. This is an emergency. Dr. Michaelson has nothing to do with this, and if you don't give me the telephone number where I can reach Dr. Hamblin, I will personally come to his house and wait until he comes home."

The baby-sitter gave him the number. He called, and Hamblin listened to Duane's story and asked softly, "Why do you need me?"

"Dr. Hamblin, mainly because the new drug is in its experimental stages. It can cause cardiac arrhythmias."

"I see. Very well, I'll be there at nine o'clock."

Pascal, the administrator, was jubilant. "You're kidding! Tell me, Dr. Novak, do you think we have the slightest chance of getting our hands on that drug?"

"It's a possibility."

"What a coup that would be for Bennet! If the experiment is successful, it would be the best advertising Bennet's had since we acquired the new CAT scanner. Let *me* call the chairman of the board. He and I can set some fires under the board members' tails and we'll be there by nine!"

The doctors and board members straggled in from 8:45 to 9:45. Everybody had just begun to get bored when Simon appeared, and the haggling over pros and cons and plans went on until after midnight.

Then Dr. Simon presented the situation to Rev. Jay Bass, who was sitting in the L&D waiting room as always. The reverend, a middle-aged man with a full head of gray hair, looked at his feet. "You say it can cause cardiac arrhythmias? That means irregular heart beats, doesn't it?"

"Yes, but experiments so far indicate that the dosage of the drug can be regulated to eliminate the arrhythmias, which only occur in some patients, anyway. We will have a cardiac monitor installed in her room," Simon said.

"She'll be on a heart monitor?" the minister asked.

"Yes."

"Call California."

At 11:45 the next morning the new uterine relaxant drug, accompanied by one of its most enthusiastic researchers, was flown by Pan Am 727 jet to the city's airport and was met by a helicopter ambulance and crew, generously loaned by Methodist Hospitals Incorporated, to pick up the meds and the nervous young doctor from California named Valasco, and fly them to Bennet Memorial.

Melinda was heavily sedated, but she had had her bed bath and her bed had been made by the time Drs. Simon, Hamblin, and Jackson, followed by the short, egg-shaped and beaming hospital administrator, came striding into L&D. Behind the administrator, the hospital's diminutive head pharmacist came carrying a plastic basket containing a half-dozen small vials which he solemnly presented to Mac at the nurses' station as exhibit number one in the trial to come.

Everybody in L&D, and no telling who else, knew there'd been some shortcuts made in the red tape, which was usually involved when experimental drugs were used in a private hospital on private patients— some arm-twistings maybe, and some bribery or blackmail even—but nobody knew exactly what or where and didn't care. The pharmacist handed Mac the print-out Valasco had given him; it showed the recommended dosages, plus the interactions and side effects that could be expected from administering the drug.

For five minutes Simon and Jackson debated about who should begin the administration of the drug. Dr. Valasco oversaw Mac's mixing of the solution at the counter behind the nurses' station and then the three doctors, the administrator, and Mac filed into Melinda Curtis' room. The pharmacist slipped in, too, hoping nobody would notice and make him leave. The isolation procedures, the gowning and gloving, had been discontinued five days ago.

Carol looked up. She was framed by the window; through its opened Venetian blind a blinding winter sun slanted in. She wore a green, baggy surgical scrub dress as usual; her reddish blond hair, gold in the sun, was smoothed up into a neat chignon at the back of her head. She was holding a fetoscope, and when the others came crowding into the room, she smiled. They were here. The medication had arrived! Thank God. Maybe this time something would work.

Melinda was sleeping. She opened her eyes and listened as Dr. Simon told her that they had obtained the new drug and asked her if she remembered that she had signed a release for the drug to be given to her last night? Simon was nervous but excited. He hadn't slept all night, couldn't eat breakfast, couldn't even get a cup of coffee down. This had to work after all the bluster, blather, and blab. It had better. Gilda wouldn't be able to face the other doctors' wives if it failed, she said. Most important, he didn't want to disappoint Melinda again. His stomach rumbled loudly, and he cleared his throat and shuffled his feet to cover up the noise.

Let's see. Mr. Curtis had also signed the release. He, Bascum Pascal, had seen to that personally because you certainly couldn't have the hospital sued if

281

something went wrong. All bases covered? Yes. Too bad they couldn't let the newspapers in on this yet. But eventually . . .

Dr. Valasco studied the vital-sign sheet. All seemed to be in order. The lovely young thing who was Mrs. Curtis' nurse, had just taken her vital signs, according to the sheet on the table—he checked his pocket watch—five minutes ago. Very well. She had also done a vaginal exam five minutes ago, according to her records, and the patient's cervix was dilated—*tsk-tsk*—three centimeters. Contractions were ten minutes apart and weak. But according to the electrohysterograph and fetal cardiograph monitor which was now operating, and which had been attached at 9:30 A.M., according to the nurse's record, the patient was definitely in labor. Vital signs were normal, FHTs one hundred thirty-eight, and . . . a glance at the monitor readout showed that they were steady. Excellent. He was ready.

Dr. Hamblin turned on the cardiac monitor temporarily installed on a bracket above Melinda's bed. He decided to use Lead II, simpler for the nurses since all they were doing was checking for arrhythmias. He attached the leads with their adhesive disks to Melinda's chest while the nurse held up the top sheet to shield the girl's breasts from the eyes of others in the room. Now. All eyes went to the oscilloscope on the cardiac monitor. The electronic blip which represented the electrical activity of Melinda's heart was bobbing happily and normally. It was a pleasure to watch. He hoped, and prayed, that it remained just this stable.

Dr. Jackson looked at the vital-sign record sheet. He didn't know how the hell to read the cardiac monitor, but he trusted Hamblin's judgment that Melinda's heart was O.K. He'd suggested the tests that Simon should order on the girl before the experiment could get under way and Simon had complied; earlier that morning, he'd ordered an EKG, a portable chest x-ray, CBC, liver function tests, and urinalysis to make sure Melinda was in the best possible condition. This had seemed to please the weirdo from California who was keeping meticulous records of everything that went on. Jackson wondered if Valasco's continual jotting of notations was because he thought they were hick Texans who didn't know what they were doing. Well, they'd show him. If California doctors could pull this experiment off successfully, Texas doctors could sure as hell pull it off. If the truth were known, the drug had probably actually been discovered at the University of Texas or at Texas A&M, or at the University of Houston. . . .

Milvern Norris stood as close to the back wall as possible, but he could see all of it. The entire scene. He'd write a book about this someday. He'd begin where the doctors had stridden decisively into the hospital pharmacy that morning and announced that a new drug was being flown in from California, an experimental drug, and that he had been chosen to meet the helicopter when it was scheduled to land on the visitors' parking lot at 12:30 A.M. Along with Drs. Simon and Jackson—and Mr. Pascal.

RH. Well, he had read a little about that one, though it was only a small article that was just published in the *AMA*—no, it was the *Southwest Medical Journal,* just this month, and he was able to speak knowledgeably about it when they came in. He was certain that the obstetricians and the administrator were impressed with his being up-to-date on new drugs, even new ones not yet approved by the AMA and the FDA. If he wrote a book about this, he might even win the Pulitzer Prize or the Book-of-the-Year award or something. He'd always made A's in English composition.

*   *   *

The patient lay exhausted in the throes of lassitude. A beautiful young nurse with furrowed brow stood beside her with steady hand on the patient's grossly protruding abdomen. The golden sunlight streaming through the window cast an ethereal glow within the room causing an aura of unreality to pervade the somber silence. The knowing clock on the wall showed 1:15 P.M. boldly.

The moment was tense. The doctors stood soberly regarding the patient with perspiring brows. Time was growing short. It was their last hope, their only hope.

I stood calmly with, perhaps, a smug smile on my relaxed face. For only I knew that the drug would be successful. Only I possessed the knowledge—that inner knowledge gained by years of experience in dealing with the chemical components and in vivo effects of drugs upon the imperfect mortal bodies of mankind. . . .

Yes, he'd remember this scene forever. Maybe if the experiment was successful, he could tell his grandchildren about it someday. If he ever had any. If he ever had any children. If he ever got married.

Whitehall was just in time. He couldn't really expect the obstetricians to wait until he had finished the operation before they began their little experiment. The room was full of people already. You'd think they were performing an artificial-liver transplant or something. He'd left Basil Novak to close the surgical incision on . . . whatever the hell his name was, so that he could witness the beginning of this experiment on . . . Lucinda. Well, this was Simon's show, so he'd just . . . back against the wall. . . .

"Ouch."

284

"Sorry."

"Quite all right, Dr. Whitehall."

They ought not to allow ancillary personnel in the room anyway.

Simon said, "Mac, you mixed the medication; you can have the honor of starting it."

Mac raised her brows. "Me?" She'd brought in new IV tubing with the IV solution and while the doctors had stood around, had replaced the tubing and checked the IV infusion site in Melinda's poor little hand. It looked fine. All she had to do now was cut off the D5W and open the stopcock to the 500 cc D5W with RH.

"Yes, you," Simon said smiling.

O.K. Fine. Mac glanced at the clock, closed the stopcock on the plain D5W, and opened the stopcock that would let the solution containing the new uterine relaxant into the IV tubing.

Carol meantime was timing Melinda's contractions. "Here's hoping," she said to her softly.

Melinda smiled sleepily and held up her crossed fingers. "Pray for me—us . . . . Knock on wood, cross your fingers, genuflect, and count your beads—whatever it takes."

"Maybe it takes a little of all of it." Carol glanced at her watch and looked at Dr. Simon. "This contraction was only nine minutes from the last one."

Dr. Simon turned to his colleagues, then to Valasco. "You say the effects are instantaneous?" as if to reassure himself.

"Instantaneous or within ten minutes at the very most," Valasco said with pen poised above his pad.

Melinda did not experience another contraction, and the electronic blip remained normal on the cardiac monitor.

* * *

The doctors left the room together twenty minutes after the infusion began. The cafeteria would be almost vacant; they could get a cup of coffee and a snack and everybody but Whitehall needed one. Nobody had eaten lunch. Besides, the cafeteria was the best place to let their success be known—in a subtle way. The cafeteria not only sustained and nourished doctors, nurses, hospital personnel, and visitors; it also nourished the hospital grapevine.

As for Carol, she would go off duty soon and she had a long list of doctors' orders to carry out, as would all the nurses caring for Melinda on all shifts.

The initial dosage given as drops-per-minute via the IV had been suggested by Dr. Valasco and seemed adequate for Melinda's case. Now Carol must monitor vital signs and FHTs every ten minutes. On the three-to-eleven shift, beginning at five o'clock, the vitals could be spaced out to every twenty minutes. At midnight, vitals could be taken every hour, provided they were stable.

The nurses would have several side effects to watch for: restlessness, nausea, rapid pulse, headache, skin rash. But these effects were no more apt to occur than they would be with most other medications. At four o'clock, if her heart rate remained stable, the cardiac monitor would be discontinued.

At 3:15, Carol left the hospital feeling light-hearted and gay; she greeted the security guard at the door cheerfully and skipped across the street toward the parking lot, taking a deep breath of the cold, clear air. The sun was still bright, the sky aqua blue. Somewhere an impatient mockingbird thought it was spring and was declaring his territorial rights in a plagiarized medley of popular bird songs. Nurses, in white, were weaving among the cars, each looking for her or his own. Carol, too, couldn't remember where she'd parked hers. She stopped beside a blue station wagon, and her eyes panned the parking lot until she saw Basil Novak's tall form beside her car. She smiled and hurried to him. He watched her until she came and stopped in front of him.

"Hi," she said squinting up at him. "Don't tell me you lost your little plastic card again."

"Never again. Your parking lot costs twenty-five cents. I could almost buy a cup of coffee for that." He grinned. "I heard the news. RH worked."

"Yes."

"And I'll bet you a chicken-fried-steak dinner that it will continue to work."

"I think so. There was a question as to whether she was dilated too much before we began the infusion. If a patient's cervix is dilated three or four, it could be too late for the medication to help. In her case . . ." She shrugged. "She was lucky. On many counts. I've gained new respect for Dr. Simon. He found out somehow about RH and had the guts to get the ball rolling on this."

"Yes. Simon's a good obstetrician."

They stood silently for a moment before Novak added, "You should know that Duane Duren was the one who found the article and brought it to Simon's attention."

She felt her spirits plummet unexpectedly. "No. I didn't know." She shook her head. "I might have known. Everything always goes back to him, it seems."

"What about you?"

She was unlocking her car door and opened it. "I haven't been invited back. And if I had been . . ."

He held the door open again and watched her slide in under the steering wheel. "If he wanted to come back to you?"

She squinted ahead through the windshield over the

287

hood of her car toward the doctors' parking lot. "No." She shook her head. "No, I couldn't let him. Not without his apologizing for the things he said to me—and Duane will never apologize to anyone for anything."

Novak shut her door, having rolled down her car window for her. "And love?"

"I think this is where we left off day before yesterday."

"I missed yesterday's episode. What happened?"

"I don't know. I missed it too."

"Shall we see what happens today, same time, same channel?"

She shook her head, smiling, and started her car. "No, because I never found out what I wanted to know about you and Shelly."

"Which means you never found out for sure whether I'm a rogue or not." When she smiled at him, he said, "That was supposed to be revealed in yesterday's episode."

"Then we'll never know, will we?" She smiled, put the car in reverse, and backed slowly out of the parking slot.

He stood watching as she waved and drove away.

"Carol, you have the honor," Mac said cheerfully. "You cared for Melinda more than anybody on any shift except maybe Hank on three-to-eleven, so you get to go with her when she has her sonograph."

Carol leaned against the wall behind the nurses' station and grinned. "Super. I've never seen one done before."

Mac handed her the requisition slip. Then with a gleam of mischief in her eye and a flourish of her hand, she presented Carol with a transfer slip. "We're going to do it all in one trip. She goes for her sonograph, then we'll transfer her from there to the post-partum floor."

Carol clapped her hands. "She's graduated!" It had been four days since they had first begun the infusion of RH and Melinda had never had another uterine contraction.

"Dr. Simon was in while you were setting up the delivery room and said that Melinda would remain on the post-partum floor about three or four weeks before she can be discharged for home."

"But why so long?"

"They'll be running the RH drip for no telling how long. Then they'll maintain her on oral RH for a while. Then they'll take her off the RH altogether and hope the baby hangs in there. If she starts labor once she's off RH, she'll go back on it again. Dr. Simon says she'll remain on the post-partum floor for however long it takes. If it's four weeks, she'll be only one month away from her due date. Then if all is well, she can go home, but she'll be on complete bed rest. Someday, when RH is approved and is on the market for everybody's use, a patient can take it at home, under a doctor's care. But for now, c'mon. I'll help you get her onto the stretcher."

"No need. She doesn't have any tubes anymore so it'll be easy."

Carol was wrong. Melinda only had the one IV now, no NG tube or urinary catheter or CVP, but she was weak. Because of her threatened spontaneous abortion, she wasn't allowed out of bed even to sit in a chair. She had been taking IPPB treatments since they'd got the peritonitis under control and that had prevented her contracting pneumonia.

Now Melinda was excited and eased herself little by little from her bed onto the stretcher. She giggled when the baby objected by kicking her in the ribs and her hand went to her abdomen while Carol covered her with a sheet.

"They told you about the sonograph?" Carol asked. "I mean about what it's for?"

"Yes, to check for any physical defects, for one thing," Melinda replied. "But it can't tell if the baby's mentally deficient, can it?"

Carol said, "No. But let's take one worry off our minds at a time, O.K.?"

"O.K. We'll work on the physical-defect worry first."

Carol watched as the girl smiled another brave smile, one more to add to the thousands she'd seen since Melinda had been admitted to L&D. "Say good-by to your room forever."

Melinda turned her head and looked at her bed, the window, the clock. "I hated this room at times; then I loved it. I was afraid of it, yet it gave me tremendous comfort. I can't say good-by forever, because maybe . . . I'll see it again."

"Like in about six weeks."

Carol wheeled her into the corridor where the bon voyage committee stood waiting, a pause of only a second or two in their busy, busy day to say good luck to a girl who had had both kinds.

Robbie paused as she pushed a stretcher bearing her patient from the labor room to delivery. "See you, dear heart," she told Melinda. "I'll visit you."

"'Bye, Robbie." Melinda watched as the stretcher turned down the hallway toward the delivery rooms and disappeared inside one.

"'Bye, Martin," Melinda said waving to Marty, who stood watching beside the nurses' station."

"'Bye," Martin said nodding and almost smiling.

Mac caught her hand and held it. "We'll be seeing you in your new room." She tucked Melinda's chart under the mattress of the stretcher.

"'Bye, Mac. 'Bye, Joy."

Joy took her hand, too, but couldn't speak. Instead

she began to cry and had to turn away in embarrassment.

Carol wheeled the stretcher through the double doors and down the corridor to the elevator, then pushed the button for the second floor.

"Will they really visit me?" Melinda asked in a small voice as they waited for the elevator.

"If I know that bunch in L&D, Melinda, they'll all visit you."

The elevator door slid open; a lab tech, dressed in white lab coat, stepped off, carrying his little case of test tubes and syringes like an oversized shoeshine kit. There were other people on the elevator so Melinda said nothing more. But she noticed a visitor staring at her abdomen, protruding under the top sheet, and she smiled at him and patted it fondly as if to say, Yeah, I'm pregnant. Aren't I huge?

The small converted treatment room where the ultrasonograph equipment was kept was not as impressive as the x-ray lab. For the magnitude of data the sonograph could reveal, the machine itself was not at all imposing. It was about the size and shape of . . . two EHFC monitors, standing side by side, with what looked like a radio tape player mounted on the top. On top of the tape player–type device a small TV-like screen was mounted.

The sonograph technician greeted Melinda happily and took her chart from Carol. He was thirtyish and bored and seemed glad to have a patient to work with.

"Do you do many of these a day?" Carol asked as she helped him place the stretcher against the treatment table.

"I have in-hospital patients . . ."—he looked at the ceiling—". . . occasionally. Mostly, though, the obstetricians send patients over from their offices. I do about one a day, maybe two. Last year I did four hundred twenty-five sonographs. Melinda, will you scoot over onto the table for us? That's a girl. Slowly, now. Into the center, sweetheart, toward me. That's fine. I'll have to uncover your tummy for this."

"Gee, I hope you do something else besides this," Melinda said.

"Oh I do. I run the CAT scanner. Now *that* dude stays busy."

"It has to, to pay for itself," Melinda said.

The technician changed the subject, for Melinda had trodden lightly upon the hospital's carefully kept bed of roses. Carol knew that when the sonograph equipment had been purchased in the latter '70s, suddenly there had been many pregnant patients who needed it. Doctors had put the pressure on hospital administration to secure the sonograph equipment, and the hospital had complied. The unwritten agreement between the doctors and the hospital board had been: if you buy it, we'll send enough patients over to pay for it. They had. If there was the slightest doubt about anything during a patient's pregnancy, the doctor would decide the patient needed a sonograph. Most patients' insurance wouldn't pay for the sonograph unless they had a suspected abnormality that might endanger mother or infant, so sympathetic doctors would write on the insurance forms that the purpose of the sonograph was to establish a diagnosis as to whether or not the fetus was abnormal physically, or that there was a question about the size of the fetus as compared to the mother's pelvic outlet, or some other cover statement. On this basis, most insurance companies begrudgingly paid part of the cost of the procedure—they knew what the doctors were up to, but they couldn't prove it. The patient paid for the rest. Carol suspected that the same thing was true of the CAT scanner, but on a larger scale.

But, oh, the advantages of having such sophisticated equipment! While the technician smeared oil on Melinda's protruding abdomen he explained.

"We use the sonograph to detect discrepancies between the size of the uterus and the expected due date of the fetus. We can measure the baby's head to determine his due date pretty closely. We can detect physical abnormalities in a fetus as far along as yours, Melinda, and see if he's developing normally. We can see if there're twins, and can determine the location of the placenta. The location of the placenta is very important. If it is too low, it could tear loose from the uterus when you go into labor. And there're hundreds of other advantages of using a sonograph, the best of which is, it is absolutely *radiation-free*. In some countries the sonograph is used routinely on every OB patient at specific intervals during her pregnancy."

"How does it work?" Melinda asked.

"Ultrasonic sound. Sound waves of such high frequency, we can't hear them. See this?" The technician held up a piece of equipment about the size and shape of a brick, which was connected by a fat cord to the tape player–type machine, and brought it down and placed it on her abdomen. "This sends sound waves into the uterus." He flipped some switches and turned dials on the machine. "A visual echo is transformed to an image on that little screen up there. Watch it."

Carol was fascinated. As the technician moved the brick thing about on Melinda's oiled abdomen, images changed on the screen.

"See his head?"

Melinda squinted. "Yes! Oh my, yes!"

It was only a black-and-white image, but unmistakable.

"Do you want to know the sex of your baby?"

"No, please. I know it's a boy, but—"

"O.K. I don't believe we can tell anyway in your case because he's facing away from us."

Melinda giggled.

Periodically, the technician took still pictures of the fetus, but the rest of the time Melinda and Carol watched the screen, on which they saw the baby move occasionally, jerk his leg, bring his arm up to his face.

And then it was all over.

Carol and the technician helped Melinda scoot back onto the stretcher. The big question still hung in the air—was the fetus normal?

"By all indications, it appears your baby is exactly the size he should be, that he is physically normal, and that even his reflexes appear to be normal. I'll study the still pictures carefully to make certain, and your doctor will give you a report. I'll even let you have a couple of the pictures later."

Melinda and Carol were both quiet as they left the room.

Modern technology. Where would they be without it? In the dark, that's where.

The post-partum floor. It was a familiar floor. Here, the routine of the maternity ward included giving sitz baths, spraying episiotomies with antiseptics and anesthetics, putting heat lamps on patients' bottoms, checking fundi, passing out lots of minor pain medications, and constantly repeating the visiting hours to anxious relatives.

Carol didn't like post-partum work, though she'd had only a taste of it as a student nurse. There was no variety in it, but one plus for working here was that it was a happy place. Almost everything related to it was upbeat. Flowers here did not remind one of funerals, but of gardens. Each patient would be going home within forty-eight to seventy-two hours, and she would be carrying in her arms her gift to the world.

When Carol paused at the nurses' station with the stretcher bearing Melinda, she observed Dr. Moss, bespectacled and introspective as always, bending over a chart at the doctors' desk, a small out-of-the-way shelf, actually, located near the revolving wheel of patient charts behind the nurses' station. She remembered the first time she had ever seen him—her first day in surgery as a student nurse, the first day she had seen Basil Novak up close.

As he stood with Betty Falk, charge nurse of the post-partum floor, Dr. Blasingame was shaking his head and saying, "That's the trouble, Falk; when you *think,* you get into trouble every time. Don't assume anything *ever* about one of my orders." He whipped out a pen from inside his coat and a prescription pad. Carol leaned over to see what he was scribbling. He wrote the word "assume" saying, "You see, Falk assuming often makes an *ass* out of *U* and *me."*

When Blasingame turned away, Betty glanced at Carol and rolled her eyes. That was an old, old . . . whatever it was. They'd heard it a million times.

But like most doctors, Dr. Blasingame didn't like to make enemies. Besides, today he was feeling more benevolent than on other days, so he turned back and patted Betty's shoulder. "But this time we'll let it go," he said hurrying from behind the nurses' station. "Hello," he greeted Carol. "How're things in the back?"

"Three in labor," Carol replied briefly with a fake smile as Blasingame passed on by.

The medications nurse for the post-partum floor came out of the medication room looking harassed as always and flipped open a Kardex on the desk to check an order.

Dr. Jackson dressed in jeans and an ox-blood leather

jacket strode up to the nurses' station saying, "What's going on?" Then he asked the medications nurse, "Hey, Toombs, will you go on rounds with me?" He pointed his thumb over his shoulder. "That woman, Forbes, in room—room—"

"One-oh-six," Betty Falk informed him.

Jackson looked at Betty. "Falk, will *you* go on rounds with me? Forbes in one-oh-six—she's . . . she's . . . God I don't dare go in there *alone.*"

Carol had to laugh. Most doctors took a nurse with them on the rounds of the post-partum floor, but Dr. Jackson usually didn't. To admit that he was scared of Forbes by asking somebody to make rounds with him was laughable.

Betty Falk was a short, slightly plump, round-faced woman, and although she maintained a permanent fixed smile on her pleasant face, she was absolutely humorless. "O.K.," she chirped in her little girl's voice. "Shall I bring her chart?"

Jackson winked at Carol. "Hell, no. Bring a baseball bat. Hello, Welles," he said hurrying from behind the nurses' station.

"Hi, Doctor."

Betty said to Carol, "I'll have Quisenberry check on our new patient—hi there, Melinda—as soon as I'm through with Dr. Jackson."

Carol nodded and pushed the stretcher down the corridor to Melinda's new room.

This room was larger than the labor room and already looked like a greenhouse, filled as it was with scads of fresh flowers and potted plants from friends and relatives. Melinda's mother and her husband John were there waiting. The post-partum nurse, Amy Quisenberry, who had already been assigned to Melinda along with her other patients, had been on the ball and already had the bed raised to its highest

296

position in anticipation of transferring Melinda from the stretcher. The bed covers were pulled down.

"Here she is!" Mrs. Bass said joyously, and John grinned and hurried to help Carol slide Melinda from the stretcher to the bed.

Carol knew that in a moment or two the nurse would come in and help Melinda out of her hospital gown and into a pretty one of her own. Then *her* part would be over.

A hand, much like her own, gripped Carol's. And she let herself look down at the wan face on the pillow. But Melinda's eyes were now bright with new hope and gratitude, and she said, "Thanks, Carol, for everything."

John embarrassedly handed her a dozen red roses. "For the nurses in Labor and Delivery," he said and met her eyes. "Thank you."

Mrs. Bass pressed a box of chocolates into her arms. "This can't begin to compensate—" was all she was able to say.

Carol was overwhelmed.

I am a nurse.

This recovery is what it's all about.

I had a hand in this.

Me and a dozen others.

Dedicated doctors, dedicated nurses, and lab techs, respiratory therapists, x-ray techs, housekeeping personnel, the laundry, Marty, and a loving family who cared.

Carol told Melinda she'd be visiting often, placed the gifts on the stretcher, and pulled it from the room.

But outside the door she leaned against the wall, and let the tears come—really let them fall. *We did it. If the baby is mentally sound, we did it, and we saved Melinda. I was a part of it all.* There was still D-day to go yet, though, and they'd have Melinda again in a few

297

weeks, so it wasn't over entirely. Not yet. But the bad part was.

Brown shoes neatly polished came into the view of her lowered eyes, then trousers creased just so, a white lab coat over a brown suit and a gold-striped tie, as Basil Novak lifted her chin with his hand. "Going my way?"

It was the first time she had seen the gentleness in him, something going deeper than a fine intellect and handsome face.

She smiled and, taking a Kleenex out of her pocket, wiped her eyes. "We did it."

His eyes glanced at Melinda's room. "Yes, we did. I just checked about the sonograph, and it's all good news."

"Yes."

"I come to see Melinda in her new room and find her nurse crying. For happy, I guess."

"Yes." She thought, I am attracted to this man and yet I distrust him awfully. I think he's curious about me, but doesn't want to interfere with any relationship I have with Duane. Well, fine. Because I could never trust Basil Novak.

He was thinking, Carol, there's a time and a place for everyone. My time hasn't come, neither has yours.

She smiled, shrugging, and put her hands on the stretcher. "I'll see you . . . around," she said as she began to push the stretcher away. This was it. Their paths had crossed because of Melinda. She had seen him periodically in L&D, because he was helping Whitehall with Melinda's case. But now—Melinda was gone from L&D. There would be no rounds in L&D ever again for Basil Novak.

Mac had admitted two more patients to L&D by the time Carol returned from delivering Melinda to her room.

"Thank God you're back, Carol. Dr. Moss is pitting two. Dr. Jackson has somebody coming in through ER and Brew says she's a gravida four and about to precip. Peusy's delivering in three. I want to hear about Melinda's sonograph, but right now—"

"Mac, she's crowning," Joy said sticking her head out the door of labor room two.

"Take Bickerstaff in one and O'Malley in five, will you, Carol?" Mac said hurrying toward room two.

And the routine in L&D was carried on.

SIXTEEN

Walking down the corridor to Elaine Bryant's office, Carol felt a little like someone going to the gallows. While Carol was assisting Dr. Moss in the delivery room, the nursing director had left word at the nurses' station in L&D that Carol should come to her office when she was off duty. When Carol, standing with her mask dangling under her chin and still wearing her surgical cap, read the note, she experienced a series of emotions: horror (what have I done wrong?), curiosity (what would she want with me?), and elation (will this be about my nine-month raise?).

Now she was simply, inexplicably, nervous. This hadn't been one of her good days because she was blue. The night before Bret had told her that he had changed jobs, that he had been accepted at another hospital—in a different city.

They had been in her apartment. He had just dropped by, had made her sit down on the sofa, and had put his arms around her.

"Carol, I love you," he had said, "but I can't make you return my love, and I can't keep living like this.

So . . . I've decided to—"

She had sat up straight and turned toward him, sensing the finality in his voice. His eyes had never avoided hers, had always sought whatever there was in her for him to see. He had searched her face as he went on. "I took the job at Veterans with great plans of changing things there. Well, fate did that for me. Since I saw you day before yesterday, we've gotten a new administrator. He's fired the riffraff off the nursing staff and the chiefs of staff for the doctors are getting their own house in order, disciplining their own colleagues, and laying down rules, as they should. I'm not going to have to do it for them." He had smiled wryly. "Such a naïve fool I was. Anyhow, I've taken a job in an emergency room, and I won't be coming back here again."

She had wept. Bret was dear to her, but she had never been in love with him; they had both known that from the beginning.

Later, as he had gone to the door of her apartment, both of them close to tears, knowing that this was good-by forever, Carol had said, "Will you remember me pleasantly, Bret?"

He had spread his hands over his chest and replied, "My school pal, we shared a lot together, as students and as tyros in the nursing profession. At least we shared stories of our experiences as new nurses. My sweetheart—" He had reached for her, but thought better of it and dropped his arms to his side. "You have a life to live and so have I, and it doesn't seem that the gods mean for us to live them together."

"Bret, oh, Bret, I know you'll go far and do great things someday."

"As a nurse?" he had laughed softly.

"If we ever do meet again, we'll have more stories to share. Perhaps I'll know by then Melinda Curtis' complete story and Shelly's and Basil Novak's. And maybe even Duane's professional story."

When she spoke Duane's name, Bret, who had opened the door, swallowed, chucked her under the chin, and smiled. "Maybe someday, Carol, somebody can tell *my* story."

Now, nervously, Carol entered the large carpeted, mahogany-paneled office of the director of nursing. Elaine Bryant looked up from some papers on her desk. "Hello, Carol. Sit down, please."

Carol sat down in the pliable maroon-colored leather chair in front of Elaine's desk. Elaine sat, seeming starched herself, in her white uniform, with her hair professionally helmeted and shellacked. Not a hair, or string, or wrinkle, or thought was out of place.

"When you applied for a job here," Elaine began, "you expressed a desire to work in the cardiac-care unit."

Carol nodded.

"Would you still like to do that?"

Carol looked stunned. "I— Well. Why? Isn't my work in L&D satisfactory?"

Elaine smiled. "More than satisfactory, but when I asked MacMillan if she thought you might like to transfer to CCU, she told me that you've been a little worried about not learning any skills other than those confined to labor and delivery. Mac wants desperately to keep you, but so do I. I've learned that once a nurse starts thinking like that, she's ready to move on. And I'd rather transfer you to another department than lose you to another hospital."

Carol folded her hands in her lap and relaxed. "Melinda Curtis' case taught me a lot besides just maternity nursing, and I must confess that I enjoyed learning something new."

"When is Melinda due?"

"She told me yesterday in four weeks. Maybe less, according to the latest sonograph they did on her about two weeks ago."

"She was a miracle. One of our great successes. But now, what about you?"

"I do love L&D, but—" Carol's eyes wandered to the window and out beyond. "But yes, I would like to learn something different."

"You understand that CCU is also a small area. But very fascinating."

"Yes." Carol's heart was racing. She had wanted to work in the cardiac-care unit from the very beginning. L&D had been her second choice.

"You'll have heart-attack patients in one area and open-heart-surgery patients in the other. Have you seen CCU?"

"Yes. I spent three days there as a student."

"Fine. Then you know what it's all about. Do you need more time to decide?"

"May I have . . . three days?"

The nursing director started fidgeting with the papers on her desk. "Can you make that one day? I have no trouble finding people to work in L&D; I have six applications for Labor and Delivery on my desk right now. But I have a lot of trouble finding people to work the critical-care areas. That's why I want to steal you from L&D. I have an opening on day shift in CCU now. I *always* have an opening in CCU since they're admitting the open hearts there. The reason I didn't have you work in CCU when you first applied for a job, remember, was because you were inexperienced and the rule at Bennet is that one must work a year in some other area before being allowed to work in any of the critical-care areas. You know that I'm having difficulty keeping people in CCU now that they're having to care for the open-heart patients."

"Oh?"

Elaine smiled briefly. "CCU nurses are accustomed to sitting a lot and watching monitors, which is in itself, a difficult job to do day in and day out. But of course CCU is a lot like L&D in that it's either feast or famine. Either it's quiet for days and days or there're critical patients crashing and CPRs several times a day. Now since they've extended CCU to include an area for surgery patients some of the CCU nurses don't like it. There's a great deal of work involved in caring for open-heart patients, though not nearly so much as in surgical ICU or in other areas of the hospital. Do you still want to consider it?"

Carol thought briefly of the conversation she had had with Basil Novak, in which he had told her of his plan to join the cardiovascular surgeon, Dr. Greenburg, as his associate next year, and of his desire that Duane do the same someday. Maybe for that reason, she should turn down the offer to work in CCU.

But no, Novak's plans wouldn't be realized for a year, if then, and this was here and now.

She nodded. "I'd still like to consider your offer. May I let you know tomorrow?"

Elaine was pleased. "Indeed yes, Carol. Thank you. Call me on the telephone and let me know what your answer is. I'll need to leave you in L&D for two more weeks while we orient another nurse to take your place."

Carol wrestled with her decision all night—another sleepless night, the second in a row. She loved labor and delivery, but a part of her yearned to learn more. The only drawback to her taking the job in CCU was that almost assuredly she'd work in the same area with Basil Novak again, as he was doing most of his last year's residency in cardiovascular surgery. And later

304

she might have to work with Duane.

But she came to a conclusion just after midnight. She'd do it.

The next day she had the switchboard operator ring the nursing director's office, and she told Elaine that she would transfer.

After all, why should she object to seeing Novak again in a professional capacity? Besides, she thought that she wouldn't be seeing Novak or Duane again for weeks, maybe even for months.

But as it turned out, she was wrong.

Name <u>Melinda Lynn Curtis</u>
Hosp. No. <u>086420</u>   RM NO. <u>110 M</u>
Doctor <u>Simon</u>

NURSES' NOTES
March 14, 1980
   8:10 P.M.—Pt. complaining of intermittent low back pain and contractions 15–20 minutes apart.
   8:15—Notified Dr. Simon who ordered vag exam.
   8:32—Vag exam done by E. Spinoza from Labor and Delivery—Dilation 4 cm, small amt. bloody show.
   8:40—Notified Dr. Simon of dilation and bloody show.
   9:00—Dr. Simon here. Orders.
   9:15—Pt. transferred to L&D via wheelchair.
                                    J. Pratt, R.N.
DOCTORS' PROGRESS REPORT

March 14, 1980
9:00 P.M. Vaginal exam by me reveals four cm dilation of the cervix and small amount of blood-

tinged mucus. Reviewed sonograph reports dated March 10, 1980, calculate fetus weighs approx. five pounds. Due to 4 cm dilation of cervix and satisfactory weight of fetus, am allowing pt. to continue labor with prospects of imminent delivery. Will transfer to Labor and Delivery and notify Dr. Whitehall in case of complications from old surgical wound and any existing diverticuli. Will follow closely.

Caleb Simon, M.D.

ADMISSION NOTES

Labor began __8:10 P.M.__ Date __3/14/80__
Spontaneous __✓__ Induction _____
Membranes ruptured at _____ Date _____
Artificially_____ Spon._____
Show: Absent _____ Bleeding Present __✓__
Scant __✓__ Mod_____ Excessive _____
Dilation of cervix _4_ Blood Type & RH _A+_
Last Meal __5:00 P.M.__
Grava _I_ Para _0_ Abortions _0_
Breast __✓__ Bottle ____
Pediatrician __Ferdinand__
Illnesses and drugs during this pregnancy:
__Diverticulitis & Diverticulosis, peritonitis, abd. surg. Demerol, morphine, antibiotics (see chart), Valium, antihistamines, Phenergan__
Lab: CBC __✓__ Urine __✓__ Sero __✓__
         X-rays __✓__ Other __✓__

NURSES' NOTES

March 14, 1980
9:15—Admitted to labor room eight via wheel chair from post-partum room 110 as per order by

Dr. Simon. In good spirits. VS: BP 110/70, pulse 86, resp. 16, FHT 144. Urine specimen to lab.

Vag exam shows dilation 4 cm. Contractions 15 min. apart. Small amt. bloody discharge.

9:45—Enema given and perineal prep.

10:45—Contractions eleven–twelve min. apart and firm. Dilation 4 cm. VS stable. FHT 148.

R. Hanky, LVN

March 14, 1980
11:30 P.M.

VS stable. FHT 148. Contractions 10 min. apart, duration 60 seconds. Dilation 4 cm.

L. Parker, R.N.

March 15, 1980

12:30 A.M. Pt. complaining of severe low back pain. Dr. Simon notified of pain and slow progression of dilation.

1:30—Dr. Simon here. Orders given.

2:10—IV with Pitocin started in L arm. Demerol 25 mg. given for pain. VS stable. FHT 142. Contractions 8–10 min. apart. Dilation 4 cm.

3:00—Pitocin drip increased. Contractions remain 8–10 min. apart, dilation 4 cm.

3:46—Pt. vomiting 100 cc emesis. VS stable, FHT 140. Dilation 4 cm.

4:30—Dr. Simon here. Ruptured membranes. VS stable. FHT 148.

6:30—Contractions strong and regular at 6–7 min. apart.

P. Smith, R.N.

When Carol walked into her room Melinda was lying on her back with her eyes shut. John, sitting in the chair beside her bed, sprang nervously to his feet as she entered. At four centimeters dilation of the cervix, Melinda should be beginning to have moderately painful contractions, but she and the other nurses and Dr. Simon knew that in spite of the Pitocin in the IV, which was given to keep the contractions strong and regular, Melinda's labor was not progressing normally. She was not dilating sufficiently.

At 6:30 Simon, forgetting that on the West Coast it was only 4:30 A.M., had telephoned Dr. Valasco in California and roused the young obstetrician to ask, "Is it possible that the RH could cause uterine atony"— which was weakness of the uterine muscle—"or dystocia?"—which was slow or difficult delivery. Valasco told him that of the several patients treated with RH, none had shown uterine atony or dystocia during labor.

When Carol had arrived at 6:45, Dr. Simon was pacing the L&D hallway in front of the delivery rooms saying, "I wish I were back in the used-car business." Raising his hands skyward, he added, *"God* how I wish I were just selling automobiles."

Carol had soon found out why Dr. Simon was longing for his pre-medical school days. A half-hour before she'd arrived he had palpated Melinda's uterus, done a painful vaginal exam, and discovered that he still could not feel the fetal head and that the fetus was "floating," not engaging at the pelvic inlet. Suspecting that the fetus was breech, he'd had Melinda taken to x-ray. X-ray had confirmed that the fetus was breech.

He'd had the eleven-to-seven nurses attach the EHFC monitor to Melinda; the contractions were real, but piddly still. The fetal heart remained strong and stable. At the rate she was going, Melinda would be in labor for days. Even Pitocin was not very effective because there was no wedge presenting at the internal cervical os to dilate the cervix. He'd seen cases like this many times before in his career; the causes of them were unknown in most cases. In the old days, the patient would be in labor for days and become dehydrated and exhausted. Some ended up dying in childbirth. These days, there was a way out. Caesarean section.

Dr. Simon had got on the telephone again to Whitehall. Damned if he was going to do a C-section on Melinda by himself. No telling what he'd run into in the abdominal cavity. She had been doing fine, no elevated temp for weeks, but just in case—

Melinda was wan and pale and still thin. Carol thought, It isn't fair! It isn't fair that she should have a difficult delivery after all the rest she has suffered.

Melinda's eyes flew open and she cried, "My friend!" and held her arms out to her.

Carol went to her, and they embraced, like friends, like sisters; very unprofessional—but what the hell.

Melinda fell back onto her small pillow.

"Are you feeling much pain?" Carol wanted to know first.

Melinda smiled. "Not much. Dr. Simon says the baby's not making any progress. Carol, I'm just a *mess*, right?"

Carol was fitting the fetoscope over her head. "No you aren't. And even if you are, Dr. Simon says it'll all be over soon."

She listened to the fetal heart—good. Always good. The fetus had remained strong and had continued to grow throughout all of it.

When Carol took the earpieces from her ears, Melinda said, "Dr. Simon says I can stay awake. Dr. Pashi is going to monitor me and do an epidural. He says an epidural anesthetizes me higher up than a caudal would, so they can do the operation and I can

309

stay awake. Carol, I won't be able to *feel* the surgery, will I?"

"No."

"Gee, and I can watch Johnathan be born."

"Johnathan?"

"Yes. You might not understand how, but I *know* the baby's a boy and his name is Johnathan."

John laughed and held on to her hand as Carol took the presurgery vitals.

Then suddenly the quiet L&D unit came alive.

First, Dr. Peusy's patient in room two was ready for delivery so Joy went with that patient. Carol knew Robbie was attending Dr. Jackson's patient in room one; Mac had come in with the stretcher just as Dr. Simon had stridden by puffing his pipe followed by Basil Novak and—was that *Duane?*

Carol went to the door and peeped out. It *was* Duane. Shit, damn it, and hell. What was *he* doing here?

Carol and Mac got Melinda onto the stretcher, and Mac took her to delivery. Mac would be scrub nurse and Carol would circulate, but what the *hell* were Novak and Duane doing here?

The telephone rang at the nurses' station and Carol hurried to answer it. Dr. Moss' patient would be coming in soon from home, admitting said, but she was a primip, so no big hurry.

Carol hung up the phone and ran back into Melinda's room to get the latest vital-sign sheet. Dr. Pashi would want it on the chart. When she turned, Duane was standing in the doorway.

"Such a big hurry," he said leaning against the doorjamb. "Busy, busy, busy. What's so important that you have to *run,* Carol?"

She put her hand on her hip and sighed loudly. O.K. He was wanting to pick a fight. But why? Why? "I've got to circulate; that's why I'm running."

"You ran the wrong way," he said, smiling—almost friendly. "The delivery room's *that* way."

"I'm getting the—" Suddenly it occurred to her that she did not owe Duane Duren any explanation. "Please stand aside and let me pass."

"What are you fetching, Nancy Nurse?"

She tightened her lips over her teeth. "Why are *you* in here?"

"Novak and I are assisting with Melinda's surgery. Didn't Simon tell you girls? He's uptight about the incision and about what he'll run into in Melinda's abdomen. Just like a GYN man. Knows nothing about anatomy—except certain parts."

"Please let me by," Carol said. When he didn't move, just kept smiling at her, she said, "I'd think if you're assisting you'd have to be scrubbing."

"Doctors scrub when they feel like it. Novak and Simon are having coffee while Pashi's doing his epidural."

"Duane, let me out of this room. I have to scrub and prep Melinda and help Mac."

His eyes flashed with meanness. "Read me her latest vitals, *Nurse.*"

"Go to hell."

"You still haven't gotten the picture. I'm a doctor; you do what I say. Read the vitals."

"I said go to hell. You're no doctor. You're just an intern."

"Nevertheless, there's an 'M.D.' behind my name, Nancy Nurse."

"One last time, get out of my way or I'll scream."

He shrugged. "Go ahead. Then maybe somebody will come in and do a vaginal exam on you to see if you're ready to deliver. *I* could volunteer."

That made her furious.

"Are you ready to . . . deliver? How long has your boyfriend been gone, a month? Yep, you should be ready to deliver."

He caught her hand before it had time to make contact with his face, and suddenly, touching her again seemed to charge him with so much emotion that he caught both her wrists and pushed her away from the door and against the wall out of sight. "Don't be so high-and-mighty with me. I slept with you, remember? Dozens of times and you liked it."

At that moment she knew that he was going to kiss her. *Macho man, eh? Wonder how he'd like a knee in the groin to go to surgery with?* But she didn't get the chance to find out, for he pulled her against him and kissed her roughly, lingeringly while she made feeble efforts to pull free. His hands moved, too, down, down, until she did manage to pull free and back away against the bed, hating herself because once she had enjoyed his kisses, enjoyed the feel of him.

"Aren't you afraid," she said breathlessly, "that someone will see us and connect you with me?"

He stood looking at her, perplexed. His hands trembled slightly.

"Well, I'd *like* someone to see us," she said; "then I can explain how we knew each other when I was a student and did a term paper on a certain—"

He gestured with one hand. "Don't think for a moment I've forgotten," he interrupted. Then he smiled and said, "Thanks for the feel, Carol. You've put on a little weight since I felt of you last."

She ran out of the room, burning all over, burning and enraged and about to cry, because he knew she hated that kind of talk. At the delivery door she handed Mac the vital-sign sheet and then went to the sink where she pulled on her cap and mask and began to scrub. She scrubbed furiously, hurriedly, fingers,

312

between fingers, nails, the backs of her hands, palms, wrists—

"Good morning." A long, slender hand reached for a cap, and Carol looked up from her soapy hands to see Novak don a disposable green cap.

"Good morning," she said shakily and went back to her scrubbing. "Is . . . is Dr. Whitehall sure everything's O.K. with Melinda's colon?"

"We are all absolutely sure there's no peritonitis, of course. There may be some diverticuli but x-rays show none. Her abdomen looks normal, and she hasn't had a temp in six weeks. We're certain all is O.K.—but we're being extra cautious. Whitehall will feel better if one of us has a look-see at things after the baby's delivered and the uterus is closed. And Simon *insisted* one of us assist. Whitehall has an important surgery schedule this morning, so here *I* am."

"May I ask why Duane is assisting?"

"He's back on surgery rotation and this is good experience." Novak, scrubbing his hands, looked at her. "There's no chance of you two going back together, is there?"

"Ha!"

Dr. Simon, just approaching the scrub area, looked astonished when he saw Carol fling Novak a wry look over her shoulder as she entered the delivery room.

Mac was prepping Melinda's abdomen with gauze sponges and Betadine, from her breasts to her pubic mound, on either side almost around to her back. Carol started to begin opening the sterile packs when Mac said, "Don't touch anything, Carol. You're going to scrub."

"What?"

"You dillydallied until I had to do the circulating stuff," Mac said smiling. "Naw, I'm kidding. I'm doing this because I want to. You've done the last three

313

C-sections, and you might as well do this one."

It was true. Carol had been scrub nurse for three C-sections in the past six weeks.

"But Mac. This one is—"

Mac held up a finger to shush her, because Melinda was awake and listening. "I'm hoping this might change your mind about leaving us for CCU," she said.

"Mac, please. I can't."

Novak came in holding his hands up above his waist and away from his scrub suit. "What's this about *you* can't?"

"This C-section should have an expert scrub nurse to—"

Dr. Simon was striding in, hands held above his waist. "Bah. You're fine, Carol. Just fine. If you've scrubbed, get on your gloves and your gown, my dear, and help me with mine, please ma'am."

Carol obeyed, trembling, and pulled on her gown with Mac's help. She gloved herself. Then she turned and gowned and gloved Dr. Simon. Then Novak stood for gowning, his incredible blue eyes laughing at her over the surgical mask, as he dried his hands on a sterile towel.

Smiling in spite of her fears, she held the gown for him.

"You should get into the habit of this," he said.

Mac tied his gown in back while she held the gloves for him. *Snap. Snap.* She was remembering when she had tied his gown in surgery as a student. *Well, Carol, next time I see you in surgery I'll expect you to be scrubbed and know how to gown and glove me.*

"You're an expert already," he said. "Sure you don't want to be a surgical nurse?"

"No."

"Especially in cardiovascular—"

314

"My God, no!"

"Just wondered." He walked over to stand on the left of the table across from Simon just as Duane entered.

The lights seemed to dim and suddenly she was trembling and perspiring. She had to gown and glove *him*. As she held the gown for him he said, "Higher. I'm not a midget."

"Only mentally," said she softly as she held the gown higher.

He thrust his arms inside, and Mac pulled the tab and tied it at the back.

Duane kept shrugging in his gown as if it were too tight and said to Mac, "Next time I'm going to ask for a cloth gown." He added in an aside to Carol, "And a disposable scrub nurse."

"You're a shit-ass," she whispered to him blithely as Mac, smiling, left them to stand beside the operating table. Carol picked up the sterile surgical glove by its cuff.

"Nurse, you contaminated the glove," Duane announced loudly.

A glance showed Carol that Dr. Simon was nervous and stewing and unaware of the two of them. Novak was hearing but not looking, Mac was laughing to herself, and Dr. Pashi was obviously enjoying their spat.

"I did not contaminate your glove," Carol said through her teeth.

"You did. You touched the palm with your thumb."

"I didn't."

"Drop the glove and give me another."

Carol had no choice but to obey. She held the new glove as he thrust his right hand into it.

"Firmer, please. How do you expect me to get it in if you don't help me?"

315

"Get it *up,* don't you mean?" she said softly.

Both red-faced, they went to stand at the table where the doctors decided that Novak would do the actual cutting and that Dr. Simon would deliver the infant and placenta. While they were discussing the procedure, Carol checked the instrument table, arranging the instruments and supplies; then she arranged the Mayo stand, her fury at Duane having completely replaced her nervousness over being scrub nurse.

Duane's mixed-up passions had got his mind off the thrill of the surgery and onto how much he . . . despised her.

Novak was having mixed feelings as he took his place beside her on the right side of the table, warring within himself about whether he wanted them to hate each other or not. If they loved each other, all the better; they could work as a team. On the other hand, if they hated each other, maybe he had a chance to make inroads with Carol himself. Suddenly, he decided he'd prefer the latter.

He looked at Pashi. "How're the vitals?"

"A-O.K.," Pashi said. "Stable. The anesthesia is up to T-six, the diaphragm."

"And how do you feel, Melinda?" Dr. Simon asked.

"I'm fine. And if Carol and Dr. Duren will stop fussing, maybe we can get on with this," she said mischievously. "Johnathan's getting hungry and so am I."

Damn Duane, Carol thought. Damn him for making all this fuss and embarrassing me before the others and for making Melinda overhear our quarrel.

Duane must have been thinking similar thoughts as they stood glaring at each other across the operating table.

Looking at Duane, Novak could see that he was giving Carol a little hell in his glare and that Carol was

316

returning the same. He could also see that Carol wasn't going to hand him the knife because her attention was elsewhere. He could pick up the knife himself and begin, but he needed to bring them both back to the job at hand. So he sighed slowly, held his palm up, and said softly, "Scalpel."

AUTHOR'S NOTE

After several years of selective testing and experimentaton, ritodrine hydrochloride has recently been placed on the market as the first drug ever to be approved in the use of premature labor.

"Melinda" in this book is now the mother of two normal, healthy children, and "Johnathan," her first, is six years old.